"...I am starting to read the series the third time, & with each read, I learn more, especially the scripture quotes. You refer them to some character, or situation, which gives it real meaning. Anyway I'm really enjoying the read, have got my friend hooked, & and we're both waiting for Book Six, can you possibly tell me when it will be for sale...?"   Ron

"...I almost feel like I'm addressing Henry Pederson instead of Henry Ripplinger! I just finished reading Angel Promises Fulfilled – which for me was a feat! I wondered if I would get through all five of the tomes you wrote, but you kept my interest! You achieved a rare thing – mixing romance, spirituality, and common sense advice into books of fiction. And I'm sure you have the Lord to thank for that!"   Cathy

"...What treasures you have placed in my heart! I'm amazed at my own thoughts and how much love I have been given by those around me. It is through your words that I'm able to realize what life is really all about. I am truly grateful to you. You are truly blessed with your gifts of art and writing."   Victoria

"...Thank you so much for writing the "Angelic Letters Series". These books are enjoyable and so inspiring. I have never found books so captivating. I couldn't put them down and yet I didn't want to finish them. You made the characters so real. You truly have a gift. I know I will re-read these books again and I look forward to "The House Where Angels Dwell"   Pat

"...All I would like to say is that your books are super good and very inspiring. You are so smart to plan all the things that happened in the books, and make them all come together so smoothly. Your books are so hard to put down! Thank you so much for writing these wonderful books. I will never forget them because they are far beyond good. :-)"   Roana

"...I am so thankful to have the privilege of reading your beautiful books, Henry. They are family to me as my own family can attest to, while I try to tell them why my heart is breaking today or why Father Engelmann has helped me get through a difficult period."   Norma

"…Your five books were marvelously entertaining! Your pleasant writing style had me "hooked" in the first book. Curiosity and the love of the characters led me on and, before long, I had read all five TWICE!"

HEIDI

"…WOW! I have now finished all 5 books and I was disappointed that I was done!! Such a good read!! I haven't read 5 books in 10 years let alone 5 books in less than 2 months! I just couldn't put the books down!! I managed to get a few girlfriends to read them as well and they are enjoying them as much as I did. It was nice to be able to compare notes with them and discuss how we felt! I am anxiously waiting for the next book and maybe another series??"

BEV

"…I have loved all your 5 books. Not just the story but all the inspiration it gave me. If I wasn't already a person of faith. I would sure be thinking that way."

GERALDINE

"…This set of 5 books was heartwarming, There were very loveable characters, people you wanted to revisit time and again. The story lines for me were just what I love to read. Book 5 was my favorite and I shed many tears along with the characters. Thank You, for such a wonderful series. I'll be watching for book six."

LYNN

"…Our mother of 8 will be celebrating her 85th birthday next March. Your Pewter Angel books were a 'godsend' to her when she was going through the difficult time of our Dad's fairly sudden illness and death 2 years ago. She hadn't read in a long time, but now has read all 5 of them and is anxiously awaiting your sixth book. She's been doing a fair bit of reading now that she's been on her own, but continually tells us that she hasn't found any to be nearly as good as the Pewter Angels"

MARGARET

"…What am I to do without Henry and Jenny and David Engelmann in my life? Such a story! Such great life lessons. Forgiveness and love being at the top of the list. It is all about love, isn't it. You have taught me so very much!!!"

DONNA

"…I wanted to share how profoundly your five books have touched me. I became very engrossed in the story you laid out, so much that I laughed and cried along with the characters. I found it to be very unpredictable - I never knew what to expect next. This created a little problem as I missed out on some sleep reading instead :) I loved your Father David!"

HEATHER

"… I don't think there is hardly anyone in our small town that has not read your books… It took my husband something like 2 and a half weeks to read all 5…It has been a pleasure and a blessing to have read your books." CHARLOTTE

"…Dearest Henry! I have never enjoyed 5 books as much as I have read these! Truly inspirational and so family oriented. With the faith of God, love and family, I soooo truly enjoyed each and every book! I don't know if I can wait for book 6." SHARON

"…There have been times that I wanted to read until finished the set without stopping, but then the experience would be over all to quickly! You have written a story that is so (I cannot think of any other word than your words) (ANGELIC). Anyway thank you for a GREAT READ!!"

CAROLE

"…Thank you again for writing such heartfelt books. I now have a much better alternative than flowers for special friends and am very excited. I love my angels and talk to them daily as I see evidence of their existence. Life is truly wonderful." KELSIE

"…I am writing to you on behalf of my husband. He has simply fallen in love with your books, I have not seen him sit down to read a book and he has read your books from cover to cover and waiting for your next book to come out. He really wants to meet you some time."

MELVA

"…I wish every senior in high school was required to read these books--so much good Christian advice for life and living. Bless you for doing this." PAT

"…, truly I am inspired by your books. I feel at peace and want to follow the message you gave us. It is a gift you provided us and I want to share my books with my friends to share your message. thank you thank you thank you!!!"   NADINE

"…I was extremely touched by the first three books of the Pewter Angels series. I found them so profound. I have never been so emotionally torn by reading a book before. They have opened my eyes to the possibility of the existence of God. I really have to acquire a Bible and to actually read it. Your books are truly wonderful and inspiring. Thank you for your uplifting works. You are a blessing to us all. God is working through you. I am looking forward to reading more of your books."   JUDI

"…What a powerful series! I love the books, I love the message, I love your writing style one question for you ... WHEN WILL BOOK SIX BE AVAILABLE *smiling*"   JO ANNE

"…you are a great inspiration to me and thousands of other people. Hopefully many years from now and long after you have left this world you will continue to be a blessing and an inspiration, to countless people around the world."   BARRY

"…You are a true angel who has the mission to inspire and lead us to have a closer relationship with God, our angels and our loved ones. You truly are an "angel of enlightenment" chosen by God to touch our hearts and spirits and make us soar to new heights. May God bless you and may his angels be forever at your side to guide you!"   DORIS

"…I have enjoyed these books immensely. Finding it very difficult to put down, being so captivated by each word and message you were conveying to your reader. Your gift of writing that places you within each character and situation. I have shed many tears of joy and sorrow along this journey with your characters. I find it hard to put into words how I felt in reading your books. They brought me such comfort, hope, pleasure, knowledge of scripture, and most of all love for all beings regardless of their actions."   SHERRY

"…I love your books to pieces, a movie would be phenomenal!!!"

NEELY

"…I have not read a novel in 20 yrs. I did read all 5 of the Angelic Series. Wow wow my my pulled at every emotion I could think of. God will be rewarding you when he takes you to His kingdom. You have touched me in so many ways you are so gifted to write a story like no other. Thank you and keep on writing. I can't wait to read your next novel!"

ALLISON

"…I almost feel I know you personally. Your angel books meant the world to me. I read the 5 and again out loud to my husband. I recommended them to MANY and bought some as gifts. Please let me know when I can expect to read the conclusion of this uplifting and wonderfully written story. I'm so eager I can't stand it. Thank you."   MICHELLE

"…Your beautiful books are ever so much more than mere stories! They are life-giving parables like Jesus Himself told to touch not just the minds but also stir the hearts of listeners. …As an avid reader who worked at Barnes and Noble, I was pleasantly expecting a nice little read. I was shaken to the very core of my being from the very first chapters of book one as your story richly unfolds in the lives and times of people who could have been my family, my neighbors."   MARY

"…. I have just finished the last book, and I must say what an enjoyable read. They were all so inspirational and I had a hard time to put them down. I just could not stop reading. You have been gifted for sure to write such books. I can hardly wait for the 6th book to be published."

SHIRLEY

"… It is very seldom that we get such a beautiful love story that makes your heart and soul sing. Please keep writing."   HELEN

"…Best books I've ever read,awesome story! I've just re-read the whole series again..,amazing every time, inspiring!! Hope it's not too much longer for Book Six."   RACHELLE

"…This is the best series I have ever read. There is tremendous wisdom, beauty, purity, and solid Christian values that seem all too rare. God Bless you. I look forward to the final book."   EILEEN

"…I have been totally blessed by your Angelic Letters Series.…I thank you for your ministry. It is truly an outreach spreading the word of God throughout the people."   SHIRLEY

"…I have just finished reading all five for the second time. I am amazed as to how much more enjoyment I received the second time around. I eagerly await the sixth book. Thank you from the bottom of my heart for the joy of your books. May God continue to assist you! With all my respect,"   NANCY

"…Your writing indeed had my appetite to read non stop to the finish line of Book Five ! "Angels promises fulfilled and Love conquers all "was so beautifully and elegantly written from your soul and elegantly described with love…"   JUNE

"…Haven't read any books I've enjoyed as much as the Angelic Letters Series. I was hooked in the first 20 pages and couldn't put the books down. I've given the books to a number of other women from our church who are also waiting for Book 6. When can we expect to see it? Can hardly wait!"   MIKAYLA

"…This was such a moving book. I love it when I read a book that teaches me something and especially one that moves my heart to make me want to be a better person. I am so thankful for people like you who can still write a beautiful story without taking the Lord's name in vain as so many authors do today. Thank you from the bottom of my heart. God Bless You.'   BONNIE

"Hello Henry. Words do not express the meaning of the Angelic Letters Series. I have read & re-read them twice already and am getting ready to read them again. Each time I do this I get so much more out of them. I have bought the set as gifts for people who enjoyed them as much as me."   MARY ANNE

"…These books are priceless. Thank-you so much for writing them and inspiring us and connecting us with our heavenly angels and our Father in Heaven."   KAY

"…My mother-in-law (86 years old) has loved reading this series of books. Just wondering if you can tell us when Book six may be out for sale. She loves the series and can't wait to finish them. She thinks you are a wonderful author."   CHRIS

"…I was very touched by the story and the spiritual depth you portrayed as well. Very touching and heartfelt. I can't wait to read more of your books. I just wanted you to know how grateful I am to have had the pleasure and opportunity to come across your work. It's very inspiring and genuine."   AIMEE

"…So many of the difficult topics you address through your characters and plot are all too familiar in our lives. Reading them strengthened me and helped me to face the difficulties of my own life. May the Holy Spirit continue to inspire your mind and heart to feed God's children through the labor of your writing and painting. Blessings on you both,"
                                                                            PAT

"…I just wanted to tell you it was an AMAZING, ASTOUNDING series, I was amazed, because I have never ever enjoyed a series so much!!!! Keep up the amazing work!!!!"   ELIZA

"…I just finished reading the Angelic Letters Series, and found all 5 books to be the most inspirational readings I have had the privilege to read - Thank you! I can't wait for book number 6 "The House Where Angels Dwell.""   SUZANNE

"…I would like to tell you how involved I became in your first 5 books – man, are they ever wonderful. Now I have been patiently waiting and watching for "The House Where Angels Dwell"."   DORIS

"…Have no idea where you get your ideas for the books from but, one word phenomenal…"   DORY SCOTT

"… It is so refreshing to get books that are spell binding without violence, cursing and blatant sexuality. Great gifts for all members of your families. Am looking forward to your next book and praying success over all your endeavors."   TANYA

"…I admire you so much I know the Heavenly Father has touched you with his presence to inspire you to write these books. you have made such a difference in my life and my outlook. bless you…"   CHARLES

"…Oh my dear lord what a wonderful time I have had reading your books. I am so glad to hear there will be (or maybe all ready is) a last book. P.S. These books have inspired me to start reading my bible. I'll say it again......Thank you, Thank you."   NORMA

"…I have so enjoyed your angelic works of story and wisdom for living life to the fullest with God in control. You have managed to weave a beautiful love story while advising and guiding the reader in the importance of love and awareness of a higher power much greater than us. Thank you so much for this series. I can't wait to share them with my daughters and friends for I know they will enjoy your work as much as I have. I so look forward to your sixth book! Never doubt that you are writing for the reader's enjoyment only,but for the glory of our Heavenly Father! May God continue to bless you as you fulfill His work."   LINDA

"… I took my time reading the books because I did not want them to end!!! They were wonderful, I laughed, I cried, and I sympathized! I loved all 5 books, and they captivated me. Thank you,"   LYNNE

"…Just finished book five.....wow I have never enjoyed reading so much. thank you ever so much for these priceless books...they have touched my heart so much. When is book six coming out....can't wait."

                                                                    SALLY

Please write to Henry at: henry@henryripplinger.com or visit www.henryripplinger.com for more information about Henry's work and art. We would love to hear from you

THE HOUSE WHERE
ANGELS DWELL

---— ✦ ——---

Also by **Henry K. Ripplinger**

THE ANGELIC LETTERS SERIES
Book One....Pewter Angels
Book Two....Another Angel of Love
Book Three....Angel of Thanksgiving
Book Four....The Angelic Occurrence
Book Five....Angel Promises Fulfilled

OTHER WORKS
If You're Not From the Prairie...
(Story by David Bouchard, Images by Henry K. Ripplinger)

Coming soon from Pio-Seelos Books:

BOOK SEVEN OF THE ANGELIC LETTERS SERIES
The Heart of an Angel

THE ANGELIC LETTERS SERIES

Book Six

———— ✳ ————

THE HOUSE WHERE ANGELS DWELL

1992–1993

HENRY K. RIPPLINGER
Best Selling Author of Pewter Angels

Library and Archives Canada Cataloguing in Publication

Ripplinger, Henry, author
    The house where angels dwell / Henry K. Ripplinger.

(The angelic letters series ; book six)
Issued in print and electronic formats.
ISBN 978-1-928142-06-5 (hardcover).--ISBN 978-1-928142-07-2 (softcover).--
ISBN 978-1-928142-08-9 (ebook)

    I. Title. II. Series: Ripplinger, Henry Angelic letters series ; bk 6.

PS8585.I565H68 2017   C813'.6   C2017-901757-8
                                                  C2017-901758-6

Author photo: Bruce Vasselin, Designer Photo
Cover concept and design by Henry K. Ripplinger
Cover design and production by Brian Danchuk Design
Page layout by Human Powered Design

PIO-SEELOS BOOKS
Ph: (306) 731-3087, Fax: (306) 731-3852.
E-mail: henry@henryripplinger.com

Printed and bound in Canada by Friesens Printers
March 2017

This novel is dedicated to my guardian angel who has been by my side to guide, protect and pray to God on my behalf. At times, your job hasn't been easy!

ACKNOWLEDGEMENTS

DEAR JOAN, THANK you for the life we have shared together as a young couple, as parents and now as grandparents! With each passing year, I've come to treasure more and more your friendship and love in my life.

Thank you, too, Joan and Jen Howie, Debbie Beedham, my American friend, Penni Royston and Sr Theresia Elder for reading through the manuscript and catching errors in spelling, punctuation and grammar. Thank you, too, for your constructive comments.

To Tracy Jacknife, thank you for editing, proofreading, and your insightful suggestions. Very much appreciated!

To Dr. Peter Van Rooyen, thank you for your time, knowledge and assistance in dealing with the medical matters in the story.

To Father Hezuk Shroff, thank you for reviewing some of the chapters for theological correctness. Your encouragement and support is much appreciated!

Once again, to all of you, my heartfelt thanks for making my writing the best it can be.

As always, I thank the Lord for the gift of the Angelic Letters Series! Daily, I am thankful for His inspiration, guidance and encouragement through His angels, Holy Spirit and Divine Providence.

PREFACE

ONE OF THE things which I am learning over and over as I journey through life is that we are co-creators with God. If we have this mindset and come to Him each day, we will know the plan He has for each of our lives. To achieve your potential on this earth is to realize that it is not about you. It is about service to others so as to bring honor and glory to God. Directly or indirectly, it's to help Jesus bring salvation to the world; to continue the atonement which He began. When we allow His Spirit to work through us, we serve perfectly because we are at once elevated to our full potential as a child of God.

Like Jesus, we are here on this earth to serve. In the same way Jesus was obedient to the Father even unto death, so too, we are to be obedient to the Words of Jesus even unto death. Jesus knew his purpose on this earth was to die for our sins and He never wavered from that path.

As we learn what our plan and purpose is, we will become more at peace with ourselves and others; we become focused and live more fully in the present. The work we do becomes a joy even though hard work and sacrifice is required.

When I started to write this story, I never at any time realized that it would take on the life which it did. It was simply going to be a story about purchasing a home with its entire contents and becoming connected to the lady who owned it with the fictional realization that she was my first love. At no time did I ever think in the beginning that this story would grow beyond a single book. Nor did I think that it would become an inspirational series of books through which so many life lessons based upon Christian values would be portrayed through the characters in the story.

But then, this was to be expected. I am a teacher at heart with an inner need and desire to help others grow and look at life in a more meaningful way. I was simply developing the God given aptitudes, talents and gifts I was given at birth. I was realizing what I was intended to do; fulfilling God's plan for my life. Although I knew I was blessed with teaching and counseling abilities, I never realized to what depth until I began writing this epic story.

I never knew that I had writing skills and yet that is what I needed to impart the abilities I was blessed with. When the Lord has a plan for our lives, He prepares us for it and also gives us all the tools to get the job done. Through this story, God helped me claim my inheritance and discover who I was.

When we become who we were meant to be, it affects others and their lives. We now work with God to make a difference in the world. This was one of the most beautiful rewards I received from writing this series. When I began receiving countless emails how the series brought people back to their faith and how it helped them in their struggle to accept others, forgive others, love others, stop blaming others and taking responsibility for their lives, I was deeply touched. I knew that this series was not about me but Jesus touching lives through the story. I knew the series was a gift to me for a purpose that went beyond myself.

In book two, I introduced the concept of God's Divine Providence. How He works through others to help draw us back to Him, but also, how He works through us to minister to others. That is why we must always be ready and willing to serve our Father. Now when I write, it is with a different purpose than I had when I first began. Then, I focused on the story and the excitement of discovering my writing ability. Now, I pray that the Holy Spirit and my guardian angel through God's Divine Providence will fill me with words that will touch the hearts of others. My focus, prayer and motivation is to help others in their search for faith and a more meaningful life. It is to give hope, direction, purpose, meaning, and love. It's about collaborating with God to bring us all safely home to heaven.

My prayer for you in sharing all of this is to make you aware that God is preparing you for some work which you may already know and are carrying out. It is not about amassing treasures for ourselves here on earth but rather storing treasures in heaven. God's plan for our lives will always have to do with serving others and glorifying Him. That should be our focus in all that we do.

There is a recurring quote from Mr. Engelmann throughout the series that he said to Henry when he started to work for him at the grocery store: "Henry, this world so desperately needs people who have thought things through and don't go through life like a leaf tossed by the wind. We need more than ever, strong people who others will want to emulate because of the wholesome way they live."

Our time on earth is short in the vast scheme of things. Each second is a gift never to come our way again. The challenge for us each and every day is how we choose to live those precious moments; in service for ourselves or for Him.

Henry K. Ripplinger
February 23, 2017

"If anyone thirsts let him come unto Me and drink. He who believes in Me as the Scripture has said, "out of his heart will flow rivers of living water." But this He spoke concerning the Spirit, whom those believing in Him would receive; for the Holy Spirit was not yet given, because Jesus was not yet glorified."

JOHN 7: 37-39

"These things I have spoken to you while being present with you. But the Helper, the Holy Spirit whom the Father will send in My name, He will teach you all things, and bring to your remembrance all things that I said to you.

JOHN 14: 25-26

"But the Spirit Himself intercedes for us with groaning too deep for words."

ROMANS 8:26

"Know you not, that you are the temple of God and that the Spirit of God dwelleth in you?"

1 CORINTHIANS 3:16

"And it happened…that Paul….came to Ephesus. And finding some disciples he said to them, "Did you receive the Holy Spirit when you believed?"

ACTS 19: 1-2

PROLOGUE

A THOUGHTFUL MAN ONCE said that the reason why so many Christians have a weak faith and don't lead victorious lives is because they lack the full power of the Holy Spirit in their lives. It is indeed unfortunate that this blessing which could fill their lives with strength, joy and victory is little used and little searched for. Many believers don't even whisper a single word, a single small prayer to the third Person of the Holy Trinity. They seem to lack the knowledge that He is even in their soul.

It is a sad observation and yet, one so true. I have witnessed it often during the years of my priesthood and zillions of times more when I was on the other side. In those few moments when I had a glimpse into the heart of man, I was saddened by so many of God's children living mediocre lives drifting aimlessly day in and day out without purpose and meaning and eternity in mind.

This is so contrary to God's plan for His children. His design for humanity from the beginning was that each and every one of His children lives continuously under the control of His Divine Spirit. Imagine, God loves us so much that he sends his Holy Spirit to live in our souls. If only we would realize the joy, strength, graces, gifts and fruits we receive if we are open to Him. Imagine being filled with the love, peace and joy of God himself in our being!

We readily acknowledge God the Father and God the Son but fail to give the same homage to God the Holy Spirit. Somehow, His importance and role in the salvation of humanity was downplayed or the message was lost over time. Somehow, the Gospel was watered down and countless people were led to believe that just knowledge of the Holy Spirit is needed to live out a Christian life.

As I gazed over the sea of humanity, I saw a huge difference between being a Christian who was a believer and one which was filled with the power of the Holy Spirit. So many souls are converted to the faith but not convicted. So many know of Jesus, but sadly, are not filled with Him. It is as if they are satisfied to push the car which they are driving rather than start the motor and enjoy the journey.

I could see from this heavenly perspective how Satan has deceived so many souls into believing they are good enough; that it is okay to lower the standards of the Gospel and its teachings. That it is okay to be independent of God and His Spirit. That saying the Savior prayer is all that is required to be saved and not necessary to be committed and obedient to Jesus and follow in His ways.

I shook my head and immediately admonished my dear brothers and sisters in Christ, "Nein, nein, meine lieben Kinder, faith without works is dead. To commit to Christ requires that we show it by the way we live. The old must be gone and a new creature must be born. There must be a transformation of our mind and commitment to Jesus. We must witness to others that the light of the Holy Spirit is truly within us. That we are alive and well because the Holy Spirit gives us the strength and power and wisdom to live with the indwelling love and presence of Jesus in our hearts! Without this burning fire and passion for the Lord, our life is hollow and our faith will remain weak. If only the world today could see what happened the day of Pentecost and its meaning for us."

Zachariah knew my thoughts and his sensitive clear brown eyes saw what touched my heart. "Yes, David, Jesus clearly said to His apostles and disciples before He returned to heaven to sit at the right hand of the Father that God would send the Holy Spirit to guide, strengthen and lead them. They would not remain alone unprotected in the midst of their enemies and evil spirits prowling the world seeking the ruin of their souls. Jesus said He would be their Advocate in Heaven pleading on their behalf to the Father and the Holy Spirit would now come to them and be their Advocate, Comforter and Helper to empower them in their faith on earth."

I nodded as the vision of the day of Pentecost unfolded before me. The disciples were huddled together weak and filled with fear when a deafening sound filled the room. Out of what was like the roar of a mighty thunderstorm, flames as tongues of fire appeared and settled on the heads of all in the upper room. They were filled with the Holy Spirit and began speaking in languages they didn't know!

No sooner had they received the Holy Spirit than they all became warriors for the Lord. Their fears and worries and lack of courage were replaced with a mighty passion for Jesus. Incredulously, in the same way that Jesus had received the Holy Spirit on the day He was baptized by John the Baptist giving Jesus the power as a man to perform all the miracles and wisdom filled teachings during His ministry, the apostles and disciples on the day of Pentecost were now empowered by the Holy Spirit to do the same!

As Jesus said, "Truly, truly, I say to you, he who believes in Me will also do the works that I do; and greater work than these will he do, because I go to the Father." (John 14:12).

I could see that the day of Pentecost was the beginning of Christianity. What happened to the apostles and disciples also happened to the people they converted; the infilling of the Holy Spirit was intended for all followers of Christ.

"That is true," observed Zachariah as he read my thoughts once more. "However, even then there were believers who were not filled with the full power of the Spirit. It was immediately detected by those who were. Look at St. Paul when he went to Ephesus some twenty years after the outpouring of the Holy Spirit at Pentecost, he noticed straight away that many of the believers lacked the infilling of the Divine Spirit."

"Yes, yes, that is true."

Instantly, I recalled Acts 19: 1-2 when Paul came to Ephesus and asked some of the disciples, "Did you receive the Holy Spirit when you believed?" Upon learning that they did not know of the Spirit, Paul at once laid hands upon them to receive the Spirit of God. He knew that without the indwelling of the Spirit, they would never know the full love nor receive the indwelling of Jesus presence in them, too. Their belief would be in their mind but not their heart and thus they would lack conviction and not receive all the blessings of their faith!

It was the same with the Apostles when they walked the earth with Jesus. Although they were faithful in the presence of their Lord, they remained weak and relied upon their own independence. Even at the last supper they argued who would be regarded as the greatest amongst them. But after Pentecost, the Lord was no longer outside of them but now He was within them through the presence of the Holy Spirit.

And that made all the difference!

So much so, that countless of them in their quest to continue the redemption of Jesus in carrying out the Great Commission endured immense suffering, torture and martyrdom for their faith!

If St. Paul were to come into today's world, he would be devastated and his heart overflowing with sorrow that so many believers are still not convicted by the Holy Spirit! I could just visualize Paul hastening from one Christian to the other, laying hands on them to receive the strength and all the many blessings that accompany the Baptism in the Spirit!

"This is the age of the Holy Spirit, Zachariah, and we are missing out on the great realization that God Himself in the Person of the Holy Spirit could dwell within us in full power! His love within us makes things in our lives possible that would be completely impossible without Him!"

Zachariah nodded, "Without being filled with the Spirit, Christians and churches will never be able to fulfill their roles as God wants. The early Christians prayed and fasted and gave their 'all' in following Jesus. They were open and ripe to receive the Holy Spirit in full power. It is in direct proportion that mankind is willing to do the same; they will receive His power and strength."

"Yes, yes, when we pray with a sincere heart, the Holy Spirit will show where we are really at in our journey in life. He will reveal to us our lingering temptations and inclinations towards sin. He will show us the obstacles and masters stealing us away from the Truth: money, possessions, materialism, unforgiveness, character flaws, the list of false gods is endless! He will convict us of Jesus' teachings and prompt and urge us to let our worldly ways go. By receiving the strength and grace from the Spirit we will finally and fully realize this and begin to pass all of our thoughts, words, actions and deeds through the scrutiny of Jesus' word. We will see the light and become a beacon to others!"

Zachariah's wings fluttered even more vigorously, slightly lifting him off his feet. He began speaking much the same as the one he protected from his birth, "Yes, yes, David, when mankind fully realizes that their body is the temple of God, they will be far more careful in what they say, eat or drink and how they act in their lives."

Tears filled my eyes over the truth of my protector's words. This was all so profound that I fell to my knees and prayed for humanity to wake up before it was too late and waste so much of their lives lived without victory!

The Church and people need a revival of the Holy Spirit!

Although we have received Him at Baptism or re-born in the Spirit, we must invite Him into our lives daily to strengthen us and bring us home. It is the choices governed by our free will which opens and closes the doors to the Divine Spirit. Everyday must be a day of Pentecost! Yes, only then will the gift of living waters flow in and through our lives as the good Lord promised and so dearly wants for our lives!

"Oh, Spirit of God, I implore you to help us. Fill our minds and hearts with the need for Jesus in our lives. Oh, Holy Spirit, convict us to come to Jesus and be transformed! Oh, Holy Spirit, let others no longer see me but Jesus who now lives in me. Oh, Holy Spirit..."

I felt the soft touch of Zachariah's hand on my shoulder and soothingly heard his words filled with hope. "Our fleet of angels is working tirelessly to prompt mankind for this very purpose, David. We desire as you, to urge those in our charge to come to the Spirit. We all know, only too well, without the Holy Spirit in their lives, they will be helpless and unable to truly live for the Lord as was intended."

The vision of angels busily flitting about in the unseen came swiftly back to me during my near-death experience; so many helpers in God's kingdom with the same goal to redeem and save mankind. How deeply we are loved and cherished and desired by the Father and Son and the Holy Spirit to come to our heavenly home.

And there, from that divine perspective, I saw my dear adopted son still struggling with the ways of the world. Henry so aspires to be like Gary and John but his attachment to the world is still too great. He is only receiving part of the joy and strength he could have of the Holy Spirit if only he would let go and be free like his dear, sweet Jenny, the love of his life.

There she was, running ahead of him in the valley as cheerful and bright as the morning sun rising in the cloudless, blue sky. Even though she is not as knowledgeable as Henry of the Holy Spirit and His workings, she is filled with Him in her heart. It is evident in her life of praise and thanksgiving! She manifests the fruits and gifts of the Spirit in all whom she encounters: love, joy, peace, patience, kindness, generosity, faithfulness, gentleness and self control. She freely witnesses the outward expression of an inner life energized by the Holy Spirit!

I smiled as I saw in Jenny that her heart was so much like the happy angel that flitted about her like a hummingbird. She truly has the heart of an angel. Yes, I thought, if Hannah were to become an earthling, it would be impossible to tell her apart from her charge.

Zachariah's wings fluttered as he nodded with a broad grin showing agreement and added, "Yes, David your observation is correct, Jennifer is an example of one who knows the secret to a joyous life. She is filled with grace and truth."

"Ah, yes," I nodded to my wise, beloved friend and protector as the words of Jesus in John 15:1-8 came into mind:

"I am the true vine, and My Father is the vinedresser. Every branch in Me that does not bear fruit, He takes away; and every branch that bears fruit, He prunes it so that it may bear more fruit. You are already clean because of the word which I have spoken to you. Abide in Me, and I in you. As the branch cannot bear fruit of itself unless it abides in the vine, so neither can you unless you abide in Me. I am the vine, you are the branches; he who abides in Me and I in him, he bears much fruit, for apart from Me you can do nothing. If anyone does not abide in Me, he is thrown away as a branch and dries up; and they gather them, and cast them into the fire and they are burned. If you abide in Me, and My words abide in you, ask whatever you wish, and it will be done for you. My Father is glorified by this, that you bear much fruit, and so prove to be My disciples."

Tears sat on the edge of my eyelids as I saw and heard my Lord repeat Himself for the purpose of stressing the importance of Christians being closely connected to Him. Each time His repetition gave deeper meaning and further consequences.

Zachariah nodded, "It is also clear that a branch that is truly connected to the vine is secure and will never be removed. But one that only appears to be connected—one that has only a superficial connection to the vine—will be removed. If it does not have the life of the Holy Spirit flowing through it, it will bear no fruit.

"And it is further clear that you will never become the person you were meant to be without Jesus at the center of your life. With the Holy Spirit in your soul and the indwelling love of Jesus in your heart you will rise to your full potential as a child of God! We have witnessed this many times over the years in those we are assigned to guide and protect."

I smiled at my beloved protector and added, "The message is clear is it not? *Invite the Holy Spirit into your heart so that you might remain in the vine and live a life of peace and joy on earth and an unimaginable life of bliss for all eternity in heaven!*"

CHAPTER ONE

J ENNY WAS DELIRIOUSLY happy as she drove to the city. The
last three years of her marriage to Henry was all still a
dream come true. The incredible miracle of her healing and
bringing her daughter and Henry back into her life was one
thing, but how God's divine providence continued to turn all
the obstacles in her path into such good, filled her with a sense
of overwhelming awe: James' conversion; reconciliation with
her son; Carlos and his wife so readily agreeing to come to
Regina and take over her home; starting up the group marriage
and Bible studies and how the sessions had grown; and on
and on. Jenny could hardly contain herself as she reveled in
God's goodness.

Jenny was certain that the few remaining challenges would
soon be resolved. Justin still had not accepted her as part of
the family. Jenny had brought it up in the group session and
tried everything that was suggested to her, yet nothing seemed
to be able to break down the barrier or reach Justin's heart.

Both she and Henry had spoken to Justin but to no avail.
She explained to her step-son that she had no intention of ever
replacing Julean as his mother, but rather only to establish
a close, friendly relationship. While Justin seemed to agree,
time revealed however, that it was more to appease his father.

Jenny always felt his subtle coolness, the look in his eyes lacked warmth and acceptance, but what hurt Jenny the most was Justin's rejection of her touch. In many ways, Justin's reaction to her was similar to that of J.J.'s.

However, there was hope. If J.J. could be turned around, surely, Justin would too. Time and prayer are great healers; she had seen it with James and J.J. Sooner or later, God would work His healing touch in Henry's family just like He did in hers. Jenny fully expected it to happen but just didn't know when.

And then, there were the challenges that cropped up in the marriage and Bible studies which were becoming more like group counseling sessions. There were so many hurts and concerns in families. She thought all the while living on the estate with James that her problems were exclusive to her, but she was wrong. Problems similar to hers existed in other families; the coolness, withholding affection, taking each other for granted, financial problems, children out of control, unfaithfulness, drug addiction, the list was endless. One thing she was beginning to realize was what Father Engelmann had maintained all of the time, without Christ at the center of a home, the problems are insurmountable.

Jenny soon learned the need to help families was so great that she established twelve groups over the last year and half. Since it was impossible to head them all, Jenny began to train other ladies to lead the groups in their area of the city. This reduced her work load down to two meetings per week; the one with her group and the other with a group which consisted of all the leaders who would meet along with a psychologist to help them understand and deal with problems that were beyond their capabilities.

Word about Jenny's groups had spread so fast that there was always a waiting list of ladies wanting to join when the next session began. Jenny limited the groups to eight ladies. Agreement to strict confidentiality was mandatory. Other than that, there were no restrictions. Ladies in general opened up their lives quite readily and at times, too readily. That was why Jenny insisted on what was said in the group stayed in the group, if the sessions became more than just Bible study. To establish trust and openness was always a top priority with Jenny. She wanted the meetings to be relevant and helpful showing how the teachings in the Bible related to a happy family.

There were times however, when ladies in the group were hurting so deeply that they shared problems that were best discussed privately or referred to someone more qualified. Her thoughts wandered to a case in point as her car drifted into the other lane. A loud honk quickly brought her back into the slow lane. Jenny smiled at the man passing her, shaking his head.

She tried to concentrate more on her driving but soon her mind was going over what Susan, a mother of three children shared in the last session. The more the troubled mother alluded to her husband's abuse of the family, the more shocked some of the ladies became. Several of the ladies in the group knew Susan's husband and had a very positive impression of him. Jenny could sense the different reactions and concern amongst the ladies present.

Susan centered more on the verbal abuse in their relationship. Jenny understood that only too well from her relationship with James but in Susan's case, Jenny suspected physical abuse was there as well. Jenny was glad the last session had run out of time as she wanted to talk with Susan in private to see where this was going and the help which might be required.

One of Jenny's concerns was always that the sessions involved the wife but not the husband. This was a case in point where the husband had to be involved. That was one of the reasons she was trying to convince Henry to start up a men's group or at least to have three or four sessions a year which involved both halves of the couples. Speakers could be brought in to address different major concerns in marriages as well as family growth and development. In any case, Jenny was glad Susan had agreed to meet with her this morning before the regular session started and thus her reason for coming into the city early.

JENNY HELD HER breath as she pulled up and stopped in front of her home on Hill Avenue. It was the last week in May and the perennials were in full bloom. She loved the way the flowers grew at different heights and the lessons she had learned from Thomas as how to plant them so each flower could be seen. The dazzling colors took her breath away. Not only were her eyes feasting on all the flowers around but also the butterflies in the sky. Jenny was surprised to see so many Monarchs in the front yard as Carlos hadn't as yet planted the milkweed in the location he was going to. Perhaps they were drifting to the front in anticipation of food soon to be here. Jenny's blue eyes sparkled as she pictured the Monarchs as angels flitting about in colorful robes.

As soon as she got out of the car, the scent of the flowers and herbs wafted towards her. The aroma of God's creation of beauty touched all of her senses lifting her spirits instantly. She bent down and tore off a tiny piece of thyme at the edge of the walkway. She wanted to break off a daisy too, but was reluctant to terminate its life span. Jenny knew the healing power of nature and had always thrived on it. She didn't want to steal away any of the delicate flower's spiritual sustenance that it could offer to someone passing by.

Rather than go in the front door, Jenny decided to go around the walkway on the west side of the house. It was the fragrance of the lilacs that drew her. As soon as she turned the corner, the lilac bushes appeared in full bloom. She loved the way the white flowers of one bush intermingled with the purple flowers of the other as if embracing lovingly. The closer she came, the stronger the scent. She drank in the aroma so deeply, she felt intoxicated. She stopped to touch many of the flowers softly and tenderly resisting the temptation to break one of them off.

She heard Carlos whistling in the back yard before she saw him. He sounded like a Meadow Lark. When he spoke, it was no different. His words carried a melody to them. She had to step off the walkway to go around the third lilac bush to enter fully into the backyard. Carlos was replacing some of the petunias that were killed by the late frost two weeks ago. Fortunately, most of the flowers survived because of all the tree shelter. At the time, Carlos was almost in tears when he went out in the morning and saw so many of the flowers had wilted from the cold. In Ottawa, there is rarely a frost that late into the spring. He was learning that weather was not to be trusted on the prairies.

"Hi Carlos," Jenny said in a soft voice not wanting to startle him. But that was not necessary as she would soon find out.

"Good morning, Senorita Jenny. I sensed you were here."

"How, Carlos?" Jenny asked quizzically.

"Look at the Monarchs, how they come to you. I saw them fly towards the front yard ten minutes ago. I knew that only something they love more than the abundance of milkweed had to be there."

"Carlos, what an uplifting greeting...thank you!"

As Jenny approached the affable gardener, he stood up and extended his arms towards Jenny's extended arms as well. He had learned over the years a handshake was never accepted by his mistress. They briefly hugged.

"Everything looks so beautiful. It was such a blessing that you and Maria agreed to come to Regina." Jenny paused and looked around, "Is Maria in the house?"

"No, Senorita. She is praying at the shrine to the Blessed Mother."

"At the shrine? Where is the shrine...? Church?"

"No, it is here, at the back of the yard in between the fir trees."

Jenny looked surprised and Carlos continued, "Perhaps, we should have asked you, Senorita Jenny. The two fir trees behind the brush were a perfect place for a shrine. I was able to easily build it between the trees and well hidden from view..." Carlos' words trailed off as he kept his gaze on Jenny, not sure if his actions were offensive to his mistress.

"Oh Carlos, that sounds wonderful! I didn't know it was there. When did you construct it?" Jenny wanted to know.

"Last fall, Senorita. I studied how the light from the sun struck that area where we wanted the shrine. I had to prune back a few branches for the glorious sun to come through most of the day, especially in the morning."

"I would love to see it, Carlos but I do not want to disturb Maria...perhaps later after my visit with Susan."

"Oh no, now is fine. Maria asked to be called when you came so she can prepare the coffee and pastries for your group of ladies."

Jenny followed Carlos all the way to the very back of the yard just beyond where the gazebo and Angel of Thanksgiving were situated. Jenny just had to stop and pick a daisy. She smelled it and then placed it in the angel's basket. She softly murmured a prayer of thanks for all her blessings. She didn't mind picking the flower in this instance as she knew it would survive longer in the angel's care than in the earth.

When she looked up, Carlos was waiting for her and a warm smile covered his friendly face. "Look up, Senorita Jenny—see how they follow you."

Jenny looked up and countless butterflies flitted all about her.

Opposite the gazebo, Carlos disappeared behind a bush that was at least a foot taller than he was. All Jenny heard was the landscaper's soft words, "Come, Miss Jenny."

Jenny had to admit that she never explored that area of the yard. It was devoid of flowers and light and she always assumed it was filled with thick brush and several tall towering fir trees growing out in between.

When Jenny entered the dark, shadow filled opening, she could barely make out the path. Just ahead, however, a light struck the edge of the brush illuminating the worn, narrow path. Excitement swept through Jenny in anticipation that she was about to see something very beautiful.

She was right!

There, before her was a shrine about three feet high and two feet wide. The top canopy was curved giving the shrine a holy, cathedral look. A two foot tall statue of the Blessed Mother Mary stood inside the structure. Lying at the base of the statue were several red and yellow roses. Carlos' strategic positioning of the shrine allowed the rays of the sun to shine on the statue, bringing it to life.

What stung Jenny's heart, however, was Maria kneeling in the shadows before the shrine. Maria was so deep in prayer she hadn't yet heard or noticed the presence of Carlos and Jenny.

Jenny now knew why certain scenes prompted Henry to want to paint them. The image before her kept Jenny breathless and speechless. In much the same way nature drew her to Jesus and the Father, the shrine did so for Maria.

Suddenly, Maria turned and smiled. Even though still in the shadows, her eyes lit up at the sight of her dear friend. She quickly got up and made her way to Jenny. When she raised her arms, Jenny noticed the rosary sparkling in Maria's hand.

"I hope we are not disturbing you!" Jenny exclaimed as she hugged her dear friend.

"Oh no, I was just telling the Blessed Mother that I must begin to prepare refreshments and finger sandwiches for you and the other ladies."

"Mary seems like a friend to you?"

"Oh yes, Miss Jenny, she is my closest friend. I pray often to her to intercede to her son, Jesus, on my behalf."

"And I pray one novena after the other to the Blessed Mother as well," interjected Carlos.

"Henry says the rosary all of the time too, and so did his former wife, Julean. She had a very close relationship with the Mother of God."

Jenny paused and continued, "Why not pray directly to Jesus or to the Father?" Jenny asked with a quizzical look on her face once again.

"Si," said Carlos. "That question is asked all the time, Senorita Jenny. Another one is, 'do we worship Mary like we do Jesus or God the Father?'"

Jenny remained silent and waited for Carlos to explain as that was a concern she often thought, herself.

"The truth is that we do not worship the Blessed Mother. We honor her and consider her as a very close friend. When we pray to her it is not for her to answer our prayers directly but to intercede for us. We know that it is God, and God alone who answers our prayers. To pray to Mary, is much the same as when we often ask friends, or the parish pastor to pray to God for us. Prayer touches the heart of our heavenly Father and encourages His children to pray for and love one another."

"We hold the Blessed Mother full of grace and in the highest regard and honor," this time Maria interjected. "After all she was blessed to give birth to God the Son. She and Joseph raised Him—who better would know Jesus and His heart. It is only natural for a mother to ask her son to grant her requests. As I said earlier, conversing with Mary is like speaking with my closest friend. She understands my concerns and helps me clarify my prayers which I want to ask of Jesus."

It was as if Carlos had read Jenny's mind concerning the statue.

"Many times people think we are adoring and praying to a plastic statue." Carlos smiled and continued, "This of course is not the case. The statue of Mary helps us to visualize her in our mind and create a prayerful atmosphere bringing us to the Lord. Holy pictures, the cross, and the rosary all help us to come to the Father in thanksgiving and prayer."

Jenny reflected for a moment and said, "In a way, it's like how God's creation brings me close to Him."

Carlos nodded and smiled, his brilliant white teeth catching a ray of the sun.

"What do you mean by saying a novena, Carlos? Henry says them, too."

"It's a special prayer to Mary or another saint to intercede for a prayer request we may have. Right now, I am saying one to Saint Anthony to protect our eldest son who is in Korea. I have family, friends and grandparents who along with St. Anthony present our deepest prayer to God to keep our son safe. All of these different ways of praying help to lead us to the Lord. Angels and saints don't just sit around in heaven. They were so holy while on earth and spent their lives in prayer for peace, the church and mankind. Now that they are in heaven, face to face with God, they continue to assist us by interceding to the Father on our behalf. Jesus, too, continues to plead to the Father on our behalf as well to have mercy on us poor sinners."

A silence settled in the holy shrine area as the sun streaming through the trees warmed their spirits. Jenny wondered if a novena to Mary would help her deepest heart's desire. Ever since her marriage to Henry, it was her hope that one day, she would realize her lifelong wish...to carry his child.

CHAPTER TWO

H ENRY NEVER DID move off the deck after Jenny left for the city. They had shared morning tea, said their morning prayers and seeped in the beauty of the valley. Although spring had come early, there was always the danger of frost or even snow on the prairies. Usually, it's safe to plant flowers after May 24, but an unexpected cold front sneaked in during the night from Alberta creating a morning frost which was fatal for some of the flowers. Fortunately, it didn't snow as was forecast, which would have been devastating for many gardens already in full bloom.

Henry scanned the valley floor looking for damage to the wildflowers but was glad he didn't see any. His eyes rested on the bridge he had built across the meandering creek two years ago. For two springs now he didn't have to replace the road and culverts which were usually washed away by the torrent spring runoff. Henry wished he had built the bridge sooner. He should have known his battle against nature could never be won. It was wonderful for him to see the water flowing freely under the bridge as it was intended from the beginning of time.

He kept glancing to see if Father Engelmann would emerge from the prayer house. Father was spending more time there and less and less at the care home. Ever since he was miraculously healed, life at the care home had never been the same. Even before that incredible event, Father had the reputation of a very holy man. But after his restoration, people saw him as a blessed, beloved person of God, favored as much as Lazarus was.

Over his tenure as priest, many healings were due to Father's intercession which resulted in many coming to him for prayer requests. After his own miraculous healing however, not only had the requests increased a hundred fold, but many saw Father Engelmann as having special powers. Over and over, he would say that it was Jesus who heals and not him but his efforts seemed in vain. It was no wonder that slowly over the past two years, Father withdrew from the care home and decided his silent prayers and Mass offerings in the Poustinia for all the people in pain and struggling with different concerns would be better heard by the good Lord.

Suddenly, the phone rang, startling Henry out of his reverie. He quickly got up and went into the sun room and answered the extension phone next to his reading chair.

"Hello."

"Hi, is this Mr. Pederson?"

The female voice sounded familiar but Henry could not put a face to her distinctive words. "Yes, this is Henry Pederson."

"I hope you still remember the interview I had with you several years ago in your café. It's Brenda Oakley from the Leader Post calling."

"Aaah, yes, yes, of course I remember you and the interview we had. If you're looking for another one, I'm afraid there is nothing new to report other than I got married."

There was a momentary pause and Brenda dared to ask, "Would it have anything to do with the girl you briefly mentioned meeting in Mr. Engelmann's store back in 1956?"

Henry was amazed by her remarkable memory! "How on earth can you remember all those details, Brenda? That interview was at least six years ago?"

"Actually, I read my notes before I called and refreshed my mind as to what we were discussing. There were two or three items that you shied away from and one had to do with the girl you had met and the other had to do with some philosophical thoughts you expressed about the materialistic world we live in. To be honest, Mr. Pederson, I was very interested about the girl, as you had slipped away from me for several minutes during our interview. I could see the young girl, whoever she was, still had a hold of your heart. I am going to go out on a limb and say, I bet she is the one you married…am I correct?"

Once again, Henry was taken aback by Brenda's astute intuition!

"That's remarkable, Brenda! Truly amazing…you certainly are an incredible reporter. Yes, you are correct! Jenny is the girl and she and I married after being apart for decades. I'm sure, however, that is not the reason for your call…and please call me Henry. It's much too formal for someone who seems to know me at such a personal level!"

"Actually…Henry, the reason for my call was to see if I could have an interview with Father Engelmann. I called the Nunnery Care Home and they informed me that I might be able to locate Father at your acreage."

"Yes, he is here, Brenda. He's down in the valley prayer house. In fact, I was just thinking about him as I sat on the deck overlooking the valley. And now that my memory is coming back about our interview, I did suggest at that time you might want to do an interview with him."

"Yes, I read that in my notes the other day as I was preparing for this call. However, we have had several people call in over the past year suggesting that we do a story about him. Apparently, he had died and was miraculously restored back to life. Can you verify that, Henry?"

"Yes, that's true. Actually when I said, not much has happened since our last interview that was not exactly correct. It was not only Father who had died but so did Jenny and I as well. We were all healed and restored back to life! But that is old news even though it was an incredible event."

Henry could have gone on and on about purchasing Jenny's house and discovering it was hers. Now that would make for an incredible story or having finally come back together only to almost lose her again to her former husband...so many healings and happenings any of which would be interesting news.

Brenda broke into his thoughts. "Is Father coming in to Regina any time soon? I could meet him at the care home... or, I could come out to your acreage. I would love to see your studio and visit Father in the prayer house."

"It would make a great story, Brenda but Father Engelmann doesn't like to talk about himself. I could tell him you called and run it by him."

"Yes, please ask him." Brenda quickly added some motivation for the holy priest, "Tell him that such a story would inspire others to follow his lead. It would be faith building...perhaps, bring people back to the Lord. It would show that it is possible to live a detached life. It would demon—"

"Whoa, Brenda! All those things you mentioned may excite many people to show others what they have accomplished. However, Father is not one to do that. He does lead by example, quietly and humbly. If he has something that his flock should hear then he might raise his voice to make sure he has everyone's attention. Like I said, Brenda, I will run it by him, I may be wrong."

"Thank you, Henry. Please try your best. I have heard so much about him and would love to meet him. It would make an incredible story. I just know it!"

"Yes, I'm sure it would, Brenda...but don't raise your hopes up too high."

"Thank you for your time and congratulations on marrying the girl from your youth. I would love to meet her, too, and learn more of all that happened to all of you."

"I'm afraid an interview in that regard is out of the question. We are all happy to have settled into a peaceful lifestyle. It was nice chatting with you again, Brenda. I will let you know of Father's decision."

Henry hung up the phone, returned to the deck and sat down. He had to admit a story about Father's life would be incredible but Henry knew Father would not agree to it. And yet, like Brenda, he too, was writing a story! Henry wondered how Father was coming along with the epic love story he was assigned to write by his guardian angel, Zachariah. That was a remarkable story in itself. Both he and Jenny wanted so much to read it but Father was adamant that they must wait until he was finished.

Henry recalled a month ago when he visited Father in the prayer house, he noticed Father had finished book three which he had titled, *Angel of Thanksgiving*. Henry was certain the title had something to do with the Angel of Thanksgiving in Jenny's backyard. Henry would give anything to read it. He also noticed that Father was well into book four. It was still untitled.

Henry took a deep breath and slowly exhaled. *Yes*, Henry thought, as he drank in the fresh, early morning air, *it would all make quite a story*. In any case, he was elated the way everything turned out. Henry couldn't be happier living with his dear sweet Jenny. He was already counting the minutes until she came home. It was amazing how easily they both slipped into married life, accepting one another with their idiosyncrasies, their former spouses and their families. They were such a part of each other's lives and yet, they were free to pursue their interests and life work. It gave Henry such joy to see Jenny realize her vision to start up group Bible studies and marriage counseling.

As Henry gazed up into the cerulean blue sky contemplating how God had turned all things into such incredible good, there in the distance, coming towards him was an air balloon. He sat up and took notice. It looked so tiny and yet Henry knew only too well how huge the balloon was. He immediately recalled his and Jenny's adventure two years ago when he proposed to his first love in the heavens. *Wow! What a thrilling ride that was*. In fact, Henry still dreamed about it along with flashbacks of his stint on the other side.

Jenny mentioned that she, too, had dreams about that time she died and went to the other side and how a flashback of that came to her just before he had proposed to her up in the balloon. She saw Father Engelmann and him waiting with her to enter the tunnel of light. She had asked Father if he would marry them once they got to heaven. Although Father thought that was impossible as marriage doesn't exist in heaven, he had to admit anything is possible with God. His ways clearly are not like our ways nor are His thoughts like ours either. In any case the proposal way up high in the balloon was near to heaven and that entire experience was divine! Henry felt goose bumps sweep up and down his spine just thinking about it.

It was a good thing Father Engelmann's memory of that entire event was so clear in his mind. Even though Henry and Jenny couldn't recall seeing their guardian angels at least Father was able to describe them to Jenny and him. Henry wished that Jenny was able to remember seeing and meeting her guardian like Father described. He told Jenny how Hannah, her guardian angel looked so much like her and when her angel got excited, she would flutter about like a hummingbird! Henry knew Jenny would give anything if she could only remember meeting her guardian. Henry prayed right then and there that someday it would happen. His heart's desire was to make his dear wife happy and fulfilled in every way.

Once again, Henry was startled by the piercing ring of the phone. It was on its third ring when he answered it. Camilla was on the other end. He knew it was his lovely daughter-in-law as he heard the baby crying.

"Hi Camilla," said Henry forecasting who it was.

"If Noah hadn't just started to cry you wouldn't have been able to foretell who it was! One of these days I am going to trick you! How are you, Dad?"

"Hi Honey. I am just relaxing outside on the deck enjoying the beautiful summer morning. I am allowing my thoughts to wander to delay having to mow the grass beside the road leading into the property."

"Oh, Dad, I know that is not the case. You love being on the tractor, we all know that you're a farm boy at heart."

"Yeah, you're right, I do enjoy the smell of straw, grass, harvest…if you're calling for Mom; she went to the city to meet with her group."

"That's the third time this week. I hope she didn't start up another group?"

"Yes, she did. She is training another lady to take it over though. In a couple of weeks she'll be down to two groups per week."

"But that may not last long. She sure loves counseling and she is so good at it," observed Camilla.

"Yeah, a natural. She is trying to convince me to get involved by establishing a men's group. So many of the concerns their groups are dealing with involve issues that the husbands should be made aware of."

"Like the man's role and leadership in the family, the importance of communication, working at your marriage… need I go on?"

"You sound just like your mother. I have to agree that it's best if both partners are involved in these sessions. It's just that, I don't know if I want to be involved with counseling any more. I want to get back into my painting now that Jeremy and Justin are taking over more of the business and then there is something else I feel called to…" Henry didn't want to get into his calling to do missionary work and so he said, "Oh, here I am rambling on, I'll have Jenny call you when she gets home."

"The reason I called was to have you and Mom and Justin and Father Engelmann over for dinner this Sunday. Can you make it?"

"Wild horses couldn't keep us away. I know Father will be on board; he loves to see the kids as much as Jenny and I. I'll check with Justin—"

"Jeremy already asked him at work this morning and he can come too. It's too bad Lauren isn't home for the summer, I miss her."

"She is a busy young lady. Her dance classes in Montreal finished two weeks ago. She wanted to spend some time exploring Old Quebec but an audition came up in Toronto."

"Oh, that sounds exciting. What did she audition for?"

"It's for a part in a new musical about the biblical story of

Joseph and his brothers who tried to kill him. Lauren will know today or tomorrow if she got the dance part."

"She is a very talented dancer, I'm certain she will get the part. In fact, I bet she will be on Broadway in New York in no time."

"That is one of her dreams which may be well on its way to coming true."

Camilla couldn't resist adding, "That's for sure, like Matti would say."

They both laughed.

"Well, I better get going; sounds like Noah won't stop blabbering until he gets something to eat."

"Typical man, Camilla. Their stomach is constantly on their mind!"

"That and a few other things! See you Sunday, Dad."

As soon as Henry hung up the phone, it rang again! My, my, what a busy morning.

"Hello."

"I don't think you will ever guess who this is."

This was the second call from an unidentified female. With Brenda, her distinctive voice triggered a memory, but this one... Henry didn't have a clue.

"I'm afraid you've got me. Who is calling?"

"Does Sarah ring a bell?" the woman answered with a chuckling tone in her voice.

Henry didn't know...Sarah...Sarah and then suddenly, he remembered it was Gary's sister and the first thing he recalled was the large purple birthmark on the side of her face.

"Sarah! Gary's sister! Is that you Sarah!?"

"That's me, Hank."

"How are you doing, Sarah? It's been years since I last saw you. I recall so many fond memories of you, Gary and me chatting on the back steps."

"I enjoyed those talks, too, Hank. Well, I'm married, but I think Gary may have mentioned that to you. What you may not know however, is that I have six children, two are still at home..."

Henry momentarily tuned out. He enjoyed being called Hank. Friends close to him called him by his nickname...he liked that. It also reminded him right away of Julean. She always called him, Hank, as well with a Mormon accent which he loved. His mind quickly shifted to shame and anger at himself... why did he remember Sarah's impediment right away?

"Are you still there, Hank?"

"Yes, I am, Sarah. Your calling me, Hank, took me back in time to when we were growing up. Ever since starting my business most people call me, Henry. I must say being called Hank, caused me to recall so many fond memories and also reminds me of my former wife, Julean who called me that all of the time. But enough of that, it's so good to hear from you, Sarah. I recall you went into nursing after high school. Are you still in the helping services?"

"No. After my third child came along, my husband, Ben and I decided that it's best for me to stay at home. We don't have the fancy home or two cars that many people have but we enjoyed the kids growing up and the close family ties."

"That's great, Sarah. Jenny, my new wife—"

"Is that the same Jenny who lived in our neighborhood back then? She was so pretty. I'll never forget her blonde hair and sky blue eyes. You were so sweet on her. So you got married to Julean and now Jenny...?" Sarah's words trailed off not sure if she should ask what happened.

Henry sensed Sarah's concern and explained, "Julean got very sick and passed away several years ago and...well, it's a long story but somehow Jenny and I got back together again after thirty years of being apart. Two years ago, we got married. In fact, our third anniversary is next week, June 3rd! Oh my gosh..."

"Almost forgot, didn't you? I have to subtly remind Ben of our special day, too."

"See, there was a reason for you calling...it's not that I had totally forgotten but I almost forgot to pick up what I had ordered six months ago."

"Well, looks like you have things under control. The reason

for my call besides wanting to chat with you is that Gary is coming home next month for three weeks. Mom's celebrating her 85th birthday this July and he doesn't want to miss it. His friend John is coming with him as well."

"That's great, Sarah!" Henry exclaimed, "It will be so good to see Gary and John, too. I think of them so much lately and the wonderful work they are doing."

"Yes, I am very proud of him. Some of the things he tells me are heartbreaking; so many children starving and abandoned on the streets."

"Yes, my heart goes out to them. I keep thinking of ways to help besides just giving financial support."

"Perhaps the Lord is calling you in some special way, too."

"Yes, perhaps he is..." Henry's words trailed off.

"When Gary is here maybe we can all meet together. It would be so nice to get caught up on everything and I would love to see Jenny again. She was such a nice girl."

"Yeah, that would be great."

"Well, I better prepare for lunch. Ben is coming home early. You have a wonderful day, Hank."

"And you too, Sarah. If you write to Gary, tell him I can't wait to see him."

Henry's first thought after he hung up the phone was why it was Sarah's birthmark that he remembered first. Why do we focus on people's impediments? Sarah was such a wonderful girl and was so self-confident. Henry admired her self-assurance and all the while growing up; she made no attempt to hide the mark. And why should she?

"Henry!" Henry blurted, as he made his way back out to the deck. "Still so controlled by externals, by what people think," Henry continued to murmur to himself... "When are you going to grow out of this nonsense? It simply doesn't matter, we are all children of God and that is what is important. We are loved more than we can ever imagine. Whether one has purple skin, or it's black, yellow, brown or white; it simply doesn't matter." What needed to happen is for this to travel from the head to the heart. We are all brothers and sisters in

Christ, each unique in our own way with all of the challenges each of us is asked to bear.

Henry was going to sit down and have a second cup of coffee but decided he better get out there and mow the grass before Jenny came home. He picked up the empty mug and just as he turned, Father Engelmann emerged from the prayer house. Coco was right behind, her nose touching Father's knee with every step. It was interesting how Ginger stayed up top and Coco befriended Father. They had become inseparable. Henry was happy that Father had this loveable chocolate lab as a friend.

Father was beginning to look more like Moses or some other great prophet every day. His hair was growing longer and he began to grow a beard; both were as white as snow and flowing. He often said that shaving is time taken away from prayer. He was wearing his brown habit and the hood hung down on his back. The top of his balding head glistened like a wet stone. He reached for his walking stick and stepped off the deck. He was beginning his morning trek around the stream near the prayer house and would end up by climbing the hill just to the south which gave him a spectacular view of the valley. Father often said how much he loved that perspective. In some pleasant way, it reminded him of his homeland in Austria. Even though it was a small hill, at his age it was like a mountain and he considered it a great accomplishment to still be able to climb that high. Often times, Henry and Jenny would watch him and when he made it to the top of the hill he would raise his hands in praise and shout thanks of gratitude to God. The re-sounding echo through the valley sent chills up and down their spines.

Henry was so pleased that he had constructed the prayer house. Even though he didn't use it, it gave such a joyous refuge to his mentor. Henry loved Father Engelmann deeply, like his own father. How long would Father live? Henry knew it all had to do with his two missions that his guardian angel had assigned to him before he was restored back to life. His first mission to write the story which was well under way and would soon be completed. But what of his second mission? What task did God request of him? Whatever it is, Henry prayed that it would be far off into the future. Henry knew when it was done, so too, would Father Engelmann's life on earth be over as well.

CHAPTER THREE

J UST AS CARLOS, Jenny and Maria emerged from the secluded shrine area, Susan was walking down the stone path towards them.

"Oh, there you are! I thought that since no one was around that perhaps I mixed up my days."

"No, this is the day we meet, Susan. I was visiting a small prayer grove that Maria and Carlos created in the back area."

Jenny approached Susan and gave her a hug. "Thanks for coming earlier. Let's go inside. There is something I want to discuss with you."

As Susan turned, Jenny put her arm around her friend and together they strolled back to the house.

The ladies sat next to one another on the sofa in the living room. After discussing a few trivialities, Jenny broached the subject she wanted to talk with Susan about.

"At our last meeting, Susan, you began to speak of your relationship with your husband, Jack. What I understood from what you said was your concern over Jack's lack of respect for you. I'm happy that you feel safe enough in the group to share the relationship you have with your husband at a deeper level. I thought it best to discuss it with you in private before opening your life up further with the group."

Jenny took a deep breath and continued, "If you like, Susan, we can talk more about it now. I feel I went through similar concerns in my first marriage and understand what you may be going through."

Susan sat in silence for a long time. Unbidden tears rested on the lower lids of her eyes, ready to fall at any moment. Jenny reached for a tissue and handed it to her troubled friend and then let her hand rest on Susan's knee. Jenny softly smiled and nodded conveying to Susan that she had her full attention and willingness to help.

"In so many ways, Jenny, Jack is a wonderful husband and father but he tends to take his frustrations at work out on the children and me when he comes home. If everything isn't perfect, he finds fault with it. If the children misbehave, it's my fault. If the dinner is overcooked, I hear no end of it...and many times it's because he is late. Some days, Jenny, I wish...I wish I were dead and gone...he's so hard to live with."

As Susan spoke, Jenny recalled similar days she had with James. Many times she too, wanted to leave. If J.J. hadn't been in the picture, she may very well have, but she didn't want to lose a second child. Jenny reached out with both her hands and grasped Susan's hands resting on her lap.

"Oh Susan, I understand what you are going through and how difficult it is to deal and cope in such a relationship...is it just verbal disrespect, Susan, or does he physically abuse as well?" Jenny needed to know.

Susan could no longer hold back her tears and broke down and cried. Maria was about to bring in tea and cookies for the ladies but stopped abruptly at the doorway and quietly returned to the kitchen.

Slowly, Susan began, "He doesn't mean to, but after a few drinks his personality seems to change and he becomes a different person. At times, I am so afraid of him...and yet, at other times, I am so thankful I married him and he is the father of our children. Oh Jenny, what can I do?"

Jenny squeezed Susan's hands, "Thank you for sharing that with me, Susan. I know how difficult this is for you and yet, this has to be dealt with—"

"But how? Jack would be terribly upset with me if he knew I was divulging what goes on in our home with others. He didn't like it when I joined the group and he always cautions me not to discuss our family affairs…I don't see any solution, Jenny."

Susan began to cry once more, only this time, the sound carried hopelessness. She shook her head in despair. Jenny had heard other stories like this over the past year and a half since starting up the groups. She had soon learned that there were too many concerns that she was not trained to deal with. Taking Camilla's suggestion, Jenny had made arrangements with a Family Service Bureau with a psychologist and psychiatrist on staff to refer people in her group to in such instances.

"Susan, I am going to make a suggestion to which at first you may be unwilling to try. I can only tell you, we have had tremendous success in dealing with concerns like this. I would like to refer you to an agency that is trained to deal with such problems. I know it's frightening and may seem impossible, yet things have a way of working out. You have to be willing to trust the process. For you and Jack to continue in your present relationship is going nowhere and detrimental to the children and to you. This is no environment in which to raise a family and it's so unhealthy for all concerned. I have seen things turn around. Jack needs help and both you and he have to be open to deal with this."

"But Jenny, how would I ever approach him about this? He would never agree to counseling and I would never hear the end of it. Just the thought of telling him frightens me to no end…I'm afraid of what he might do."

"I understand how you feel, Susan. Counseling services are trained to help you with how to approach your husband. You have to consider it, Susan. What else can you do? You know this isn't any good for you and the children nor Jack. To just let it continue would be devastating and harmful."

"Well, perhaps I could talk to them. If I don't want the Family Service to get involved will they leave me alone?" Susan asked with fear in her eyes.

"Yes, Susan, if you don't want them to get involved, they will respect your decision. I will go with you at the start."

Jenny looked at Susan with compassionate, trusting eyes and added, "Together, we can do this Susan."

"Oh Jenny, you are such a true friend..." Susan began crying once more and the two ladies reached out to one another and warmly embraced.

CHAPTER FOUR

S HE WAS A mile away driving down the grid road when Henry noticed Jenny. He knew it was her as he gazed across the flat prairie; it wasn't just the blue color of the car that made him so sure, it was what he was feeling in his heart. There was only one person that made his heart race the way it was now. Henry stopped and turned off the diesel engine without looking at the key in the ignition. He couldn't keep his gaze off the convertible as it suddenly came to the top of the valley and began to meander around several sharp turns that followed the contour of the valley floor.

There was no mistaking the driver of the blue BMW convertible. Her golden, wheat colored hair fluttered in the wind as she turned the car into the lane leading to the farm. Ginger was already there ready to greet and lead her to the farm house. Henry thought it was odd not seeing Coco alongside her side kick, Ginger. They were always rivaling to be the one at the lead and the first to get patted by whoever came home.

Jenny pulled up beside the tractor and winked at Henry. Keeping her gaze on Henry, she too, turned off the motor. They stared at one another as if lost in another world but it wasn't enough. Henry climbed off the tractor and Jenny opened the car door and slid out. Within seconds they embraced and their lips met for a long time.

Ginger wriggled between them pleading for affection too, finally separating them. Henry reached his hand down and patted Ginger. "Good girl, Ginger."

Jenny bent down and gave Ginger a hug. "You're such a good girl, Ginger. I love you, too!" Jenny looked up at Henry and continued, "Is Coco still with Father Engelmann?"

Henry nodded, "Yeah, I never thought I'd see the day Coco would leave my side but I'm no match for Father. Coco is completely smitten by him. Her nose never leaves his side as she did mine. It's always touching his knees whether he's sitting or walking or just standing."

"It's such wonderful companionship for Father. Coco is so loyal and faithful…" Jenny's words trailed off as her eyes grew watery and red.

Henry immediately sensed something was troubling her. "What's wrong, Honey?"

Jenny began to weep. "Oh, why can't people be as faithful and loving as dogs? I promised not to bring my problems home from the group work but…"

Henry put his arm around Jenny and gently pulled her over to the white railing fence. Both horses were running towards them. Henry loved that sight more-so than riding them.

As they slowly strolled over to the horses already waiting for them at the fence, Henry gently asked, "Some of the ladies having more than their share of challenges, Honey?"

Jenny pulled a tissue out of her pocket and dried her eyes. "So many of the ladies opened up today; Susan is not only dealing with verbal abuse but physical as well. Her husband drinks too much and at times can't recall in the morning that he beats her and the children, Later, when the regular session began with the entire group, Jill broke down as she shared how she found a love letter in her husband's sports jacket's pocket from a lady he has been seeing for over a year. I don't know which is worse; a husband who is faithful but abusive or an unfaithful spouse. Oh, Honey, my heart breaks listening to the women. How can a man with a loving wife and three children cheat on them?"

Henry kept one arm around Jenny and stroked the nose of Valley Seeker. "It's hard to understand, Jenny, but it's a common problem for both men and women. It's more prevalent with men; that's for sure. I see it all the time in the café. If I'm talking to a group of married men and an attractive girl walks by, no matter how interesting my story is, I see their eyes either wandering or casting a furtive glance."

"Not you, I hope?" Jenny interjected.

Henry smiled, "I'm guilty at times but I quickly rein myself in. It doesn't take much for a man to get excited. That's why it's important for women to realize how they dress and behave—not that I'm saying it's a woman's problem—it's just that a woman can have tremendous power over a man."

"I know what you're saying, Henry…"

"With you, you always dress modestly and I love and respect you for it."

Jenny gazed at Henry and forced a smile. "I was so overwhelmed by all the concerns the ladies brought up. Of all the groups I have had, this one is the most challenging. I just kept praying to the Holy Spirit for wisdom and guidance in dealing with all of the difficulties that arise within their families."

Jenny turned back to the horses as both were nodding their heads vying for her attention much like Ginger was. It gave her a momentary respite from her heavy heart before she turned back to Henry and continued, "The trouble is, Henry, in so many marriages, there is a lack of Jesus in the home. I loved when we got married and vowed to keep Jesus at the center of our marriage. There is such strength and security in that which many families are missing out on. From what the ladies share, there is little faith and spiritual leadership in the home. Some go to church occasionally but most do not go at all. Most say there isn't any prayer time, grace at the table and Jesus' teachings in the Bible are never brought up. Most have Bibles in the home but are rarely opened. Many expressed the hope that this study group would get them started and find help for improving their lives and family."

Henry nodded but remained silent allowing Jenny to express her concerns.

"I was so relieved when Connie shared that they pray every morning and evening as a family. They bring up challenges in their lives and the entire family prays for that member's concern. They attend church on Sunday as a family, pray at meal times and even have her children giving part of their allowance to charities and missionaries."

"Sounds like the ideal family, Jen. She and her husband are instilling very important values to live by in their children."

"Yes, and I loved the way she added that she and her husband have special days together. And like we do, they go out to dinner twice a month and surprise one another with little gifts just like they did when they were courting!"

"Wow, what a great member to have in your group. There is nothing more powerful than hearing someone proclaim the value of having Jesus not only at the center of the family but also how important it is to receive His grace and strength to make a marriage work from day to day. So often after a year or so, couples take one another for granted. They slip into a daily routine and get caught up in work, making money and are too tired or filled with so many concerns that they ignore one another and each other's needs."

Henry took his arm off Jenny and leaned both arms on the fence. Jenny turned to the horses once again, too, and continued talking as if speaking to them. She stroked their foreheads and said, "Jesus is a big part of the answer. I am so glad that our groups are faith based and use the scriptures as our guide. For many of the women in the group this is so new to them. I can see the power of praying for one another and witnessing. It was wonderful to see James turn around as he began to read the Bible and see how God's words were alive and present and lived out on the estate by Matti, Thomas and the other staff."

"Yeah, that's the key, Jen. Witnessing by the staff was important but I still say it was your love and acceptance of where James was at when he was most difficult to live with that helped him to see himself as he really was and he began to grow as result. *So many couples can't do that.* In many relationships, love is so conditional…if you do this or are that way, then, I will love you and be nice to you…"

Jenny's eyes widened and nodded in agreement. "One of the ladies shared that exact point the other day. She would give her husband the silent treatment or withhold sex and just let things simmer until she would get her way. Or, at times her husband, too, would not give in until eventually it became so unbearable that they would have a huge quarrel even in front of the children."

Henry turned to Jenny keeping one elbow on the fence, "Being kind, respectful, forgiving, not holding grudges, talking things out, wanting the best for your partner has to be the top priority everyday for a good relationship to grow and stay alive…"

"See!" Jenny nodded, her blue eyes brightening, "You're basically saying what First Corinthians, Chapter 13 verse 1 to 13 says about loving one another! It's all in the scriptures how we should be; I'm learning that over and over, honey. We can discuss issues week after week but without the grace and strength and guidance of God and His word it's just too difficult. We need Jesus at the center and the Holy Spirit to help us stay committed to Jesus and obey His word and apply it in the family."

"Wow! You are sounding a bit like Father. The key is to get people to understand that. Father Engelmann has been preaching that for years and years; we're just too self-centered and proud to try and change and make things work on our own. Even Jesus said in one of the scriptures, "'Without Me you can do nothing.'"

"Oh, Henry, I know it was my idea to start up these groups and I'm glad I did but it just seems so one-sided. Somehow, the men need to get involved. They need help and guidance as much if not more…even though women can express and share their feelings easily, men need to open up as well. So many men must hurt so deeply, trapped by feelings they bottle up and can't release."

"Yeah, many men think it's a weakness to show tears or hurts, yet, I agree, they need to let it out and get new thoughts about their concerns and their role within the family."

Jenny was comforted by Henry's words and that encouraged her to ask him something she had been considering for the past few weeks. She looked pleadingly into his eyes and said, "I wonder if we had a social get-to-together and both you and I speak..."

Jenny hesitated for a moment, "You are a counselor and such a wonderful husband...would you consider forming a men's group?"

Henry tightened his lips and gazed tenderly into his dear wife's eyes. He didn't know if it was Jenny or Ginger or the horses who wanted his attention more. Henry looked down at Ginger's nose nudging repeatedly against his hand hanging at his side. He held off gazing into Jenny's pleading eyes as he didn't want to commit. Now that he had more time on his hands, he wanted to get back to his painting and then there was also this tug at his heart to help Gary. For years he felt called to help out in missionary service and yet...

"You know, Jen, you are raising many issues, some so serious that they require professional counseling, but for the most part, you are right. What you are trying to do must involve both parties at least some of the times. I agree, talking to the ladies is a great start and opens the door but men need to be involved too. I thought at first your groups would center more on bible study and social events but I see it's turning out to be much more and that's wonderful. Reading the Bible lets people know what they are lacking in their lives and sharing where they are at and what they need to do to make their family come together in a more wholesome way. You are looking at the spiritual side of life which many people and families ignore or are missing."

Henry paused, and went on, "I can help to get a men's group started and maybe we can train men with leadership potential to take over just like you have trained women to lead other groups. Perhaps we could bring in guest speakers in the fall to get things started—"

"Oh, Henry," Jenny thrust her arms around him and gazed lovingly into his eyes. That would be so wonderful…"

As they tenderly kissed, Ginger quickly nudged her cold nose in between them, once again. They parted and looked down at their friend wagging her tail pleading for more affection that could never be satisfied.

"I have to make just two or three more passes with the tractor and the grass should be done."

"Yes, it looks so nice and trimmed driving up the lane. I noticed you cut around the fir trees on either side of the road, too."

"Yeah, it's tricky, but I'll finish off with the weed cutter. By the way, I took chicken out of the freezer for dinner and left the recipe book open on the counter."

"Chicken Marsalis with wild rice…right?"

"My favorite, sweetheart. That was the recipe you had open on your kitchen counter when I bought your house on Hill Avenue. It will always be my favorite recipe."

"I'll make it extra special, just for you! Thank you so much for deciding to help me, Henry!"

Jenny checked her watch and added, "It's only a bit past four, I think I'll change and go for a horseback ride before dinner."

They both turned towards the horses, "I can saddle up Valley Seeker and have her ready for you."

"That would be wonderful, Henry. She is a tall quarter horse and I do have trouble putting the saddle on her."

Henry climbed over the fence and just before he turned to head to the barn with the horses, he said, "Oh, Camilla called and asked to have us over for Sunday dinner."

"Wonderful! Love you!"

He loved the way she said she loved him. He loved the way her lips formed each word. How many times had he wished he were a word to be cuddled by the sweetness of her lips. Henry gazed into Jenny's sparkling eyes, bluer than the blue sky and mouthed to her, "I love you more, Jen."

Just as Henry was making the last swipe with the tractor, Jenny galloped past him on Valley Seeker. She threw him a kiss and waved. He immediately stopped and gazed at her. Shortly after they married, Jenny began horseback riding. Instantly, she loved it. She was a natural; her balance was perfect and her posture, excellent; she was one with the horse. Henry was certain, Valley Seeker enjoyed the run just as much as the graceful rider on her back.

Henry could feel his dear wife release the cares of life into the prairie wind as she cantered along the ditch. He loved how her golden blonde hair glistened in the sun and fluttered, wildly in the wind. He could feel the freedom soaring through her. Although he wasn't the rider she was, Henry often had similar feelings of abandon when he used to ride his bike speeding down the streets and avenues when he was growing up.

When Jenny reached the end of the lane leading into the property, Henry was certain she would head south down the dirt road and then turn east into the valley but she surprised him. She turned and headed back his way. Henry turned off the tractor as she rode to his side.

"Come on, Honey. Let's have a late dinner. I just remembered that Justin is staying in the city and it's such a beautiful day. Saddle up Lucky and let's go for a ride together."

How could he resist. "Okay, I'll finish cutting this last bit of grass in the ditch on the way to the barn. Bring Lucky up to the corral."

Within fifteen minutes, they both were off down the dirt road Henry thought Jenny was going to take earlier. Where the road led through a coulee, they chose to go off the road and follow a trail which descended down into the valley about two miles south of the Poustinia. From there, they would follow the meandering stream to the prayer house and then return back up to the barn.

About half way down the steep hill, two deer darted out from the brush startling Jenny and the horse. She quickly got control of Valley Seeker and continued on. Henry wondered if he would have remained that cool and collected. He had to admit, he enjoyed watching horses run more than riding them but just being next to Jenny was having a calming effect on him.

It took longer than expected to make it to the prayer house. By the time they stopped several times by the stream to let the horses drink and enjoy the different scenery in that part of the valley, the sun was getting close to setting in the west. They decided not to visit with Father and instead head straight up to the barn before dark.

When they reached the top, there was hardly a breeze in the air. It was a calm summer evening. A few distant clouds were scattered into a strata formation near the zenith and some more billowing ones further to the south, guaranteed a typical prairie sunset. Henry and Jenny were almost touching as they slowed their horses to a walk. Riding into the sunset was one of the beautiful wonders of the prairies and they wanted to fully take in the spectacular show.

"I remember when we first met; you said one of the things you would miss if you ever moved away from the prairies was the sky. I can see why."

They both came to a stop and gazed at the scene unfolding before them. They knew the prairie treasure they were about to see would quickly be over.

Against the canvas of the prairie sky, stretched from a perfectly flat unobstructed horizon, to a clear blue zenith overhead, the colors and the light both quickly changed. The sun's rays created a kaleidoscope of colors in all directions illuminating the undersides of the clouds and everything in its path. The edge of the tall elevator in the distance, standing as a sentinel over the land, seemed to be burned off as the sun slid behind it. In the next breath, the horizon itself seemed destined for the same fate, as the glowing yellow sun dipped out of view. Thousands of shades of oranges, yellows, mauves, violets, purples, blues, dashing from warm to cool spattered across the sky... changing from one canvas to another, ever changing from a cool palette to a warm... now slowing, softening.... bringing peace and stillness to the close of another day. Henry and Jenny were held captive in a rapturous embrace as if cradled in the boundless beauty and glory of God's creation.

"Unbelievably breathtaking, are inadequate words to describe this, Henry. This is something we rarely saw growing up in Ottawa. I just keep catching my breath at the magnificent sight before us."

"For years as an artist, I would watch this show with such a critical and analytical eye that I would literally miss the natural beauty of what was before me. When I finally accepted the fact that I would never capture it all, I slowly began to relax and started to truly appreciate its spectacular magnificence. God and God alone is the Master Painter. I will be His apprentice forever. Furthermore, the more I relaxed about it all, the easier it became for me to try to capture it on canvas in some small way. Along with this resigned acceptance, came a better painting. The painterly part of my mind was no longer inhibited by struggling thoughts of trying to become like the Creator and reproduce what He so effortlessly has achieved with a slight twinkle of His eye or soft whisper of His breath."

"That's a beautiful thought, Henry. I think the same would apply to an author trying to find adequate words to describe the yellow glow surrounding a blinding core, causing colors to change so quickly in all directions. But once again as you just said, Honey, trying to analyze each second seems to destroy the beauty of the entire scene. Don't complicate and clog up your mind trying to describe something that was meant to give joy and peace; to soothe the cares of the day and take them along with the setting sun. Release it all … just let go, and enjoy the moment…be still and know that I am God, our Creator and Creator of everything."

Henry nodded. There was much truth in what they said, yet there was that creative part within us that always tried to capture the beauty of God's creation whether it was by word, brush or pen. We can't help ourselves but try.

By the time Henry and Jenny got up to the barn, the brilliant hues which were before them just moments ago were gone. In its wake, an emerging twilight spread across the horizon.

Jenny made her way over to the fence and leaned on it as she waited for Henry to feed the horses and close up the barn.

"Now comes your favorite time of the day, Henry," Jenny said as Henry joined her by the fence.

"Yeah, the stillness and peace is ever more enhanced as the darkness grows, bringing to an end another day. Look how the dark silhouettes which were not that evident before, pop out here and there." Henry pointed to a farm homestead with a twinkling light, groups of trees, granaries, the sheen of the water atop a slough reflecting the soft light; all were coming into view, carrying their own beauty.

"Oh, Henry, with each sight and thought I feel the tension of the day go. If only it were possible for everyone to see how God intended for us to unwind."

"That's why Father Engelmann follows the cycle of the day. He rises with the sun and gets ready to retire shortly after the sun sets. He would compare everything to the light. Just like the Word of God is a beacon of light, the sun seems to start it all by luring one's attention to the beauty of God's creation."

"Only if they take the time to notice it! The sun is coming up somewhere now to begin the day. I pray they rejoice and are glad in it and at day's end they too, can take in the greatest show on earth which is ever changing and never a re-run!"

CHAPTER FIVE

⟫⟩⟨⟪

E ARLY THE NEXT morning, Henry and Jenny decided to
walk down to the prayer house and visit with Father. It
was only six thirty, but they knew if they didn't go soon, Father
may already have said Mass and they wanted to celebrate the
Sacrament with him. Father didn't have a phone and so there
was no way of communicating with him other than going
down there.

They both took a deep breath of the morning fresh air.
Ginger was out of her dog house the instant they opened the
front door and ready to greet them with excitement.

"See, this verifies what I said yesterday; dogs are so friendly
and ready to do anything to make you happy. We can learn so
much from them; always ready to forgive and forget, affection-
ate, accepting…the perfect example of unconditional love."

Henry bent down and patted Ginger wagging her tail in
appreciation. "I have to agree, Honey."

Jenny winked and blurted out her favorite phrase, "Quickly,
hold my hand."

She didn't have to ask twice before Henry slid his hand
into Jenny's warm soft hand and they were off at a brisk pace.

They had only walked a few steps when Henry suddenly
stopped. Jenny turned to look at him. Henry was staring

towards the sky, "Jenny look, there's the same hot air balloon I saw yesterday floating over the valley!"

"Oh, my gosh, Henry!" Jenny said excitedly, "It takes me instantly back to when we went up on one and you proposed to me! I'll never forget that morning. I was so afraid to go and yet, once up there, it was truly heavenly!"

"Yeah, what a morning that was and to watch the sun come up from that perspective was amazing! What do you say we do it again, Jen?"

"No, once is enough and I don't ever want to forget that experience. It was so special, honey!"

The air cooled as they descended into the valley. Jenny wrapped her arms tighter around Henry's arm trying to draw more warmth from his body. Soon the road winding around the hill turned the bend which exposed the panoramic view of the valley. Both stopped instinctively to catch their breath and take in the incredible beauty of the valley floor surrounding the Poustinia. The meandering stream snaking in and out amongst the bright green shrubs and wildflowers highlighted by the rising sun was breathtaking, indeed!

"I never get tired of this view, Jenny. The prayer house nestled in all this beauty just naturally makes one think of God. No wonder Father loves it here so much."

Jenny didn't speak for the longest time. She was lost, completely living what Henry had just said without hearing his words. Nature truly was her refuge and strength; the channel through which she related to the heavenly Father. It was the source through which the Holy Spirit filled her with the power and strength to love unconditionally. Henry looked at his sweetheart and knew what she was feeling.

Silently, slowly, they walked ahead, occasionally squeezing each other's hands to convey the love they held for one another as well as expressing their deep appreciation for God's creation.

"What is going on at the island?" Jenny inquired.

Henry wanted to keep it a secret from Jenny that he was planning to build a gazebo for her on the small mass of land that was surrounded by the meandering stream.

It was across the pond from where the prayer house was situated, just far enough to make another wonderful refuge site and not interfere with the solitary sereneness of the prayer house. What Jenny was noticing was a make shift bridge made out of two long telephone poles that provided access to the island.

"Oh, I want to make a little clearing for a rest spot for Father when he takes his walk…and for any of us for that matter." Henry quickly changed the subject. "I am surprised that Coco has not come out of the Poustinia, yet. She usually hears us coming long before Father is aware of our presence."

Father must have intuitively heard Henry's words as both Father and Coco came out of the house onto the deck and waved.

"Hi Father!" shouted Jenny, her eyes sparkling in the growing light.

Henry smiled and waved and watched as Coco struggled with the decision to stay with Father or come to him and Ginger. Amazingly, she stayed at Father's side.

Father shook his head as he watched the radiant couple hurry towards him. It immediately brought back memories of the first few times Jenny came to the store to visit Henry. He was taken aback then and again now over Jenny's buoyant spirit. He recalled the scripture now as he did then, "Ah, Proverbs 13:15," Father muttered as he saw the sun dancing in her twinkling eyes, lighting up her features. "A happy heart makes a cheerful face!"

Father Engelmann's smile broadened and said, "I suspected you might be coming down this morning, so, I held off from saying Mass."

Jenny quickened her pace as she approached the deck and hurried to give Father a warm hug. "Oh, Father, I love the way your white hair tosses about in the breeze and your beard is getting longer. You have the image of a wise prophet in the Old Testament."

"Yes, that's for sure!" echoed Henry as he climbed onto the deck and embraced Father.

They all looked down at the two dogs excitedly greeting one another by sniffing and touching each other's noses. Henry bent down and patted his once inseparable sidekick. "Hi, Coco…good girl. I see you don't miss me anymore." Coco licked Henry's hand and then returned to Father's side.

"Come in, let us celebrate Mass and then we will have a nice visit and enjoy some fresh fruit out here on the deck," said Father, as he turned and entered the prayer house by way of the kitchen. Coco immediately followed her new master, her nose touching Father's knee with every step he took.

Jenny loved the Poustinia. The small kitchenette opened up to the living room. The large five foot tall wooden cross on the opposite wall immediately drew one's vision upon entering the room. The wood carving of Jesus hanging on the oak cross was so lifelike it was difficult to pull one's gaze away from it. The small altar directly below the cross immediately gave the room with its high cathedral ceiling a small country church atmosphere. Father had turned the two wicker chairs that normally faced the pond from the patio doors towards the altar in anticipation for their coming to the morning Mass. A padded oak kneeler was already in front of each chair.

Jenny and Henry made the sign of the cross and knelt far enough away from the altar for Father to move about in front as he celebrated the Mass. While Ginger lay on the deck, Coco lay right beside the altar watching Father's every move.

Incredibly, one of the readings that day was Ephesians 5:21-30. With a twinkle in his eye, Father turned to Jenny and said, "I know where your heart and mind are these days. God not only instituted marriage but He also defined the roles of husbands and wives." Father turned to the altar and picked up the Bible, turned again and handed it to Jenny. "Please read the scripture Jenny and then we can take a few minutes to discuss it."

Jenny knew of the scripture and had read it many times in her groups. The one stumbling block that many women felt was the word 'submit'. Jenny rested the heavy Bible on her lap and began to read:

"Honor Christ by submitting to each other. You wives must submit to your husband's leadership in the same way you submit to the Lord. For a husband is in charge of his wife in the same way Christ is in charge of his body the church. (He gave his very life to take care of it and be its savior!) So you wives must willingly obey your husband in everything, just as the church obeys Christ.

"And you husbands, show the same kind of love to your wives as Christ showed to the church when he died for her, to make her holy and clean, washed by baptism and God's Word; so that He could give her to Himself as a glorious church without a single spot or wrinkle or any other blemish, being holy and without a single fault. That is how husbands should treat their wives, loving them as parts of themselves. For since a man and his wife are now one, a man is really doing himself a favor and loving himself when he loves his wife! No one hates his own body but lovingly cares for it, just as Christ cares for his body the church, of which we are parts."

Jenny stared at the words she had just read and then looked up at Father.

"Those words are filled with much wisdom." And as if reading Jenny's mind, Father continued, "Over the years when I have given homilies on that chapter and counseled couples in their difficulties, the wife many times feels that she should not have to submit to the husband—"

"Yes! That's exactly what comes up so often. I don't have any trouble submitting to Henry's leadership in the home but for many wives they find that difficult to swallow."

"Yes, someone in any relationship, whether family, company or business has to have the final say and God chose the man to be the one in charge but note how the husband is instructed to treat the wife; to love her as his own body. In some Bibles, it is interpreted as the man is to cherish and nourish his wife as he would himself. God is not saying the husband is to be dictatorial nor so strict as to turn the children away either.

"To be clear, Jenny, the marital union is a voluntary self-giving in love. Submission must be interpreted in that light. A woman is not the slave of a husband and neither is the husband the slave of the wife. There is mutual submission; the husband and wife are servants to each other. Such a relationship is marked by faithfulness, respect, care and equal dignity.

"Yes, the man is at the head of the household. However, only after discussion and careful weighing of all the facts and consequences the man is left with the awesome role of making final decisions for the family. If the relationship is filled with love and respect for each other both are to mutually submit to one another just as Christ submitted to the Father even unto death. That is why it is so important to have Jesus Christ at the center of marriages. He is the example, the model to follow. He asks no less of the spouses than was asked of Him. He chose freely, willingly to obey and submit to the Father and to us out of His great love. What do the verses say? We are to love each other just as Christ loved the church; just as He loved us."

After a momentary silence, Henry said, "It is important for husbands and wives not to keep score; I will submit to you if you do in return. In a perfect marriage this may happen but most, if not all marriages it is never so. Out of love for the other, we accept them where they are at and love unconditionally. We die to ourselves. Remember Christ died for us while we were yet sinners."

"I'm happy you brought that up, Henry as I was just going to say how difficult it is for so many women to do that. The word love always comes up in both the Bible and in our groups so often. We look to First Corinthians 13 verses 4-8 for an answer: Love is patient, love is kind…it is not self-seeking or easily angered or keeps records of wrongs and so on. These are wonderful words to live by but in so many marriages, Father, they are not put into practice. Over and over women express the lack of affection and appreciation they receive from their husbands and children…" Jenny's words trailed off, the luster in her usually sparkling eyes fading.

"Yes," said Father Engelmann, "being taken for granted is an all too common problem in marriages. When couples first meet and court, they take the time to show love and affection but once married and the love bug begins to wear off, work, career, getting ahead and as children arrive, slowly these things take precedence over what should be our top priority; loving God and each other."

Jenny nodded. "I will never forget what Linda said to me two weeks ago, 'Sometimes, I feel like I'm living in a desert thirsting for a drop of affection.' I've felt like that in my relationship with James. It's so hard to cope with all of the demands in a marriage when a husband's awareness of the importance of showing appreciation and affection becomes so shallow or non-existent. And to be fair, so many men find it difficult to show affection or their feelings and many times it is what they have seen their father do."

Henry finally interjected, "That's why I have always maintained when I was a counselor in the school system that we need to have courses for students about their roles in a marriage; how to relate to their spouse and children, finances, mortgages, community, worship and so on. Parents should be leaders in this first and foremost but reinforcing these things in the school is vital as many children never learn how to have healthy and fulfilling relationships."

"Yes, yes," said Father. It's important for children to see exactly what a family should look like. That's why it's so foundational for parents to realize the tremendous importance and power of their role. One of the best things that a father can do for his children is to openly love their mother—"

"What a powerful observation, Father David!" interjected Jenny, the light in her eyes returning.

"Yes, concurred, Henry, and it should be the same for the mother."

"Yes, yes, to love another is to do so not only in one's thoughts but in their words and deeds. To love, to accept, and to be kind, caring, patient, forgiving requires action! When children see this, it is deeply internalized and they will want their marriage to be the same when it is time for them to raise their family. Of all human relationships, marriage is the most important. Family is the foundation of society. God knew that from the beginning and that is why he instituted marriage whereby a man and woman shall come together and become one flesh. No other earthly relationship can become so close, deep and binding.

"Eventually, spouses become naked to one another in every way. They learn of each other's strengths and weaknesses and it is their greatest responsibility to die to their self and live for the other. *It is only if couples put Jesus at the center can they acquire such acceptance and help each other become the person God created them to be.* Within such an environment, even though children may not be able to verbalize it, they internalize what it is like to have a happy family in which God must be at the center. Through spiritual leadership and prayer all members of the family see the importance of obtaining the strength and wisdom of the Holy Spirit to live selflessly. When the teachings of the Bible are taught and lived by in the home, it gives children instruction on how to live from day to day. Today's reading is but one teaching that instructs us how God wants us to live and how men and women must lead within the home."

Jenny looked at Father and hesitantly, she said, "What you have said is so wise, beautiful and filled with truth. When couples are of the same faith, know God and accept Jesus into their hearts and both openly talk about their relationship and how to improve it, then what you said has a chance to work. But... but, what if there is a lack of spiritual leadership in the home? What if Jesus isn't at the center of their marriage? What if the couple has difficulty communicating their concerns and feelings? What if one or both spouses do not want to see a counselor? How does one change such a situation? What is the ingredient to make a marriage that is failing or in trouble begin to grow? What is it that I can suggest to the ladies to do that will begin to turn their marriage around and make it better?" Jenny took a deep breath and slowly exhaled trying to dispel some of her frustrations along with it.

Father Engelmann turned his face and gazed through the glass patio doors to the placid pond just beyond the deck. He reflected on what Jenny said and was somewhat surprised. Of all people he knew during his life time, Jenny had seen over and over how God turns seemingly impossible circumstances into good for those who trust Him, yet in this situation, she had doubts and lacked trust in God. Perhaps the Evil One is clouding her usual clear perception of the situation and how to respond to it. She needed to be reminded that God is at the heart of marriages and quick to respond to bring healing to them.

Slowly, Father turned his gaze back to Jenny and said, "I understand your concerns, Jenny. You are overwhelmed by the magnitude of trying to find ways to restore families in the midst of all the obstacles which marriages face. It is through His divine providence that God touches the hearts and minds of all marriages—"

"Yes, that's right! That's what happened to my father," interjected Henry. "Do you recall when my parents had marital difficulties and dad ran off with another woman, Father?"

Father nodded.

"Even when he returned, I still felt insecure that he might do that again and hurt mom and me once more but the day he brought home a paper bag of rosaries and led us into saying the rosary daily for the blessed Mary to intercede for the family, from that day on, I knew we had a family once more."

"That's wonderful, Henry. What caused your father to change?" Jenny wanted to know.

"I think listening to Bishop Sheen on TV had a lot to do with it. The Bishop's motto was, 'The family that prays together stays together...' and, Mom was always praying...and so was Father Engelmann," Henry quickly added.

This time Father Engelmann interjected, "See, that's how God's divine providence is always at work. In all of those instances you just mentioned, God was at work. If we pray and trust God, He will turn any situation into good."

Turning to Jenny, Father continued, "Trust in the Lord, Jenny, God is at work especially in marriages that invite God into their lives. Take your group for example, it is no accident that you started this and the other groups. Through groups such as yours, through the pulpit, books, Christian counselors, by the example of our lives, our marriages, reading Christian literature, involvement in the community and perhaps most of all it is through prayer that God's divine providence works most powerfully."

Father sensed that Jenny still had concerns. He paused for a moment and then went on, "Of all of the things I have just mentioned Jenny, the two which I consider the most important and suggest you stress to the ladies in your group are: placing Jesus at the center of their marriage and life and second is prayer. Now, I say this in part because I have seen both work so powerfully in your life as it has in mine. Your life has been a prayer of thanksgiving and praise to God. Despite a loveless marriage, you accepted your husband and focused upon the man God created. You could have focused on his character flaws and became angry and hateful and resentful as many spouses do, but you chose to love. And what sustained you? Your daily prayer life helped you to love like Jesus. As Henry said moments ago, Jesus loved us unconditionally while we were still sinners even unto the extent of dying for us so that we might have life with Him and the Father. Jesus directly and perhaps indirectly was your teacher, mentor, and example of how to live and die to yourself.

"Jenny, recall when you were so critically ill and near death in the hospital, how you saw the connection of your pain and suffering with the pain and suffering of Jesus. Because He so loved us, you repented and accepted your cross in the hope that God would use your suffering like He did of Jesus for the redemption of mankind. In this, you found meaning and purpose. Jenny, you are an exceptional woman and the ladies in your group are blessed to have you as their leader. Daily, I see you die and resurrect with Jesus. Many women would not be able to accept and love like you did in your relationship with James. They would be focusing mainly on their needs and wants rather than helping their spouse to grow. Yet, look what happened in the end to your marriage?

Your love transformed a life and saved a soul and restored a family."

Father studied Jenny to see if she was even aware of what her example of daily living was doing for others. Jenny always tried to avoid drawing attention to herself and yet how can a light be hidden? Jenny's angelic heart naturally drew others to her.

Father was about to continue when Henry softly said, "That's very true, sweetheart. I may not have witnessed the power and beauty of your love in your marriage to James but I will never forget how you forgave the man who assaulted you when you were fifteen years old. In the Calgary airport that day, you showed us what it means to die to oneself and resurrect with Jesus. The lives you changed and the freedom you released in so many people's lives that day must have caused heaven to celebrate for days on end."

Jenny tenderly smiled at Henry and bowed her head. She was obviously unsettled by Henry and Father's kind words and didn't know how to react; her face blushed. Father appreciated her humility and so he said, "This may be too close to home for you to see and accept what you have done and are doing in your daily life and the wonderful affect you are having on others. Perhaps, it will be clearer if I share with you another life experience; my own. Something similar happened in my life which shows beyond doubt how God can transform the life of the most hardened heart in a marriage. However, before I share that with you, let us continue with the Mass and consecrate the bread and wine at the altar so we may receive nourishment and strength and enlightenment.

Father turned and said, "Dear heavenly Father, we offer up this Mass to You for the restoration and healing of marriages and families. Through You, all things are possible!"

Gazing up to the cross, Father continued, "Eternal Father, we offer You the body and blood, soul and divinity of Your dearly beloved Son, our Lord and Savior Jesus Christ in atonement for our sins and those of the whole world. Dear Jesus, help us to see the power of the cross. How You gave up Your heavenly throne, humbled Yourself to become man, born in a stable, endured poverty, abuse, pain and suffering unto death so that we might have life. How dare we be so proud in the face of such immense humility which You have shown us that we refuse to die to ourselves for our good and the good of our spouse and family. Help us to see our great need to completely dependent upon You, as we too, pick up our cross daily, repent of our sins and pray for the Holy Spirit to give us the strength and wisdom to follow in Your footsteps. We trust in You, Jesus, to be our guiding light as we live by Your example and teachings in the Living Word, that our lives, our marriage and family will turn into such good that is meaningful and acceptable to You and the Holy Father."

Father bowed and continued with the transubstantiation of the bread and wine. It took several moments for Henry and Jenny to get back into the Mass. Their thoughts still lingered on what it was that Father was going to share with them. Whose hardened heart was he referring to? They could hardly wait to hear about Father's personal experience.

Soon Henry and Jenny were swept into the celebration of the Mass. Without words, Father conveyed his deep devotion to the Lord. When he held up the host, he gazed at it for the longest time as if reluctant to put it down on the altar. One knew Father was looking at Jesus and not just a large circular disc of unleavened bread. With deep conviction, Father said, "Take this, all of you, and eat it, for this is my body, which will be given up for you." Then with the same deep faith, Father took the chalice filled with wine as Jesus did at the last supper and gave the chalice to his disciples, saying, "Take this, all of you, and drink from it, for this is the cup of my Blood, the Blood of the new and eternal covenant, which will be poured out for you and for many for the forgiveness of sins. Do this in memory of me."

The holy Eucharist is the mystery of faith which has been passed down since the early fathers of church said the Mass as Jesus requested them to do. For so many years, Henry had to admit that all he saw was bread and wine being offered. But Father's belief was so strong, he transformed so many lives. With faith, the Mass becomes alive. Henry knew at that moment when Father consecrated the bread and wine, it changed into the body and blood of Jesus, true God and true Man sacrificing Himself on the altar as He did on the cross. Henry bowed his head in homage and recalled the scripture reading in John, 6:53 which Father Engelmann often quoted; 'If you do not eat the flesh of the Son of Man and drink His blood you will not have life in yourselves.'

Henry couldn't get over how Father was changing. It was difficult to notice his weight loss because of the brown Franciscan habit he constantly wore but it was evident on his face. It no longer was as round as it was but more slender and drawn. The white hair and beard made him look older but holier. What a true, remarkable disciple of the Lord, Henry thought. What a blessing it was to have Father as a friend over the years. How would their relationship end? When would his time on earth...be no more?

Chapter Six

A FTER MASS, HENRY and Father went outside to the deck while Jenny prepared what little she could from Father's meager supply of food. Jenny made tea and added slices of the remaining half lemon she found in the fridge for color and flavor. She also cut up half of a whole melon and half a cantaloupe and put it into a bowl. Jenny looked for something else for them to nibble on but the fridge was empty except for two and half bottles of spring water and left over fruit.

No sooner had Jenny set the fruit down and filled the glasses with tea, than she exclaimed, "Oh Father, I can hardly wait for you to share your personal experience which demonstrates how God works in our lives. I have seen it so many times in my own and others and yet, we need to be reminded again and again to overcome the doubt created by the problems we see as so insurmountable."

"Yes, Jenny, God is constantly at work through His divine providence. We must trust in Him and not rely on our own understanding which is constantly influenced by evil spirits prowling around the world seeking the ruin of souls."

True to his style, Father began by first sweeping his gaze across the mirror like surface of the still water and then up towards the ascending morning sun. It seemed as if an insight from the heavens was about to illuminate his mind as it had done so many times before. Henry knew that look, he had seen it so many times when they were out back behind the grocery store sitting on old weathered gray crates discussing concerns he was facing at that time. Henry sat at the edge of his seat in anticipation of Father's wisdom to be revealed once more.

Jenny, too, straightened up and sat nearer to the edge of her chair than Henry. She hoped Father would enlighten her even more than he already had that morning. More than anything she wanted to find and know of ways in which she might help many of the women in her groups renew hope in their lives, marriages and families. As Father had already pointed out, Jenny would soon discover that she knew of the secret to transform lives all along, in fact, she lived it every day. Perhaps witnessing it through Father's sharing will objectify it for her and bring it all together.

With the sound of the moving stream seeping soothingly through the twigs, mud and branches of the distant beaver dam, Father slowly began, " When Anna and I married, we were very much in love and for the first while, I was fortunate enough that Anna accepted habits and attitudes of mine that she really didn't appreciate. I was stubborn, opinionated, proud, arrogant and grew more so when I became an instructor at the university. I tended to devalue many things Anna said or believed in. As the years passed and Anna became less accepting of my character flaws, we would get into heated arguments. I could see that many of my comments which were colored with an arrogant, display of superiority and condescension were hurtful to Anna and affected her self-esteem, but I was too proud to say I was sorry or give in.

"Fortunately for us, the Lord had his foot in the door. Occasionally, we prayed together when someone in the family was ill or some friends asked for prayer or there was a personal need on our part. One day after we had finished praying on such an occasion, Anna wisely suggested that we should begin our day by reading a chapter of the Bible and end with a short prayer. Although I downplayed the suggestion, Anna continued to take leadership everyday even though most days, I was in too much of a hurry or didn't want to mainly because it was not I who suggested this practice, *but I noticed*!

"Since our apartment was small, many times I overheard her praying or rather praising God for me and our marriage! Rather than focusing on how difficult it was for her to live with me or change me, she was giving thanks to God for everything just the way it was! On one occasion when she was not at home, I read a scripture she had underlined in her Bible and one that I heard her repeat many times. It was Hebrews 13:15, 'By Him therefore let us offer the sacrifice of praise to God continually, that is, the fruit of our lips giving thanks to His name.' I began to wonder if the practice of this verse was the reason I noticed a growing peace and joy surrounding Anna.

"It began to touch me. Anna's praising was bearing fruit in her life and mine!

"Next, I saw her determination to bring God into our marriage. She began to use an entirely different approach in our discussions which were heading towards an argument; she invited Jesus into the conversation! She would quietly listen to my concern and simply say, 'Let us pray and praise God about that David.'

Father Engelmann stopped and shook his head, "My, my, such wisdom…she knew that I would not talk to God in the manner in which I spoke to her…so, if she disagreed with me and knowing of my impatience, stubbornness and defensiveness, while in prayer and with God present and listening, she would calmly pray, 'Dear Lord, help me to understand David's concerns and help David too, dear Lord, to pray about his request and bring to mind the consequences of what he is asking according to Your Word.' Sometimes, I would feel she was manipulating me and I would become defensive but she would raise her hand to her lips and say 'Ssssh, David, God wants me to finish my prayer and for you to listen. When you pray, I will listen, too.'

"But after she prayed and the matter we were discussing was brought out into its full objective truth in the presence of God the Father and the teachings of Jesus in the Bible, more times than not, I could see the wisdom of her words and the truth in her prayer. With my defensiveness down and not focusing on how to rebut her or put her in her place, I actually listened in the presence of Jesus to her point of view! At times, after or during prayer, she would agree with my side as her defensiveness was down as well. In all cases, whether for my benefit or hers, she would praise God for bringing that concern into our marriage and helping us to deal with it.

"*Soon, we began to feel a peace settle in our home.*

"Slowly, I began to see my character for what it was. I began to understand why so many times people shunned away from me. Why they found me unapproachable. I could see my pride, arrogance and stubbornness sticking out like thorns in my relationship with Anna and others. Anna's spiritual leadership, which I should have been showing, and her love for God and Jesus and the Holy Spirit was so great, so strong, that it not only gave her the strength to put up with me but penetrated through the hardness of my mind and heart.

"Anna knew me inside out, the good and the really bad; yet, she accepted me and praised God for it! As I said, she no longer dwelled on how bad our marriage was or how miserable I was making her life but rather she was trusting God to turn it all into good. By praising God for all the circumstances in our lives, she kept the door closed to Satan and his destructive thoughts in her mind. This is what kept her at peace and amazingly happy. Her unconditional love and daily prayer had opened the door to the core of my being and allowed Jesus' sacrificial giving of His life for me to mold and shape me into the child of God that I was meant to be.

"It was as if I was blind and began to see!" Father paused and looked at Jenny. "In many ways, I was like your former husband, James. I, too, lived in the darkness but the light of your and Anna's example took our blinders off. I used to think it was how Helen Keller must have felt in the beginning to try and understand a world she couldn't see or hear. Imagine how excited Helen was as her patient loving teacher guided her to the light! You and Anna led us into a world we never knew and perhaps never would have without your sacrificial love! I came to love Anna and make her happy like never before. Her increased joy in our marriage caused her to appreciate me more which in turn increased my efforts to do anything for her. We had decided to love one another with all of our hearts no matter what the sacrifice. I was no longer a stumbling block for her to sin by being angry towards me and thinking unkindly. I was now helping her become the person God wanted and loved, ready to welcome into heaven.

"*It opened my eyes to a great truth.*

"I could see through the faith of my dear wife what our most important responsibility above all else was to each other."

Father stopped and looked at Jenny. "Even though you may not have realized it Jenny, you were carrying out this responsibility in your marriage with James, too."

Jenny crinkled her forehead, not sure of Father's meaning. Henry straightened his posture and leaned forward as Father went on.

"Finally, one day, I tried to express this great obligation to Anna during our prayer time.

"*It touched Anna to the core.*

"With tears in my eyes, I held Anna's hands and looking into her tear-filled eyes as well, I said, "Anna, from this day forward, we shall never retire without forgiving or asking for forgiveness from one another and God our Father. The sun will never go down on our anger. As God does not keep record of our wrongs when we repent neither shall we...

"*Each day is a new day and a new beginning.*

"Anna, you have shown great wisdom by bringing Jesus into the heart of our marriage. Through prayer and meditation on His Word and your living example of it, I have come to deeply appreciate the immense sacrifice Jesus has done by laying down His life for my sins and those of all mankind. You have taken His sacrifice to heart and have picked up your daily cross; whether it's having to deal with my shortcomings or the trials of life that come your way and instead of focusing on the evil, the problems or flaws that are injurious to you, you offer it up as a sacrifice to God thanking and praising Him for it. Through this sacrificial loving, Anna, you have given birth to much fruit, in others and especially me. You have helped me overcome my many weaknesses which resulted in me growing closer to you and to God.

"I want to return this love to you!

"I will love and support and encourage you to live more and more for Christ through my example and no longer be a stumbling block for you. He is our mentor and through His example of dying for us, each day with the strength of the Holy Spirit, I will die to myself and resurrect with Jesus. In all things, I will give praise and trust in God to turn it all into good according to His will. We have only to see the great good God brought out of the sacrifice of His Son by dying for us while we were still sinners. He died so that we may be reconciled with the Father and come to heaven at the end of our journey and spend everlasting eternity with Him and the Father. I will not let His sacrifice go in vain and neither yours on my account. This is my most important responsibility; *to bring you safely home into His arms, my dear Anna.*

"Needless to say, Anna was totally changed that day. Her trust in the Lord was complete. From that day on until the day she went home to the Father, I never heard a harsh word from her. I was now in God's care. She gave up any and all control to Him over herself, me and our marriage. *The practice of repenting and going to confession, reading the Bible daily and asking the Holy Spirit to help us to obey and put into practice its teachings, praising God in prayer in all circumstances, keeping Jesus' sacrifice on the cross for us ever in the forefront of our marriage to remind us that death to our ego brings true life and trust in God to turn all things into good and receiving Holy Communion as often as you can for strength and nourishment; that my dear children leads to unshakeable faith and a happy family that brings peace and light into the world."*

No one spoke for the longest time. If couples lived with such a dedication of mind, heart and spirit for their spouse, there would be no such thing as divorce, families would feel secure. Depression, separation, suicides among young people would be no more.

"What a sharing, Father. It made me recall the many times Anna prayed for others in the back storage room at the store and praised God for the problem they were having! It never made sense to me at the time. That was the first time I heard of the scripture Hebrews 13:15 in which we are to praise God continuously and yet there is one which I had memorized when I attended university each time I got anxious over things. Now that I think of it, the verse says sort of the same thing. It was Philippians 4:6-7, 'Be anxious for nothing, but in everything by prayer and supplication, with thanksgiving, let your requests be made known to God; and the peace of God, which surpasses all understanding, will guard your hearts and minds through Christ Jesus.'"

"Yes, Anna said that one as well. See, how the scripture says to pray with thanksgiving and also why it's so important to have Jesus at the center of your life and marriage."

Henry nodded, "*The peace of God comes through Jesus!*"

Father nodded and with growing excitement, said, "There is another one in 1 Thessalonians 5:18 which I say daily: 'In everything give thanks: for this is the will of God in Christ Jesus concerning you.'"

"Isn't there a Psalm that suggests praising—"

"Yes, yes! Interjected Father, "I say Psalm 34:1 every day, too: 'I will bless the Lord at all times; His praise shall continually be in my mouth.'"

This time Jenny chimed in, "You two are wonderful! How you can rattle off one scripture after the other is amazing!"

"I always thought that my calling was in the priesthood," Henry said with a wink in his eye.

"Yes, you would have made a good priest, Henry," observed Father.

"Well, I'm happy he didn't! But I will do everything I can to keep him on the right track, Father!"

They all laughed.

Henry then said, "I know Jenny has a strong affect on me but I didn't realize that Anna had such an impact upon you. I always thought it was through your faith that Anna was influenced to be such a strong spiritual leader. I would never have thought of you being a proud man as you described either." Henry paused and then asked, "Did you or Anna ever consider separation or divorce?"

"No, that never entered our mind. We knew the seriousness of our oath to one another. It is not just a commitment or agreement but a sacred covenant between the man, woman and God. It is clear in Mark's 10th chapter in which Jesus says, '...from the beginning of creation, God made them male and female. Therefore a man shall leave his father and mother and hold fast to his wife, and the two shall become one flesh. So they are no longer two but one flesh. What therefore God has joined together let no man separate.'

"It is clear what God intended when two people make such a vow to each other to be faithful and honor their marriage for better or worse, in sickness or health, to death do they part... it's a sealed covenant. If couples have this kind of commitment in their hearts when they marry, they will make their marriage work. And for those who put Christ at the center will soon find out the beauty of marriage. Unfortunately, all too many are not taking their marriage vows seriously, especially amongst the young people. No sooner does the strong feeling of attraction begin to fade and the character flaws in their spouse begins to rear its head that many think they married the wrong person. Rather than pray and put effort into making their marriage work, many begin to think they can do better and open themselves up to affairs and the evil one to fuel thoughts of being worthy of more or someone better. Unfortunately, many couples that divorce soon find out the same thing occurs in their new marriage.

"Marriage is a golden opportunity to grow up, to mature, to heal and be healed by their spouse. I am a prime example! There is a wonderful mystery in learning to die to yourself and self-centeredness. Jesus said, 'to find yourself you must lose yourself, to bear fruit you must die to yourself.' The more you achieve this with the help of the Holy Spirit, the more you will truly love and respect yourself and be able to love your spouse and others. This is how we become the child of God we were meant to be; we become the flower that came from the seed that first had to die in the ground in order to show its beauty and bear fruit!"

"That's beautiful, Father..." Jenny's words trailed off.

After a long pause to reflect on Father's words, Henry said, "To live for the salvation of your spouse's soul is an incredibly wonderful goal in a marriage! That would take quite a commitment and definitely require Jesus to be at the center like you said. In all of the years I was involved as a counselor, couples would go into counseling for months, read the best books on marriage, hear talk after talk on how to grow into a relationship but until a personal decision was made to put Jesus at the center of their relationship and put into practice His teachings, many marriages just spin their wheels and are mediocre at best."

Father nodded and said, "Yes, there are many good insights in books we can buy in a book store, but upon analysis you will find they are merely saying in a different way what is in the Bible. It's all in there, how we should live and be. That is the only book which is necessary and sadly the least referred to.

"The Bible is the Living Word of God."

"It comes with complete instructions all laid out for us and it comes with a bonus which no other book can offer; the grace of God. The wisdom and strength to carry out the teachings with the help of the Holy Spirit will fill one's heart and continue to motivate them beyond measure as we all here can attest to and I'm certain what other couples who have stuck it out will agree to as well. Without Christ, it's too difficult for us to overcome our self-centeredness. Jesus is the way, the truth and life. Without Him at the center and praying daily, our lives and marriages will be a struggle."

Henry wanted to say more, but Jenny could hardly wait to burst in,

"Wow, Father, there is so much in what you said, it will take me days to sort it all out. If only couples would see and understand that!"

"Jesus is the glue which keeps a marriage and family together. The Holy Spirit will convict your heart to follow Jesus. His great sacrificial love for me as a sinner is what makes it possible for me to draw strength from His example to love my spouse in return even when it is difficult to do so. But Anna took it one step further as I have already shared. Rather than bite her tongue and hold back anger or frustration over some incidence, she would praise and thank God for it.

"That is the sacrificial offering we are asked to do which in turn bears much fruit!

"God is in control of the universe. By praising Him and trusting in Him to turn it all into good, releases His power in our lives and deepens our faith. God instituted marriage and laid out the instructions as to how we shall live within this sacred covenant between a man and a wife. Through the teachings of the Living Word, we are taught through scripture after scripture how to make it a wonderful union on earth."

Turning once again to Jenny, Father said, "Earlier, during Mass, you mentioned St. Paul's letter to the Corinthians: Chapter 13, verses 1-13, on love for example; the words to be patient, kind, caring, forgiving…these are not just idle words but words that require action. If spouses commit to one another with Jesus at the center of their lives and marriage, they will receive the strength from the Holy Spirit to live such a life for their spouse. Even if one of the couple isn't spiritual or doesn't pray to God as to a large degree was my case, miracles can happen. If the women in your group put into practice prayer, praise, reading the Bible and obeying its Word, I promise you, Jenny, families and lives will be transformed."

Jenny nodded, "Yes, I can see what you mean, Father. The power of prayer and calling upon the Holy Spirit can do amazing things in a marriage."

Father was going to speak but Henry interjected, "Hold that thought, Father. I want to get a bottle of water, care for some?"

"Yes, Henry, bring out the water and the remainder of the fruit that's left."

"Hurry, Henry, I am anxious to hear what else Father is going to say…"

CHAPTER SEVEN

H ENRY RETURNED WITH water and the rest of the melon
and cantaloupe clearing out the fridge completely. Father
would need some more groceries before the end of the day.
Jenny and Father were sitting quietly waiting for him to return.
Henry set the fruit on the table, handed Jenny and Father each
a bottle of water, and sat down to enjoy the respite from the
insightful conversation they were having. Jenny was beginning
to get answers as to how to help the ladies in her group mainly
through prayer and calling upon the help of the Holy Spirit
but Father would next expound upon the power of example.
Jenny would soon learn that she was very much a part of
Father's next lesson.

The morning sun was climbing high into the cloudless, blue
sky warming Father's woolen habit. Beads of perspiration were
forming on his forehead. He reached into an invisible pocket in
his robe with his left hand and took out a white handkerchief
and patted his brow. With the same magical move, he made
the hanky disappear into the loose sleeve surrounding his
right arm. Without looking at Jenny or Henry and as more of
an observation he said, "Anna and Jenny are perfect examples
of how lives can be transformed and marriages fulfilled. I
never met Jenny's former husband but from what you have

shared with me in the past, I'm certain that if I had had the opportunity to talk with James, we would have said similar things to say about our spouse and how their love changed us and motivated us to come to God."

Tears came into Jenny's eyes and softly, she spoke, "During the years of our marriage, I never resented James or felt anger for his ways. Rather, I felt compassion for him. Daily, he would go into the world creating untold stress for himself and those around him. His main goal in life was to amass more wealth and power. He rarely took time for family or to smell the flowers in his beautiful estate.

"I always tried to envision him, however, doing the various things that he was missing. I pictured him as a loving father and husband and a man of God, I knew he could be. It was that James which God created, that I focused on and loved. Towards the end when James was ill and he began to read the Bible and his heart mellowed, I thought I would love him more but that was not the case. My love for him was the same but my joy escalated that he had found himself before his life was over. To this day, I am thankful to God for allowing James to see the truth to real life in Jesus."

Father nodded, "You brought the light to James as Anna did to me. Without you ladies in our lives, James and I may never have known the life in God which you both knew. In the same way James began to read the Bible to discover what made you so beautiful, I began to pray and read the Bible every morning as well. I wanted to find out what it was which gave Anna the heart of an angel and I'm sure that same question haunted James for years. It's unfortunate James discovered the Light so late in life."

"It took an illness to slow him down and stop to analyze his life," Henry offered and then turning to Jenny he said, "You may not realize it, but as Father just observed, it was through your unconditional love of James which turned his life around. Just think, Jenny, where many wives would have focused on their husband's faults you always focused on the person which God created. If you had dwelled upon how miserable and unhappy your marriage was, instead of loving him in such a deep sacrificial way, your days would have been filled with resentment, hatred and anger. I have seen this so often in my counseling of couples where a spouse chooses to be a victim in their marriage and allow their life to be controlled by the shortcomings of their mate.

"But you didn't!

"How we respond to circumstances in our lives is the important point of all this. Rather, you chose to love him unconditionally which eventually saved his soul. You did exactly what Father promised to Anna, to bring James home to the Father. That's amazing, Jenny! Your special gift of love and caring and example of loving others the way they are, is a tremendous gift and example to the women in your group."

"That's a wonderful observation, Henry." Father leaned towards Jenny and patted her hand and said, "To that, I can only add the wonderful blessing you received from the Lord. Anna had received it as well; you both possess a peace that surpasses all understanding. In the midst of the storms of life, you are calm and centered because you trust God to turn all things into good. You live lives of praise and thanksgiving in all circumstances. Daily, Anna would praise the Lord and revel in the way God worked so miraculously in her life and in those she prayed for.

"You, too, Jenny visit your garden daily and give thanksgiving and praise. Your offering of flowers in the Angel of Thanksgiving's basket every day for all of God's blessings for you and others focuses your heart where it should be for all of us. It is a way of life in which God is glorified and if we follow it, He has no choice but to shower us with more blessings!

"If our attention is on His greatness and goodness rather than on our lack, there is nothing which cannot be accomplished. God is the God of all possibilities. Who better can we trust and put in control of our lives! No matter what the situation, accept it as the will of God just as Jesus did in all of the circumstances that came His way when He walked the earth, including His crucifixion. Just as we can be joyful and thankful for His dying for us on the cross and the tremendous good which came out of it, so too, do we accept our daily cross and thank God for all circumstances for we know He will turn it into good."

This time it was Jenny that placed both of her hands on Fathers which were resting on his lap. "My dear Father David, pray that I can touch the hearts of the ladies in my groups with your wisdom and love of God as you have done to mine this morning. Thank you."

Henry sensed such a deep love and similarity between Jenny and Father Engelmann. Their lives exhibited the humility of Jesus without realizing it. That's what made them so loveable, so approachable and why others wanted to be around them and be like them. They lived Jesus in their lives and became a beacon of light which gave hope and faith to all they met. Unbidden tears surfaced in Henry's eyes just thinking on his beautiful, dear sweet wife and Father Engelmann, his lifelong friend.

With her hands still resting on Father's, Jenny said, "You still miss, Anna, Father…"

Those understanding words of compassion were all that was needed to cause Father to weep. He nodded and slowly, he said, "Yes, I miss making her happy." Turning to Jenny he took in a deep breath of fresh morning air coming off the rippling pond and continued, "In the same way James wanted to do more for your happiness when he realized the great gift God had given him; he commissioned another angel of thanksgiving, offered up flowers in thanksgiving for you, prayed for your healing, brought Henry and his family to the estate and in the end he refused to be sustained by drugs and machines to quicken his death so you were free to marry Henry. I was the same with Anna, I wanted to do all I could for her not just because of what she did for me over the years, but because it gave me so much joy to see the sparkle in her eyes and smile on her lips and happiness in her heart.

"That's what God's love does in our hearts!

"When she became ill, the doctor tried to convince me to put Anna in the hospital for better care and Anna agreed mainly because she thought looking after her was too hard on me.

"They both had it wrong; what others thought was a burden, I considered a blessing. In fact, I had selfish reasons for keeping her at home. I wanted Anna and needed to have her in my life. It lifted my spirits when ladies in the neighborhood came to see her. Anna would derive great satisfaction in helping them out. She loved when I shared what happened in the store especially when Henry started to work for us."

Father paused and looked at Henry. "You were the son we never had. We were so grateful to your parents for sharing you with us. I cannot put into words the joy and love you gave us." Father wiped a tear rolling down his cheek with the back of his hand and continued, "When I came upstairs at the end of the day, if she was at all capable of getting out of bed, she would not only have a simple dinner ready but soft music playing and a candle flickering on the dinner table. Right to the end, she never lost being romantic in our marriage. I will never forget what she said to me on the day of our last anniversary, "David, as wonderful as our first anniversaries were, the man I am in love with now gives me more joy and happiness than I ever dreamed possible."

"If only young couples starting out could see the immense happiness they can derive out of a marriage that has matured in the Lord through sacrificial love and caring. The euphoria they feel, no matter how powerful at the beginning of their relationship, is nothing compared to the deep, true love it can become.

"So much good comes out of knowing what our greatest responsibility is in marriage."

"When Anna died and she was buried in her wedding gown which she requested near the end, I knew in my heart that I had fulfilled my obligation as a husband; to bring her safely home to her eternal Groom."

Father lifted his head until his gaze rested tenderly on Jenny's eyes and said,

"You have done the same for James. As wealthy and powerful as he was in the world, he knew that it was your love that brought him into the Light and saved him. It was a free gift you gave him in the same way Christ freely gave us His life for our salvation. No amount of money or all the gold and silver in the entire world can buy this love. My Anna, too, gave me the gift of that kind of love."

Such a soothing peace was present amongst them as if they were seated just this side of heaven. Every now and then the flutter of wings could be heard and a warm gust of air felt ever so softly on their skin; they knew their guardian angels were near enjoying their conversation too and perhaps prompting them to share more. When Henry noticed Father gaze up into the rising sun, he knew his mentor was about to share something from the heart or rather a whisper from his protector. Slowly, Father began...

"Later in our marriage when things were healed and working better, Anna shared with me her dream as a young girl; she prayed that she would marry a man who would be kind, faithful, loving and her best friend; someone who would sweep her off her feet; someone who would nourish, cherish and protect her. It made me think that if I hadn't changed, Anna would have spent her life with someone who was furthest from fulfilling her dream. It made me think further of so many marriages in which women, and it can be said for men as well that are caught in an unfulfilled relationship because either spouse doesn't grow and mature and try to meet the needs of their mate. If only husbands and wives would stop and look tenderly at their spouse and see the hope and dreams they had when they were young and growing up that one day they would meet their perfect mate. When they married they had that kind of hope in their heart. We may never be perfect but such thoughts can motivate us to think more for our spouse than ourselves.

Tears came into Father's eyes as he said, "Often I would envision Anna as a young girl, her eyes reflecting that dream in her heart and I sometimes think back and regret the many years how my own lack of maturity was hurtful to Anna and how it marred her dream of marrying a man who was at times the opposite of what she hoped for. That is why as I began to grow in the footsteps of Jesus as my model, teacher and guide, I could see how her eyes began to light up. I desired all the more to be her knight in shining armor. I longed to make her happier. That is what I miss…seeing her happy as a result of how I loved and treated her.

"How sad it is when one or the other or both lose sight of the aspirations they had of their marriage and fail to work on it. The rise in divorce and separation attest to this fact."

Father uncrossed his legs and sat forward placing more emphasis upon what he would say next, "It just takes a moment in time to decide that from this day on, you will make a difference in your marriage. Decide to put Jesus at the helm to be your teacher, example and guide to keep you focused and committed. No longer will I be a passive participant but an active one that really cares about their marriage and family. To achieve anything in life worthwhile requires, work, effort, and sacrifice. To make your spouses' dream come true is a natural outcome of a goal to bring your spouse home to the Father. Any marriage, no matter how failing or what state it is in, can be restored with a new mindset. God can heal and make a new creature out of you just as he did out of me. You can make your spouse's dream come true.

There was a long pause and then Father simply nodded, "Soon, I hope to be home."

Father's words stung in Henry's mind. He loved his friend and second father so deeply. The thought of his lifelong mentor passing on swept untold sorrow through Henry's being. He didn't want to contemplate it, yet he knew it was inevitable. Father returned from his stint on the other side to carry out two missions: the one was to write a love story which incredibly included Jenny and him. Henry wondered if Father knew what his second mission was…when that was completed, Henry knew Father would soon be gone thereafter.

Henry waited until Father was more composed and settled and then dared to ask, "Father, I recall you sharing with us that your guardian angel, Zachariah, gave you two missions to carry out upon your return to earth. One was to write a lengthy story, but what of the second? Do you know what that is?"

Father shrugged his shoulders, "No, that still has not been revealed to me. I am waiting anxiously for the Lord to tell me what it is."

"And how are you coming along with the book series? Jenny wanted to know.

"I finished book four and am well into book five, "Father replied.

"Really!? What is the name of book four?"Henry asked.

"IT CAME TO me just the other day; *The Angelic Occurrence*. It's based upon the remarkable incidence which brought you and Jenny back together."

Both Jenny and Henry wrinkled their foreheads...

"How soon one forgets such an extraordinary experience. Did you not purchase a revenue home on Hill Avenue and discover a secret diary which led you to find out the home had belonged to Jenny, the girl that swept you off your feet when you were fifteen!?

"If that wasn't an angelic occurrence, then what is!?"

Henry and Jenny let out a nervous chuckle.

"Yes, yes, of course!" Henry replied, sounding like his mentor. "It truly was an angelic occurrence. What an amazing discovery that was!"

"Just thinking on it sends shivers through my body," added Jenny.

"It's just wonderful how our guardian angels brought us back together! Have you thought of a name for book five yet?" asked Jenny.

"No, it's still in the early stages and... perhaps what you just said gives me an idea of what the title might be."

Henry turned sharply towards Jenny, "What did you just say to Father?"

"Oh, my, it was something to do with how our angels brought us back together or how they kept their promise..." Jenny's words trailed off.

Turning abruptly back to Father, Henry asked, "Was that it, something to do with our guardian angels fulfilling their promise?"

Father looked at Henry and reflected what his adopted son just said. "Mmmm, that gives me food for thought...yes, that just might be it."

"Oh, Father, I'm sure the title will come to you in your dreams as the others did. In any case, I can hardly wait to read the books!" exclaimed Jenny.

Father nodded. He was happy that the first mission was coming to an end. He now thought what the second one might be. He recalled that he was allowed to see what it was in the future but it was removed from his memory immediately after he agreed to return to the land of the living...

Henry interrupted Father's thoughts. "Gary and John are coming home in a couple of weeks, Father. Gary's mom is celebrating her 85th birthday."

"That is wonderful. It will be good to see them both and hear what they have been doing for the Lord."

"I am so excited to talk to them, too," said Jenny, her eyes sparkling. "Henry keeps talking about their work in India and the challenges they are constantly facing."

"Missionary work is very important. They are carrying out the Great Commission that Jesus instructed his disciples to do; to bring the Gospel to all people over the world. Gary and John have been specially blessed."

Henry wanted to talk about the tug he constantly felt to get involved some way in that work too, but it was getting late. He checked his watch and said,

"Well, Father, it was a pleasure attending Mass with you and as always, the discussions are stimulating, but we have to go. I have a meeting with an art collector who is interested in one of my paintings."

Henry looked at Jenny, "Perhaps we should begin our trek back to the house."

Reluctantly, she got up and made her way to Father. As soon as Father stood to receive Jenny's hug, Coco stood immediately as well ready to move along with her master.

"It's so peaceful and beautiful here, it's hard to leave. Do you need any groceries, Father? I noticed the fridge is bare. I'm afraid we ate the last of your fruit."

"Perhaps Justin can bring down water and a bit of fruit. Other than that, some sour dough bread from Borden's would be nice if you're in the area and just a few bags of tea. I will be going into the city on Friday to take an article in for the care home newsletter. In fact it's on the very topic we have been discussing; *The Power of Prayer.*"

"Oh, I can't wait to read it, Father! And thank you for your insightful sharing, too. I can't wait to meet with the ladies and share what our most important responsibility is in marriage."

"Yes, Jenny, we get so caught up with our earthly lives and challenges that we forget to keep eternity ever in the forefront of our mind. What greater gift can a husband or wife give to their spouse and family than to lead them home to the Father. Everything else and I say again, everything else is secondary. If only couples would stop to think about the impermanence of this life and that most of our efforts are towards material possessions that have no value in eternity and in trying to change others to have our needs and wants met.

"We seek happiness in dead ends.

"A person's life on earth can be over at any moment. Every second all around the world hundreds if not thousands of people are dying whether they are young, middle aged or old.

"Where will they spend eternity? Are they prepared? Have they been a stumbling block or rather a promoter, encourager and an example of how to be for others?

"Unfortunately, it is when we are lying on our death bed that we see the light. We finally realize that all our possessions, wealth, gold and silver have absolutely no value to where we are heading. And if we haven't used it to help others then it's completely worthless. We see that it is the love, care, kindness and compassion we have shown that is the important thing in life. This is what we bring to the Father at the end of our days. This is the kind of legacy we want to leave and the one that will be remembered.

"Love lasts eternal; everything else rots, rusts out and decays."

"Amen," said Henry and turning to Jenny, he added, "You know, Jen, Father would make a great guest speaker when you bring the wives and husbands together next fall or winter. I could briefly speak and then introduce Father to share what he did to us this morning."

"Oh, Henry, what a wonderful idea!" Turning to Father, Jenny continued, "What you shared with us this morning would be perfect for both the men and women to hear. Please consider to do so, Father."

Father smiled and nodded, "Yes, Jenny, perhaps in the fall you can arrange to bring your groups along with their husbands together and we can share God's words with them."

Jenny ran to Father and gave him a hug. "Oh, Father David, you are such a blessing to all of us. Thank you for everything!"

"Oh, by the way, Father, Camilla has invited us all to dinner on Sunday, I'm sure I don't have to remind you not to eat too much before you come!"

They all laughed, knowing how Father continually fasted.

With a twinkle in his eye, Father said, "I can hardly wait. Your daughter is an excellent cook, Jenny."

"Yes, I know. Unfortunately, she didn't learn from me! It was her other mother, Valerie Breckhart, who raised her, that taught Camilla how to cook like that!" And turning to Henry with a playful sparkle in her eyes, she thrust out her hand and said the magic words that always made his heart race;

"Quickly, Honey, hold my hand!"

CHAPTER EIGHT

HENRY DROPPED FATHER Engelmann off at the Chancery office. The Archbishop wanted to see him the next time he came to the city.

The Archbishop was somewhat startled when he saw Father Engelmann. It had been almost nine months since they last spoke and the Archbishop hadn't seen how long Father's beard and hair had grown and how white they had become.

"You look like what I would picture Moses to look like, David."

"Perhaps, I best get a haircut and shave soon, my appearance is getting too much attention."

"That is not necessary, David, it is rather becoming of your holiness."

Father turned a bit on the red side, "All the more reason to do away with it all together. But then that may draw even more attention!"

"Come, sit down, David. There is a matter which I wish to discuss with you. It concerns the healings and miracles which occurred three years ago."

"Surely, they have stopped investigating that matter."

"Time moves slowly, David. There are countless miracles reported annually and all must be given consideration and investigated."

"Will it be the same Monsignor who came at that time?"

"Perhaps, they did not say. Your age came to their attention. They did not realize that you have long since been retired and yet, were still celebrating Mass at the care home chapel voluntarily on your part. In any case, they want to meet with you for the purpose of going over what had transpired but even more so, to get to know you better."

"But why, John? I am just a retired priest who has served a parish like any other priest."

"Besides the miracles which have occurred, our office has received countless letters from parishioners who have testified of your holiness and healings which have been due to your intercession, David. Another reason is the power of your confessionals and ability to see into the hearts of those confessing to you. Now, I know you don't wish to hear of this but Rome is interested when they learn of one of their reverent brothers whose work is extraordinary, shall we say."

"Well, all I can say is, I pray the Lord calls me before any more fuss is made over one who is simply doing the Lord's work."

The Archbishop didn't want to say any more on the matter. He could already see the great discomfort of the holy man in front of him whose humility had been exalted more than he could tolerate. The truth of the matter was, David was already being considered as having met the first step towards sainthood; Servant of God.

"Just one more thing on the matter and then we can move on. I did mention to the Cardinal I spoke with that you were spending more and more time at the prayer house on Mr. Pederson's property. When I described the prayer house and that it was a Poustinia with a small chapel inside, they expressed an interest in interviewing you at the prayer house. Would that meet with your approval, David?"

"Yes, yes, that would be fine."

"So, what brings you to the city on such a beautiful day, David?"

"I was asked to write a short article on 'prayer' for the newsletter. Today is the deadline for getting it into the next issue."

"Yes, I have read many of them over the years, David. Some excellent articles and much wisdom has been shared by the residents. My prayer on several occasions as I read through the newsletter was the hope that more and more young people read what the elderly have written. And, I must add, the touches of humor throughout are excellent."

"All too often children treat their parents with condescension or feel that they are not able to understand their problems. The newsletter has done much good to dispel this notion and help children to realize the treasure of friendship and knowledge and insight into life's challenges that is available to them through their parents. It is important for grandchildren to be in constant touch with their grandparents and the tremendous love and knowledge about life which they receive from them, too. In any case, you are a busy man and I best be off and get this article over to the care home."

"Do you mind if I peruse it before you leave?"

"Yes, go ahead. I will chat with Bernadette for a few moments and she can call a taxi for me."

When Father returned to the Archbishop's office, he had finished the article David had written.

"This is an insightful article, David. I love the picture you paint of prayer; to go into a room alone (in secret) with a sincere heart like a child coming to talk with their father. And to do so daily as you strongly urge, begins the work of grace in a person's life and prepares them for the trials which inevitably will come their way."

Father nodded, "People who don't pray and rely on their own strengths, have found struggle with life and often are in unnecessary turmoil. They have not developed a relationship with Jesus and thus do not know Him. They have not called upon the Holy Spirit to teach them how to pray and come before the Lord in their brokenness. As a result, they have not learned to believe, trust and wait upon the Lord. Because of sin, as we know John, there is so much sorrow and pain in the world. There is no one on earth who can escape from the multitude of afflictions which can beset us. The surest way to maintain peace and cheerfulness is to bring everything to God in prayer."

"And the scriptures you quote attesting to this are some of my favorites. Philippians 4: 6, 7 is one I say regularly: Be anxious for nothing, but in everything by prayer and supplication with thanksgiving, let your requests be made know unto God: and the peace of God, which passes all understanding shall keep your hearts and minds through Christ Jesus."

Father nodded, "And as the psalmist says in 50:22, 'Call upon me in the day of trouble, and I will deliver thee, and thou shalt glorify me.' People who pray without ceasing have learned to trust and praise God in all situations and thus have maintained peace of heart under the most difficult of circumstances."

The Archbishop nodded and handed the article back to Father and said, "I hope this message touches the hearts of all who read it. Prayer is the language of communicating with God. As you say, we cannot get to know our heavenly Father without prayer."

Father smiled at his superior and added, "Prayer is as essential to our existence as the air we breathe!"

Just as Father got out of the taxi and made his way up the walk to the front door of the care home, he heard someone shout out his name.

"Father, Father Engelmann!"

Father turned to see a lady in her forties running up the walk. When she got in front of him, she stopped and took a deep breath. "Oh, I am so glad to finally meet up with you. I have been here since eight thirty waiting for your arrival. The receptionist in the care home said you would be in this morning." She stuck out her hand towards Father and said, "I'm Brenda Oakley, a journalist with the *Leader Post*."

Father furrowed his brow and met her hand with his. "How do you do, Miss Oakley…"

Brenda's eyes widened and brightened, "Did Henry

Pederson mention that I would love to do an interview with you for an article in the paper—"

"Ah, yes, yes, Henry did mention that someone from the *Leader Post* wanted to do that."

"I hope you will say yes, Father. I have heard so much about you and the wonderful things you have done. And then there are all of the miracles which happened several years ago. It would make a wonderful story and…" Brenda's eyes flashed as she thought of how to motivate the man in front of her, added, "It would be so inspiring for many readers and perhaps bring them back to their faith. I know just hearing all you have done for others certainly has helped me think about my faith and—"

"Oh, my, you are very good at your job, Miss—"

"Please call me Brenda."

Father smiled and nodded, "Yes, Brenda. It would be inaccurate to say that; I am just an instrument for God to use. Everything which I do is due to the grace of God. On my own, I can do nothing. I'm afraid my story would be very boring for your readers."

"But, Father, your story would inspire others perhaps to go to church, wouldn't you want that? And, and…it could be more directed about where society is heading, about prayer, about family and why we are here. And I recall Mr. Pederson expressing concern about materialism and our focus on wealth and possessions and our pursuit of more and more. There is much you could say about these issues which would be so helpful to us who are searching for a more meaningful life!"

"My, my, Brenda, the Lord has given you a gift—"

And before Father could say no, Brenda thought of another argument for the holy man to consider before making his decision, "On at least two occasions when I came to the care home hoping that you might be here, I read several of the newsletters which you started. The staff said it has done very well due to a large part because the residents write about their experiences and offer their wisdom to young people. Well, Father, your advice and wisdom for the *Leader Post* would be similar to the newsletter only on a larger scale, wouldn't it?"

Father Engelmann's smile broadened. Brenda reminded him of Henry and his enthusiasm when he had an idea or was excited about something. In fact, Father recalled how excited he got when Henry discussed the idea of the newsletter in his café so many years ago. And then, he too, was writing a story which he was assigned by his guardian angel for the purpose of inspiring many readers. He had to admit, Brenda's task was no different.

"Very well, Brenda. Let me pray about it and I shall let you know either directly or through Henry. I am certain, the good Lord will approve."

"Oh, Father you are making my day! If you would like, I could make a list of questions and issues and concerns and you can decide the direction in which the interview can go. It will be so helpful to all of us."

Father nodded, "It was very nice to meet you, Brenda."

"The pleasure is all mine, Father. Have a wonderful day!"

CHAPTER NINE

N₀ SOONER HAD Jenny opened the door to Camilla and Jeremy's home than the smell of bread baking in the oven wafted to her nose and to the three men following close behind her. "Oh, that smells so good!" Jenny exclaimed.

"Hi, Mom, Dad...Hi, Father, Justin," said Camilla as she came out of the kitchen wiping her hands on her apron.

After they all greeted one another with a warm hug, Henry said, "Over the aroma of all the beautiful flowers in the front yard, I detected the wonderful odor of your baking even before we came in. It immediately reminded me of the days I came home from school or work and Mom was baking bread. I could hardly wait to get inside and have a slice loaded with butter."

"Yes, yes," said Father Engelmann. "It reminded me not only of Mary's baking but also how wonderful it is to enter a home that has the smell of bread baking in the oven. It's one of the most welcoming scents there is. I compare it to the comforting love of a wife welcoming her children and husband home."

"That reminds me of the sermon you once said, Father, about the double loaf of bread. I don't think there is a parishioner who forgot the homily that day."

"Well, please share it at dinner. First, I have to see my grandchildren," said Jenny, excitedly.

No sooner had those words left Jenny's mouth than she heard Joshua shout from his bedroom, "Grandma and Grandpa are here!" In the next split second, they could hear him running down the hallway to the front door. Both Henry and Jenny had their arms open. He ran into the middle of them and quickly received a warm embrace from both his grandparents at the same time.

As soon as they parted, Father Engelmann crouched down and opened his arms. "Does the Great Grandfather get a hug, too?"

Joshua ran to Father's waiting arms. "I'm playing with the Tinker Toys you gave to me for my birthday."

"I recall playing with Tinker Toys with my father many years ago and they still bring family together. My, my, I wonder what an eight year old boy would be constructing."

Reaching out for Father's hand, he said, "Come, see! Come too, Justin."

"Yeah, sure, Josh," said Justin, as he followed Joshua and Father to the bedroom.

"So, is Jeremy at work, Camilla?" inquired Henry.

"He's in the bedroom changing Noah. He had to run into the café shortly after noon as one of the servers didn't show up. It wasn't too busy and so he came home shortly after."

Jenny turned to see Jeremy heading towards them carrying their two and half year old son. She ran towards them, quickly kissed Jeremy on the cheek and took Noah from his arms. "Ahh, Noah, how is my darling, little boy?" Jenny asked, as she hugged and kissed him and brought him to Henry.

"Who is this? Noah?"

"Papa…" Noah shouted, a coy smile covering his face.

"That's right," said Henry, as he poked his finger into Noah's tummy. "Got a kiss for Grandpa?"

Jenny brought Noah over and up to Henry for a quick kiss on his cheek.

"Oh, I forgot about the bread!" exclaimed Camilla. "I hope it didn't burn. Get everyone a drink Jeremy. Dinner won't be ready for another half hour."

Jenny followed Camilla into the kitchen still holding Noah. "Oh, Camilla, Noah is so cute and cuddly. I am trying so hard to get pregnant. I would just love to give Henry a child."

"Ahh, Mom…" Camilla's words trailed off as she gazed at Jenny for a moment before turning and bending down to take the golden brown, crusted bread from the oven.

Henry heard just part of Jenny's comment as he sat in the living room with Father Engelmann. He shook his head slightly knowing of Jenny's wish but it was too late for them.

"What would you like to drink, Dad?"

"Iced tea would be wonderful Jeremy and I think that would work for Father. He likes iced tea, as well."

Jenny passed Jeremy entering the kitchen as she was going to the living room. "Henry, would you take Noah, Camilla needs a hand in the kitchen. Isn't he just a darling, honey?" said Jenny, as she handed the little boy to Henry and rushed back into the kitchen.

Just as Jeremy was bringing in the drinks, Father Engelmann came back to the living room. "That Joshua sure knows how to build with those Tinker Toys. Justin has got him started on erecting the Eiffel Tower! I'll check in on them later."

"Yeah, he sure is fascinated with that toy. It's all he plays with lately and…I have to admit, I enjoy erecting different things with him too! I got you an iced tea, hope that's okay, Father?"

"Yes, yes, some iced tea would be fine."

"Just set my drink down, Jeremy, I want to see how Joshua and Justin are coming along with the tower. I'll be right back."

Henry put Noah down and holding his hand, they slowly walked down the hall to Joshua's room.

"So, what do you think of Don Matthews, the Roughriders' new head coach, Father?" Jeremy asked, as he gave Father his drink and set the other one he was holding for Henry on the other end table."

"I haven't been following it. The last I heard, Kent Austin was doing a great job as quarterback. Seems to me, I have heard of Mr. Matthews, however. He led the B.C Lions to a Grey Cup, I understand?"

"Yeah, that was in 1985. He's a risk taker and so far has a very good record. We're hoping he'll take us to the Grey Cup this year."

"Those two are sure constructing that tower in a hurry; it's well over a foot high already!" Henry said as he came into the room still holding Noah's hand.

Just as Henry was about to sit down, Camilla shouted from the kitchen, "Jeremy, can you please put Noah in the high chair, we are just about ready to serve dinner. And...maybe dad can keep an eye on Noah while you carve the ham."

"You and Dad can sit there," Camilla said to Jenny. Looking at Justin, Camilla continued, "You can sit beside your Mom."

"She's not my Mom," Justin muttered and sat next to Henry. There was a moment of silence and Jeremy plunked the high chair next to Justin. "Okay, Justin, you can help me feed Noah."

"I'll get the potatoes and we should be all ready." Camilla rushed back into the kitchen and returned with steaming scalloped potatoes straight from the oven.

"This all looks so delicious, Camilla; just like many of the dishes prepared by chefs on TV!" commented Jenny.

"Thanks, Mom." Camilla took a deep breath and then asked Father to say grace. Just as Father was about to begin, Joshua pulled at Jeremy's sleeve. "I think Joshua wants to say Grace, too. Perhaps, after Father—"

"Yes, yes, that would be wonderful! Please, Joshua, go ahead!" exclaimed Father.

Joshua brought both hands together and slowly said, "Thank you, God for making so many good things for us to eat and enjoy and keep us healthy. Bless this food and Mommy for making it. Bless our guests and what we talk about so our home is a happy place to be." Josh looked up at his dad who simply nodded and then Josh concluded with, "Amen."

"Well done, Son," said Jeremy as he put his arm around Joshua.

Father's eyes reddened a bit and he simply nodded with approval. "It is wonderful to see the beauty of family coming together to give thanks and especially to see the children growing in the Lord like this."

"So true, Father," Jenny commented, her eyes sparkling. "That was a beautiful grace, Joshua, thank you."

"Yes, very nice, Josh," Henry added with a broad smile as he picked up a slice of bread. "The bread is still warm; please pass the butter, Justin." Henry was going to ask Jeremy about the staff at the café but they had made an agreement long ago not to bring up work at the dinner table. Instead, he mentioned a trip coming up.

"You all remember the musical Lauren auditioned for; *Joseph and The Amazing Technicolor Dream Coat?* Well, she was hired to be one of the dancers!"

Before Henry could continue, everyone at the table made joyful comments. When the excitement subsided, Henry continued, "The musical opens up around the middle of June and Jenny and I were thinking of going. We are trying to convince Father to come along."

"That would be a perfect musical for you to go to, Father. That's a great story in the Bible about Joseph's brothers who were envious of his relationship with their father and how they tried to get rid of him," commented Jeremy.

"Yes, it would be wonderful to see Lauren perform. The last time I was in a theatre was in Austria. Anna and I would go whenever we had enough money to attend. Father Knuka's mother is ill again and he asked if I could cover for him should an emergency arise, so hopefully, I will be free to go."

"How is Alison doing at the Bible College? Is she still helping out there?" Camilla wanted to know.

"We just spoke with her the other night," answered Jenny, as Henry's mouth was full of food. "She surprised us. We thought she might consider entering a convent because of her close relationship with the Lord but apparently she has found some interest with a young man at the college."

Henry had swallowed his food and added, "I think it's more than interest. I know Alison and just by the tone in her voice as she spoke of Carson, indicated to me that it was a more serious relationship developing. She did say he was a Métis. His father was white and mother native so there might be some cultural challenges."

"I'm excited to meet him!" said Jenny. Alison and Carson are planning a trip home sometime this summer."

"I hope to meet the young man, too," said Father. "Perhaps, I may be able to perform another wedding!"

"This meal is so delicious, Camilla. I'm amazed how you find time to prepare it with two children and working part time at the tutorial school for unwed mothers."

"Jeremy is a big help. And I only work on the two days Jeremy has off, so, one of us is always at home. I considered terminating my employment but I enjoy it so much."

"The girls would miss you terribly," added Jeremy.

"Still, how you can prepare a meal for so many people is overwhelming. I'm afraid I don't think I could do that. Valerie did an excellent job teaching you that and being able to bake bread from scratch is wonderful!"

"Almost every week as I grew up, relatives would either come to our home or we would be invited to their place. It was always a large gathering and we all helped. It's a matter of getting organized and preparing some of the salads and whatever you can ahead of time."

"Well, I would love to do this some time. You will have to help me."

"My mom could cook for a lot of people," observed Justin.

Before it came too obvious the slight Justin intended against Jenny, Father quickly added, "Yes, yes, Julean was a fine cook. She developed those skills raising a big family. Bringing up you and Jeremy and the girls, all with big appetites was always a challenge."

"And, Julean was brought up surrounded by large families as well," added Henry in further defense.

"When I grew up, I was the only child and we moved around quite a bit with Daddy's job. Some of the times we had a cook live in but the last time in Ottawa, Mom didn't want a live in cook and so I did learn to prepare some meals but never on this scale. When I married James, the estate did have a lot of help and Matti, as you know, was the cook there. I tried to help but she discouraged me from doing so as she felt it was her job to always prepare our meals and look after us."

"Well, you grew up with a different life style," commented Jeremy.

"But, I would have loved to be surrounded by lots of relatives and family. It was very lonely so much of the time."

Henry put his arm around his dear wife, and said, "Well, you have lots of family now, Honey. Henry pulled Jenny in and then changed the subject, "I am going to have another piece of that bread, Camilla, which reminds me once again of Father's sermon about the double loaf of bread."

"So, Father, what was the sermon that Henry and the other parishioners remember that had to do with baked bread in the oven?" asked Camilla.

Father swallowed the food he was chewing and then said, "That was a long time ago but I still recall most of it because it was my grandmother's recipe for a happy and contented home. Perhaps you can help me, Henry."

"Actually, Father, it was such a great sermon that I typed it out and gave it as a handout to families who I counseled in the years that followed. In fact, I think I have a copy in my wallet." Henry set his cutlery down and pulled out his wallet. Yeah, I think this is it." Henry opened a folded piece of paper and muttered, "No this is a different one about never giving up…" His words trailed off as he replaced the one he took out with another and opened it up.

"Yes, this is it: Father Engelmann's recipe for a Double Loaf of Homemade Bread." Henry took a sip of water and then began to read: "The more this bread is baked every day, the happier your marriage will be. Just like flour is to a loaf of bread, the main ingredient in a marriage is our Lord; putting Jesus into the marriage first keeps it sticking together, while prayer and faith leavens it. To this we should add: 1 cup caring, 1 cup kind acts, 1 cup understanding, 2 cups sacrifices, 5 cups forgiveness and a whole lot of—acceptance!

"Thoroughly mix the above ingredients. Add tears of joy, sorrow, and compassion and a pinch of spice. Now roll it and hug it all over. And after it rises a bit, beat down all of the fault finding, resentment, and especially the anger. Never let the sun set on anger and carry over to the next day's baking. It will lose its freshness and quickly spoil for sure.

"Once well formed, place it into a home with walls made of loving arms and bake in an oven of human kindness. Never take making good bread for granted, as it quickly becomes stale and hard, even overnight.

"Start each day with a new double loaf so when you pull it apart, it is always warm and fresh inside, ready to be spread with the butter of love and served with a smile."

Henry folded the paper and said, "Doesn't that summarize the heart of what makes a happy marriage!"

"Yes, those are wonderful ingredients for a good marriage, Father!" said Jenny.

"Essentially, what my grandmother did was to put into practice St. Paul's scripture to the Corinthians on 'love' by relating it to something practical that she loved to do. And I would have to add that your home, Jeremy, is an excellent example of putting it into practice not only my grandmother's recipe for a happy marriage but also of what Henry, Jenny and I were talking about the other day at the prayer house. I can see that you have Jesus at the center of your home and have your family's best interest at heart."

"I was brought up in a Christian home," said Camilla. "We went to church every Sunday, said grace at every meal and did charitable works but what we didn't do, which I learned from Jeremy, was to take time to read the Bible and meditate every morning and when we are all ready to leave for the day we pray together. It's such a wonderful ritual to get into and starts the day out in such a purposeful way."

"Yes, yes, that's wonderful," chimed in Father Engelmann. "You have learned the secret to baking Grandmother's double loaf of bread. You have gone to the source. God made the earth, sun and water to grow the wheat. All things come from Him and thus are ready to live out the ingredients of the baked bread! You have filled your mind and heart first thing with God's word and received the Holy Spirit's grace and strength to live it out in your family and with people you meet throughout the day. It was Anna, who taught me to do that every morning and after a time, she would immediately notice by my demeanor if I hadn't spent time with the Lord. She would be quick to say, 'David, did you read the Bible yet this morning?'"

"My gosh," interjected Camilla, "That's exactly what I said to Jeremy last week when he was running late and grumbling around!"

Everyone laughed.

"Your grandma was very wise, Father, to come up with that recipe," said Camilla.

"I'd have to say Honey, that you are, too! You not only bake bread but you put into practice the entire ingredients Dad listed! In fact," he added with a wink, "there are many days, I can't keep my mind on my work just thinking about coming home."

"Ah, that's sweet, Jeremy!"

"Yeah, that explains why Jeremy neglects the customers so many times," jested Justin.

Everyone chuckled.

"Never mind, your day will come soon enough," Jeremy retorted. "I can just see you ogling all the pretty girls when you start high school this fall."

Justin blushed. "Yeah, yeah, sure…" His words trailed off not sure how to reply.

"My, my, how the time flies; already starting high school. I can still remember the day Julean took you to begin elementary school and now you're a young man ready to go to the next level. If I'm not mistaken, you have a birthday coming up soon?" Father observed.

"Yeah, I'll be fifteen this August 3rd. I can hardly wait. Just a couple of more months and I can get my learner's license!"

"Can I be excused, Mom?" Joshua interjected, "I want to work some more on the tower."

Jeremy put his arm around his son. "Are you sure you don't want to visit with Grandma and Grandpa and Father some more? You couldn't wait until they got here."

"It's just that I want to show them the tower when I finish it."

"Well, you did a good job on your dinner, Son. Yes, go ahead."

"Thanks, Dad. Want to come, Justin?"

Justin looked at Henry who was already nodding his approval and got up, "Thank you for the dinner, Camilla. It was really good."

"You're welcome, Justin. I will call you both for dessert later. It's strawberry shortcake with whipped cream!"

"Sounds great!"

"That was a delicious meal, Camilla. It will last me for a few days," said Father.

"I think you need to eat a bit more, mind you, perhaps, I should consider fasting more like you do. I could easily afford to lose a few pounds," observed Camilla.

"It does have the benefit of cleansing out the body of all its toxins and the energy which results is a wonderful bonus. I can still walk the hills and valleys very easily at the prayer house."

"Why do you fast so much, Father?" Camilla wanted to know.

"Fasting and prayer draw us closer to God. Fasting helps free us from worldly attachments, especially the flesh. I always want to know what God's purpose is for me. What is His will...I want to be in touch as much as possible. And the Bible teaches us to fast and pray. Jesus did, His apostles did and many leaders in the Old Testament did."

"Do your prayers get answered better if you fast?" Jenny wanted to know as she was planning to do a novena. Instinctively, she moved her hand until it touched Henry's hand resting on the table. Would Henry know what her motives were?

Father straightened in his chair and studied Jenny for a moment. "I have witnessed many breakthroughs to having prayers answered in the lives of others and also myself. However, fasting is first and foremost to develop a closer relationship with God. It is about changing you; coming to know God more intimately and His will for you. It is best to keep your motives pure and not just fast to get something. As you grow closer to His will, the Holy Spirit will teach you how to pray."

"For how long do you fast, Father," inquired Jeremy.

"I have done forty day fasts similar to that which Jesus did before he began His ministry. However, one can begin simply by skipping a meal or fasting for a day. Many people choose Monday not to eat or again choose to eat only fruit or drink juice for the day. When fasting, it's important to set a time for prayer; prayer and fasting work together to produce wonderful results in so many ways."

"In what ways?" asked Camilla.

"As I alluded to, the purpose of fasting is to change you, to repair what needs fixing from the inside out. You will come to understand yourself at a deeper level and things that are roadblocks to God. Remember, where your treasures lie, there will your heart be also. The very first commandment of God is that thou shall not have false gods before you. As you examine your life, you will be amazed how many idols you have in your life. Food itself can be an idol as can money, possessions, drugs, one's talents and even one's spouse. God must be master of your life and we come to Him through Jesus..."

Father's words trailed off as what he just said struck a deep chord within Henry. He knew exactly what Father was talking about. He still struggled with so many masters in his life; his abilities, wealth, possessions, accolades from others and Father was right, the list was endless. Henry realized lately, more and more how far he was missing the mark by not having Jesus at the center. A sense of hypocrisy tugged at him as he slowly straightened in his chair and tuned back in to Father's words.

"...detaching yourself from food helps to discipline and strengthen your will to overcome the constant cravings and temptations we face."

"I never realized there were so many benefits from fasting," observed Jeremy.

After a long pause, Father added, "Besides helping to gain control over attachments and idols in your life, when one fasts for several days, you begin to know and understand firsthand what it feels like for most of the world that goes to bed hungry; your compassion and concern for suffering of all kinds increases tenfold."

"There are so many things I am praying for, perhaps fasting would help to get some answers and clarity," commented Jenny.

"I may try it, too," Camilla chimed in. Some of the girls at the tutorial school have so many issues in their lives: their boyfriends have abandoned them, should they keep the child they are carrying, give it up for adoption or have an abortion, estranged with their parents and the list goes on. Sometimes, I just want to bring them all home and love them to bits." Tears surfaced in Camilla's eyes. Jeremy reached over and put his hand on hers resting on the table.

Jenny immediately reached over and put her hand on Camilla and Jeremy's, "Oh, Camilla, you have such a compassionate heart. If I can help you in any way…it hurts my heart too, just thinking about those young girls as unwed mothers and facing such huge decisions. To decide whether or not to terminate the child within your womb would be so overwhelming. There are so many couples wanting to adopt a child…oh, Camilla, it must be so difficult for you…" Jenny's words trailed off. She sat back up and brushed off a tear rolling down her cheek with her finger tips.

Father studied the caring young woman and added, "Yes, Camilla, the Lord is calling you. I feel the heaviness of your heart and He wants to carry the load for you. Give thanks for all these concerns and trust in God to work in the lives of these young women. He will lighten their lives as He will yours. If any of you wish to spend a day or two at the Poustinia, please come. The peace and quiet surrounded by the beauty of nature will heal your heart and may give you the breakthrough you need to know God's plan and purpose for you. Since you already pray and meditate every morning, fasting would take you to the next level."

"Can I be first on the list, Father? I would love to meet with you in the next day or two and spend the day in fast and prayer. There is something I wish to discuss with you if you have time."

"Yes, yes, of course, Jenny."

"That's wonderful, Father. I will start my fast right after I have my strawberry shortcake and whipped cream desert!"

Everyone chuckled except for Henry. He remained silent. How many times had Father invited him to come to the prayer house, too? What was holding him back?

CHAPTER TEN

"**H**i, Mom, it's Camilla."

"Hi, Camilla, it's Mom!" They both laughed, "I still can't stop saying that even though it's been over three years. Sometimes, I still think it's all a dream that we found each other after all those years."

"Yes, I know what you mean. I have the same feelings. Actually, one of my students who was adopted just tracked down her biological mother."

"Oh, that's wonderful, Camilla—"

"In most cases it is, but in Natalie's case it hasn't got a happy ending, at least so far. Apparently her mother is married and has four children and doesn't want her past known to her husband or children."

Jenny was silent for a moment and then said, "I can understand that could be a problem for some women but still, it is her child and there is such a strong instinct to be re-united with the biological parent."

"Well, it certainly was in our case and we both desired and prayed that we would one day be together again but that is not always the case."

"Has the mother talked to Natalie?" Jenny wanted to know.

"Yes, they spoke just briefly and the mother told Natalie not to call the house again. She said she was sorry but doesn't want to bring back the past or have her life disrupted."

"That must be very difficult for Natalie to accept. Knowing one is adopted at times leads to feelings of rejection and then to find out that they really have been, it reinforces the pain."

"Fortunately, Natalie's adoptive parents are very loving and supportive but she has another issue to deal with: a very abusive boyfriend. Since she won't have an abortion, he wants her to give up the child for adoption."

"But then she would be doing exactly what her biological mother did to her."

"Exactly, that's why she is so torn and stressed out. She is so in love with her boyfriend that she can't see things clearly and accepts his disrespect and intimidation towards her. We called in a speaker to talk about healthy relationships and communication which contains mutual respect, consideration and understanding. The speaker is open to talking with the girls one on one, Natalie has agreed to see him."

"Verbal and physical abuse is more common than we think. One of the ladies in our group has agreed to see a counselor at the Family Service Bureau and so far it seems to be helping. She told her husband that the family doctor advised her to seek therapy because of her stress level, which was true and the counselor she was seeing advised her to invite her husband."

"I'm sure that didn't go over well."

"No, he was outraged at the start but when she said she would leave if he didn't co-operate, he agreed to go. They have had two sessions now and Susan informs me that her husband is making a concerted effort. The goal is to restore the marriage, not to separate or divorce if at all possible."

"Creating a crisis like that often works when the victim takes a stand and won't put up with that kind of behavior any longer. It opens the door to at least trying to change. Many negative behaviors and thought patterns like this are deeply entrenched and so difficult to deal with. It takes time and great effort...and great love."

"Well said, dear. We will have to keep them in our prayers

and others in the group, too. Since Susan opened up about her situation at home, several other women have shared similar situations. One of the ladies made a good observation that a spouse who uses verbal abuse usually is very insecure and tries to control the partner with derogatory comments and intimidation. Another said, her husband came from a home in which his father was an alcoholic and very abusive. Sometimes behaviors are learned at an early age and repeated."

"That's the case with some of the boys the girls go out with at the school. Many have been shown little respect in their upbringing and seem to pass it on."

"Yes, abusive relationships don't necessarily apply to marriages but all relationships, even friends can be abusive and controlling of one another. I was surprised when one of the ladies in our group admitted that she was the one who was guilty of abusive behavior. She confessed to being very critical and judgmental of her husband and can see the constant stress it's creating in their marriage.

"I am convinced, Camilla, that it all comes back to having Jesus at the center of relationships and marriage. Father Engelmann has stressed that so much over the years and I have to agree. When we stop and pray and read what Jesus has to say about loving one another; being kind, considerate, respectful and forgiving, it just makes such good sense. So many marriages are caught up in the rat race to keep up with the Jones' or just forget about one another. If we don't take the time to examine our lives on a daily basis, we perpetuate the state we are caught in. The relationship journeys along aimlessly with no purpose or direction. There isn't any accountability if God isn't at the center of the marriage. Who can we learn from? Whose example do we follow? How do we break the negative cycle?"

"That's so true, Mom. It's so easy to fall into that daily grind trap," remarked, Camilla. "Working, coming home for dinner, watching some TV, going to bed only to get up the next morning and repeat the cycle; taking each other for granted slips into a relationship so easily if, as you say, we don't take the time to stop and examine our lives and see what really matters."

Jenny nodded, even though Camilla couldn't see her affirming what she said, "The problem with taking each other for granted is we fail to acknowledge each other almost as if our partner has little value."

"Yes, and we all need to be affirmed, and accepted, respected, loved, we need to feel secure and appreciated for who we are. If our basic needs are not met, we begin to drift apart."

Jenny nodded again, "If Jesus is at the center of our relationship and we take the time to pray to Him and ask for guidance and strength from the Holy Spirit, it's amazing how things improve because our needs as you pointed out would begin to be met. The ladies in the group who have tried prayer and bring Jesus into the home and marriage say the results are unbelievable. When we die to ourselves as Jesus did for the Father and begin to submit and serve one another with love, how could the results not be for the better!?

"The best marriage is two servants of each other in love!"

"I have to agree, Mom. I know with Jeremy and me, as we shared at dinner last evening, if we don't say morning prayers together and stop to pray and mediate before the kids get up, our peace and sometimes the entire day is disrupted.

"The key is not to fit God into your day but rather build your day around God!"

"I wish you were part of our group, Camilla, your marriage would be a great example to share. You are a beacon of light, Honey!"

Camilla hesitated for a moment and decided to share something which she and Jeremy were doing in their marriage. "Jeremy and I have started to bless one another and I must admit, Mom, I love when I am prayed over by my husband and Jeremy does too, when I bless him."

"That sounds wonderful, Camilla, tell me about it."

"It all started one day when I was so worried about one of the girls who decided to abort her baby. It was getting me down because I had said all I could to Marcia and in the end she decided to have an abortion. Normally, Jeremy and I pray for the girls and ask the Holy Spirit to guide them and also give us the strength to accept their decisions. But this one was so difficult for me to accept. She was three months pregnant and the fetus was healthy and well developed.

"Anyway, one morning, Jeremy asked me to sit down on the kitchen chair and he put both of his hands on my head and prayed that I let go of my worry and give it God. He prayed that God bless me with His grace and love so I could accept the decisions that the girls make. He let me know how much I love and care for the girls. He reminded me how thoroughly I explain to the girls all the options available to them and the consequences of the decisions they make. He reminded me of how I work with the girls to examine each of their concerns and all the services available to them. 'Honey,' he said, 'you have done all you can and now the decision is up to them and God.' As Jeremy blessed me in the name of the Father and the Son and Holy Spirit, I can't tell you, Mom, how at peace I felt when Jeremy did that. It was so wonderful to feel my husband show such deep love for my welfare and being. It was such an outpouring of his love and care for me. And it was not only his love and care I felt but God's as well. It was almost as if Jesus was right there."

"Oh, Camilla, I am so happy you shared that with me. The way you described it is so meaningful. It just isn't words which we so often hear like, 'God bless you' or 'may the Lord bless and keep you.' Most times, we just pass that off as a nice gesture but with little meaning. What you said however, Honey, was such a deep evoking of God to bring good into the life of another. What Jeremy did was to ask God to do something for you which he was incapable of doing. He asked the all knowing God of the universe to shower you with blessings for your good! Oh, Camilla, that can be such an act of deep care, concern and love for another."

Jenny paused and then added excitedly, "See how that brings Jesus and our heavenly Father into the marriage! Look how He blesses us and fills us with love through our spouses!"

"You know when Jeremy first did that, he reminded me of something Father Engelmann would do because he is a priest and thus it would be an accepted and expected thing to do. It seemed a little awkward at first for my husband to do this but then why should it be? Praying to God is personal but it's also central to our lives and so important in healing our emotional and mental sides. I just love when my husband prays that God look after me and blesses me with grace to deal with life's challenges."

"It's odd that we can talk about sports and politics for hours without giving it another thought and yet to talk about God in the home and to pray, people find so difficult. Anyway, I must tell the ladies about this. I'm sure many of them will find it hard to introduce blessing one another and yet once they start after a few times it begins to feel like the natural thing to do."

"That's what happened to me. Following Jeremy's leadership, I pray over and bless him as well. Two weeks ago I noticed Jeremy was so stressed out with work, I asked God to bless his relationships with his staff and the customers he greets. Dad has taught Jeremy to act the way Father Engelmann did when he used to run the grocery store; to be a light to others and that his staff should have the same frame of mind. We are here to serve more than food. The nice thing about all this, too, Mom, the boys have started to join in with us. When Joshua and little Noah lay their hands on me, that's when I feel and know, God is at the center of our family."

"Oh, Camilla that is so wonderful it brings tears to my eyes. It's such a good example to the children to see their parents showing love and care for each other. It will help them in their future marriages and have a positive effect on them for the rest of their lives! See, how just talking about praying and blessing each other is so uplifting and healing! I wish our group sessions could go on over the summer but today is our last meeting until the fall. Henry is going to line up speakers for the men and he hopes to be one of the speakers, too, either next fall or winter. Men need to take leadership in the home to pray and put Jesus at the center. Men have such an important role in this entire area. Oh, Camilla I wish I could shout it from the rooftops!"

"Once the husband and wife see the tremendous benefits of prayer and taking the time to examine their lives and marriage they will kick themselves for not doing it sooner. Having my quiet time and praying sets the tone in the home. It gets me into a good mood and frame of mind to think of others. I find I am more cheerful, considerate, encouraging and it's contagious! Everyone gets a good start to loving one another within the family and gives them the encouragement, motivation to be a beacon out into a world that is so desperate for love and care and kindness and a friendly smile."

"Oh, Honey, I wish we had this discussion in the ladies group. I can't wait to get there and share it all with them!"

Jenny paused and then said, "What about the girls who decided to keep their babies? How do they manage if their boyfriend has abandoned them? There are two ladies in our group: one who has two children is divorced and the other has three and the father has walked out on them. It's such a challenge for them to carry out such a huge responsibility to try and be both a mother and father."

"Yes, over the years I have worked with so many single girls who are raising their child and it is difficult. It's so important for a father to be in the home. You can see just from what I have shared with you how much Jeremy supports me in raising the children and is such a strong role model for the boys. Jeremy belongs to a volunteer program called Big Brothers Big Sisters and often helps out as a big brother to the boys of single mothers who haven't any family to help out."

"That's wonderful for Jeremy to give of his time like that."

"It's not a chore to him, he loves to help out and sees the joy in the children's eyes when he takes them out to a movie or lunch or just plays ball or games with them."

"I recall Father Engelmann saying when a spouse dies or is divorced it's so important for family and relatives to help. Grandfathers and grandmothers can be such important role figures for children. In any case, it's so critical for spouses to make every effort to make their marriage work."

"That cannot be stressed enough, Mom. And as you have said many times, if Jesus is at the center of the marriage and spouses make their relationship and family the number one priority in their lives, their children's need for identity, love and security will most assuredly be met."

"Oh, my, how did we get started on all of this? Actually, I had called for another reason."

"Yes, you are calling early. I know you don't have to have a reason to call other than to just chat and hear each other's voice."

"I do have something on my mind. It's what you said in the kitchen last evening. I know you had mentioned before your desire to get pregnant and have a baby but you hadn't said it for some time and I thought that wish had passed but you said it with such feeling, I thought perhaps we should talk about it."

"Oh Camilla, that's the counselor in you coming out. The truth is, my dear, I want more than anything to carry Henry's child. It's been a long held secret and desire for as long as I can remember."

"But Mom, you're over fifty years of age, I think you may be too old to have a child. Do you still menstruate?" Camilla wanted to know.

After a brief pause, Jenny said, "No, it's been over a year and half, I think, why do you ask?"

"Well, if you haven't menstruated for over a year it means that you're in menopause and it's very difficult if not impossible for you to conceive." And before Jenny could answer, Camilla quickly added, "and what about the cancer and all the radiation and chemotherapy treatments you had, hasn't that damaged the ovaries?"

"That's just the thing, Camilla, when Doctor Kreake thoroughly examined me after I was miraculously healed and ran all of the tests, he was stunned to find out that there wasn't anything wrong with any of my organs. I had asked him specifically about my ovaries and if I was still able to conceive a child. He couldn't answer that question directly and so he referred me to a gynecologist who was an expert in fertility reproduction."

"My gosh, Mom, what did he find?"

"Like Dr. Kreake, he was amazed to conclude that my ovaries were in excellent condition similar to that of much younger women. He found it difficult to believe, knowing of my history and how cancer had ravaged my body. He did say, however, that although my ovaries seemed fine it may be my age which might restrict me from becoming pregnant."

Camilla remained silent for a moment to reflect on what her mom had said and then inquired, "How does Henry, I mean, Dad feel about this?"

"We have discussed this several times. I think he is okay with a child but tries to play it down. He knows how much I want to have his child and he's concerned that it's too late and doesn't want me to get discouraged if it doesn't work out. He tells me over and over how much he loves me just the way things are."

"And what about Justin, I noticed at the dinner table that he didn't want to sit beside you and made it obvious that his mother was a better cook than you."

"Oh Camilla, you don't miss a thing do you? Yes, there is still some tension between us. He dearly misses, Julean. Henry tells me they were very close and not to be concerned about it as time will heal everything."

"It's been three years, Mom and I still don't notice him warming up to you."

"Yes, I know, somehow I have to convince him that I am not here to replace his mother. Both Henry and I have had a talk with him about it but he just brushes it off. I am going to ask my ladies group if any of them had the same concern and how they handled it. I think there are one or two ladies in the group that have had children from previous marriages."

"Yes, that's a good idea. Would you like me talk to Justin about it?"

Jenny reflected for a moment, "It may not hurt, Camilla, He likes you very much and may not feel as threatened by you as he does by me."

"He is staying with us more often lately rather than going to the farm. Perhaps one evening, I may have a chat with him."

"That would be wonderful, Honey."

There was a long silence between them.

"Are you still there Mom?"

"Yes, Camilla, I was just thinking if I should share this with you or not that I was thinking about making an intercessory novena to Mary. Carlos's wife, Maria does all the time. Last week, they showed me a little shrine they had built in the back yard behind all the shrubbery in front of the tall fir trees. It's just across from the gazebo. They have a statue of the Blessed Mother there to provide a mental image of Mary and pray to her all of the time for intercessory prayer. They both have such deep faith in their prayers for Mary to intercede to her Son, Jesus to heal their son who is suffering from some health issues."

"Yes, I recall Mary, or Grandma Pederson, rather, Dad's Mom, who also made novenas to St. Theresa all of the time, too. It's worth a try, Mom. And, what about fasting and praying? Father Engelmann is big on that and seems to encourage it all of the time. Have you given any thought to that?"

"Yes, as a matter of fact, I have. I was planning to visit Father at the Poustinia tomorrow morning and discuss that very thing with him. I do pray all of the time but he seems to think fasting may just make a breakthrough with God."

"So, you want another miracle, do you?"

Jenny paused for a moment, and then said, "Yes, I guess I do, Camilla. Yes, I may be getting on in age but after having my body in such a mess and to be back alive and in complete health...yes, I do expect another miracle!"

CHAPTER ELEVEN

RIGHT AFTER HENRY and Jenny said their morning prayers, Jenny decided to walk down to the prayer house. Henry had an early meeting at the gallery and felt it would be okay for her to make the trek down there accompanied by Ginger. Even though it was going to be a hot day on the prairies, Jenny put on one of her heavier sweaters. She knew as she descended into the valley the air would get cooler. She understood why Father always wore the heavy hooded robe.

"I love you so much, Jenny. Are you sure you don't want me to drive you down?"

"No, that's fine, Henry. The walk will do me good and give me time to reflect on what I want to talk to Father about."

Henry wrinkled his forehead and remained silent hoping Jenny would share with him what concerned her, but she too, remained silent.

"Does it have to do with Justin?" Henry wanted to know.

"I am concerned about my relationship with Justin, but that wasn't what I wanted to chat with Father about. I don't want to upset you, Honey, but I want Father to say a Mass and pray that …that, I get pregnant." Tears surfaced in Jenny's eyes. "It's something I wanted since the day we met, Henry…even when married to James, I felt guilty so many times just thinking on it. And I keep thinking that perhaps my healing was in part to bring me back so that I could realize my lifelong wish. I know it's foolish to think that at my age....but..., but, why are all my organs all perfectly healed? And the gynecologist said that my ovaries are similar to that of a much younger woman... why? I just keep thinking and hoping that it will all come true."

Jenny began to sob and fell into Henry's arms and buried her head into his chest.

"Honey, if that's what you want, I am okay with it, but I don't like to see you hurt if it doesn't happen. We are getting on in age and it will be difficult to raise a baby...when the child is twenty, we will be in our seventies, you know."

"Yes, I know, but age doesn't matter so much as loving a child and bringing it up in a Christian home. And, I want something that you and I have created together. Just think, to have our own child...it's been my lifelong dream."

"Well, Honey, I'm all for trying," Henry winked, "some days I can't wait for night fall just so that I can hold you in my arms and make love. Perhaps, talk to Father and share this all with him. And I promise, I too, will pray that you realize your heart's desire. What makes you happy, sweetheart, makes me happy. But please know that you could bear ten or more children for me and I still couldn't possibly love you any more than I already do."

Henry and Jenny embraced and tenderly kissed once more. They finally became aware of Ginger snuggling in between them. They were so engrossed in their conversation that they hadn't even noticed her squirming the whole time.

They both reached down and patted her. "Okay, Ginger, let's go."

Henry watched Jenny and Ginger walk down the road. Unbidden tears surfaced as he softly whispered a prayer. "Dear Jesus, I know it's late in our lives to think about bringing a child into the world but if this is Your will and that of Your heavenly Father, please let Jenny conceive."

Henry had to admit that it had been his desire and prayer for all those years since Jenny and he had met to have a child, too.

How many countless times had he remembered over and over the time when they went to Wascana Park and almost made love? How many times had he wished, even though it wouldn't have been the right thing to do, that they had? He often wished that they had and Jenny had conceived a child so somehow it could have kept them together. Henry shook his head to dispel the foolish thoughts he was entertaining and once again whispered into the crisp morning air, "Miraculously, Jesus, we were brought back together again and if it's possible, please let us have a child."

JENNY SOFTLY TAPPED on the front door and opened it. In a low voice, she whispered, "Father, good morning, it's me, Jenny." She entered the small foyer and looked into the living room but Father wasn't there. She thought he might be saying Mass but since he hadn't expected her, he may have already said it earlier as he usually did. She looked straight ahead into the kitchenette but he wasn't there either and a quick peek through the doorway into the bedroom also didn't reveal him. Perhaps, he was out for his morning walk.

She thought she would pray.

Jenny knelt down on the kneeler and made the sign of the cross. She looked up and locked her gaze on the large crucifix hanging on the wall above the altar. The wood carving of Jesus looked so real. She recalled her suffering in the hospital and how she related it to Jesus' sacrifice of love for her. It had touched her so deeply then and did now. "Thank You for giving Your life for me, dear sweet Jesus," Jenny said, with deep emotion. "Thank You for giving me eternal life by opening the doors to heaven but also for restoring my health and allowing me to live on earth for a while longer. I long to serve You and the Father in any way I can."

She paused for a moment and then continued, "I have often wondered, dear Lord, for the reason or reasons of my return. There were so many miracles and things that happened: James and I were reconciled and he came to know You before his death, Peter and I were reconciled and I have developed such a wonderful relationship with him and his family and my lifelong prayer to find my daughter who I had given up for adoption. I am so thankful Jesus for these miracles and especially for re-uniting Henry and me. It all turned out so wonderful! I am so happy Jesus and thankful for all my blessings and yet, in my heart, perhaps, I have also been brought back to realize my deep desire to bear a child for Henry. His previous wife gave him four beautiful children and I at least wish to give him one. Please, Jesus, please, dear heavenly Father, hear my earnest plea. You are the God of all possibilities. You are merciful and generous. It is in You who I trust. Please, I entreat You to hear my plea, listen to my prayer to bear Henry's child..."

So overwhelmed with grief, Jenny began to sob.

WHEN JENNY HAD come into the Poustinia, Father Engelmann didn't hear her. He was at the bedroom closet putting on his garments to say Mass. It was then he heard someone speaking or rather praying. He thought it was an angel, the voice was so gentle and appealing. He silently went to the door and was surprised to see Jenny kneeling before the altar in deep prayer and petition. He froze at the doorway and just quietly listened to her deeply pleading to the Lord.

Her lips quivered so fervently.

He was spellbound by the pouring out of her heartfelt prayer and supplication. He felt her deep desolation and emptiness. Father had never seen or heard Jenny in such a state of anguish. It reminded him of a story he had read so many times in the Old Testament.

Not wanting to startle her, he quietly entered the living room and with tears of compassion sitting on the edge of his eyelids, he softly spoke, "My dear child..."

Jenny turned towards Father, surprised to see him. She quickly got up and embraced the holy priest. "Oh Father, I don't know what to do. I want to bear Henry a child so much."

"I am certain the Lord has heard your cry, and I, too, pray the Lord grant the prayer you have requested." Father swept his hand towards the chairs, "Come, let us sit and watch the stillness of the pond and reflect upon your request."

Jenny and Father sat in the two wicker chairs in front of the patio doors and gazed out into the valley coming to life by the rising sun. The dark shadows were scampering in all directions revealing the fresh green colors of early summer. Jenny began to feel the peace of nature as it seeped into her heart and calmed her breathing.

Father turned to Jenny and said, "I had forgotten your heart's desire, Jenny. I recall you shared that with me when I visited you when you were ill in the Santa Maria Care Home. Now that you are married to Henry, I can see it is still a wish you want so dearly to be fulfilled. From the earnestness of your prayer to God, I am certain that He has heard your plea. You have brought your deep faith before the Lord and entwined your suffering with that of Christ."

Father shook his head in disbelief, "I am astounded by the similarity of your cry to God to that of Hannah in the Bible. Are you familiar with the book of Samuel in the Old Testament, Jenny?"

Jenny wiped her eyes with the tips of her fingers and shook her head, "No Father, I am not."

"It's a story about a lady named Hannah—"

"As you know, Father, that's the name of my guardian angel, too! I have been dreaming of her so much lately. She knows of my prayers to Jesus and in a dream I had last night, she was flying around Camilla's home listening to our discussion about fasting and praying. This is one of the reasons I came down for you to help me get started on a fast. Perhaps this is what God wants me to do. I have already started an intercessory novena to Mary."

Once again, Father shook his head. "It's remarkable how it's all so similar to Hannah's story. In the Old Testament, people often brought animals to the altar to be sacrificed to the Lord for their prayers to be heard. Hannah brings no animal or food for sacrifice only her pain. Hannah, too, prayed and fasted and came to the Lord pouring out her life."

Jenny thought Father was going off on a tangent and she was more interested in the woman named Hannah in the Bible. "How is Hannah's plea similar to mine, Father?" Jenny was anxious to know.

"Yes, yes, I was just coming to how this all fits together."

Father sat back into his chair and crossed his legs. He took a deep breath and began to tell Jenny the story of Samuel 1, in the Old Testament. "Hannah was married to Elkanah who also had a second wife, Peninnah who had borne him many children. Hannah, however, was miserable because she was barren, unable to have children. Even though her husband loved her very much, in fact, more so than his other wife, Hannah desperately wanted to give Elkanah a child. One time when the entire family made their annual pilgrimage to the shrine of Shiloh a little ways from Jerusalem, Hannah, out of exasperation left the festivities and went into the shrine to pray. She pleads with God to give her a child just like you did this morning in the prayer house. What also is remarkable, Jenny, is that when Hannah went to the shrine to pray, Eli, the priest at the shrine also witnesses Hannah praying so intensely just as I did you! Anyway, Eli approached Hannah and talks to her just as I am to you now!"

Father leaned forward in his chair to emphasize the hope he held for Jenny's plea and said, "He, like I, came to the same conclusion that God will surely grant your request. Besides prayer and fasting like you are doing, Hannah even promised God that if she bears a son, she would dedicate the child to the Lord from birth—".

"Oh Father," Jenny cried out, no longer able to wait, "Did she conceive, Father? Did she bear a child!?'

Father sat back, and lifted his hands and shook them with his affirmative response, "Yes, yes, she bore a son and she named him Samuel, a name whose meaning recalls that 'she requested him from the Lord.' It would ever remind Hannah of how God answered her tearful cry for help."

Jenny's heart exulted, "What a wonderful story, Father, if God answers my prayer, I too, will offer the child up to Him.

You have always been such a wonderful example of one who has dedicated his life to God through the vocation you have chosen. I will pray every day that it is the child's vocation to have a special place in Jesus' heart!"

Father couldn't believe what Jenny had just said, "Jenny, not only was Hannah's son given to her but Samuel went on to have a special place in history beyond anything she could have imagined! Hannah would claim her place in the salvation history."

"What do you mean, Father?"

Father sat up in his chair once more and went on with excitement growing in his voice. "Young Samuel grew up to be a great prophet who anointed both Israel's first king, Saul, and its greatest king, David, who was the ancestor of Jesus! It was King David who established Jerusalem, proposed the building of the temple, and established the house into which Jesus the savior of the world was born."

Jenny looked at Father, flabbergasted.

"In the same way Hannah's child was preparing the way for King David to show Israel a different way, later on, Mary the Blessed Mother, who would bear Jesus, is preparing the way for the one who will be called 'Son of David.'"

After a long pause, Father added, "I am astounded, Jenny that you have not only decided to make the sacrifice of fasting to God but you have also decided to make a novena to Mary to intercede to her Son on your behalf as well!"

Father paused and then stepped out in faith and added, "This seems to me that your prayer is doubly heard."

A serene silence fell in the holy room. Both were quietly meditating on what they had discussed as they gazed through the patio door windows at the still pond. Every so often, tiny ripples formed from insects striking the mirror like surface. Jenny could see in the water that clouds had begun to build up without looking up at the sky. It made her think of how Father, too, reflected Jesus here on earth without looking up to heaven. *Such a holy man of God, she thought. It would be so wonderful to have a child who would go into a vocation which would follow his footsteps.*

"What does the name, Hannah mean, Father? Jenny asked, softly breaking the silence

"The name, Hannah, calls to mind the Hebrew verb that means 'to show favor.'

"So, Hannah was favored by God."

Father simply nodded and sat back in the chair, his twinkling eyes revealing his fondness for the woman seated across from him.

"That's so beautiful, Father. Perhaps, my guardian angel is favored by God as well." Jenny said, with a warm smile covering her words.

"Oh, I'm sure your angel Hannah is, Jenny, as I am certain that you are, too!"

"I see you are wearing your liturgical vestments, have you celebrated Mass, yet?" Jenny wanted to know.

"I was about to do just that, Jenny. I was busy writing early this morning and wanted to finish the chapter I was working on. Actually, I was about to ask if you would join me in the Mass and also present your heartfelt petition to bear a child at the offering when Jesus' sacrifice on the cross is re-enacted and lifted up to the Father."

Jenny wrinkled her forehead. "I'm not sure I understand what you mean."

"Although I have been a Catholic all my life, my parents were not really strong in the faith. While I knew it was the Church's belief that the bread and wine turn into the body and blood of Jesus, I have to admit I'm not sure if I understand it or what really goes on during the Mass. I love how it is such a holy ritual."

"Yes, many Catholics don't understand nor believe the transubstantiation either and as a result they miss out on the tremendous benefits which the Mass offers. Come, let us celebrate Mass together and I will refresh your memory of what goes on and how you can participate with your offering as well."

CHAPTER TWELVE

JUST AS FATHER rose and made his way over to the altar, there was a tap on the door and Henry walked in.

"Hi, my meeting in town was cancelled and so I thought I would come down. Am I too late for Mass?"

"No, we were just about to start. Your timing couldn't be better, Henry. You can help me as I review different aspects of the Mass for Jenny,"

"It wouldn't hurt for me to be reminded too, Father."

Jenny got up and gave Henry a hug and peck on the cheek. They both turned and stepped forward in front of the kneelers. Father kissed the altar and then made the sign of the cross. Jenny and Henry followed Father's lead as he went along as he usually did until he came to the readings.

"Over a two or three year period, Jenny, we read from the Old Testament, Psalms and New Testament. During that time almost all of the scriptures are read to the parishioners. And I don't have to encourage you to read the Bible and attend Bible study classes as I know you are already doing that in your daily life and ladies groups. But what we are doing here in Mass, Jenny, is telling people the Word of God. In the Gospel readings, we let parishioners know the teachings of Jesus and how we should live. We want our sheep to grow in their relationship with God and His Son and the Holy Spirit. What I have to say in the homily supports and explains what is read and how it applies to daily living but neither the homily nor the readings are the main things in the Mass."

Jenny was surprised by Father's comment and said, "But the Holy Scriptures are the word of God, Father..."

"That's true, Jenny, they are and should be taken as such and obediently followed. However, it is what Christ does in the Mass which is the main and most important event. He gives of Himself for us in the same way He did on the cross.

"Here, at this altar, Jenny, just as Jesus did on the cross at Calvary, He offers His body and blood for us. The only difference is that on the cross His body and blood were seen by all those present, but here in the Mass we are about to celebrate, His body and blood are hidden under the appearances of bread and wine. It is an un-bloody sacrifice."

Henry looked at Jenny and could see she was unsure of what Father said and added, "This is where faith comes in, Jen. We have to believe in what Jesus said and what He asked us to do. At the last supper, He took the bread and broke it and said, 'This is My body,' and in the same way, He took the cup of wine and said, 'this is My blood which shall be shed for the forgiveness of sins. Do this in memory of me.'"

"Yes," said Father, "And in John 6:53 Jesus said, 'Very truly I tell you, unless you eat the flesh of the Son of Man and drink His blood, you have no life in you.' At the last supper, He made a new covenant with the people. There would no longer be animals offered on the altar, He now would become the sacrificial Lamb out of His immense love for us!

"The Mass established by Jesus at the Last Supper is the 'source and summit' of our faith, Jenny. It is here the Paschal Mystery takes place; the suffering and death of Jesus and His glorious resurrection. When we receive Holy Communion, we receive the resurrected Lord. It is this which gives victory for us as followers of Christ."

Henry nodded and added to what Father had just said. "Every time I stop to think about this, it is really an amazing plan God conceived how, we, who were in sin were justified with the Father through His Son who died for our salvation. And then to be remembered through the Mass in this way down through the ages is incredible! Through the institution of the Holy Eucharist, Christ is here in body and blood to be received in our heart! We are re-living the day He died for our sins so that we may have life!"

After a moment of silence and awe, Henry added, "What an incredible plan! The entire New Testament is really about the Eucharist. In the Liturgy of the Word, we are nourished with the words of sacred Scripture, as well as giving glory to God through the readings as Father Engelmann said earlier. We learn of Jesus and how He wants us to live and are prepared for His offering of Himself to us in the Eucharist as the resurrected Christ! In receiving Him in Holy Communion, we receive the strength and grace and nourishment to live out His teachings."

"That is well said, Henry. It's like we are walking with Jesus to Calvary. Imagine re-living Jesus' sacrifice and resurrection each time we attend Mass! But there is more, Jenny, here is where we can make our own offering to God along with Jesus' sacrifice as I said earlier; be it our petitions, our suffering, pain, work , illness, whether ours or someone else's or whatever!"

"Yeah, this is the part a lot of people miss in the Mass. I remember as an altar boy that our offerings can be placed alongside the presentation of the gifts of bread and wine and just as they are transformed into the Body and Blood of Christ, so too, may we be changed to become more like Him and our petitions heard by His grace."

"Yes, that is correct, Henry. At Consecration when the priest announces the words, "This is my Body; this is the chalice of my Blood" our mere gifts of bread and wine which we brought to the altar are changed into the Body and Blood of Jesus, true God and true Man. But we can become even more entwined with Jesus' sacrifice at this moment of the Mass if we offered up our own petitions along with the presentation of gifts. That is, we can place our prayers, needs, struggles and our lives on the paten beside the hosts and in the chalice with the wine.

In doing so, Jenny, at Consecration not only is the bread and wine changed into the Body and Blood of Jesus Christ but also our personal offerings will have divine value. Our petitions are elevated into a divine state!

"Our lives become entwined with Jesus!

"As we go through Mass this morning, I will stop and let you know how you, or members of the congregation in a church, and my offering becomes part of the Mass and sacrifice."

"That's wonderful, Father. It's such a beautiful way God has designed for us to be part of what Jesus did for all of us as if we were there at Calvary but, I can see how this requires faith as Henry mentioned earlier."

"Yes, Jenny, that is the key to all this, we must have faith otherwise this is just a re-enactment of the last supper and simply becomes a meal. But Jesus said He is the Lamb of the New Covenant. He was giving us a precursor to His crucifixion. He was letting us know that He was offering Himself up freely as a sacrifice for our salvation. What happened the next day on Good Friday would simply have been an execution of a man if Jesus hadn't explained at the Last Supper that He was preparing to give up His life for us!

"Believe, Jenny and you shall live and have new life. The Eucharist is the most wonderful gift God has given to us. Imagine, all over the world at this moment thousands of Masses are said in remembrance of Jesus and what He did for us."

Jenny listened intently, nodded and remained silent.

"You see, Jenny, in the Word we come *to* Christ, in the Mass He offers Himself *for us* in the crucifixion and then in Holy Communion, He gives Himself *to us.*"

"What a gift that is, Father!" exclaimed, Jenny. "I am sorry to say, I have been missing out on the full meaning of what is actually happening here."

Father nodded and then said, "When your faith is stirred and you look at the Host in the next few minutes when transubstantiation takes place, one cannot help but say, "My Lord and my God. Thank you, all praise and glory be to God for this wonderful gift to strengthen us and deepen our faith."

"The soul needs nourishment much more than the body. The more often we can go to Communion and see the tremendous love Jesus has for us, the more we are transformed by His grace. We follow more closely in His footsteps. It becomes easier for us to die to ourselves, too, and fulfill His commandments with love. We can forgive others of their transgressions because of our love for the Lord and what He did for us."

Father continued with the Mass and during the presentation of the gifts of bread and wine, he invited Jenny and Henry to offer up their petitions so that their offering was combined with the Lord's sacrifice and became holy and acceptable to God. Father Engelmann concluded the offering by inviting them to pray with him. "Pray, brethren, (Jenny and Henry), that my sacrifice and yours may be acceptable to God, the almighty Father."

Henry and Jenny responded, "May the Lord accept the sacrifice at your hands, for the praise and glory of His name, for our good and the good of all His Holy Church."

Father was about to go on with the Mass but stopped and said to Jenny.

"Unfortunately, as Henry said, all too many parishioners pass over this too lightly and miss out on the offering they can make and the tremendous blessing they can receive when they put part of themselves into the sacrifice. What a wonderful gift the Mass is when we come with faith and love and free from sin to receive the Lord in Holy Communion."

Jenny had tears in her eyes; she was so moved by Father's faith and words.

The Mass had become alive with new meaning and purpose and deeper faith. She offered up her covenant to the Lord that if she was blessed with a child, she would give the child back to Him to do His work just like Hannah did in the Old Testament.

"I love the way we can offer up our thanks and petitions and how they combine with Jesus' sacrifice. I pray that God stirs up my faith to see it the way you do."

Father nodded. "Faith is crucial, Jenny. What did Jesus say to Thomas after he rose from the dead? 'Thomas, because thou hast seen me thou hast believed. Blessed are they that have not seen and yet, have believed.'"

Father turned and continued with the Mass. He said prayers of thanksgiving and exchanged further words with Henry and Jenny but at Consecration, Father became very solemn. Up to that point what was on the altar was still bread and wine but as soon as Father uttered the words which came from the lips of Jesus at the Last Supper, Jesus Christ was present.

Father raised the consecrated host and chalice and turned to Henry and Jenny. It was plain to them that Father did not adore the appearances of bread of wine but rather the Lord himself. It was as if they were all on Calvary; Jesus, offering himself on the altar just as he offered himself for us on the cross.

After Father placed the host and chalice back on the altar, he genuflected in reverence to the Lord. Once again, Father turned and faced Henry and Jenny. He raised his hands and invited them to say the Our Father, the prayer which Jesus taught us. They briefly mediated on the seven petitions in the Lord's Prayer which cover our important needs as God's sons and daughters, together in Christ, not as isolated individuals.

Finally, Father prepared for Communion. He raised the Host and said, "Behold the Lamb of God, behold Him who takes away the sins of the world. Blessed are those who are called to the Supper of the Lamb."

Henry and Jenny responded in unison, "Lord, I am not worthy that you should enter under my roof, but only say the word and my soul shall be healed."

After giving Communion to himself, Father picked up the paten containing the two remaining hosts and turned to Henry and Jenny.

Jenny's eyes grew wide and sparkled with wonder and awe as she gazed at the Host which Father Engelmann held before her. Father could see the seriousness of Jenny's new faith written all over her face. He made the sign of the cross with the Host and said, "The Body of Christ."

Jenny already had such a deep love of Jesus but now her heart filled to overflowing knowing she would really receive Him with new understanding, deep affection and love. Tears came to her eyes; she no longer saw a white host of unleavened bread before her but Jesus, fully God and fully Man, resurrected!

"My Lord and my God," Jenny softly whispered in a spirit of reverence and adoration. She took the Host and ate it.

After Father gave Henry Holy Communion, he turned to the altar and took the chalice filled with wine and once again offered the cup to Jenny, saying, "The blood of Christ."

Jenny nodded and once again whispered, "My Lord and my God." She took the chalice and drank of it.

When she knelt down, her heart and prayers were completely different from other times she had received Communion. She felt the love of Jesus in her heart. She never felt more united with His humanity and His divinity.

Henry gazed lovingly at his dear wife. He suspected what her offering and request to the Lord would be. What Henry didn't yet know, however, was that one day, not too far in the distant future, the heartfelt offering which he would make to God, would transform his life forever!

CHAPTER THIRTEEN

THE SUN HADN'T been up for more than ten minutes when J.J. emerged through the patio kitchen doors. He paused for a moment and inhaled a deep breath of the early morning, crisp air. He thought he was the only one up but Thomas was already getting ready for the day. The silence on the estate could be easily penetrated by any sound coming from the work shed.

J.J. slowly made his way to the gazebo, taking note of all the beautiful flowers and herbs blooming in the garden. Since his father's death, J.J. had acquired the habit of taking the time to prepare for the day. He was amazed by the dramatic change in James when illness forced him to stop and smell the roses and take stock of his life. Perhaps more than anything else he had learned from his dad, the most important thing was to take time to meditate, pray and give thanks for all his blessings. It was his mom though, who had really started it all. If she hadn't begun this practice in the first place, J.J. was certain that neither he nor his father would ever have learned the secret to inner peace and contentment.

Yes, indeed, he was blessed: Nora and he had reconciled and couldn't be happier as a family, seeing his father develop such a deep friendship with the staff was a practice which he had the good sense to continue. Matilda, Thomas, his wife, Neela and George had become like an extended family to him. He marveled at their insight and common sense about problems which he and his group of executives sometimes overlooked. He missed Carlos, who decided to accept Jenny's invitation to live in her home in Regina but they still called each other regularly. Carlos was a strong man of faith and fortunately some of that had rubbed off on him.

But then, Thomas too, had the same faith and in more ways than one had become his mentor and a man J.J. wanted to emulate. Thomas' previous knowledge of the corporate world from when he was a lawyer in London had on more than one occasion saved him from entering into mergers and deals which could have cost the firm millions. Once again, he was glad he acted upon the advice of his father; never make a big decision without running it by Thomas. *The gardener has more savvy than all the executives put together.* His father's words rung true; knowledge, common sense and integrity is a rare combination in the world of big business, "Son, trust me, Thomas will prove to be your best secret advisor in the entire firm."

Yes, J.J. was a fortunate young man to be surrounded by such a loving, loyal and trusting entourage of people. Outsiders would never understand how such a relationship could be established with estate staff. His father's decision to give a guest house to each of his main staff was brilliant. It was Jenny who had suggested it early on. The homes were just sitting there empty for the most part year in and year out. J.J. was glad James had taken Mom's advice to heart. They had all become one big family!

His peace and contentment at home also reflected itself in the work place. For a young man of twenty three years of age, he had gained the respect of all the staff from the custodians to the top executives. At first, most of his senior staff were convinced that when James died the company would falter. J.J. was simply too young and hot tempered. Fortunately, many of the snap decisions he made were caught in time by James to prevent disasters. But he had proved them all wrong. In that last year of James' life, J.J. grew up almost overnight. And with the help and support of his home team, he was proving to not only his staff but also to his competitors that he was a brilliant, formidable leader.

He was firm and decisive when needed and yet, caring and understanding when the situation called for it. He was honest and fair in his dealings and perhaps his strongest character trait was how he treated the people in the firm. He took time for his staff, not just his executives but the secretaries, clerical staff, commissioners and custodians. At times he would spend fifteen minutes or more chatting with the doorman getting to know his family.

J.J. stooped down and plucked several daisies from the garden patch in front of the Angel of Thanksgiving. He liked the way several rays of the rising sun sneaking through the tree branches illuminated the face of the angel revealing the veins in the white marble. The angel wasn't exactly the same as the original one his mother had but it reminded him as it did Jenny that every day is a gift full of blessings. For as long as he could remember, his Mom came here most days to give thanks for her blessings and pray for others. He was thankful that his father followed Jenny's example and that he now did so, too.

Such a simple practice and yet, so life changing!

J.J. smelled the rest of the flowers he was holding and placed them into the angel's basket in thanks for his parents. He was so pleased with himself for reconciling with both of them. He was never happier and more content in his life.

He stepped into the gazebo and sat down on the swing, putting it slowly into motion. Lying beside him on the seat was Thomas's old, worn Bible which he had given to James. Several Monarch butterflies were huddled together on the Holy Book, perhaps, drawing warmth from the black leather cover and the content inside. He was reluctant to disturb them into the cool morning air. However, the sun had moved into a large opening between several large trees allowing more sunlight to enter near the gazebo. Thoughts of his father entered his mind as he picked up the Bible. It was the last thing that James learned to love so much. Every time J.J. came to visit him in the hospital his father was totally absorbed in the Book. This past year since he had made it a daily practice to read a chapter or two, he was beginning to understand why his father had made such a dramatic change in his life in the days and months before his death.

Just as J.J. was about to open the Bible, he heard soft footsteps. Thomas was walking softly, careful not to disturb his employer and friend.

J.J. looked up. "Morning, Thomas. One of these days I'll be up before you."

"As you get older, J.J., you don't require as much sleep but this time of day is God's time. There's a peace and serenity in the air that's hard to explain to someone who sleeps away this glorious time."

J.J. nodded. "I have to agree Thomas. I hope the edge cutter you're carrying is for the younger staff. You should be delegating more than doing."

"Can't give all the fun away, J.J. This is what keeps me young. I love the smell of new grass and the feel of soil in my hands," said Thomas and then added, "Can't seem to figure out why some of the grass in the south area needs replacing each year. Perhaps there's something in the soil. In any case, we plan to put new top soil down before replacing it with the new sod which arrived yesterday."

"How are you coming along with your land purchases for the Monarchs?"

"Yes, I meant to report back to you about that yesterday. Another farmer in Nebraska agreed to sell forty acres and plant milkweed and several other flowers that produce nectar which the Monarchs like. It's difficult to convince many of the farmers of the importance to leave some land available for the butterflies to protect their survival as they make that long trek back to Mexico. Many just feel it's a waste of productive crop land."

"Well, keep trying to convince farmers otherwise. You're doing a great job in Texas. I noticed some of the farmers there are even allowing more of their land as feeding and resting stops."

"Yes, it's a matter of education and people understanding that we're all in this together. Local schools are encouraging residents to plant milkweed and other flowers such asters, verains and purple cone flowers which are popular among Monarchs. They are also taking students to see Monarchs eating and laying eggs on the milkweed leaves on a larger scale in farmers' fields. It gets the entire community involved."

"It would be quite something for everyone to see what we did on our trip last February to that area near New Mexico where the Monarchs migrate to every year."

Thomas nodded and shifted his weight on the grass edger he was using as a cane to rest on and said, "Yes, I'll never forget our trek up to the mountainous forests in eastern Michoacán. Before that trip, it was hard to visualize branches so heavily laden with butterflies, clustered together to keep warm, could make a heavy tree branch sag!

"And what a sight it was to see when the sun warmed the air and thousands upon thousands of brilliant orange butterflies burst from the trees, rising and falling and swirling around us like a great living blizzard. I thought a light rain had started to fall."

"Quite the sound, that's for sure, as Matti would say."

J.J. smiled. "Well, it's reassuring that the President of Mexico has declared that area a Federal reserve even though there's still a lot of illegal logging and farming practices that destroy the forests. In any case, we will continue to do what we can." There was a momentary silence and J.J. added, "Perhaps, Thomas we could produce a movie...wouldn't that be a great way to bring attention to this amazing species!"

"Now, that's something to contemplate on!" remarked Thomas. "Showing how Monarchs lay their eggs on the underside of a milkweed plant, turns into a caterpillar which eventually transforms into another butterfly is an amazing miracle. But then how the last generation of butterflies to be born at the end of summer have the added longevity to make their incredible 3000 mile trek to Mexico, has to be an even greater miracle! Yes, that would make for an interesting movie all right, J.J."

"It's easy to see that rising early in the morning also gives rise to creative thoughts, indeed!"

They both studied one another contemplating the idea. "Well, I best be going and get ready for Ramon and the others. You have a nice day now."

"You, too, Thomas."

J.J. watched his friend continue to stroll down the walk and then opened the Bible for perhaps another insight that would help improve the world. After a short while, he set the Bible down and made his way to the angel now glistening fully in the sun. Ever since he had reconciled with Jenny, he still felt twinges of guilt for his past behavior towards her. He knew she had forgiven him and had gone to confession, sorrow every now and then, like now, prompted him again to make further amends with his soul. He picked a white daisy with a yellow centre. It was the wildflower which was his mother's favorite. Softly he muttered, "Thank you, Mom, for being you; I deeply regret the years I so foolishly wasted by rejecting you. All the days, months and years of joy we could have shared. I am sorry for my stubborn pride that shut the door to your love, your guidance and example of how to live and enjoy a peaceful life. I am thankful for Dad's illness which made him and me stop and realize what we were missing and get us both back on track. I love you, Mom and I am so blessed because of you."

J.J. placed the daisy on top of the other flowers in the basket. The flower immediately brightened as if its glowing white petals had caught the sun in its center. If the truth were known however, the shimmering light was due to the heartfelt outpouring of gratitude of a prodigal son who had come home.

MATTI WAS BUSY in the kitchen when J.J. came in from the garden. Knowing J.J.'s schedule, she had anticipated his return and had his breakfast table set and his food ready to be served.

"Morning, Matti, it's a beautiful day out there. Thomas is helping to unload the sod. Perhaps bring him in for morning coffee or think of some other excuse long enough so the younger workers do more of the heavy lifting. He won't listen to me to slow down."

"I know what you be saying, J.J. He's always believed to be an example to others never expectin' they be doing what he ain't willing to do."

"Yeah, but everyone knows that and so setting an example is harder on him than the lesson he still wants to convey to unappreciative workers."

"What you be seeing as hard work, he seein' as a labor of love. There be no way of changin' that picture at this point, J.J Your raisin toast be popping up any minute and here's your hot oatmeal." Matti brought over the steaming bowl and set it in front of J.J.

"Would you do me a favor, Matti?"

"Sure t'ing, J.J. What you wantin' me to do?"

"Call Henry and let him know the angel sculpture he wanted me to order is finished and is going to be shipped tomorrow. He wanted it before their wedding anniversary next week. I put a rush on it and so I hope it gets there in time. It should have been completed last week but artists have their own timetable. I saw it the other day and I think Mom will really like it. He sculpted an angel with a both arms outstretched in a welcoming pose. The sculptor absolutely refused to have the angel carrying a basket like he did with the other two he created. Anyway, I think it's good to be different. Mom's Angel of Thanksgiving is so special and look at all of the good that happened from Mom's daily thanksgiving."

J.J. stopped talking. He blew on his porridge and began to eat. Matti was always surprised by J.J.

"That be a nice t'ing you sayin', J.J. From day to day, I just don't know what good things be coming next out of that mouth of yours. I have to say, it makes my heart skip a beat...in a good way, know what I'm sayin'?"

J.J. pretended he didn't hear Matti but he loved and respected her. She was like another mother to him. He soon finished eating, wiped his mouth and stood. Matti outstretched her arms, tilted her head and a warm smile covered her face. He looked so much like his father with his dark flashing eyes, shining jet black hair and ruddy complexion. There wasn't anything in the man in front of her that bore any resemblance to the fair skinned, blonde woman who gave birth to him. However, he did receive her heart which was revealing itself more and more with each passing day.

J.J. approached Matti and walked into her greeting arms. He stooped down and gave her a peck on the cheek. "Have a nice day, Matti. Tell Nora to call me at the office. She thought she might be coming into the city and we can have a late lunch. And just as J.J. turned to head for the door he added, "Please call, Grandma and let her know we are expecting her for Sunday dinner. A limo will pick her up around 3:00 in the afternoon."

"You have a nice day, too, J.J. and I have to say you lookin' mighty handsome this fine morning."

"Don't I always?" winked J.J.

"Now don't you be testin' me, Son. You be no match, hear?"

They both chuckled. .

Just as J.J. left, Thomas came in through the patio doors.

"Morning, Matti. Just wanted to let you know that Ramon and I are heading over to the artist's compound to crate up the angel he created for Miss Jenny. He adamantly claims that he is a sculptor and not a shipper. J.J. wants to make sure it gets out today if possible so we thought we'd look after it. So, don't bother making coffee or cookies for us."

"That be a good t'ing you told me as I was about to make them chewy, chocolate chip cookies you boys be dyin' for."

"Just the way you said that makes my mouth water already! We'll miss them today, that's for sure, Matti. Did J.J. get away already?"

"Yes, he left minutes ago. Just have to say, that boy making me more mellow every day. Why, Thomas, I ain't lost my temper and be judgin' this and that for a long time! I no longer have anythin' to be critical about! Why every day be sailing along so smooth, I afraid of slipping on all those kind words floating around here".

"That's a good thing, I'd say, Matti. Learning to live right can be such a blessing. All too many folks live a lifetime before they realize what they missed."

"And many don't at all. Like you be sayin' all along; heaven right under our noses if we be makin' the right choices. It takes the same amount of time to be kind as it takes to be miserable. Both be takin energy from the well, except the one opens the portal to heaven on earth while the other produces feelings that ain't good for nothin' for yourself or anybody else! Know what I'm sayin?"

"Couldn't have said it any better myself, Matti."

"I'm so happy J.J. is taking the time to smell the roses while he still be young. Jim waited a spell too long but his boy be learnin' a big lesson from his daddy before he be goin' to see his Maker. J.J. could have learned sooner from his mommy if he were open to her. See, there be an example of takin' things for granted too much and for too long, Thomas. As soon as we stop and put the Boss in control everyt'ing' falls into place and we soon learn not to take God's creation and each other for granted. No sir! Look at that young man how he reads the Bible every day and how it spreads to everyt'ing. Just the way he looks at the flowers, the butterflies, the garden and how he be appreciatin' his work, his family and people around him is a blessin' of the first order. That for sure!"

"Matti, you got the makings for being a fine preacher, I'd say."

"I 'spect I could, Thomas. I can see my words become so sweet and chewy just like my cookies! The people would be beggin' for more. Why, I would have the congregation eatin' out of my hands in no time."

Matti stopped and winked at her dear friend. "See, Thomas, you been saying things like that for so long, my ears finally startin' to hear what you be preachin' over the years. The student be catchin' up to the teacher...that for sure!"

MATTI CARRIED OUT J.J.'s instructions. She called Nancy and relayed her grandson's Sunday dinner invitation. She hoped it would be a quick call, however, Nancy went on and on about her arthritis for the first half hour and then how much she missed James. All she talked about was the miracle which happened in the Hamilton family. She never thought she would ever see the day a Hamilton would swallow their pride and learn to show love and affection. Nancy just didn't think it was possible.

'How is it possible for water to come out of a stone?' Nancy would often start and then go on and on how Jenny's love and forbearance finally broke through the tough, hardnosed, impenetrable coat of steel barrier that surrounded the Hamilton men for generations. Nancy so loved the new James in the weeks leading up to his death that after his demise that was all she would talk about and still did to this very day! It gave Nancy a new hope in life, in people and especially, God.

At the start, Matti enjoyed Nancy's rambling on because she too had the same opinion about James but after the millionth time, Matti grew tired of hearing about James' miraculous conversion and it was only out of sheer respect for the aging woman, Matti listened for as long as she could. Finally, Matti resorted to telling a wee fib that she had to go and make lunch for the landscape workers.

Matti knew this is why J.J. had asked her to call Nancy. Better it was her time that was tied up than his. She resolved right then and there that that would be last time she would do J.J. a favor like that. She was so flustered with the call to Nancy and guilt ridden over the little white lie she told, Matti fell to her knees and asked for God's forgiveness. Feeling sufficiently cleansed from her venial sin, Matti resumed her daily chores forgetting to call Henry and relay J.J.'s second message to him until late in the afternoon. Fortunately, Regina was two hours behind so the gallery would still be open. When she called however, the lady who answered the phone said Henry was gone for the day. At the risk of spoiling the surprise for Jenny, she decided to call the farm and hoped that Henry would answer.

When Jenny answered the phone, Matti assumed God was still punishing her and quickly resorted to lowering her voice in disguise, "Would the man of house be in?" Matti said, holding her breath.

There was a momentary pause and Jenny said, "Yes, just a moment please and set the receiver down much to Matti's relief. However it didn't last long as Jenny returned to the phone and asked suspiciously, "Is this Matilda Bellafonte?"

"This be she," Matti sheepishly replied.

Jenny laughed, "Oh Matti, you've never done that before! Never knew of you as a prankster!"

"I just feels so giddy lately, Jen," Matti started out trying to avoid answering the possible question as to why she directly asked for Henry so she quickly decided to bring up a diversion of something that she wasn't yet ready to talk about…but this was the only thing which came to mind.

"Charles asked me out to a movie. It be the second time this month …"

"That sounds exciting, Matti. Is it just a movie or is there more to it?" Jenny wanted to know. She immediately thought of the time Matti was leaving the estate to move into James' downtown condo and the going away party she and the other staff had arranged. It was such a wonderful sight to see her and Charles dancing together in the garden.

"Well, we be goin' out for lunch on our days off several times and I have to admit, Jen, his British haughtiness which goes with his occupation does irritate my skin at times but…I am fond of him." Matti giggled softly in the background.

"Oh, Matti, that sounds wonderful! You both have been employed by the Hamilton's long before I ever showed up. Was Charles there when you were hired?"

"No, I be there two years before Charles came to the estate. It was Thomas who recommended Charles to Mr. Hamilton senior. Both men were from London. At one time, Charles worked as a butler for Thomas! Fancy that!"

"Isn't that something, Matti. I do recall now that Thomas was a lawyer in London. How are Thomas and Neela doing?

It's been awhile since I spoke to either of them."

"They be fine. Actually, Thomas is busy buying land from farmers which follows the path that the Monarchs be takin when they head south for the winter. It was James' request that J.J. and Thomas make sure they do all they can for the survival of the very insect that the master didn't like one bit."

"Yes, that's wonderful of James. So how does buying land help the Monarchs?" Jenny wanted to know.

"Farmers be makin' more and more wild land into crops which destroyin' the natural wildflowers that fed the butterflies on their way to Mexico. Thomas buys small acreages of ten to fifty acres from farmers who also agree to grow milkweed and flowers on that plot of land. Ain't that somethin', Jen?"

"What a great idea. Thomas is doing on a larger scale what he taught me to do in my backyard garden. I am so glad I learned to plant milkweed and flowers that take turn blooming from May until late in October. A butterfly's home and garden is out there in nature and if we all start to plant crops that are not nourishing to them, they will die. It s heartening to see J.J. and Thomas do what they can to keep the Monarch we all so love, alive!"

"Both J.J. and Thomas still be so takin' by their trip to Mexico last winter to see where the Monarchs migrate to that they now want to do anyt'ing they can to protect the butterfly."

"Yes, I spoke to J.J. several times about their trip. He sounded more excited by that trip than any merger he or James ever put together. Anyway, Henry and I decided to go next winter as well. The most visited of the butterfly colonies is El Rosario. It's in the state of Michoacán where J.J. and Thomas visited. That tour site was full so we are going to the other sanctuary in Sierra Chincua. Oh, I am so excited to go! We also heard that in February of next year the community is beginning a Monarch Butterfly Festival which not only celebrates the Monarch but also promotes the culture and arts of the area."

"That be soundin' so wonderful, Jen. You and that man of yours be enjoyin' the trip so much and for you to be seein' where the butterflies spend their winter and where they come from will be heaven for you! That for sure!"

"In any case, Matti, I can't get over what Thomas and J.J. are doing. That's a wonderful project they are carrying out to protect and save a dying species."

In the silence which followed, Jenny reflected on their discussion while Matti struggled to figure out a way to relay J.J.'s message about the angel gift for Jenny on their anniversary. Matti didn't want to suffer the guilt of another white lie and so she finally said something which she figured the Lord would forgive and understand.

"Anyway, Jen, I best be getting supper ready. The other reason for my call was to relay a message to Henry. J.J. wants him to call first t'ing in the morning...I think it has somet'ing' to do with art."

"Oh, is J.J. making an art purchase?"

"Hmm, yes, Jen, it be somet'ing' like that..."

CHAPTER FOURTEEN

THE MOMENT JENNY opened her eyes; she saw a card dangling in the air no more than six inches from her face! At first she thought she was dreaming, how on earth a greeting card could be suspended in the air like that. Perhaps, it was her guardian angel holding it there for her!

Jenny reached up and noticed it was attached to a string which led up to a balloon supposedly filled with helium to make it stick to the ceiling. She pulled gently on the card and opened it in midair:

> *Happy 3rd Anniversary, Honey!*
> *Love you more than words can say!*
> *Henry*
>
> *PS. Want to go up in a hot air balloon again!?*

"Oh, no! Henry you didn't!?" She quickly turned over but he was already up. He must be joking as they had arranged to meet with Father that morning. She checked the clock on the night table: 6:45. She looked at the note again and smiled, "What a wonderful surprise!" She got up and made her way to the shower only to find Henry had draped a cotton towel over the door on which he had written:

It was love at first sight on that
memorable summer morning in 1956!
From that moment on I have loved you for:
36 years
432 months
13,140 days
18, 921, 600 minutes
and I have to say I loved every
11,352,960 seconds of it!

"Oh, Henry!" Jenny exclaimed. She took the cotton towel and brought it lovingly to her heart. "You are such a dear."

Jenny opened the shower door only to see another two towels taped to the back wall. On one it read: YOU WASH and on the other, I'LL DRY!!

Jenny shook her head in delight and disbelief!

After she showered and got dressed, she made her way over to her dresser and sat down to put on her make-up. Her mind kept swirling over Henry's creativeness and didn't notice what he had written on the mirror until she flipped on the string of lights overhead:

MY DEAR JENNY,
YOU LIGHT
UP MY LIFE !!!
('_')

Tears surfaced in Jenny's eyes. She was so elated, she thought she would explode with happiness at any moment! She got up and ran out of the bedroom and down the stairs. Henry was in the kitchen preparing a breakfast to take down to the prayer house when Jenny burst into the room, "Oh, Henry, you're so full of surprises, I love you so much!" cried Jenny as she flung herself into Henry's arms.

"I didn't think you could ever possibly out do what you did on our last two anniversaries and here you go again!"

Henry smiled, "The day is just beginning, Honey!"

"Do you mean there is more to come!?"

Henry's face glowed with love. He just shrugged his shoulders and tenderly kissed his dear sweet wife.

FATHER GAZED AT the happy couple before him and began, "Since it is your intention to re-affirm your marriage vows, join your right hands and declare before God and His church."

Jenny and Henry turned towards each other, looked into each other's eyes and joined their right hands. Then Henry began:

"I, Henry, do promise to be true to you in good times and in bad, in sickness, and in health. I will love you and honor you all the days of my life."

Tears came to Jenny's eyes and Henry brushed a tear away from her cheek.

"I, Jennifer ...," she paused, her voice cracking. "I...I... promise to always be true to you in good times and in bad. I will love you—"

Once again, Henry gently wiped another tear away and in the same motion brushed away tears welling in his eyes as well.

"I will love you," she repeated, "and honor you all the days of my life and into eternity." Jenny leaned into Henry and tenderly kissed him. She stepped back slightly as Father Engelmann moved closer and looked into Henry's then Jenny's eyes. He took a deep breath to gain his composure and said,

"May the Lord in His goodness continue to strengthen and fill you both with His blessings."

Then taking Jenny's right hand and Henry's with his other hand, Father brought them together until they touched. He then began to bless their rings.

"Lord, bless these rings in your name..." Father made the sign of the cross over the rings and with hands outstretched over Henry and Jenny's hands he continued.

"May these rings be a symbol of your true faith and fidelity for one another and always remind you of your love.

"May Jesus always be at the heart of your marriage and be there for you in sickness and in health and in good times and in bad. May the Holy Spirit continue to fill your hearts with love and joy and compassion and understanding and wisdom and truth. May you continue to be beacons of light giving witness to Jesus' love for all that you meet.

"And, may these rings be ever mindful of the covenant of love you have pledged to each other through the sacrament of marriage and never fail in your responsibility to lead one another home to the Father and together shall praise Him forever."

Then Father raised his right hand and said, "May almighty God bless you both in the name of the Father and the Son and the Holy Spirit," and in unison all three said, "Amen."

Father gazed at the radiant couple and exclaimed, "Henry, I know you cannot wait another moment lest you heart should burst, you may kiss your lovely wife!"

Father gave Jenny a hug and then Henry. He turned and continued with the Mass to consecrate the bread and wine into the body and blood of Christ. Upon receiving the Holy Eucharist, Jenny and Henry are not only one flesh but from one body in Christ! What more perfect way is there to seal their commitment to one another and make Jesus the heart and center of their marriage.

After Mass, they decided to sit on the deck and have breakfast. It was a gorgeous day in June, almost a repeat of the day they got married three years ago. Henry had prepared some fruit plates along with yogurt and the cottage cheese that Father liked so much. "I filled the fridge with a loaf of Borden's sour dough bread, some Roma tomatoes, cheddar cheese and slices of ham and chicken. Can we get you anything else?" Henry asked.

"No, that is more than enough. I usually end up throwing some food out. I don't eat very much anymore."

"So I have noticed," Jenny observed. "Oh, I also put twelve bottles of water in the fridge as well."

Jenny set some food on the table and filled the glasses with orange juice and then sat down.

Father raised his glass and made a toast, "To Henry and Jenny on their third anniversary. From the bottom of my heart,

I wish you both all a year filled with much happiness, good health and peace and...your heart's desire!"

Father had to add a wish of hope for what he knew Jenny wanted...a child!

"What a beautiful way to begin the day of one's anniversary!" commented Henry. "Thank you so much for renewing our vows."

"Yes, it is a wonderful practice to do so. Anna and I did every year except the year we escaped from Austria during the war to come to Canada. It is a wonderful practice not only for people who are strong in the Lord but especially for couples who are not and struggling in their marriages. It is important for couples to realize the sacred covenant which they made is a permanent commitment to one another. There is no back door...they have to make it work.

"Coming to the foot of God's altar each year to reaffirm vows also reminds couples of the crucial importance of having Jesus at the center of their marriage each day. Without Him, we are like a leaf in the prairie wind floundering and helpless with no guide, no example, no teacher, nor without purpose and meaning! It is He who shows us through His Word how to rise above the daily routines of life in which we easily slip into the grave malady of taking each other for granted. It is He who is the constant light leading us out of the darkness. It is He who refreshes our marriage daily. And it is the Holy Spirit who gives us the grace and strength to die to ourselves and follow in obedience Jesus' direction."

"Oh my gosh, Father, I think you may have to come to one of our meetings! Your words are always so inspiring! I brought that up in our ladies group the other day; the importance of having Jesus at the center of their marriage. It was well received as most ladies realize their helplessness and many days are at a loss of what to do."

"Jesus' sacrifice and teachings, Jenny, is the key to life and marriage. In John 10:10, Scripture says, "He has come in order that we might have life and have it more abundantly." And if we are not living an abundant life, it is because He is not at the center of our lives. What did Jesus say in John 15:9,10,11, 'If you keep My commandments, you will remain in My love, just as I have kept my Father's commandments and remain in His love. These things I have spoken to you, that My joy may remain in you, and that your joy may be full."

"It doesn't get any clearer than that, Father," observed Jenny. Since our last conversation with you the other day, Henry and I have been working on a morning prayer for couples to say that captures the essence of what you said the other day when you shared how Anna helped you grow into the Lord and what you just said helps, too, in giving us further direction. I hope I can remember it all."

"That is a good idea Jenny and one which will please the Lord. The Holy Spirit will guide you and Henry. Remind your ladies of this: in spite of having a beautiful home, a nice car or perhaps two, a career, money in the bank, a spouse, a family and on and on and yet, something is lacking. On the surface everything appears to be going their way. The world promises happiness and inner peace but we know the promise is empty. It is Jesus and Jesus alone who can fill the void and promises the abundant life. It may not all be a bed of roses but He is there to guide, lead and comfort you.

"Just as Jesus picked up His cross and carried it each day, so too, must we.

Just as He was obedient to the Father, so too, must we to His Word. Just as He had to die to Himself to bear the fruit which the Father wanted Him to produce, so too, must we die to ourselves so our lives and marriages bear fruit. At times this will require much sacrifice, pain and suffering just as Jesus incurred. However, as I pointed out several days ago and it doesn't hurt repeating since it is so critical in dealing with all of the challenges we face in life."

Father leaned forward in his chair as if to make sure Henry and Jenny would get what he was about to say, "The secret to bearing the crosses which come along is to do what Anna and…" then looking at Jenny he continued, "you did. After discussing your concerns with your spouse, you then offered it up to the Lord. Rather than grin and bear it, become upset and angry, feel as if you were a victim, you both gave praise and thanks in all circumstances. You both counted it all as a blessing and trusted in God to turn it all into good. In doing so, neither of you allowed Satan to get his foot into the door and expand any gloomy or destructive thoughts floating around in your mind. What the mind thinks on expands. If thoughts are of anger, resentment or ill will towards your spouse is what you entertain, these thoughts quickly fester which leads to more destructive thinking such as, 'I deserve better, I married the wrong person and open to all of the evil things which are out there like affairs, flirting and on and on. If, on the other hand one gives thanks to God and sings praises, it lifts one's spirit; one remains centered and not controlled by others shortcomings or the challenges of life."

"What you say is true, Father, yet it's difficult to praise God for trials that come into our lives."

"Yes, it seems like a paradox to be thankful for a trial that causes suffering and pain. One day when I challenged Anna about this approach to life's difficulties, she made a startling statement which snapped me out of any lingering doubts I still had about praising God in all things. She said, 'David, God is happy to hear you sing and praise over the death of His Son. He rejoices to hear that you are thankful that Jesus suffered, died and was crucified for our salvation. Yes, God accepts our thanks even for this horrific circumstance.'

"And it was at this juncture, Anna made her point.

"'David, if you can be joyous and happy over Jesus' death, the Lord and King of the universe, than surely you can give praise for trials that come along your way. If Jesus can lay down His life for us while we were still a sinner can we not lay down our self-centeredness for our spouse or accept their shortcomings no matter how difficult it is and give thanks for it?'

"*Look at the good which God brought out of Jesus' sacrifice!*"

Father sat back and raised both of his hands and cried out, "That is the good news to this story; an amazing thing happens when we give praise and thanks to God in all circumstances.

Anna soon learned that it releases God's power to answer prayer and shower blessings on those whose lips constantly give praise and thanks. He is the God of all possibilities! Look at the wonderful things which happened in your life Jenny. You have been confronted with so many challenges in life and look at the peace which you maintained through it all and the wonderful outcomes. Look at me, a proud, arrogant man who has humbly acknowledged his sinful self and great need to have total dependence on God in all things. Can you imagine the joy Anna received to see my conversion of heart? It is in this way we assist one another in carrying out our greatest responsibility to our spouse, and children...to bring them home to the Father. A good exercise for your ladies group would be to search the Bible for passages that ask us to praise and thank God in all circumstances."

"Those were my very thoughts as you spoke, Father. I praise God that we have been so blessed to have you in our lives," said Jenny.

"I'll say, Amen to that as well. What you just shared Father about scriptures that say we should praise God continuously is something I have done for a long time. Unfortunately, it was more of a thought distraction to keep me from worrying or entertaining thoughts not good for me. You however, have made me aware that these are not just empty words. Jesus' words in the Bible are Living Words with the power to change lives. I will no longer just repeat them without thought or meaning but rather with faith and belief and acceptance of God's will in the matter whatever it may be."

"Ach mein lieber Gott, danke, danke! Mien geliebter Sohn sieht das Licht! You see the light, my Son, well said. Yes, we must accept what God's will is in the matter. This is the proper motive to have. We should not try to control God. Praise and thanksgiving should come freely out of our love for God and what He and the Son did for us."

With great reluctance, Henry said, "Well, Father, I always enjoy our conversation so much but we have a busy anniversary day planned. Just give me a minute; there is a package in the truck I want to get." As soon as Henry got up, Coco suddenly came to life and stood, too. She was not sure if she should follow her former master.

Henry ran to the truck and returned with a package for Jenny. As he handed it to her, he said, "Happy anniversary, Honey!"

Jenny felt the soft cloth through the package and said with a wink, "Not more messages on cotton towels like the ones you left for me in the shower!?"

Henry smiled and said, "Keep in mind where it all began."

When Jenny opened her gift, she was surprised to find a white cotton tee shirt. On the front Henry had drawn a partial map of the east end of Regina. In large letters running across the city map were the words: 'Where it all began!' A tiny red heart was also on the map located between Henry's house on Broder Street and Jenny's home three doors down. Jenny laid the tee shirt down on the deck and all three studied the map.

"There is our place and there's your house, Henry! Jenny exclaimed and running her finger along the map, she added, "And just down the street is where Engelmann's Grocery is!"

"Rather was, Jenny. Remind me to show you some photos of the store and the day it was torn down."

"Oh, Honey this is wonderful, are we going to visit the old area...where it all began?"

"We sure are. I want to retrace each and every step how the girl of my dreams came along and instantly swept me off my feet. And I'd love to hold your hand and walk down the streets we walked back then."

Unbidden tears surfaced in Henry's eyes just thinking on it. Father too, was already wiping tears rolling down his cheeks as well. Very softly almost in a whisper and pointing to where his store was on the map, "That is where my Anna and I spent fourteen wonderful years."

Both Henry and Jenny quickly got up and went to Father and put their arms around him. "Ah, I'm sure Anna is looking down at you right now, Father. We know you miss her so much."

Jenny hugged Father and added, "we love you so much, too. You are still a romantic at heart!"

Coco who was amazingly calm that entire morning suddenly stood and began to lick Father's hand which was dangling at his side. Henry reached over and patted his former sensitive sidekick.

"I still remember that morning when Jenny came into the store and a few minutes later you came in as well. I knew you were looking for her. I could see it in your eyes. What happened next, I will remember for the rest of my days." Looking at Jenny, Father said, "When you helped Henry pick up the salmon tins he had knocked over and you looked into each other's eyes the entire store seemed to brighten. You both stood still, locked into each other's gazes and stood up as if lifted. Both Herman, the man I was serving at the time and I were momentarily spell bound by the sight. It haunted me for months and then years until finally when we went to the other side, my guardian angel explained what had happened."

"Yes, you told us that Henry and my guardian angel had imparted their heavenly energy into the gaze Henry and I shared. Was that it, Father?"

"Yes, that is what Zachariah told me. You were not only smitten with each other in an earthly sense but spiritually beyond to connect your very souls! It is little wonder that your love for one another has stood the test of time. As I write about your love story, I am amazed that no matter how many people tried to keep you both apart or destroy the last letters with the pewter angels inside were faithfully kept intact over all those years by your guardian angels. Truly, they had fulfilled their promises to you both."

"Oh, I can hardly wait to read the books, Father."

"Yeah, same here, can we have a peek?"

"No, not until I am done. You may have to complete the last one for me…"

"What do you mean, Father? Why…?"

Father just shrugged his shoulders not wanting to get into the possibility that he may not live long enough to finish the series. He simply said, "You two best be off and enjoy your day! This is the day the Lord hath made, you shall truly be glad and rejoice in it!"

Henry and Jenny said their goodbyes and jumped into the truck and sped off. They didn't even get fifty yards down the lane when the truck abruptly stopped and Jenny opened the door and jumped out. Henry did the same on the driver's side. Jenny began running through the wildflower field picking different wildflowers.

"Get some red poppies over there, Henry, and don't forget one or two black eyed susans."

Henry finally caught up to Jenny and twirled her around into his waiting arms. He gave Jenny the flowers he had picked and then took Jenny at the waist and literally tossed her upwards. Jenny thrust her hands to the sky gaining even more height!

"Oh, Sweetheart, I am so happy to be surrounded by heaven. Let's pick the most beautiful bouquet of wildflowers to put in the Angel of Thanksgiving's basket. I want God to know that my cup is running over with blessings! Thank you, thank you, dear Father, thank you for my dear, darling, Henry!"

Father watched on with tears of joy in his eyes. "Such a happy heart," he whispered, "so much like my Anna."

Father looked upward to heaven, brought the tips of his fingers to his lips, and kissed them and then trying to mimic the exuberance of the joyful couple in the meadow; he thrust his hand upwards carrying his heartfelt kiss to Anna!

CHAPTER FIFTEEN

WHEN THEY GOT back up to the house, the rest of Henry's plan for the day began to unfold.

"I know you want to visit with Maria and Carlos for a bit and so perhaps we can each take our car into the city and I'll meet you at the Gallery around eleven thirty. We can visit with Jeremy and Justin, have lunch at Henry's, my favorite place by the way, and then we can go in separate cars to, *where it all began.*"

"What do you have to do?" Jenny was inquisitive to know.

"Well, I want to pick up the mail at the Lumsden post office and then meet with a carpenter I know about doing some work around the farm."

"Oh, you haven't mentioned anything...what work, Honey?"

"I'll explain later."

They both got out of the SUV and Ginger was right there to meet them. Henry patted Ginger and then approached Jenny. He kissed her tenderly and said, "Do you need anything from the house or do you want to leave right away?"

Jenny looked at Henry quizzically, "Do I have the sense that you are trying to get rid of me?"

Henry chuckled nervously and shook his head, "What on earth makes you think that?"

"I don't know…well, I have to go to the washroom, put on my new tee shirt and then I will be off. So, should I put anything out for dinner?"

"No, I'll look after it…it's getting late, honey, we should get going."

Jenny went into the house and came out momentarily, "I didn't know we were going into Regina this morning and I had planned on giving you this." Jenny handed Henry a gift bag.

Henry smiled as he opened the bag and pulled out a felt box with the name *Birk's Jewelers* stamped in gold on the outside. A silver watch with dark brown leather straps was inside. "Jenny, this is beautiful!" He lifted it out of the box and read the inscription on the back:

I love you
more each
second!

"Wow, I like that, Honey! Thank you so much." He moved closer to her and kissed her. "Here, let's put it on." Henry held out his arm and Jenny strapped it on his wrist. She then said something which surprised him, "Leather is for the third anniversary so the straps will help you remember when you got this gift from me."

"Oh! I thought it was cotton! But that was last year!"

"I was wondering why all your little notes and gifts were on cotton."

Henry tapped the side of his head, "I'll make sure I remember next year. Anyway, this looks great, honey. Each time I check the time I'll think of how much I love you more!"

Henry checked his new watch and said, "It's close to ten o'clock, we better be off if we're going to meet at the gallery before noon." As Henry turned to go to his SUV, he said, "Yeah, I…I have to go to the washroom, too. Okay, Honey, see you at the gallery. Say hi to Maria and Carlos for me."

Henry ran into the house. As soon as he closed the door he peeked outside to make sure Jenny was leaving. He watched her go into the garage with Ginger beside her. She was out of sight for a minute and then he was relieved to see her blue BMW back out of the garage. She backed up to the dog house, shifted gears and sped off.

"Good!" said Henry as he dashed upstairs and prepared the bedroom for the evening. He got the flowers he had stored in his studio next door and arranged them strategically in the bedroom along with numerous candles. He went back downstairs, took two chicken breasts out of the freezer to thaw and then set the table in the sun room for dinner out there.

On his way back to the kitchen he stopped at the record changer to make sure the records he wanted to play were there. Love me Tender was the first record on the changer. It was Julean's and his favorite record. He was going to remove it but thought otherwise. She had wanted him to find Jenny. No, she should be a part of his relationship with Jenny as Jenny was with theirs. "I miss you Julean..." he whispered.

Henry went to the kitchen and took a deep breath "Well it's all set." He checked his new watch: five minutes past eleven. He would never be on time to meet Jenny at eleven thirty. He quickly called the gallery. Justin answered.

"Hi Son, it's Dad. How's it going?"

"It's been busy. Three framing orders came in. I handled one of them and Michael did the other two. I thought you were coming in this morning?"

"Yeah, I'm just leaving. Jenny is going to meet me there at eleven thirty. Tell her I'll be a little late. Perhaps chat with her for awhile. Is Jeremy in the café?"

"He just walked into the gallery; do want to speak with him?"

"Yes, put him on the phone."

"Hi, Dad, what's up?"

"Hi, Jeremy."

"I tried to reach you around nine. A huge crate came in for you from Ottawa, and I think it's the angel you ordered."

"Oh, it came. That's great. Would you do me a favor? Right after the noon lunch rush is over, can you escort the movers out to the farm, have them take the angel out of the crate and set it beside the front door. If Jenny wants a different spot for it we can move it later. Don't tell Jenny about it as I want it to be a surprise. And one other thing, would you mind asking Justin to stay at your place for another night, I thought Jenny and I would have a quiet dinner at the farm."

"Geez, Dad, it's your third anniversary. Congratulations Dad! Oh yeah, Camilla sent you guys a card. Did you get it?"

"No, I ran out of time to get to Lumsden, I'll try later this afternoon on the way home. Anyway, Jenny and I are coming for lunch. Reserve a table near the bay windows at the back and put two flowers in a vase on the table."

"Sure thing, Dad, was there anything else?" Jeremy wanted to know.

"No, that's it for now. Thanks for looking after the angel shipment for me."

Both Carlos and Maria were working in the backyard when Jenny got there. She had never seen the garden look more beautiful. Most of the flowers were in full bloom except for those that were timed to flower as the summer progressed. It was amazing how skillfully Carlos had added to the flowers she had planted to take advantage of nature's clock. Just when one flower made its exit from the scene and took its final bow, another was ready to come on stage to show its beauty. From spring to fall, the backyard was in full color!

"Carlos, the yard looks so beautiful!"

Carlos and Maria got up. "I was expecting you. I noticed the Monarchs suddenly became very agitated."

"Si, Jenny, it is true what Carlos observed, I too, saw them suddenly take flight. You are like nectar to them!"

Jenny didn't know whose words she found more comforting. Whatever they said seemed to be covered with kindness. "What a nice thing to say, Maria." Jenny went over and gave them both a hug.

"I hope you do not have a meeting today, I never prepared any lunch," said Maria.

"No, it's our third anniversary today and I brought in a bouquet of wildflowers to put in the Angel of Thanksgivings basket."

"Si, Miss Jenny, I noticed them right away. They look so beautiful and congratulations on your important day! I, too, noticed on our calendar that it is three years you have been married to Senor Henry. My, how quickly time goes by."

"It's been much longer than that, Maria—"

"What do you mean, Carlos?"

Jenny, too wanted to know what Carlos meant.

"I remember talking to Miss Jenny one day in the garden when she lived on the estate with her parents. She was writing an important message in her diary when a blue butterfly revealed her heart. It was then I could see the love in her eyes for someone special, no?"

"Oh, Carlos, you always were so insightful. It was like you saw right through me."

"You are easy to read, Senorita, you hide nothing. Your thoughts, words and actions always reveal your heart." Carlos put his arm around Maria and continued, "Beside my Maria, you are a special lady, too."

"Oh, Carlos, you and Maria are such dear friends. Henry wants me to meet him at the gallery for lunch so I better put these flowers in the angel's basket and say a little thanksgiving prayer."

"Have you started your novena to the Blessed Mother?" Maria asked.

"See, there you go, just like Carlos. Am I that transparent!?"

They all laughed.

"As a matter of fact I have, Maria. There is a special favor I want Mary to ask her Son to grant me..." Jenny's words trailed off, she wanted to tell them but felt a bit shy. Perhaps they would pray for her heart's desire, too.

"I will keep you in my prayers, Jenny," said, Maria. "Next time I visit the shrine I will talk to the Blessed Mother about your special request. She will know what is in your heart. If you have a moment to visit the shrine, Jenny, I have something for you which I left at the foot of the statue. It is more of a special gift to you and not really an anniversary gift."

"Oh, thank you, Maria. Yes, I would love to say a prayer and have a few words with Mary."

Jenny gave them both a hug once more and then made her way to the gazebo. She placed the flowers she had brought from the farm in the angel's basket and then went into the thicket where the shrine was located. As soon as she got to the shrine, the rosary at the base of the statue caught her eye. The solid white beads were glistening in the rays of the sun streaming through the trees.

Jenny went over, knelt down, and picked up the rosary. She noticed a pink note tied to the cross:

> "*Dear Miss Jenny,*
> *I pray the Blessed Mother's intercession on your behalf answers your heartfelt prayer.*
> *Maria.*"

Tears surfaced as she gazed at the beautiful gift. She brought the crucifix to her lips and kissed the cross. She made the sign of the cross with the crucifix at the end of the rosary and then kissed the cross again. She thought of Jesus' sorrowful mysteries and mediated on them as she prayed each decade of the rosary.

When she finished, she went to the gazebo and sat down. She set the swing into motion like she had done so many times before and prayed. Would this be the day her prayer would be granted? Would this be the night she would conceive?"

IT WAS JUST before noon when Henry pulled into the café parking lot. Two of his customers recognized him. He waved and decided to go in through the back kitchen area to get to the gallery.

He hoped Jenny wouldn't be upset with him.

When Henry entered the gallery, Jenny was behind the counter next to Justin going over a framing order.

"Hi, Honey, sorry I'm late. Hi Justin."

"Its fine, Henry. Justin was showing me the framing order he took in this morning. Just look at how the mats suit the painting. He just explained how the frame color and mats work together to enhance the painting and take the viewer to the center of interest. That's amazing, Justin."

"Don't give him all the credit, he had a master teacher," Henry winked. "Justin, do you want to take a lunch break now and then Jenny and I will go. It's busy in the café for a Monday. It's a good thing there was no school today and you were here to help out."

"Jeremy asked me stay at their place for another night and he'll drive me to school in the morning, is that okay?"

"Yes, that will be fine."

CHAPTER SIXTEEN

WHAT WAS SUPPOSED to be a romantic lunch at the café turned out to be a chat with one customer after the other. Nevertheless, it gave Henry an opportunity to introduce Jenny to many of the people who had never met her. After lunch, they decided to each take their own car to the east end, *'where it all began.'* Henry told Jenny to wait in her car until he got there then they would take a walk around the neighborhood.

Henry pulled up behind Jenny's car which she had parked on 13th Avenue. He noticed that she wasn't in the car. He got out of his SUV, walked to the corner, and looked up at his old home. It was painted a different color, but other than that, everything looked the same. He recalled looking out of that same front door the day Jenny walked by. His heart began to race just thinking on it. He looked three doors down and saw Jenny sitting on the front door steps, her hair glistening like gold in the sun. She was looking at him just like that morning they first met thirty seven years ago. Her adorable, oval face was covered with a radiant smile as he walked over to her and stood at the fence gate. "You looked like an angel then and still do now." Tears surfaced in Henry's eyes as he gazed at the love of his life.

"I still remember the bashful look on your face when I asked if the bike you were riding was the same that was lying in front of the steps to Mr. Engelmann's store. The moment you said yes, I knew you left it there, so you could walk me home."

Jenny got up and walked towards Henry and kissed him on the cheek. She placed her hand on his which was resting on top of the fence post. "Do you remember the game we used to play?"

"I not only recall the game but every word we said to each other. When I didn't hear from you for days, months, years that's all I could think of to keep the memory of you alive. I re-lived that summer over and over."

"I did the same. There was a time when I was going to destroy the little notes but I just couldn't..."

"If it hadn't been for your last note you left the day you went with your dad to Ottawa, I don't know if I would have made it. It was two weeks after you had gone and I walked by this gate and noticed a torn, weathered note barely clinging to the post with the frayed elastic. I sat on the steps here and read it over and over..."

Henry paused for a moment and brought back the image of the note on the screen of his mind's eye and said, "I still visualize the torn, damp note and the words:

> *"Oh, Henry,*
> *My heart just aches and feels as if it's being torn*
> *in two. Being with you has made this the happiest*
> *summer of my life. The thought of not seeing you*
> *anymore is more than I can bear.*
> *Always remember:*
> *True love lasts forever, it never says goodbye.*
> *For you and I have a guardian angel,*
> *On high with nothing to do,*
> *But to give to you and to give to me,*
> *Love forever true.*
> *Jenny"*

And just as Henry was going to say the last sentence, Jenny joined in and in unison they said:

*"P.S. If you were a heart, I'd want mine to beat
inside yours."*

"Oh, Henry those were such difficult days for both of us... but, we're together now. She tenderly kissed Henry and said the magic words, "Quickly, hold my hand," and off they went down Broder Street heading south. As they walked along, Jenny began singing, "True Love" and Henry joined in. Every now and then, they couldn't help themselves but tenderly squeezed each other's hands out of deep love and affection. Perhaps, their guardian angels prompted them to do so as well out of sheer delight!

When they came to College Avenue they reminisced over how Henry tried to scheme a way to hold Jenny's hand. Jenny admitted that she wanted to hold hands as much as he did. Knowing how shy boys could be, she took the initiative whenever the moment was there.

Henry was happy she did.

They walked all the way up to Balfour High School and returned back on Toronto Street passing the confectionery just like the day Henry had taken Jenny to Balfour to register. They laughed how they walked home in the rain storm and how hilarious they both looked soaking wet!

"What a day that was, Jenny. Up until that day, I had never felt that free inside. I was only half alive to my feelings and surroundings. Your charm, spontaneity and playful spirit were so contagious and still are! Sometimes I have to pinch myself to make sure you are really here beside me and not just some dream I used to dream."

"Oh, Henry, I feel so much the same."

The tender memories were so vivid, they squeezed each other's hands all the more just like they used to and strolled down the street savoring the moment and their togetherness. If it hadn't been for the fragrance of the lilac bush in the front yard of one of the houses they were passing by, they might not have noticed that it was the same two storey house with the two bedroom dormers Jenny had pointed to when they had taken a stroll in the neighborhood that memorable summer. It was her wish at the time to have a home like that someday and one of the bedrooms with the dormer would be her daughter's room; the daughter whom she would name Camilla.

Henry abruptly stopped and gazed to the second level of the home. "Yes, this is the very same house when you mentioned the name of your daughter you would have some day. I never forgot that name and never heard it mentioned again until years later when Jeremy brought this adorable young blonde haired girl home with that very name! I knew in my heart that it had to be your daughter. She was the very image of you!"

Henry went over the bush and picked off a clump of the lilac and gave it to Jenny without saying a word. Once again, they squeezed each other's hand and slowly walked on reveling in the miracle of it all.

They got back to their cars just after four thirty and were going to head home when Jenny excitedly asked if they could walk down the street to Victoria Avenue where Engelmann's Grocery was situated. This time it was Henry who stole Jenny's line, "Quickly, hold my hand!"

When they were a third of the way there, Henry looked into Mr. Miller's front yard and immediately concluded that he must have passed away as the beautiful array of flowers in a rock garden was replaced by a lawn that obviously wasn't looked after. However, it made him think of that time when Jenny made up a fun game to cheer him up. Jenny had said, 'If you were a tree, Henry, I would carve my heart into your bark.' It was Mr. Miller's flower garden at that time, just like now, which inspired Henry to respond to Jenny by saying out loud, "If you were a flower, Jenny, you'd be the one I'd pick"

"Oh, you remembered! I was just thinking of that very same game that we started too! Then almost verbatim of what she said back in 1956, Jenny replied, "That's really sweet, Henry, if you were a book, I'd not only read and caress every page, but also never close the cover."

Henry squeezed Jenny's hand, "If you were the sun, I'd want to feel your warmth all the time. I would never want darkness to ever come again."

Jenny chuckled, "And if you were the ocean, I'd want to be a fish and swim in you all of the time."

Henry stopped abruptly and gazed tenderly into Jenny's eyes, "Oh, Jenny, if you were the stars, I'd be the sky that held you for eternity."

Jenny smiled up at Henry, and replied just like she back then, "You've got me there, Honey. I can't top that one."

As they neared the corner a silence fell between them. They were overcome with one memory after another. Henry noticed that the lights that were erected especially for seniors to cross the busy street to shop at Engelmann's Grocery were gone. He remembered now that they were removed within months after the store was torn down. To Jenny it would appear the same as the lights weren't there when she lived in Regina. It made Henry think of the near mishap that happened to Jenny.

"I think it was the time a car almost hit you when crossing this street that made us aware of our guardian angels," said Henry

"Yes, I was so close to being hit. How I was snatched up and away in that last split second was a miracle."

"Yeah, you should have been hit. My vivid imagination already saw you being tossed in the air like a rag doll."

"It was my guardian angel that saved me. Father Engelmann confirmed that, too. Oh, how I wish we could remember meeting our guardians, too, when we went to the other side. There are so many questions I would ask Hannah and I would have loved to have seen her."

There was a long pause and then Jenny said, "It was amazing when we learned that we both were reminded to say the same angel prayer the night of accident."

"That's right, after that it seems I became more and more aware of my guardian angel."

"I believe that the more we acknowledge our protector and lifelong guide the more we do become aware of them in our lives."

Almost simultaneously, both Henry and Jenny reached for the Pewter Angel hanging at the end of a chain around their necks. "What are the odds of both of us within the same week, hundreds of miles apart, mailing each other the same pewter angel with the same inscription!?"

Jenny leaned into Henry's chest and began to say the guardian angel prayer. Henry immediately joined in:

"Angel of God, my guardian dear,
To whom His love commits me here,
Ever this day be at my side,
To light and guard, to rule and guide
My life … and Jenny's…Henry's
Amen."

"I vaguely remember the store," Jenny said as they turned to head back to their cars.

"I have some great photos of the store before and as they tore it down. Maybe later in the week when Justin is at home, we can go over them."

"That would be so nice, Henry."

HENRY TOOK EVERY shortcut he knew to make time to get home before Jenny did. He had asked her to pick up a loaf of crusty French bread at Safeway and he would pick up the mail at Lumsden. It couldn't have worked out better. Five minutes after Henry got home, Jenny drove into the yard. It just gave him enough time to position the angel beside the front entry door so it would look like the angel was welcoming visitors to the farm. He sat beside the angel as Jenny slowly approached the garage and signaled for the garage door to open. As she was doing so, she waved to Henry and turned her attention back to the driveway, but for only a moment when she hit the brakes and took a second look.

She noticed the new angel statue by the entry. The canopy over the entrance way cast a shadow in that area but the white marble had an inner luminosity of its own. It exuded a light

Jenny had become accustomed to over the years. She knew instinctively that it had to have come from the same quarry and been created by the same sculptor.

She was certain of it.

She turned off the engine and quickly got out of the car and walked slowly to the front door, her eyes fastened on the angel.

"My gosh, Henry! What a beautiful angel to guard and greet us and visitors to our home. I love the way his arms are outstretched in such a welcoming manner." Jenny touched the white marble statue and let her fingers slide across the smooth surface. After studying it for a few minutes, she knew her instincts were correct. "The sculptor, Henry, it was the same artist who created the Angel of Thanksgiving…wasn't it?"

Henry nodded, "The very same. It just came from Ottawa this morning and Jeremy had the carrier deliver it out here after lunch. It couldn't have been timed more perfectly!"

"Henry, it's beautiful!" She had noticed a card was tied to the right arm of the angel and dangling underneath almost hidden from view. "Is this for me to read?"

Henry nodded.

With tears streaming down her cheeks, Jenny took the card, opened it and silently read its message:

*Happy third anniversary, honey! I love you more
than words can say! May this angel ever remind
us of our wedding day and always light and guard
our home.*
    With all of my love,

                    Henry

"Oh, Henry," was all Jenny could say as she fell into Henry's embracing arms.

When Jenny and Henry entered the house, they both were in for another surprise. Jeremy had a huge bouquet of flowers on the kitchen counter. It was from all the children. They had gotten in on it together. When Henry and Jenny read the card, the beautiful wishes from the children seemed to fade when they looked at the signatures and personal wishes that each had written on the card. Lauren, Allison, Jeremy and Camilla had all wished their mom and dad a happy 3rd anniversary; it was Justin's greeting that stung their hearts:

> *Dad and Jenny.*
> *Happy anniversary*
> *Justin*

Henry had hoped that his son would be addressing Jenny as Mom by now but they did give him the option. He recalled Jenny telling him how she longed for her son, J.J. to call her Mom. Henry understood this wasn't the same, yet he prayed every day that Justin would be more welcoming of Jenny into the family. Or, even if he continued to call her Jenny, the name would carry more affection and acceptance. It was unfortunate that his son didn't realize how much he was missing and the needless pain he was inflicting upon himself. If Jenny was hurt by it all, she didn't let it show. She just went on and on how beautiful the flowers were and how thoughtful it was of all the children.

After Jenny went through the mail and read the cards she had received from Ottawa, she announced that she was going to take a shower and then prepare dinner. Henry convinced her to wait until later. It was already 7:00 and soon it would be dark in the valley. The descending sun in the west was already beginning to cast long shadows across the valley floor.

Henry poured a glass of chilled white wine and together they prepared their favorite meal, chicken marsala.

The dinner was quiet except for the soft music playing in the background. They talked about the wonderful day but most of all, they gazed into each other's eyes finding it hard to believe that they were actually married and together.

After dinner, they went out onto the deck and stood at the railing and looked down at the prayer house. The sun had set but its rays still lingered long enough to create that special mood of twilight time. A serene sheen glowed off the meandering stream on the valley floor. The moon hung low in the sky and reflected deeply in the pond beside the Poustinia. The first star of the east was shining brightly sending its shimmering rays of light to the happy couple.

Henry put his arm around Jenny as she snuggled closer in the cool evening air.

"I am so happy," Jenny whispered, breaking the silence. Her warm breath caught in the still, crisp air. "There is our star. I feel your love surrounding me from close and afar."

Henry too, could feel the glow of the star enter his heart. For so many years the star's rays were the only compensation for Jenny's absence and yet if offered hope that someday like now, they would be together once more. He had always felt there was an angel guarding the star. It made him think about other angels he periodically saw.

"Since you've been here, Jenny, have you ever seen numerous angels flying around the prayer house?"

"No, but I feel that I am entering on holy ground when I walk into the Poustinia. Perhaps it's Father Engelmann. He is so Spirit filled one can't help but feel surrounded by a loving presence. Why do you ask? Have you seen such a vision?"

"It's hard to explain... often when I am out here at night, there seems to be a sudden brilliance surrounding the prayer house and sky above is filled with angels flying all around. It's over in a flash, a blink of the eye, if it wasn't for the singing, I would think it's all in my imagination."

"You hear singing, too!?"

Henry nodded and didn't respond right away. He seemed to be reliving those rare times when the unseen becomes seen. "Yes, Jenny, it's not just one angel, but a whole host of them like a choir. That's what initially got my attention to get up and look down at the Poustinia. The sound was so sweet and soothing. When I stood up, I thought the bright light was the moon but it was then I saw the winged spirits; dozens of them flying here and there. Some were almost stationary hovering above or near the prayer house.

Jenny turned towards the valley and gazed at the Poustinia, "Father is very well protected. Perhaps that is why he doesn't mind being alone…well, he really isn't alone, is he?" Jenny thought for a moment and then added, "It could very well be…, the house where angels dwell."

Henry reflected on what Jenny had said. He nodded, "That's a very nice way of putting it…"

Just then the record changer began to play their song: *True love.* As Patsy Cline sang the song, Henry and Jenny began to dance and sway on the deck to the music, lost in another world. When it finished playing, Henry took Jenny's hand and led her back into the sun room, through the living room and into the kitchen. He turned off the lights as he made his way through the house and together they climbed the stairs to their bedroom.

Jenny took a shower first while Henry lit the candles he had set out earlier that morning. The covers were drawn and three roses rested on Jenny's pillow. The helium balloon was still stuck to the ceiling with the note dangling and moving slightly to the soft evening breeze coming in through the open window.

Henry went into the other bathroom and took a shower.

When he returned to the bedroom, Jenny was standing next to the bed wearing a white satin nightie. They gazed at one another for the longest moment.

"Thank you my darling Henry for everything. You have made my life complete."

She raised her left hand to her right shoulder and slowly pushed the almost invisible strap off her shoulder and let it fall. She made the same moves with her right hand to her other shoulder and the short nightgown fell to her feet. Her luminous skin glowed in the candle light.

There were no words to describe the emotion of desire and love Henry felt for Jenny. The sight of the flickering candles and soft romantic music playing which so impressed him when he walked into the room, faded instantly into the background. He was completely mesmerized by her beauty and intoxicated with the faint lilac scent of her perfume.

This was one of those moments in time that becomes a forever moment.

Jenny walked to the bed, removed the roses from the pillow, smelled them and laid them on the night table. Henry loved and watched every movement.

She slipped into bed.

Henry walked to the other side and lay next to his beloved. He slid his arm beneath her neck and shoulders and she drew near touching his skin. The warmth and softness of her body set him on fire. He looked down into her sparkling eyes not sure if he wanted to lose sight of her radiant beauty or close his eyes and savor the sweetness of her lips. "I love you so dearly, Jenny..." was all he could say as their lips touched and their bodies meshed into a passionate embrace.

The dance of the heart and soul had begun.

CHAPTER SEVENTEEN

THE PLANE HAD landed ten minutes ago and the passengers aboard still hadn't started to come into the airport terminal. More and more people were beginning to congest around the entry doors each looking for someone just as Henry was.

He hadn't seen either Gary or John since the two men attended their wedding three years ago. Henry was anxious to see them both and get caught up on all they had been doing in India. He stood on his tiptoes dodging people from side to side trying to keep some channel of vision open to the door. Finally, passengers started to come in.

Suddenly, a broad grin grew on Henry's face. He didn't have to be so anxious about spotting them come through the doors. Henry had forgotten how tall John was. He was at least two heads taller than the tallest person arriving in the terminal. In addition, it was hard to miss John who was wearing a colorful Indian tunic and finally, his gleaming bald head reflected the ceiling lights almost as if he were a lighthouse shining his beacon.

Henry waved and was immediately spotted by John. Gary must have sensed John had seen Henry as he instantly looked his way and waved. Henry began to work his way through the crowd to greet his friends.

"Great to see you Gary, John."

"Great to see you too!" responded the men almost simultaneously.

Henry hugged both of them even though it was awkward to embrace John. "The luggage comes in at that end of the terminal." Henry pointed the way.

"No need to Hank, everything we've got is on our back."

"Yeah, right, you guys travel light."

"Well, it's really all we've got."

Henry chuckled. They were just like Father Engelmann; very few attachments. And, Henry would bet his last dollar that both back packs were carrying a Bible. It immediately brought back the memory that the Bible which Gary has in his backpack would be Anna's. However, that was a long time ago; back in 1957. Now Henry wondered if it could have survived all those years.

Henry drove Gary and John to Gary's sister's place in Uplands. They decided to stay there since Sarah had more room and was better able to deal with two guests. Besides, Gary wanted to surprise his mother who still lived on Broder Street. On the way, they mainly talked about the flight overseas and how large airplanes were getting. Henry kept the conversation light as he had invited Gary and John out to farm tomorrow.

"So, if you can't get Sarah's car, I'll come in and pick you both up."

"I'll let you know if there is a problem getting a set of wheels. And the directions you gave me are straightforward, so, I shouldn't have any problem."

"Great," said Henry as John and Gary exited the car. "Say, hi to Sarah and tell her that I look forward to visiting with her at your mom's 85th birthday!"

Henry stood on the driveway as Gary and John drove up in Sarah's car. Jenny was in Regina with the ladies group and Father Engelmann was waiting to say Mass for Henry and his friends.

"Have any trouble finding your way here, Gary?"

"No, none whatsoever, the map you drew was easy to follow.

Wow, Hank, this is some place you have here!"

"Thanks, Gary, it's a work in progress, always building or adding on. I love construction."

They gave one another a hug and Henry introduced Ginger who was already nudging up to Gary with a friendly greeting.

"I love Golden Retrievers," commented Gary as he stooped over and patted the dog.

John hadn't said anything yet, he was overwhelmed with Henry's acreage. Henry, too, was set aback by the Indian apparel John was wearing. It was a white cotton cape with a hole in the center to pull over his head hiding both his arms and hands. Instead of the white sarong he was wearing yesterday it looked like a loose makeshift pair of trousers that came just above his knees.

Out of curiosity, Henry asked, "What do you call the pants you're wearing?"

"It's a Dhoti. They're made to look like shorts; actually it's a six foot long strip of cotton folded and tucked in here and there to end up looking like this. It is what I wore yesterday as a sarong."

"Really? I'd be interested in seeing how that's done."

John lifted the front of his cape exposing his hands and waist ready to show Henry how a Dhoti is waist-wrapped but Henry interrupted him, "Maybe you can show me later. Father Engelmann is waiting for us down in the valley at the prayer house. There is a road to drive there, but I thought we would walk and take in more of the valley view."

"I can't wait to see the Poustinia, Hank. Father keeps mentioning it in his letters to me.

"Yeah, Father sure likes it there, Gary. Wonderful place for prayer and reflection."

"You must go there often."

Henry was a bit embarrassed to say, "Actually, Gary, Jenny and I go to daily Mass but I've never made a retreat in all the years that the prayer house has been there."

"Really..."

AS THE THREE men and Ginger started their trek around the hill, Henry explained how the deep gorge to the side of the road they were on fed into the main valley which would come into view as soon as they turned the bend.

"The sides are sure steep, Hank. It would be tricky driving up and down here especially when it is wet."

"When it rains, we can't use this road. In places it's too steep and the tires start spinning. Sometimes, the truck stops and starts sliding back down the hill. Then it gets scary."

Just then, they turned the bend around the hill exposing the valley and the prayer house reflecting in the pond. Gary and John stopped in their tracks and so did Henry.

"Wow, Hank, what a view!"

John muttered a similar comment under his breath. The white prayer house with the red roof surrounded by wildflowers and the rich greens of summer was breathtaking. They noticed Father sitting on a chair on the deck with Coco lying beside. Father saw them and waved. The three men waved back.

As they progressed further down the hill exposing the length of the valley, Henry's friends said one adjective after the other over God's creation. John began to say what Father Engelmann often said when he walked the valley, the 23rd psalm: "...He leads me beside the still waters...He restores my soul, He leads me in the paths..."

"I can't believe you haven't made a retreat here, Hank. What possibly would keep you from coming here...?"

Henry didn't answer Gary. They all walked silently towards Father who was now standing wearing a broad smile and his arms outstretched ready to welcome his children. Ginger and Coco were already greeting one another.

"It is a blessing to see all of you. Come Gary, come..." Father was going to say, 'John' but rather said, "is that Mahatma Gandhi I see wearing garments of simplicity and poverty...?"

"And is this St. Francis?" John retorted as he admired the Franciscan habit Father was wearing also reflecting the same virtues.

The men chuckled. The observations of both men couldn't have been more right on, Henry thought. That's how Henry perceived them both as well.

Gary embraced Father, while John went to his knees. Even then he was tall enough to give Father a warm hug but Henry was surprised when John bent down and kissed Father's sandals. Quietly he said, "Father, thank you for teaching me to be a servant to others. Your example has led me to know Jesus and follow him. I have never known greater peace."

It was evident that Father was uncomfortable by the gesture of respect and immediately placed his hands to the sides of John's shoulders and squeezed him in a lifting motion, "Rise my son, the Lord is well pleased with you."

John stood and stooped low to warmly embrace his benevolent teacher.

"Come, let us celebrate the sacrifice of Jesus to our heavenly Father."

Father entered the prayer house with Coco close at his side. John and Gary couldn't get over how the interior of the prayer house looked like a church. John was instantly drawn to the cross above the small altar and went over and kissed Christ's feet. The carved wood had been worn at that spot from the touch of people's hands reaching up there over the years but in John's case, he was tall enough to show a more intimate expression of the Savior.

Henry paid more attention to Gary and John during the Mass than to the Mass itself. He could feel their love of the Lord. At communion time, while Henry stood and received the host from Father on the palm of his hand and then placed it in his mouth, both Gary and John knelt and received the Lord on their tongue. It reminded him of the way communion was distributed when he was growing up.

After Mass, they all went out onto the deck to enjoy the beautiful summer day and each other's conversation. John sat directly on the deck in a yoga position as there were only three chairs. Henry offered to get a folding chair, but John declined adding that they always sat on the floor in the chapel in India.

"So, tell me boys, how is Mother Teresa doing?" Father wanted to know as did Henry.

"She is still as spry as ever for her age; much like you Father. She did suffer from a heart attack a couple of years ago but she is committed to serve the poorest of the poor. Where the most destitute, most outcast, most ill members of society are, you will find Mother Teresa and members of her order. She is dearly loved, particularly by the poor for her kindness and compassion." Gary paused for a moment and added, "This August she will be turning eighty one."

"Truly a remarkable servant of the Lord," said Father. "She radiates pure, selfless goodness in a world that is too often filled with darkness and indifference."

John looked up at Father, as if referring to him as much as Mother Teresa, "She is a beacon of light and hope to countless people. I have often seen her kissing the hands of lepers, removing maggots from the wounds of people found lying on the street."

Gary added, "She is constantly encouraging us to hold and comfort people on the doorstep to death. All people deserve dignity and love."

"That must be an amazing experience for you and John." Henry commented.

There was a long pause and finally Gary answered, "It's not so much of an experience as it has become for us a way of life. We have come to love the people of India and long to serve and be with them in the midst of all their challenges. In this way, we bring the Gospel of Jesus to people who have never heard of Christ."

"You are carrying out the Great Commission that Jesus asked of his disciples?"

"Yeah, Hank, at the end of the day, that is what we are doing."

Henry shook his head, "Yeah, that's wonderful what you guys are doing."

"Well, you can do the same. We have talked about this on several occasions, Hank, for people in the western world are needed to spread awareness to help meet the needs of their brothers and sisters in third world countries. They need financial support, teachers, doctors, engineers and contractors who have skills to teach and build for these people a better way of life. As for missionaries to spread the Gospel, we are finding that by training the people of India who have turned to Christ to help evangelize their own people may be more effective than volunteers from the west. They know the language, are used to poverty and eating what the poor people eat out of necessity. They are familiar with the customs and practices of the people; their fears, superstitions, Caste system and sanitation…" Gary's words trailed off and then looking directly at Henry he asked, "Do you still feel called to do this kind of work here in the west, Hank?"

Henry took in a deep breath of the morning air and let it out slowly. He had felt a tug in his heart to do that for years. He nodded and said, "Yes, Gary, I have felt called to help out in that way for years and I am embarrassed to say, I haven't acted upon that conviction…" Henry shook his head, "I know the need is great and somehow other things come up distracting me from this important work."

"Well, pray and fast about it, Hank. It's a powerful way to breakthrough with the Lord. He will show you what the barrier is and how to overcome any and all obstacles if the heart is sincere."

A silence fell amongst the men. Praying and fasting had come up again. Just the other week, Father Engelmann was talking about it. Jenny had already started to skip meals every Monday. Henry hadn't acted as yet, on anything!

"I can see by your slim physique that both you and John must fast all of the time."

John remained silent but Gary spoke. His friend could see Henry was struggling with it all. "Yeah, Hank, we fast and pray regularly. It really helped me draw closer to Jesus. It helped to love others in a way I never thought I could. I often see children who are scarred or have cleft lip and hide their faces. My heart goes out to them so strongly that I want to kiss away every inch of their lips and deformities to let them know how much I love them.

"Fasting also answered many of my prayers in powerful ways; sometimes not at all what I expected. There are countless scriptures that tell us to fast and pray. Jesus did for forty days before he began his ministry and many times he withdrew from the crowds to pray and fast. So, too, did his apostles and many leaders and ordinary people mentioned in the Old Testament. If your heart is calling you to have a deeper relationship with Christ, fasting and praying is the sure way to do it."

Suddenly, John came to life. He kept his gaze upon the still water and softly spoke with a tone of reverence in his voice. "The day that Father Engelmann walked into the hospital, I was on my death bed. I no longer wanted to live. My life was in a mess and I had no hope for the future. I considered myself a rotten, corrupt, worthless, good-for-nothing. I loathed myself and was completely filled with darkness. Although my mother cared for me, I considered her love as a mother's love. She did so out of duty as a mother. But I will never forget the day a complete stranger walked into my hospital room showing his care and acceptance of me where I was at. It stirred something deep within me that I had never felt before...I now know it was Jesus' love for me channeled through a very holy man. It was through Father Engelmann's unconditional acceptance and love of me that I began to see myself as loveable. It was this seed of love that began to grow in me.

"As I began to read the Bible in the hospital and with Father Engelmann's support, I started to overcome my alcohol and drug addiction. I still had many temptations to go back to my old way of life; but somehow through support groups and Father's prayers and encouragement, I managed to stay clean. Without realizing it, I was developing a new character based upon trust in myself and for Jesus to always be there for me.

"As my health got better, so too, did my appetite for food. However, my craving for drugs and other temptations remained. If it wasn't for Father who I later learned was praying and fasting for my full healing, I may very well have fallen back. Seeing that I was healthy enough, Father suggested I begin to fast along with my prayers. Taking his advice, I quickly learned that by denying the flesh which we are constantly in the habit of gratifying at its every urge is the beginning of control, not only of your craving for food, but over all your temptations.

"Fasting spreads to your soul.

"Not only did I want to control my appetite but to cleanse my spirit of sin. I wanted to better myself in other areas too. Little by little I could feel my will power strengthen and become more disciplined ...slowly, I was gaining control. Through prayer and fasting, I had opened myself up to receive the grace and strength from the Holy Spirit to live the way God intended from the beginning. It is true what people say who have Jesus at the center of their lives; you are blessed with a peace that surpasses all understanding."

John remained silent for a moment and then turned and directly faced Henry. "Without Jesus, I can do nothing. I am completely dependent upon Him. He is the truth and the way and the life."

A long silence fell over the men. What else was there to say? It was difficult for Henry to accept that a man he once critically judged as being a terrible, evil person was now bringing him closer to Christ? Henry would have never ever expected to one day see John sitting on his deck dressed in clothing that would reflect his utter poverty and yet exhibit such joy! As Henry gazed at John contemplating on where he was at, at one point in his life to where he was now, Henry realized that the most beautiful people he has had the privilege of knowing were those who have known defeat, pain and suffering; who have had struggles and loss and yet have found their way out of the depths of despair.

Those who realize their total dependence on God.

Henry recalled deeply those dreadful days when Julean lay dying in the hospital and Father Engelmann reached out to John, the man responsible for his dear wife's illness and eventual death...that was the only time Henry had ever felt Father Engelmann had betrayed their friendship. Henry could see now once more how terribly wrong he was. Father knew

John was a child of God just like we all are and that was what Father Engelmann focused on. Father also knew that out of the most terrible atrocities can come such good if we trust in the Lord and do not rely on our own understanding. The man seated before him was the result of such unconditional love and faith in the heavenly Father.

Like John, Father Engelmann had known pain and suffering only too well. He had shared with Henry the dark moments and hardships he and Anna had endured during World War II. The loss of their family, all they owned, the poverty and their education certification not recognized in a new country. And yet, they accepted their lot and forgave the Nazis. By doing so, they understood what it was to love, to be free and go on in service of the Lord. Father had grown to have an appreciation, sensitivity and understanding of life; he was filled with compassion, gentleness and a deep loving concern for others. John McBryne was a perfect example of one being influenced by Father Engelmann's light. Both men had let go their pride and grown into a state of life which most people do not even understand the true meaning of; humility.

Gary interrupted Henry's thoughts, "You seem to have drifted off, Hank…"

Henry was startled. He was deep in another world, yet still in the world. "Yeah, I was just thinking of the effect we have on one another…" He was going to say more when John suddenly spoke with something else he wanted to share.

"Making people aware of the problems abroad and their responsibility to them is very important however, we must not forget the missionary work that needs to be done at home, too. I am a perfect example of one who was lost. If it hadn't been for Father Engelmann and my mother who also never gave up on me, only God knows where I would be today. There are many out there like me, lost with no purpose or meaning but the same is true for many who seem to have everything. Mother Teresa talks of the loneliness and spiritual poverty of the west. It is true that people who have to work hard and struggle to stay alive are closer to God and thankful for any blessing they receive."

"That's a good point John made not to forget the needs of people here but I wanted to add that it's a matter of education in the home to teach children to be charitable. Sure, my parents helped out the neighbors or gave to the church but we were never taught to be charitable or even be aware of all the starving people around the world. To make a child give part of their allowance or to sponsor or adopt a child in the third world and send money through one of the many trusted agencies is a wonderful thing to do. There is just a lack of awareness, Hank. Together we can make a difference here and abroad," declared Gary.

Father Engelmann remained silent and just listened to the men speak on such a meaningful topic.

Suddenly John got up and stood at the edge of the deck. Henry and Gary tilted their heads way up to John's face. They shielded their eyes with their hands from the bright rising sun. Father sat further back and more eastward so it was easier for him to see John.

The tall man raised his hands upward as if he was seeing Jesus before him. "Lord, we praise You and thank You for all our blessings. Thank You, thank You for this wondrous creation, for life, for each other."

He said it with such deep meaning; he groaned to express his gratitude beyond what he was capable of. A beautiful sound began to flow from his lips. Henry immediately knew it was the Holy Spirit taking over and expressing to God prayers which John was unable to do. And then, Father Engelmann and Gary joined in praying in tongues as well. The sound and words were foreign to Henry but so beautiful it brought tears to his eyes. It was touching his heart.

After a long while the sounds and words slowly faded into a peaceful silence. It was so serene; their souls had expended themselves. Their love of Jesus was so complete, so committed, so yielding; the Holy Spirit filled them with a burning passion of faith. The scripture of John 7:38 came to Henry's mind: "Whoever believes in me, ...rivers of living water will flow from within them."

Henry looked in awe, unable to speak...as his friends prayed in tongues. Henry tried so many times over the years to be prayed over to receive the gift of tongues from the Holy Spirit but it never happened. He could see the difference between his friends and himself. They prayed and fasted and filled their minds and hearts with praise for their Lord. He recalled reading in Acts how the apostles and disciples prayed and fasted before the Holy Spirit descended upon them on the Day of Pentecost. They were ready and prepared to receive the Spirit but was he? Was he truly ready to give up his old life and ways? Does he really want to fully commit to Jesus to become holy and work for the Lord as how his friends are now?

"Do you mind if I go for a swim, Hank?"

John's request startled Henry. "No, no...not at all, John."

"Often when I am walking the dusty roads of India, I think of being in a pool of fresh water. The pond looks so inviting."

"It may be muddy at the bottom. I have never swum in the water and it may be filled with blood suckers."

"I am used to all kinds of water and pollution. I am certain the moving stream through the pond keeps everything fresh and clean."

Then, right in front of the other men, John took off his cape by pulling it off the top of his head. He then began to unravel the cotton Dhoti. Within moments what had appeared as loose puffy shorts was a long strip of cloth as he had mentioned earlier. Lastly, off came the boxer shorts. John stood there fully exposing his humanity on the deck and without hesitation jumped into the cold pond. Several mallards that were hidden amongst the tall grass and reeds suddenly took flight. John had disappeared for a long moment and then stood up raising his hands in praise of it all. The water came up to John's belly button indicating how deep the water was. Henry had never given it much thought before until now. John swam off towards the middle of the pond exuding a joy on his face as if he had struck gold.

Henry asked Gary why there were so many sores all over John's body. His back and legs were covered with red scars and black and blue bruises.

Gary nodded, "While I work pretty much in the city, John travels from village to village bringing the Gospel to the people. Many times the high priests in the village feel threatened and have him stoned. At times when I have travelled with John, I have seen him curl up in a ball with his hands over his face and top of his head to protect himself. I have not seen anyone more committed to bring the Word of Jesus to the people. At times his praying over the sick brings miraculous healing which results in converting entire villages to Christ. He tries to be like one of them in dress and even has learned some of the many dialects from region to region."

Henry shook his head in amazement over the commitment of his friends to bring Jesus to all regions of the earth. Twinges of guilt swept through Henry.

"Do you ever get overwhelmed by it all, Gary?"

"It is an immense challenge with the caste system, their belief in reincarnation, the poverty, lack of education and on and on but Mother Teresa encourages us to take one individual soul at a time and simply spread the love of Jesus from day to day.

We try to live in the moment that is before us."

Father nodded, "We often feel helpless and that what we do doesn't amount to much and yet God multiplies our efforts. Look at the ripples that John is generating and how they expand and grow and grow. I am astounded how a steel rope that supports bridges consists of hundreds of frail strands yet joined together create immense strength. So too, each light that is lit adds to the others becoming brighter and brighter with the potential to become like the sun capable of illuminating the world. Trust in God to use and take each act of kindness, compassion and love that we offer and expand it tenfold for His purposes. The power of His divine providence is perhaps the greatest miracle in the world."

The complete freedom both John and Gary exuded all morning made Henry envious. His friends were living in the light just like his mentor. How soon would it be for him to light the candle? *If you want the world to be a better place than you must be better. You must become the light, the beacon.* He could see how the example of his friends were taking hold of his heart and influencing him to become lit with the light just as Father so eloquently shared in his analogies.

Henry recalled what Mr. Engelmann said to him when he first started to work in the grocery store. They were sitting out back on the old grey crates when he said words that made such a deep impression on him: 'Henry, this world so desperately needs people who have thought things through and don't go through life like a leaf tossed by the wind. We need, more than ever, strong people whom others will want to emulate because of the wholesome way they live.'

Henry realized he was still like a leaf!

Henry turned his gaze from Father and Gary to John who was thoroughly enjoying the simple delight of swimming. The sunlight sparkled like tinsel in the spray of water John created through the air with each stroke of his long arms. It was clear to Henry, John possessed the light of Jesus in his heart. He could see it in his clear, peace filled eyes, the heartfelt words he spoke, the way he walked, the freedom he exuded! He once was dead and is now a new man, a new creature full of life! The old had fallen away and he was made anew. Henry now understood 2 Corinthians 5:17 completely: 'Therefore if any man be in Christ, he is a new creature: old things are passed away; behold, all things are become new.'

Henry had a glimpse of what was holding him back. He knew Jesus but according to the flesh and the eyes of the world. It was all in his head. Father Engelmann, Gary and John, however, knew Him in this way...no longer...

They knew their Lord in their heart!

CHAPTER EIGHTEEN

HENRY TOSSED AND turned for most of the night. Finally, Jenny flicked on the light and turned towards Henry. She snuggled up to his back side and whispered, "What's the matter, Honey? I noticed something was on your mind all evening."

"It's that obvious, is it? Father always said I wear my emotions on my sleeve."

"I love that about you. So, do you want to talk about it?"

Henry turned over and gazed into Jenny's sparkling eyes. "Oh, I've been thinking about the conversation I had with the fellows yesterday morning at the prayer house. Gary and John seem to have it so much together. John's openness and honesty about himself is such a powerful display of total acceptance. This is who I am, no pretense, no masks and such humility. They're just like Father, free as a bird and filled with a joy that's hard to explain. I, or rather we, have more than they will ever have in their life time and yet who is the richer? Despite their poverty in terms of world standards, they clearly are the richer. They live with eternity in mind just like Father Engelmann keeps saying. They all have a personal relationship with Jesus. The truth of the matter, Jen, is that I know Jesus intellectually but not from my heart. After all of these years, why is it that I still don't really know Jesus?"

Jenny nodded her understanding and remained silent, suggesting that he go on.

"The subject of fasting came up again. Gary suggested that I try it. He said that it answered his prayers and helped him make a major breakthrough with God."

Jenny raised herself from the bed and rested on her elbow for support. She looked down at Henry and said, "I started fasting on Monday and almost immediately the cravings began. One certainly has to use their will power to restrain themselves."

"Yeah, that's what John said. You become aware of your will power and the need to develop discipline and control if you want to look after yourself. I like what he said about the body being the temple of the Holy Spirit and it is our responsibility to keep it undefiled."

"That's true, however, I don't think many people look at it that way though."

"Myself included, but we should. It all makes sense if we want to have a long healthy life and yet, we are not disciplined to do what we should to look after ourselves."

Henry paused and then added, "Besides being good for the body, how does fasting answer prayers?"

"I think your motive has to be sincere; you are fasting not just to lose weight, but to show God that you want to draw nearer to Him. You are sincere and willing to make a personal sacrifice in order to achieve this."

"That's nice Jenny, and seeing how Father and my friends are fasting all of the time, there must be something to it. It's clear that they are doing something right."

"Well, Honey, you will just have to try it for yourself. I am going to bring up fasting in my ladies group, too."

"Be sure to advise them to check with their doctors before trying it out as some may have health issues."

"Yes, for sure."

Jenny slid her elbow forward and lay back on the bed. "I wish your friends would have stayed longer, it would have been nice to visit with John and Gary. We had such little time together at our wedding."

"I tried to convince them to stay for dinner or at least come back after they served lunch at the Marian Centre but they had other plans for the afternoon. Gary wanted to visit his mother and also a care home that his uncle was in."

Henry was hesitant to ask Jenny but he decided to go ahead. "Does it still bother you to see John?"

Jenny thought for a moment and said, "I still get a few fluttery feelings but I think it's more so the embarrassment of a memory trying to bring back what they did. However, like Peter, John was so sincere and sorry when I met him at the wedding. It was a serious mistake, but to forgive is the right thing to do and move on. I try to avoid thoughts of unforgiveness like the plague. Once it starts it seems to fester and soon you're trapped in a quagmire of negative feelings which gets one nowhere. It's like giving the one who hurt you added power over how you feel...And the biggest reason of all to forgive is to free our heart of a spirit of unforgiveness in order for us to receive His mercy and forgiveness."

"That's well said, Honey. I will never forget when I was fifteen, Mr. Engelmann and I spoke about forgiving others. He said, unless we forgive others, Jesus cannot forgive us. How can He come into a heart where anger, hatred, revenge and resentment reside? How Jesus wants to forgive us but it is us who keeps Him out." Henry raised his arm and Jenny snuggled in and laid her head on his chest.

"I wonder what happened to the third boy who remained in the car that night. He tried so hard to discourage John and Peter from hurting us. Have you ever run into him, Henry?" Jenny wanted to know.

"His name is Bud. Believe it or not, Jen, he bought our house in Regina. I see him occasionally when he comes into the gallery asking for painting tips. He's an amateur artist, not sure what he actually does for a living. I met his wife a year ago; a very nice lady. They have three grown children."

A silence fell over the room for the longest time. Jenny assumed Henry had fallen asleep. Just as she was about to roll over and turn off the light, Henry said, "I think I'm going to talk to Father in the morning. I recall a long time ago, he said to me it's not good to procrastinate but rather take action. I think I have avoided dealing with this matter of missionary work long enough. In the meantime, turn off the lights and let's see if I can get my mind on something else. Like Father always says, "what you think about expands and before you know, it arouses your feelings and we both know what that leads to…?"

Jenny giggled "…action!"

It was almost a replay of the day before. Henry found himself sitting on the deck with Father after Mass. The serene mood of the valley was the antithesis to Henry's inner world.

"I don't know why I'm holding back, Father. Gary and John are doing such great work and I know I couldn't do what they are doing. However, to carry out missionary work here and perhaps the rest of Canada is something I have felt tug at my heart for years. You warned me about procrastination for as long as I can remember and here I am at it again feeling all of the anxiety which accompanies inaction."

Father nodded, "Yes, we have revisited this several times and yet, you are still moving towards that vision. I know you are struggling with it but I see it in your heart and eyes every day. It takes an encounter with people who are fully committed to see the huge difference between where we are at and where we would like or need to go."

"What I don't understand is that Gary and I have had similar upbringing, yet look how close he is to God. With John, it's easier for me to understand. He hit the bottom and saw…" Henry's words trailed off.

Father completed them, "Yes, Henry, John saw his immense need of God. He came face to face with his emptiness. That is a painful place to be when darkness has completely enveloped you, yet at that point, Henry, it is easy to see the light. "

"Well, I hope I don't have to hit bottom for me to get closer to Jesus."

"I pray that you don't have to either, Henry, but this I know, if you seek Him with all your heart, you will find Him. Many Christians today, have one foot in the light and yet are still held back by the other foot caught in the darkness. At times you see the light like now and the rest of the time consumed by the world. We are so blessed in North America, Henry. Just look at all you have: wealth, possessions galore, so much talent and ability. When one is so blessed it is more difficult to see our need of God until we face some calamity. We are led to believe we are doing what we need to, to get into heaven."

Father gazed into Henry's eyes and went on, "Look at John, he has nothing and yet his lack of worldly goods has given him freedom from attachments. Emptiness is more preparatory to receive Jesus than fullness. When one realizes that they are poor in spirit and lack the ability and strength to change, this leads them to Christ."

"Does that mean I have to give it all away?" The thought swept through Henry like a terrible nightmare. He could never do that. Father knew Henry wasn't ready to do that either.

"No, that is not necessary, Henry, but to use what you have for the service of the Lord is what is required. The treasures you have been blessed with are to be used to store up treasures in heaven. Take John for example, he may not possess the talents you have and certainly not the wealth, yet he knows he has been granted an abundant grace of God; the Word of God has come alive to him and the Holy Spirit filled his being. He shows his thankfulness by doing all he can to serve others, advance the kingdom of God and give glory to His name."

"And their willingness to suffer so much and make sacrifices to give service to the poor," Henry quickly interjected.

Father nodded. "Yes, when you are called to do something great the road is never an easy one."

The men remained silent for a moment while each reflected on what was said. Henry was momentarily distracted by two barn swallows busily rebuilding a nest which had fallen off the top of the door frame just under the eave. Father's next words brought him sharply back to the critical importance of their discussion.

" In Luke 12:48, Henry, it is written: 'From everyone who has been given much, much will be demanded; and from the one who has been entrusted with much, much more will be asked.' If we are blessed with talents, wealth, knowledge, time, and the like, it is expected that we use these to glorify God and help others."

"But I believe I have, Father. I help others, tithe, give to the missions, my art gives enjoyment to others…am I not doing what I should?"

"You have come down here bearing a sense of guilt that perhaps you are not doing all you can. You say that for years you have felt a calling to be more involved in missionary work."

Once again, Henry withdrew into a reflective silence. Father was trying to bring further clarity to the point on hand by reminding Henry of the Parable of the Talents, "In the parable each is given according to what they gave. For Jesus said, "For to everyone who has, more will be given and he will grow rich; but from the one who has not, even what he has will be taken away." The Lord was not referring to wealth so much as He was referring to His grace and blessings. In other words, the more we give of ourselves to advance His kingdom, and give Him glory and honor by using our talents in serving others, giving to the poor, showing mercy, forgiveness, kindness, love… being obedient to His words is what we will receive in return. Furthermore, we store treasures not on this earth, Henry, but use our treasures, whatever they are, to store for ourselves treasure in heaven. We are blessed both here on earth and in heaven!

"As we can see in John's life, he may not have much in terms of worldly standards and yet it is clear that his cup runneth over. It is because he gives all he has and in return he is filled with the peace which surpasses all understanding. This is what you are seeking and yet eludes you."

Father's wisdom and truth always cut into Henry's mind and heart like a knife.

"At first I considered myself as the first servant who gave his all and invested wisely but perhaps there are areas in my life in which I am still like the timid servant. I know I have the ability to help Gary and John in advancing their missionary work but I keep holding back."

"What do you suppose that is?" Father had a good idea of what was troubling his adopted son but it was best for Henry to search his own heart. Father waited quietly giving Henry time.

"I am fearful of doing God's work in that area, Father."

"In what way, Henry?"

"Fear of rejection, other's approval, being seen as overly religious, fear of what others may think, fear of being asked to give it all away…" Henry's words trailed off.

"This is a very common malady in our society; seeking the approval of others. It is the result of conditional love in most instances. If, if, if! If you do this, I will love you. If you stop doing that you will receive my love. Parents, friends, teachers instill fear of rejection from the moment we learn to speak as you well know. That is why it so hard for many of us to perceive a Father in heaven who loves us just the way we are; unconditionally. If we come to Him with a repentant heart, He forgives. If we choose to go our own way and reject Him, He loves us no less, however it is our sinful way which will keep us from drawing near to Him and may prevent us from gaining salvation. We have free will, Henry, just like the three servants in the parable. Learn from the lesson which the parable teaches."

"But how do I overcome these concerns, Father? I could never do what John did here the other day, undress in front of us or bear his soul as he did. He totally accepts himself… he …he seeks only the approval of God."

"Oh, mein lieber Sohn, that's the heart of the matter. He knows who he is Henry; a child of God. He has claimed his inheritance and knows he is loved beyond words.

We all are!

"John and Gary know they are truly loved and in Him is all they need. Just as we should be obedient to our earthly father, they are to their heavenly Father and look at the peace, joy, and blessings they have received in return!"

Once again, the sound of birds chirping and the soothing trickle of flowing water through the nearby beaver dam, calmed the spirits of Father and Henry as they sat there quietly contemplating the discussion at hand. The mallards gliding silently through the smooth surface of the water soothed the men still further.

While Henry was caught in a moment of respite by studying the reflection of the hills in the pond, Father wondered if perhaps this was his second mission; the reason why he returned to earth from his stint on the other side. At that time, he was allowed to see into the future what his task was but then all memory of it was removed from his mind upon his return. Could it be to help Henry find himself and lead him away from worldly living to living more with eternity in mind? To save his son's soul was always his top priority and for the most part, Henry knew what he had to do and acknowledged his shortfall both to himself and to God. Somehow, Father didn't think the good Lord would return him for this as there were so many priests and Christian counselors Henry knew that could assist him. Father was nearing the end of his first task; to write the love story of Henry and Jenny but what could the second mission possibly be? Father was anxious to go Home.

Father gazed at Henry who seemed to be deep in thought. He knew Henry was an insightful guidance counselor and over the years had helped many people. However, it was sometimes more difficult to see into one's own soul without the help of another counselor or close friend. Father thought of another approach which might lead his son into the light.

"Jesus said we must love our neighbor as ourselves," Father began, startling Henry. "To fulfill our Lord's commandment, Henry, we must begin by having a wholesome love of ourselves. Perhaps, the Lord through His divine providence brought Gary and John here yesterday for this very purpose. We both know John didn't have a healthy love of himself. He clearly told us that yesterday. However, as he also related, he learned to love himself through others unconditional love of him which eventually led him to claim his inheritance as a child of God loved beyond his wildest imagination."

"I consider myself a child of God, Father and—"

"You may intellectually, Henry but do you really believe it in your heart? More importantly, are you acting upon that belief? A few moments ago, you said you have a fear of rejection and seek other's approval. So, let's step back a moment, how realistic is your love of self? How different is it really from how John originally saw himself? Here's the point for you to reflect upon; do you consider yourself better than John? I could say Gary but I think this will make you see yourself in a truer light."

Henry was taken aback by Father's question. He had never thought of such a thing and yet...Henry had to admit that he did consider himself better than John. He was ashamed to say it but he had to be honest. "Yes, I do, Father...I'm not exactly sure why...?"

"I think you know why, Henry. Look inside of yourself and all you have."

"Yes, perhaps because I have more than John; have had a better upbringing, I'm richer, have more talents perhaps, have a home, wife, children, status in the community, I'm respected and looked up to and on and on. But this doesn't make me better, Father?"

"Of course it doesn't make you better; only if you equate your value to all those things which you mentioned. Do you only see yourself as loveable when you have other's approval or you have more than others or revel in your possessions and abilities? How different is this from the way John saw himself? For years John, too, saw himself as unlovable and confirmed this daily by other's view of him. In John's case it was more obvious and horrific, but at the end of the day you may not have a healthy love of yourself just as John didn't.

"What made the difference, Henry?

"Could it be that the main cause of all your concerns is that you still have not developed a close relationship with Jesus just as John hadn't for years and years? Since he claimed his inheritance as a child of God, however and realizes that he is loved unimaginably by his Lord, John now accepts himself totally; no masks, no pretense, no pride, just humble, plain, John. What you see is what you get. He lives for the aproval of his heavenly Father.

"Isn't this why you envy both John and Gary?"

"And here I felt sorry for John, feeling superior when I am in the same boat as he is or rather...was."

"This is a blind spot for many Christians, we go through all the correct motions appearing we are doing and living the way God wants us to live but upon close inspection like now, we see that most of what we do is from the head and not the heart. It's out of service for ourselves and not really our neighbor or God. Most of western society is caught in this trap.

"If we take this one step further it will become still more obvious the fallacy of our thinking. What if you suddenly went bankrupt and lost everything; became crippled and could no longer paint. Would you now consider yourself equal to or less than John?"

Father's words hit Henry hard. "What is going on here, Father?" Henry shook his head. "It's all an illusion, isn't it? I know it is and yet I have to be made aware of it time and again."

"It's nice to receive accolades and be appreciated, as long as we don't derive our worth from it. It's the same with money; it's good in itself, as long as we are not controlled by it and equate it with our value. We both know that neither you nor I are better than John or our neighbor just because we possess more wealth or are gifted with more talents than them. Yet we have been conditioned to think that and silently we are in constant competition with one another to derive our worth! It spreads to how we think of others and judge them for what they do or have. In turn, how easily we are threatened and hurt if someone is critical of us or suddenly makes gains over us."

"So how do you handle praise and compliments, Father?" Henry wanted to know.

"I simply acknowledge them and repeat as fast as I can in my mind, 'Not for me oh Lord, not for me but glory to Your name!' Everything I or you or anyone has is God's. There is nothing any of us can take credit for. God made everything; we are just stewards of everything we have. That's why we give all glory to Him.

"Needing or seeking others' praise, approval, equating our worth with what we own and our status is a highly insecure way to live. We are controlled by others rather than by an inner purpose driven life. We build our lives on the sand and not a rock to withstand the storms and challenges of life. We look in the wrong place for security and constancy and inner peace.

"We fail to recognize who we are."

Father sat back in his chair and crossed his legs. As soon as his teacher gazed up at the morning sun, Henry sensed that his mentor was searching for some illumination to reinforce or clarify what he had said. He loved when he first noticed Mr. Engelmann do that when sitting on the old grey crates behind the store. So many times over the years, his teacher repeated that gesture. Henry hoped his instinct was correct. He sat up in anticipation.

"Many years ago, I either heard about this or read it somewhere. Ach, es ist nicht wichtig, it makes no difference. A farmer had built a chicken coop around the base of a large elm tree. Each year the birds of the sky would build a nest in its branches. Even though the nest was securely nestled in the arms of the tree, one day a strong prairie wind came along and shook the tree so hard the nest along with three eggs fell to the ground inside the penned coop. Two of the eggs broke but one landed in the bird's nest still intact. Incredibly, a hen sat on the egg keeping it warm and within a few days the egg hatched and the newborn bird became part of the flock. Since he was raised as a chicken, he didn't know he was a bird.

As the years passed he would often see birds fly above and rest on one of the tree branches. He often wished that he could fly like that too and his instincts told him that he could but he didn't believe it. One day with the motivation of the farm dog that strayed into the coop, he not only hopped away but took flight. He soared into the prairie sky and became what he was meant to be.

"Can you imagine the freedom and joy and exhilaration that bird must have felt!?"

Father gazed lovingly at his adopted son and continued, "We too could be as a free as a bird as the saying goes, Henry. We could be flying up high in the heavens daily with our Lord if we remember that we are His children and could have fullness of life! Unfortunately, we ignore our very inheritance and spend years and sometimes a lifetime searching for happiness and peace but in the wrong places. We wallow in the illusions of what the world offers. We keep going around in circles until one day like now Henry, God reminds us again of who we are! We are His children! He wants us to come home, to fly into His waiting arms so He can fill us with His light and set us free! Henry, we are restless until we rest in Him who created us. God desires to bring you to your highest level! It is only by claiming your inheritance and doing the Father's will that can achieve that!

"The good news, Henry, is that you see it. The flesh may still want to indulge in the world. The flesh may try to convince you that true happiness is here in the world but the years of life have told you differently. It is all a lie, Henry; an illusion that you have been reminded of again and again."

Father Engelmann paused and then added, "Only humans have a mind and conscience. Only humans feel guilt and understand the need to forgive and be forgiven. Only humans can stand in awe before a sunset or gaze into the star studded sky with wonderment. Only humans can appreciate their bodies and the life force which makes billions of cells work together in perfect harmony. Only humans cry out in despair in loneliness for something to hang on to, cling to and get comfort from. Henry, these and millions of other human conditions are just a deeper sign there is something beyond this life.

"Yes, Henry, we have a spirit and a soul that yearns to return to the Father who created him. Can you not see your constant internal struggle between the two masters you continue to serve? One day it's the world and next it is God because the first master fails to fulfill you. We are restless and insecure until we rest in Him! Sadly, it is all too late for many before they realize this. All too many lay on their death bed filled with regret over a life that was wasted on things of the world that had no value!"

Henry could feel deeply Father Engelmann's care for him and his soul. His teacher so desired to bring him back into the light.

"I feel so confused and lost, Father. I understand what you are saying and at times I wish I wouldn't talk to you because the truth shatters my mind into pieces and I don't know how put myself together again."

"I cannot help you, Henry; only God can. Sooner or later you have to come to terms with all of this."

Henry shook his head, "For as long as I can remember, I have tried to build my house on a rock, only to realize that it is still on the sand. After all these years having you as a teacher and guide and best example possible, I am still struggling with all this; stuck in the dirt of life. Jesus must see me as one of the Pharisees; a hypocrite!"

"No, Henry, Jesus loves you for He is constant in His love. You can always trust Him. His heart is full of mercy and understanding and forgiveness. Trust in him and do not lean on your own understanding. Keep this vision in front of you and pray without ceasing. Henry, you are moving towards the light. I can see it. Your flesh may be wallowing in the world but your soul knows its destiny. It is constantly tugging you to go Home.

"God wants to give you everything, Henry. His Spirit is constantly working within you. More than anything, you are afraid of losing what you have worked so hard for in the world; success, prestige, wealth, recognition. You are afraid that you will lose what you have if you yield your will to the Father. You have relied for so long on your wealth and abilities for your worth and identity that the thought of leaving that for what is still unknown to you in your heart is terribly frightening. You have been duped into believing that you can do without God, look at all you have achieved. You are still unwilling to admit deep in your being that it's all due to God's blessings and nothing you possess is yours.

"A man who thinks he is rich and can do everything for himself is in grave danger. Don't let the evil one cloud your thinking and what our heart truly desires. Recognize your spiritual poverty, Henry. Emptiness of self rather than fullness in the world is necessary for true, lasting fulfillment in this life and the next. We are His, Henry. We are restless until our spirits rest in Him. What did Jesus say to the rich young man who asked what he must do to enter the kingdom of heaven? He too, like you, obeyed all the commandments and did everything correct but when Jesus asked the man to give all his wealth away, give to the poor and follow Him, he turned and left. What did Jesus say? 'It is harder for a rich man to enter the gates of heaven than it is for a camel to go through the eye of a needle.'"

Henry you are at a crossroad...

Father sat up and reached over and touched Henry's hand and continued to plead with his adopted son. "Come to Him as you are and share your burden with Him. His yoke is easy. Start to fast along with your prayers, give of your resources until it hurts and draw near to Him. Come and make a retreat. Ask Him to remove the barriers and false gods. Ask Him to put your wealth and abilities and all you possess into proper perspective. They are not what defines who you are. They are not your value or worth or what makes you loveable and accepted. They are gifts from God to use for others to bring them home to the Father. They are used for Him to store treasures in heaven for you. No more or less, my Son. Ask and He will give you His grace. His love will touch your heart and you will know who you really are; His child who He dearly loves. You are loved beyond measure. Henry, if you knew just an infinitesimal amount of His love for you, you would soar into the heavens like an eagle!"

Father Engelmann saw Henry's eyes flicker like a glowing ember struggling to stay alive, wanting to burst into flames. Father so deeply wanted to see the light in Henry's heart come to life. Oh, Holy Spirit, please fill my son's eyes with the brightness of Your love. Grant him peace and the grace for him to come home to the Father.

Father Engelmann lowered his head and continued to pray.

A silence fell between the two men. Henry was so thankful and fortunate to have Father's friendship. Father always received him so openheartedly, with such intense interest and non-judgmental attitude. His teacher saw into his very soul and could reflect back to him with words that so accurately portrayed where he was at in his journey. It was as if Father were an artist painting vivid pictures of Henry's life with his words. Yet still, Henry was wallowing in things that had no lasting value. He was rolling around in the mud of life when he could claim his inheritance and be free like the bird in Father's story.

Father raised his head and gazed compassionately towards his dear son. Unbidden tears surfaced in his eyes as he reflected on Henry's struggle. Was his addiction to the world so strong that like John, he would need to hit bottom for him to fully realize his utter emptiness and total dependence upon the Lord?

CHAPTER NINETEEN

J ENNY SIDESTEPPED SEVERAL pieces of art in progress on the floor as she made her way through the studio.

"My gosh, honey, how do you know where everything is?" Jenny asked as she made her way to the master artist painting at his easel.

"Julean asked me the same thing all of the time, Jenny. It's the casualty of a very creative mind," Henry replied with a twinkle in his eye.

"As you can see some of the art is works I started and left to begin something else and the rest of the stuff all over is the fall out of this and that which I want to keep in mind either as I do paintings or they are the seed of an idea which I want to explore and don't want to forget. So I keep it out hoping I will be able to get at it someday, soon!"

"But, how do you know where to even look for something? Look there." Jenny pointed to one of the counters piled high with books, notes, photos, and sketches. And sweeping her hand further around the large room she continued, "And look there and there..." Jenny's words trailed off.

"Trust me, Honey. Everything is filed up here." Henry pointed to the side of his head. "As long as no-one comes in and doesn't touch anything, I know exactly where to look for what I want to find."

Jenny smiled and took that as a hint not to even think about coming in and trying to organize what she perceived as a huge mess. Yet, she had to admit, despite all the clutter, she loved Henry's studio. She loved his art; she loved watching him paint; she loved to look at his sketches and most of all, she loved him.

Jenny made it to Henry's side and saw that he was working on a scene of a young boy flying a kite on a hillside. A photo and sketch of the scene that Henry was working from were pinned on the side of the easel. The canvas was toned with a light burnt sienna hue and Henry was just in the beginning stages of filling in the sketch on the canvas with color.

"Oh, Henry, I love that painting. That's Justin in the scene, isn't it?"

Henry nodded as he added ultramarine blue to the kite, "Yeah, it's a sketch and photo I took of him when he was eleven or twelve and finally getting around to making a painting of it. I like doing paintings with the kids in it; it makes them a part of my work."

"That's a nice thought, Henry. I love how the kite is sailing in the wind."

"Yeah, it captures a feeling of freedom, doesn't it? Just like the old saying, "I'm as free as a bird." Here is a young boy feeling his freedom and experiencing it through the kite. He is at one with the world. He and nature are working together to make something extraordinary happen!"

"Trying out the kite!" Jenny exclaimed. "Oh, how exhilarating and exciting that must have felt for Justin. I've always wanted to do that. Do you still have the kite?" Jenny wanted to know.

"I think it's in the basement. Ask Justin, he'll know."

Jenny hugged Henry and gave him a tender kiss. "Someday, I would like to paint you, Jenny, if you would pose for me. I may never get it done with all of the interruptions but it would be fun trying," he added with a wink.

"I would be too shy for that, Honey. I can hardly wait to see this painting finished though," she said trying to change the subject before Henry got any ideas. She knew how his vivid imagination got the better of him. "I'll check in on you later, Honey. And, oh, just a reminder, you have to start packing for our trip to Toronto. We leave the day after tomorrow."

"That's right. I'll start this evening."

"I put out some of the things you will need in another small suitcase. There is room in mine if you need more space or you can take a larger suitcase."

"I'm sure the small one will be fine."

"After Mass this morning, Father sure was excited about the trip. I guess this is the first major travel he has made since coming to Canada."

"Yeah, I'm sure glad he decided to come along."

"I called Lauren and told her there weren't any changes to our itinerary. She said she would try to meet us at the airport."

"Great. I'm getting excited about the trip, too. What a wonderful experience it will be to see Lauren in a major musical."

"I can hardly wait, too." Jenny kissed Henry again and left.

Henry had a hard time concentrating on his painting. His mind kept thinking about the trip and how thrilled Father must be. It was hard to believe that Father was over a hundred and still hadn't been on a plane yet.

About half an hour later as Henry went to turn on the stereo, he could hardly believe what he saw outside of the north studio window. There on the hill towards the back of the house were Jenny and Justin with the kite he was painting on his canvas at that very moment! At first, he didn't see Jenny as she was about fifty feet away holding the spool of string.

Justin was motioning for her to move back and make the string taut. Henry could see the leaves in the elm and popular trees rustling and so a good breeze was in the air. He hoped when Justin released the kite it would soar into the sky.

Henry's wish came true. No sooner had his son thrust the kite into the air a sudden gust caught the diamond shaped kite sending it quickly upwards.

Jenny was gleaming with excitement and Justin looked so pleased it worked on the first try. Jenny began to run letting out more string sending the kite higher into the sky. It gladdened Henry's heart to see how happy his son was for Jenny. The sight of them playing like two little children uplifted Henry's spirits even more than the kite soaring into the heavens! It was the most beautiful sight of Jenny with his son that Henry had seen since they got married. He could read his son and knew that the young boy was thoroughly enjoying himself. He was caught in a loving moment. He was immersed in the now of life and that's when God is fully present in our lives. Thoughts of the past are gone and the future is in the present making. All judgmental thoughts and critical thinking have vanished, at least for the time being. Justin was free perhaps for the first time to see the jewel in his midst!

It's rare moments like this when love and acceptance touches our hearts.

Henry couldn't hear their cries of victory but he felt their feelings of exhilaration and joy; it was written all over their gestures with gaiety. How God works through His divine providence Henry thought. They had tried so hard to reach Justin and then just like that out of the blue it suddenly happens.

Tears surfaced in Henry's eyes as he prayed for his son to hang onto this feeling of freedom. *Don't close the door to this new life which you and all of us can enjoy. Let the seed of this new relationship grow!*

Henry knew that even if his son slipped back and the guards went up again, Justin would not be able to keep the door shut for long. He would want to re-capture this joy and the beauty of a relationship with someone who loved life and lived it fully just as much as his mother did but only in a different way. He was now seeing Jenny perhaps for the first time.

Henry brushed away tears blurring the beautiful vision before him. How he had prayed for this moment. How happy Jenny must be. He wished he could be next to her and see the joy in her happy eyes as if the sun were caught in them.

A deep wave of appreciation surged through his being. "Thank You Jesus for healing my son and helping him to love and accept Jenny. Thank You for opening the door of his heart to new life. Thank You for helping him to receive Jenny's love and through her, Julean's continuing love, too!" Henry knew his son needed and missed the love of his mother. It was always Jenny's main desire to give Justin both. She would never shut out Julean's memory or presence but do everything she could to nurture and sustain it.

Henry had been blessed with two wonderful women in his life. Both had accepted the other's presence in their marriage with Henry. His heart at that moment soared higher than any kite ever could.

He gazed out the window and saw Jenny running to the top of the hill; her golden wheat colored hair fluttering like a flag in the prairie wind. Justin was trying to keep up to her. His gait was so buoyant, his feet hardly touched the tall grass. Although Henry was too far away to see the joy in their faces, he could only imagine the sparkle of gladness in Jenny's blue eyes and the veil of loneliness lifted from his son's heart to make room for another mother's love.

Henry returned to his easel with new energy and life. With the skill and passion of Rembrandt, he picked up the brush and dipped it into his palette of favorite colors. He began with the sky. With his brush loaded with his coolest blue, it touched the canvas with such finesse, skillfulness and control the sienna under painting shone through giving the cool color a subtle, delicate warmth. Henry knew this painting would glow with an inner luminosity of light and love.

For a moment, he wanted to paint Jenny in the scene and then decided that she would always be there in spirit. But when she was in earlier and first looked at the sketch, she gave him the title to the painting.

Trying Out the Kite.

"Yeah, that's exactly what Justin was doing that day. We had worked on constructing it all morning and he couldn't wait to get outside and give it a try," Henry muttered as he went back to the window. Jenny and Justin were still at it. This time Justin was controlling the kite. He let out almost the entire spool of string; the kite was barely visible. But it wasn't the kite soaring in the heavens which gave Henry such elation in his heart. It was the budding friendship between Jenny and his son, two precious loves in his life which made him glow with more inner light than any painting he would ever create.

CHAPTER TWENTY

IT WAS A week later after Henry had finished the painting of his son trying out the kite; he decided to do a waist high portrait of Jenny. At lunch time Henry told his dear wife of his desire to paint a picture of her since the day he first saw her passing by his house in 1956. Rather than keeping that image only in his mind's eye, he wanted to capture her on canvas well.

Henry could tell that Jenny was in a playful mood when she walked into the studio later that afternoon.

She strolled by his easel pretending to be fifteen again and alluring him with her feminine wiles. But Henry resisted and asked her to sit on a high stool next to the north studio window. He was immediately taken by her beauty and hoped he could capture the luminosity of her skin. She noticed his hesitancy and said, "Better get started and finish it quick before that tummy of mine grows so big that your portrait will show two of us."

Henry chuckled, "You are not pregnant yet, Honey. Perhaps some time off in the future."

"Oh, ye of little faith."

Henry dismissed her remark as he stood at his easel studying the subject before him. For the next hour or so on top of a toned yellow ochre canvas, Henry sketched in Jenny's face down to her lap with a black charcoal pencil. He was just drawing in her hands which rested on her knees.

Jenny was wearing a long sleeved white blouse that was buttoned up to her neck and a black skirt. She sat on a high stool next to the north studio window. A soft light fell gently on her glowing features. Henry could hardly contain himself. Her luminous skin, sensuous wet lips and sparking blue eyes drew him in into a more erotic mood than an artistic one. He was more desirous of holding and kissing his dear wife than concentrating on correcting ever so slightly the drawing of the shape of her nose and that of her left eye.

Jenny sensed Henry's mood swing and had seen that same look in her dear husband's eyes all too often. A gentle smile began to grow on her lips. Henry looked down momentarily at the colors on the palette he had just squeezed out trying to conceal a growing motivation to make love with Jenny rather than paint her.

In that split second, Jenny disappeared. He looked up, his mouth opened and eyes widened in surprise. And before he could turn, Jenny pulled the brush he was holding out of his hand from behind him and ran out of the studio laughing and shrieking at the top of her lungs.

"Jenny, Jenny, come back. I promise I just want to paint you."

Henry quickly set down the palette and ran after her. Just as he came out of the studio he looked down the open stairwell and caught her shadow running towards the kitchen. He had hoped she would have remained upstairs and ran towards the bedroom like a good wife should!

"Yeah right!" he muttered.

Down the stairs, he scampered and stopped when he entered the kitchen. She could have turned left into the living and dining room which also led into the sun room or she could have passed through the kitchen and down the hall into the family room.

He decided to go towards the family room.

Slowly he tiptoed his way down the hallway until he came to an intersection; to his left was the small office area where

Justin's roll top desk stood. This also led to the sun room and straight ahead was the family room. He quickly peeked into the room but Jenny wasn't there. Perhaps she went into the sun room. He pictured her sitting in his chair near the window with the sun streaming through the glass highlighting her golden wheat colored hair.

The sun room was empty too. But he heard a noise back in the living room area. He ran down the length of the sun room and turned back into the living room. "Jenny, I know you are here. Come on, where are you?"

He heard a laugh in the kitchen. She must have circled back in there after he went down the hall.

Henry rushed into the kitchen, catching a glimpse of her just as she turned left where Justin's desk was and back into the sun room. Henry ran after her in hot pursuit. It was like going around in a merry-go-round. Jenny kept circling that area. Just when Henry thought he would trick her and go the other way and run into her, Jenny quickly turned and ran the opposite way. But Henry was now making ground. This time as Jenny came into the kitchen, rather than go straight ahead as before she turned back into the foyer which led back upstairs to the studio and bedroom area.

Just as she entered the foyer, Justin came in the front door.

"Oh, is school out already?" Jenny said as she ran past him and began climbing the stairs.

"Yeah, it's four thirty and the bus just dropped me off."

As Justin gazed at Jenny climb the stairs two at a time, Henry came into the foyer and skidded to a stop but not before bumping Justin off balance. Henry's face which was red to begin with just got a lot redder. He was momentarily speechless. It reminded Henry of the time when he and Julean had made love in his studio back in Regina. When she went downstairs to take a shower, the three older kids at the time saw her in the foyer. Now Henry knew what his dear Julean must have felt like.

"If you're looking for Jenny, she ran upstairs...maybe I shouldn't tell you..." Justin chuckled.

"Oh, we are just playing tag..."

Justin studied his dad for a moment and trying to conceal a grin, he said, "Tag---inside the house? Come on, Dad, give me a break. What goes on here when I'm in school?"

Henry could see his son was quite enjoying the awkward position he found him in. "Well, why don't you go into the family room and watch some TV."

"Nah, I'd sooner stay here and watch you two!" Justin chuckled once more.

What goes around comes around, Henry thought. He recalled doing the same thing to his dad when he was Justin's age. It was the day his mom removed the twin beds from their bedroom in exchange for a king sized one. Henry could still see the look on his dad's face when he came out of the bedroom and knew what that meant!

Sheepishly, Henry rolled his eyes and made his way upstairs. When he came to the second floor, he thought Jenny might be hiding in their bedroom...a logical place to end their little foreplay of sorts. He stepped inside their room but once again she surprised him by not being there. He checked the other bedrooms as well but she had disappeared.

Maybe she did go back into the studio.

Yes, there she was sitting back on the stool wearing a beautiful smile. Her clear, cerulean blue eyes sparkling playfully in the late, dim afternoon light coming through the north windows. When he came to his easel he stopped and could see he would have to redraw part of what he had sketched earlier. Jenny was revealing her more seductive self. In public, she always dressed modestly but in the privacy of their home, she was willing to give more of her herself to her dear husband.

She had unbuttoned several buttons in her blouse revealing the shinny pewter angel resting at the end of silver chain just above her breasts. Her legs were crossed and her skirt rucked up well above her knees. Her smile changed to a more alluring expression and Henry grew helpless.

A battle was building inside him.

A part of him wanted to scoop her up and take her into the bedroom and yet a stronger part him wanted to capture this moment on canvas. A passion to do the latter was growing rapidly inside of him. It is rare when moments of true inspiration like this come along but when they do an artist must seize the moment.

Jenny looked surprised as Henry picked up the charcoal pencil once again and re-drew several parts of the earlier sketch to reflect more of what he was seeing now. This was the Jenny he knew that no one else did. After making the changes, he took hold of his wooden palette, slipped his thumb through the opening to secure it in his hand. He took a brush from the jar and dipped it into one of the blobs of his favorite pigments circling the palette.

He was now ready to paint.

As the image began to come to life, he noticed so many things about Jenny that he had taken for granted; the shape of her slightly turned up nose, her sweetheart lips and the shape of her eyes.

"Are those the same silver studs in your ears that you had on the day I met you at the grocery store back in 1956?"

Jenny just nodded.

"I recall looking at them as we waited to cross the busy Victoria Avenue. The wind lifted your hair and the sun glistened off them.

Jenny smiled. The subtle hint of her lilac perfume reached Henry and he breathed deeply. It was like opium to him. He seemed to stand taller feeling in total command of his subject and exactly how he wanted to portray her.

The light was growing dimmer; he would soon have to stop. He preferred to paint in natural light. He recalled seeing Jenny in Engelmann's store that memorable morning squatting before him to help pick up the cans of salmon he had tossed all around. He could see her in his mind's eye now how utterly beautiful she was. How the sun streaming in through the front windows of the store caught the light in the strands of her golden wheat colored hair. He didn't need the afternoon light anymore after all; he was now painting from a memory that was so much a part of him that it was just as real as the image of Jenny before him. How many times over the decades they were apart did he go over and over that scene in his mind and heart?

Jenny softly spoke pulling Henry from his reverie back to the moment. "I was just thinking of that morning I came into the store to see you and when I left how I was almost hit by a car when I crossed the busy Avenue."

Henry stopped painting and gazed at the love of his life. "I will never forget that moment, Jen. The car should have hit you but your guardian angel saved you."

Tears surfaced in their eyes as they recalled that moment in time. Jenny reached up and took hold of her pewter angel. Henry unbuttoned the second button of his shirt, reached in, and took out the identical angel he had incredibly received from Jenny. It was clear to both of them that God's divine providence was at work that morning. Out of something which could have been so tragic so much good had resulted over the years. From that moment on, their guardian angels which were always at their side, now had come into their awareness.

Henry walked over to Jenny. He let go of the angel and bent down to kiss her. The angel dangled from the end of his silver chain and touched the one Jenny was holding.

"I love you so much, darling."

"I love you all the more, Henry."

And as they gazed into each other's eyes, a prayer which they hadn't said together for a long time bubbled out of both of them:

"Angel of God, my guardian dear,
To whom His love commits me here,
Ever this day be at my side
To light and guard, to rule and guide my life
…and Jenny's …and Henry's
Forever and ever.
Amen."

At supper time that evening, Justin continued to tease Jenny and his dad about what happened earlier that day.

"So, after supper, should we have another game of tag?"

"You'd never catch her, son. She's pretty quick."

"Oh, I don't know about that. I kept up with her pretty good when she was flying the kite."

"That's right, Henry. I could barely keep up with him. After all, he's one third my age. But anyway, it was so much fun. I just loved the way the kite scooped up and down and wiggled through the air. It reminded me of a fish wiggling in the blue sky like it was swimming in the water and other times when it soared up into the sky it was like an eagle. I found it so exhilarating. Sometimes I wish I were like a bird or an angel flying so freely in the air."

There was a moment of silence before Jenny's words hit Henry like a ten-ton truck.

"Jenny!" Henry suddenly blurted out startling both Justin and his wife out of their skin. In fact Jenny dropped her fork. Both of them stared at Henry with wide open eyes."

"I know your birthday isn't until next March, but I'm going to give you your birthday present early this year..."

"What are you going to give her, Dad?" Justin asked excitedly.

"Yes, what is it, Honey?"

"I'm going to take you sky diving! If you want to fly like a bird, that's the closest way to do it, Honey! We will jump out of a plane into the clear blue sky and fly like a bird! Like an angel! ...like a butterfly!"

Jenny looked at Henry in total disbelief...skydive out of a plane? Almost in slow motion, she keeled forward imprinting the look of sheer terror on her face in the mound of mashed potatoes on her plate.

Chapter Twenty-One

J ENNY BOWED HER head and led the women in prayer, "Dear Father, we ask the Holy Spirit to enlighten us and give us wisdom and insight as we share Your word as to how it applies in our lives and family. Help us to realize our great need of Your Spirit if we are to accomplish anything worthy which gives honour and glory to Your Holy Name. We ask this through Jesus Christ your Son and our Lord, Amen."

Jenny smiled at the nine ladies sitting around her in the Hill Avenue residence. At the last meeting, many of ladies expressed so many worries and concerns within their families that Jenny decided to introduce into the morning meeting, scriptures that Henry and Father Engelmann so often referred to in dealing with anxieties.

"Perhaps, ladies, we could begin by discussing how the following scriptures which Jesus said at different times are very connected and how they might apply to our lives.

"Philippians 4:6-7 says the following: 'Do not be anxious about anything, but in everything, by prayer and petition, with thanksgiving, present your requests to God. And the peace of God, which transcends all understanding, will guard your hearts and your minds in Christ Jesus' (Phi. 4:6-7).

"Wow! That's quite a command not to worry and give it

to God in thanksgiving and in return we will receive peace."

"The second is Proverbs 3:5-6, "Trust in the Lord with all your heart and do not lean on your own understanding. In all your ways acknowledge Him, and He will make your paths straight.""

"And the third is one which we have discussed several times, Roman 28: 8, 'God causes all things to work together for good to those who love God, to those who are called according to His purpose.'

"We all know that life has trials and challenges. There isn't anybody who goes through life without having some concerns, pain and suffering. Jesus asks us to pick up our cross daily and follow Him but He also teaches us through these scriptures the best way to do it. That is, the way to a peaceful life is how we respond to our griefs and troubles. Most of us grin and bear it, get angry, frustrated, and anxious or worry. We often feel that we are the victim...why me?

"And then, there are those who have learned the secret of doing what the Bible says to do in all circumstances. To accept it as part of God's will for them and trust that He will turn it into good. We trust God so much in this regard that we can give thanks and praise the Lord for the trials which come our way. Imagine praising God for an illness, or heartbreak.

But think on it.

If we believe, really believe that God is in control of our lives then no matter what comes our way, we know that an all powerful, all knowing God is looking after us and perfectly capable of doing what we think is impossible! Praise and giving thanks is stepping out in faith and trust. It changes our attitude towards life and everything we do. Worry vanishes, anxiousness vanishes, unforgiveness, and hurt vanishes. We are centered in God. We live uplifted in spirit and are joyful people no matter what."

Jane shook her head and responded to Jenny's remarks. "Those are scriptures that I have said countless times in my life and all you just said sounds so good Jenny, but when it comes right down to it in the nitty gritty of life its easier said than done. It's so easy to say don't be anxious, fret or worry but putting it into practice is another thing. I was even having trouble concentrating on the scriptures you were reading as part of my mind was still on problems we are having with our son at home."

Jane paused for a moment and then went on, "I have two boys at home; one excels in school, sports, is respectful and obedient while the second is almost the opposite. He is getting into trouble at school; we found out that he is on drugs. The other day Wal-Mart called to tell us he was caught stealing. My husband is constantly arguing and fighting with him. We are both at our wits end. How on earth can we not be anxious or very concerned?"

"That's true, Jane," interjected Donna. "But what good does worry do? Most of us react to life's difficulties by being hurt, frustrated and/or angry as Jen pointed out, but it does little good. Yet, I succumb to worry, too. Sometimes my entire mind and heart is so focused on the problem that it mushrooms in my head to the point I can't do anything. It's confusing; if only I could do as the scriptures suggest to praise and give thanks in all circumstances and trusting God to look after it. I'd love to have a peaceful spirit even in the worst-case scenarios."

"Look what happened to Jesus," chimed in Crystal. "He was tortured, suffered horrifically and was crucified. I recall in one of our meetings that we were to praise and be thankful to God for Jesus' pain and suffering. As terrible as it was Jesus trusted and was obedient to the Father unto death because He knew that God would bring good out of it. And he did! Jesus' death on the cross won the victory over sin and death for all of us. That is why God wants us to praise Him for it. If we can be thankful for Jesus' crucifixion then can we not be thankful for our trials."

"What do you think, Dianne?" asked Jenny.

"Well, we have been meeting for over ten months and Scripture after Scripture that we study promises the release of God's power if we praise and have a thankful heart. God is obligated because of our faith and trust in Him to make it all good. Think on it this way; it may go against our logic to praise God for our circumstances be they illness, cancer, family concerns or whatever but the alternate is worse and gives us no hope."

"Good point," said Shelly and then added, "We have a choice, don't we? We can choose to feel bad and anxious or we can trust and give thanks. Which attitude is more productive and makes our lives easier to live? Which person suffers more; the one who turns it over to an all powerful God to deal with or keeping it to ourselves and trying to solve it on our own strength?

"Clearly, praise lifts us up, worry presses us down. And Jesus does say in another scripture to come unto Him all who labour and are heavy laden and He will give us rest. It's true that so many scriptures talk of this but at the end of the day many of us unfortunately resort to being anxious and worry warts."

Jane broke the temporary silence in the room, "All of what has been said makes such good sense but it's so hard to do when you are in the midst of a crisis. I'll try to praise and be more thankful but I just know it won't bring any good results. Sorry to be such a doubting Thomas."

"I appreciate your honest remark, Jane. I, too, had a lot of doubts but something happened in our home a few years ago, which changed my mind. I feel prompted to share what happened as it's a very similar situation to the one you are having in your home. A few years ago, Blaine and I went to counseling to see what we could do about our son, Todd. In our case, he was in competition with our daughter who was two years younger. Through counseling we learned that Todd was trying to get attention in the only way he knew how. From the day Connie came into the family, Todd felt dethroned as the eldest and it only got worse as the years progressed. He knew that his sister had our complete love and attention by being good and excelling at most things she tried. Todd didn't think he could ever live up to those expectations and so he found another way to get it by getting into trouble."

"So what did you do, Tracy?" Jane wanted to know.

"Counseling helped to give us a better understanding of the family dynamics, but mostly we prayed for guidance, strength and patience. Blaine has a short fuse but he really tried to be there for Todd as he went through a similar situation in his upbringing. Even though Blaine was very busy at work, he made the extra time to talk with Todd. Blaine set up woodworking projects they both could work together on which provided opportunities to give honest praise and encouragement. At first, Todd was suspicious of our motives and rebelled somewhat to Blaine's reaching out to him but Blaine remained patient much to my surprise, actually.

"Todd also liked fishing when he was younger and so once again much to my surprise, Blaine made time and revived that outing, too. It got so that our daughter missed the attention she was getting before and so we stepped up to the plate there as well. I found time to spent a little more mother daughter time with her and eventually Blaine took both of them out on the fishing trips and I even went along though I don't care much for fishing.

"I am amazed at the progress we made and how much Blaine enjoyed his time out with the kids. After a while, he did it not so much for Todd but for himself as he had so much fun. I'd have to say we are closer now as a family than ever before."

Jenny surveyed the room and said, "This has been an excellent discussion. Some of us are still sitting on the fence about these scriptures and understandably so. They make perfect sense and yet, difficult to claim. Worry, stress, anxiety and so on over the years have become a very strong habit for most of us. When problems arise, worry is the first thing we resort to even though we know it doesn't do us any good. It destroys our spirits, affects our relationships in the family and God. In fact, is it not an insult not to trust God when He asks over and over again to come to Him with our burdens?

"Something seems to be missing here that we haven't hit on. God wouldn't have given us those scriptures if they are too hard for us to implement or adopt. The words in the scriptures are so powerful that for us not to follow the advice and wisdom they contain is foolish.

"Maria, you have been silent so far, is there something you can share with the group?"

In her quiet unassuming way, Maria softly spoke in a calm sincere voice, "The scriptures we spoke about this morning are so beautiful and filled with promise. I have said them many times during my life. What I found though is that as powerful as those words are if they remain only in the head, they will lack power in our lives. The scriptures may sound hopeful for the moment but they won't take root because we do not truly know Him.

"To be alive to us, the teachings of Jesus must be in our heart. I think about my mother who had great faith but it was very simple. She just loved her Lord and believed in Him no matter what. She never read one sentence in the Bible because she didn't know how to read. What she knew was handed down to her through the spoken language from her parents, the priest and the holy pictures and statues in the church. That is how many people in the early church and down through the ages learned about Jesus and the Father and the Holy Spirit. She may have heard of those scriptures but she would not have studied them like we do today, and yet she lived them. She trusted God, she knew He would answer her prayers according to His will and she shouted and sang hymns and songs of praise and thanksgiving to Jesus and to the Father for all the blessings in her life.

"Prayer is the way to God's heart. It is the path to developing a relationship with Him? In Tracy's sharing it was through prayer that they achieved much the same results. It's wonderful how her husband went down on his knees to pray and how their family grew and came closer together. I'm certain Tracy and her husband are now much more trusting and grateful to the Lord for all the wonderful things which God brought out of the difficulty with their son. Isn't that evidence of Romans 8:28 working in their lives?

"It is through prayer that we develop a personal relationship with Jesus and the Father. It is through prayer that the

Holy Spirit comes into our lives. It is through daily prayer that we read the Bible because of our growing desire to know more and more about Him. It is the same as we got to know and love our spouse. When Carlos came into my life, I met him at a local festival in Mexico. When he asked me out, I initially said no because I did not know who he was. Through friends and relatives, I got to know a little about him and I felt more comfortable about going on a date. Even after five dates although I was fond of him, I still was not ready to go steady and marriage was the furthest thing from my mind. But over time, I got to know Carlos. I got to know his strengths, his character, his moods and how kind he was and eventually, I fell in love with him just like all of you did with your husbands.

"It is through prayer, mediation and reading about Him and His life and teachings and the great sacrifice He did for me and all of us, I came to love the Lord with all my heart. He waits for us to grow closer to Him. The closer we draw to Him the more He draws to us. When I come to Him now, it's like two people talking to one another. Scriptures come alive and Jesus speaks directly to me. It's not just words in a book that we understand in our mind; rather the words are alive and touch my heart.

"And for me that made all the difference.

"When we know Jesus in our heart as real and alive, then we can begin to trust Him and believe in His word. Then, gratitude and praise bubble up from the well spring of living waters within us. Then that scripture has real meaning as do all the others. But to simply read a scripture it may sound hopeful and help us for a moment but it won't take root because we do not know Him.

"Daily we must come to the Lord on our knees with sincerity of heart to follow Him and do His will. We ask Him from the heart to fill us with His Holy Spirit to do so. Then we know Jesus in our heart as real and alive. It is through knowing Him that we come to love Him. Then we can begin to trust Him and believe in His scriptures. Then we will be ready to trust God and in all things. Then we will continually have praise and thanksgiving on our lips. Then rivers of living waters will flow through us.

"Oh, I am so sorry ...I did not mean to go on so ..."

It was as if a light suddenly went on in the room. Maria's words were simple but very poignant and so passionate. Her comments carried a sincerity that led everyone to examine their own heart as to how committed they are to the Lord. Jenny kept looking around for Father Engelmann. Maria's words were so much like his. This was something that Father could never encourage his flock to do enough and her words couldn't have come at a more perfect time.

It was clear what they all needed to do ...

After a long silence, Tracy spoke again. "That's a great sharing Maria. I would like to add to the comments you made about your mother not being able to read the Bible and yet, God answered her prayers and she was just naturally grateful and full of praise for her Lord. Before joining this group, I never read the Bible nor did Blaine. But, like Maria's mother, we did pray and as you pointed out, Maria, that was the key to dealing with the difficulties and challenges in our lives and family.

"When I look back and see what happened in our family in light of the scriptures we are studying today, it is clear God used our son's problem through our praying to Him for help to bring so much good out of it. Like I said, our marriage improved, our relationship grew better, I respected Blaine for taking the time to be a better father to the kids. The atmosphere in our home became more loving, closer and peaceful. We are definitely less anxious and even though we were not that familiar with the Holy Spirit, I believe that through our sincere prayer from the heart we did receive strength from Him.

"In fact, something which I often thought about was if we had prayed as a family and brought God into our lives sooner, maybe Todd wouldn't have developed the problems he went through. This in my mind reinforces what Maria said about praying more and praying from the heart. The lesson we have learned is not to wait until a crisis comes into your life but to come all the time every day. I am not making excuses but in all too many families we get caught up in work, with the children, the struggle to get ahead and we don't think about praying or examining where one's life, marriage or family is heading--"

"Until a crisis comes into the family or marriage," interjected Jenny.

"That's exactly right, Jenny. God gives us a wakeup call and we better listen. Because before you know it a much bigger problem develops. When one member of the family suffers so does the entire family. I have to agree with Maria; it's best to live in such a way where Jesus is at the center and you come to Him daily."

Jenny surveyed the room to see if anyone else wanted to say something and said, "I think this would be a good place to stop for today. I just loved what Maria said and to say more would cover up the beautiful message she said. And thank you, all of you for your sharing too. I found this morning's discussion so meaningful and helpful and I hope you all did, too!"

Jenny reached out her hands to the person on each side of her and the other ladies did the same. With bowed heads, Jenny prayed, "Dear Jesus, thank You for being present with us through the Holy Spirit. Thank You for the wisdom and insight we gained through the sharing of Your Words and teachings. Help us to see the great benefits in praising You for all of our circumstances.

"We ask the Holy Spirit to bless us and we especially lift up our sister, Jane to strengthen and help her in dealing with the concerns on her heart. We lift up her children and especially her youngest son that he finds his way and is healed of the difficulties he faces. We lift up Jane's husband as head of family to have the wisdom and strength to relate to his son in a wholesome way that guides his son back on the right path with patience and understanding. In the days ahead, we will continue to pray for Jane and her family and also for all the members of this group and all families everywhere with their concerns. And help us daily to rejoice and be glad for all our blessings. Touch our hearts so that through our example of gratitude that we teach ourselves and our children that prayer, trust, praise and thankfulness are the antidotes to worry and anxiety. Just as Jesus is our mentor and example let our lives be a light and example to our family by practicing this wonderful gift of praise to the Lord."

Just as Maria got up to go into the kitchen to bring out the tea and coffee and dainties, Carlos came in with his guitar. One day the ladies had heard Carlos singing in the garden through an open window and from that day on they invited him to end their prayer group meetings with a song.

"Buenos dias senoritas!"

"Your timing couldn't have been better, Carlos."

Carlos smiled revealing his bright white teeth. "Si, Senorita Jenny, when I see the Monarch butterflies heading towards the house, I know my guardian angel has signaled me to come."

The ladies chuckled but Jenny knew that Carlos was serious.

"We were just talking about praising the Lord for all our blessings and not to be anxious. You always seem to be showing gratitude and are filled with joy. You are a powerful witness to others; a beacon of light, Carlos. Do you have any advice for us before you serenade us with your beautiful voice?"

"Gracias Senorita, for those kind words. If only we knew how much Jesus loves us, praise would be continuously on our lips. We would be jumping up and down with gratitude and joy! Our Holy Father in heaven, Jesus, and the Holy Spirit have done everything possible to bring each and every one of His children back to Him. All I can say is the Lord is my life and happiness. I am His child and He is my Father. I often think of Him as my papa! Every thought, word and deed I do, I do for Him. I see His love and goodness around me every day; the gift of life, the beauty of His creation and the tremendous sacrifice that Jesus has done for me and for all of us; we have to be happy and filled with joy, no!?

"Imagine, this is all a free gift given to us by the grace of God while we were all sinners. What more can They do to show their great love for us? That is why we walk the worthy walk in great appreciation and thanksgiving to our almighty

God. When this touches our understanding and hearts we are filled with trust and praise for the Lord; there is no room for worry or anxiety. Ladies, this is why I am happy every day and so should all of us, no!?"

"Then looking directly at Jenny, he said, "I am prompted to place a flower in the Angel of Thanksgiving basket daily for all my blessings just like you do, Senorita."

Jenny smiled. "Thank you, Carlos. You truly are a beacon of light for all of us. We are ready for our theme song; The Servant Song:

> Will you let me be your servant,
> Let me be as Christ to you;
> Pray that I may have the grace
> To let you be my servant too.
>
> We are pilgrims on a journey,
> We are travellers on the road;
> We are here to help each other
> Walk the mile and bear the load ...
>
> I will weep when you are weeping;
> When you laugh I'll laugh with you.
> I will share your joy and sorrow
> Till we've seen this journey through ...

Chapter Twenty-Two

A FTER SEVERAL WEEKS of trying to convince Jenny to go skydiving, she was still adamant not to do it.

"No Henry; never, never, never, would I ever jump out of a plane. Just the thought of it so overwhelms me it takes my breath away."

"But remember when we went up in a hot air balloon, you were frightened then and so was I, but when we did it was the most exhilarating experience we've ever had. This will be the same but so much more!"

"Henry, I would faint just looking out of the plane and never open up the chute. I'd fall to earth like a stone and shatter into pieces!"

"But I checked into it, we could both fly in tandem."

Jenny looked at her husband, quizzically, "What do you mean?"

"A trained instructor who has done hundreds of jumps would be at our side. We would be strapped with him and jump out together. It's safer than getting into your car and driving to the store. In fact, Jen, the statistics are much safer than flying in a plane or even walking across the street. Remember you almost got hit that morning in front of Engelmann's store."

Henry took a short breath and rambled on, "Jen you often

said that you wished you could fly like a bird or had the wings of an angel. I see how you ogle butterflies, too. Well, Honey if you want to feel what it's like and stroke it off your bucket list this is the only way you are going to come close to doing it."

Henry studied his dear wife. He could see she was weakening. "What do ya' say, sweetie? I'm nervous about it too, but we only live once. Come, let's at least check into it. We are dealing with fear of the unknown. I'm sure once we learn more about it and what's all involved, it may be a great fun experience! Come on, let's talk to the instructor and then we can make up our mind. We don't have to commit ourselves; all we are doing is checking it out."

"Oh, Henry, just the thought of jumping out of a plane two or three miles above ground into the open sky terrorizes me!"

"You won't be alone, Jen. You will be strapped to an experienced sky diver who's done it hundreds of times. ..."

"Oooooh, Henry, you are so persuasive."

JUST AS HENRY and Jenny drove up to the airport hanger a group of first time divers drove up after their jump. Two men were in their early twenties, two ladies in their forties and a senior in his seventies! The two men in their twenties dived solo while the women and elderly man jumped in tandem with an instructor.

They were talking excitedly about their experience as Henry and Jenny drove up.

Jenny was so nervous; she was even reluctant to get out of the car. One of the women saw Henry coaxing Jenny and came over. She motioned for Jenny to roll down the window.

"I can see you are nervous about this. I was terrified but honestly, this has to be one of the most exciting things I have ever done. The rush of adrenalin takes your breath away and those precious moments after you jump before the chute opens up you spread your arms and you can feel what a bird must feel like when it flies through the air. It's hard to describe the amazing feeling but you can do it!"

The words, 'flying like a bird' was exactly what Jenny needed to hear. She had dreamed of doing that so many times. Even watching butterflies flit about in the sky flapping their wings was something she desired to do, too! Perhaps, she should at least check into it. It didn't mean she had to go through with it, did it?

Jenny slowly opened the door and slid out of the car.

"That's the spirit Honey! Let's check it out."

"HI, MY NAME is Daredevil Jones. When you're strapped to me I'll give you a ride like no other."

That was not what Jen wanted to hear.

Jones laughed. "Just kidding. I see that look on your face so many times every day.

"*Fear.*

"But fear can be overcome and that's what I love about this business. Helping people face their fears and being rewarded with one of the most exhilarating experiences of a life time. Please sit in the other room while I finish up with the people that just came back from their jump. When I come in, I want to show you a video of how you would be strapped to me and how we would jump out of the plane together."

EVEN AFTER WATCHING a video of how safe this sport was and all that it entailed to skydive in tandem, Jenny was not willing to try it. For the next few days, Henry tried to convince Jenny further to try it but all to no avail.

Then, suddenly two weeks later about 6:30 in the morning, Jenny woke Henry up abruptly with news that he wanted to hear.

She jumped up in bed and got on her knees and began shaking Henry.

"Wh...what's wrong, Jen?"

"I've decided to go! I have always wanted to soar through the sky like a bird. Yes, I'm going to do it...eeeeek!"

HENRY MADE THE appointment for the following Monday, four days away. As soon as he did, he suddenly began to feel the spectrum of emotions; from excitement to nervousness to fear. He had been so focused on Jenny but now on himself as well.

What on earth have I just done!? Are we crazy to think about jumping out of a plane!?

He knew such talk would not be good for Jenny to hear. He tried to put on a brave front but just below the surface he wondered who was more afraid of this adventure; Jenny or him?

WITH EACH PASSING day, Henry and Jenny grew more nervous in anticipation of the big day. Henry's philosophy of living in the present was shattered. He recalled feeling this way about going up in a hot air balloon but this was the ultimate; his vivid imagination got the best of him.

Time and time again he caught himself visualizing himself and Jenny standing at the open door of the plane and thinking about jumping out into the sky 15,000 feet above the ground. *My good Lord*, Henry thought, that's almost three miles heading straight down at 120 miles per hour! Henry knew if he kept thinking about it, he might be the one to chicken out.

Neither Jenny nor Henry could sleep well Sunday night. Father Engelmann gave them both a special blessing for safety and calmness and inner peace; neither of these seemed to register. There was just this all pervading sense of impending doom!

Finally, Monday morning came and Henry dared to ask Jenny, "Do you feel nervous about this, Honey?"

"Terrified, Henry...absolutely terrified. I hope when I get there I will still do it. How about you?"

Henry thought for a moment hoping his next comment would mask or hide his true feelings. "Ah, it's going to be a great day, Jen. It will all go just great. The experience of a life time!"

"How can you be so calm and positive about it all? You're kidding me aren't you?" Jenny poked at him.

"Na, I'm just a brave, courageous guy..." And then he started to shake..."No, dear, I'm nervous, too. Actually, very nervous, but we can do it!"

And then, mustering up all the courage he could, Henry jumped out of bed.

"Let's go downstairs and have breakfast and sit in the sun room and quietly pray. God will fill us with His peace. The Holy Spirit will give us courage and make us fearless!"

Jenny shook her head and slowly got out of bed. "Did you say our appointment is for 10:30 this morning? Is that when we go up in the plane or is that for orientation?" Jenny wanted to know.

"That's when we go up, Honey. Jones wants us there an hour and half earlier to go over everything and then we have to suit up."

"Oh, Henry, I am getting the jitters just talking about it. Going up in a hot air balloon is one thing but jumping out of a plane is quite another. What if the parachute doesn't open?"

"There is a back up Jen and the probability of that happening is one in thousands. Remember the statistics; it's safer than driving in a car or plane."

Henry made his way over to his dear wife and took hold of her shoulders. "Just see yourself as flying like an angel, honey. It will all be good."

Jenny fell into his arms. He could feel her trembling. He had to admit though that staying focused on his wife and encouraging her did help to keep him calm and instilled courage in himself. But he too, was nervous, very nervous. He hoped Jenny didn't sense just how much fear was gripping at him too!

Hi Dad. Morning, Jenny," said Justin.

"You guys are sure lucky to skydive. I can hardly wait until I am old enough to do it. I can't wait to see you two come down to earth. I wish I could be right there in the plane to see the look on your face when you jump!"

"Actually, I hired a photographer to do just that, Justin. He will jump a second before Jenny does and then take pictures of her all the way down. I have one taking a video of me as well before and after the chutes open."

TENSION FILLED THE SUV as Henry, Jenny and Justin drove into the parking lot. Henry tried hard to stop shaking. He could only imagine how Jenny was feeling. He was having second thoughts. Maybe this wasn't such a good idea. They were both in their fifties and could get hurt when they landed and there was always the possibility that something could go wrong and there was no insurance what so-ever.

Jones knew how they would be feeling and thinking. No sooner had Henry parked the truck when Jones came walking towards them.

"Hi, Henry, Jenny…is this your son?"

"Yes, this is Justin, He wants to watch us land."

"No problem, nice to meet you, Justin. I can see you're just a bit too young to try this but in a few years, you may want to give it a shot."

"Yeah, I can hardly wait."

"This is a great day," Jones continued. "The sky is clear and very little wind. This is going to be an experience you will remember for the rest of your days! I know how you feel and the second thoughts which may be floating around in your mind. That's all normal but trust me, you will be in very good hands. Jenny will be strapped to me and Thomas; the other instructor will be strapped with you, Henry. Everything will be just fine. Come on in. I need you both to sign a waiver and then I will go over everything again of what is going to happen and then we will suit up and head to the plane"

Jenny's hand was so sweaty; she could hardly hold the pen to sign the pile of waivers. They covered everything; one virtually agreed to take responsibility for any and every eventuality. You were agreeing to allow yourself to be killed and have no recourse to anyone for compensation or insurance. You were in this all alone. Each time Jenny and Henry signed the stack of papers they were feeling a sense of deep finality with each signature.

After last minutes of instructions, Henry and Jenny gave Justin a hug. The hugs were more firm that usual just in case it would be their last embrace but more so, to instill that last bit of courage to do something which was insane!

"See you at the landing area, Dad...Jenny..." Justin wanted to say Mom but just couldn't bring himself to it. He waved extra hard to her trying to compensate for his stubborn pride. If anything happened to her, he would regret this moment for the rest of his life.

Justin watched as the two instructors, another diver who was going to do a solo jump and Henry and Jenny boarded the small, rickety looking plane. The door that they would jump out of was off and a small platform was on the outside edge of the open door. For the first time, Justin began to feel fear for them. Softly he whispered, "Dear God, please keep Mom and Dad safe. Please help them not to be too nervous and really enjoy flying in the air." Unbidden tears surfaced in the young man's eyes as a spectrum of emotions and chemicals rushed through him; excitement, adrenalin, concern and nervous fear and others that he wasn't aware of.

On the way up, Jenny's knees began to shake and bounce up and down. The anticipation of what she was about to do overtook her. As the small plane climbed into the sky so too did her heart rate. The noise inside the plane from the motor and the wind blowing wildly into the cabin from the open door was so loud that the rattling of her harness didn't give way the incredible nervousness and total fear she was feeling. She tried to speak but her heart was caught in her throat. She wondered how Henry was feeling.

At about 9000 feet she saw the solo jumper move towards the open door. He held his hands up on each side of the door and began sort of pumping himself to gain enough momentum to throw himself forward into the sky.

One second he was there and in the next, he vanished!

Oh my gosh, thought Jenny, *what am I doing here!? This is crazy. I just can't do this.* Just as she was about to turn to the instructor to cancel the entire thing, she thought she heard him say something to her but wasn't sure. She was so frozen with fear she could barely turn towards him. When she did, he motioned her to stand up so her harness could be attached to his. Henry was already standing behind her attached to his instructor. He was adjusting his goggles.

Jenny felt the click of the harness snuggling her up to the instructor. It gave her some relief and a sense of security. The camera guy was already at the open door waiting for Jenny. She felt the prod of her instructor to begin moving towards the door but she couldn't move. He pushed harder and shouted, "It's time to go Jenny!"

She tried to move forward but the fear overwhelmed her. The instructor fortunately was much taller than Jenny and literally began to lift her off her feet. She started to kick. She put her hands towards her mouth and began to scream. "Noooo, I can't do this!"

The air rushing in felt cool on her face and yet the sight of the open door only made her all the more terrified over what she was about to do!

The camera guy stepped out and positioned himself on some kind of platform as the instructor also positioned himself with Jenny in front. He yelled to Jenny to step out on the platform but she didn't hear him.

She was in a completely different zone.

All the instructions that she and Henry received about what to do were gone. Her mind raced with lightning speed from one thought to the next; will I faint and miss it all, will the chute open, will the harness break and fall away from the instructor, will we hit the tail of the plane, will the camera man be in our way? There was such overload blitzing through Jenny's mind it suddenly went blank.

Fear totally consumed her.

She was terrified and filled with panic; her heart palpitated so hard it threatened to break through her rib cage. She tried to resist; hold back but she was no match for the strength and power of the instructor. At once he thrust himself out of the plane following the camera guy a split second later.

"Eeeeek!" cried Jenny as a surge of adrenalin swept through her entire body. Never in all her life did she feel such intense emotions!

Incredibly, within seconds of her jump an overwhelming feeling of expansive, peaceful delight and victory pushed out the terror. The unbelievable view before her of the clouds and sky and landscape below was breathtaking. The more she breathed in with deeper breaths the more relaxed she became even though wind rushing against her body and face pushed against her with incredible speed.

And then it happened. She would have forgotten the reason she did this in the first place. The instructor reminded her during their training that when he tapped her on the shoulders to spread out her arms out wide like they were wings.

Jenny knew she would only have seconds to know and feel like a bird. She stretched her arms out and waved her hands gently up and down and imagined she was flying like a bird like she always imagined she could. She arched her body and flew effortlessly through the sky!

She savored each split second...not wanting it to end...

And then, a huge sudden jerk as the parachute opened immediately slowed her descent. Her head snapped back slightly as her lower body sank down and assumed an upright position.

Her flight as a bird although short-lived would be one she would never forget.

She breathed in a sigh of relief that everything was going as they said it would. Calmness and a feeling of absolute peace surrounded her now in the present moment. She felt immensely grateful to this large stranger escorting her through the sky.

He was her guardian angel made visible in the seen!

And for the first time, she noticed the photographer just off to the right of her broadly grinning from ear to ear as he continued to snap picture after picture to record this amazing adventure.

Jenny was now totally relaxed and enjoyed this divine view from the heavens. She whispered a prayer to her guardian angel and began wondering how Henry was doing. She tried to look up but the between the huge instructor and the open chute, she couldn't see where her dear husband was.

She decided to just enjoy the remaining moments as she gently floated down. The green and brown patches of farmland quickly grew larger as they drifted towards the earth. She felt the instructor pull on the cords and they began to spin around giving her a complete view of what lay before her. She instinctively reached out for something to hang on to but there was nothing except air. She thought she saw Henry and his instructor just off to the left. They were gaining on them.

The landing area was coming into view. There were several spots on the ground which she assumed were people. One of which probably was Justin. She could hardly wait to share this experience with him.

The earth was coming towards them faster and faster. She should have been more frightened but was gaining confidence in the ride and ability of her earthly guardian angel she was secured to. She could feel him pull hard on the toggles slowing their forward speed and descent. She remembered that she was to stretch out her legs and raise her feet and land more on her rear to allow the instructor to touch the ground with his feet in a running forward motion.

About thirty or so feet above the ground Jenny once again felt their descent slowing as the instructor flared the chute. She raised her legs and prepared for the landing. It was just as she expected. It was as if she and the instructor were as one giant bird and came resting down as gently and softly as a dove.

Ground crew immediately came rushing towards them to help gather the chute. Jenny saw Justin in the distance waving excitedly. Seconds later, Henry landed not more than fifty feet from them. Jenny could hardly wait so they could share their experience with each other.

Jenny was still on the ground when one of the workers freed the instructors harness from Jenny's. She tried to stand up but her legs were so shaky from the whole jump, she was unable to stand. The instructor and one of the helpers had to lift her up and hold her from falling.

Justin ran towards her from one direction and Henry with a slight limp from the other.

"You did it Jenny! You did it!" shouted Justin.

Henry and his son got to Jenny at the same time. It was a bit awkward to hug her with the two men on either side of her who were still holding her up. Jenny was so elated and pleased with what she done tears of ecstatic joy filled her eyes. Henry and Justin couldn't hold back their tears either.

Through tears streaming down her happy face, Jenny cried, "I did it Henry, I did it!" Then taking a deep breath she continued triumphantly,

"For a few seconds I felt what it was like to be an angel flying through the heavens!"

CHAPTER TWENTY-THREE

O F ALL PEOPLE Jenny enjoyed sharing her life experiences with most was her dear friend Matti. Just the way she responded seemed to heighten whatever they talked about. She had the natural talent of a comic and Jenny often thought that Matti had missed her calling.

"Oh, Jenny it be so good to hear your sweet voice. I could tell straight away it was you. We can hardly wait for you all to come to Ottawa on the way home from seein' Lauren perform on the big stage. My, my, so much talent in that Pederson family."

"Yes, we are so looking forward to visiting with you all, too. But I called to share something I never dreamt I would ever do."

"Now you not be tellin' me that you and that man of yours be goin' up in a hot air balloon again?"

"Matti! You are so close to guessing what it is. It's similar but much more daring and exciting!"

There was a long pause and then slowly, cautiously, Matti asked, "Good, Lord, Jen you don't be tellin' me you jumped out of a plane...please, tell me that ain't so. It frightens me to death just to be thinking such a foolish thought in my mind for a split second."

"Yes, Matti! Henry and I went skydiving!"

After a brief silence, Matti said, "My, my, I jus' can't believe that you two be doin' such a dangerous t'ing. Please tell me you be jus' foolin' with me. Say it so, Jen."

"We did do it, Matti! I could barely sleep last night, I kept waking up and giggling and laughing and so did Henry. We kept recalling and going over the incredible experience which we had. Even this morning, it's consuming my thoughts. I can't seem to put my mind on anything else. I keep recalling those last seconds before the jump! Oh, Matti, I just had to call and tell you about it!"

"It sends shivers up and down my spine…I jus' can't believe it!"

"The entire jump from the plane until we landed took three minutes or so and yet we have been talking about it and reliving it for hours. Each second of the experience going up in the plane, getting attached to the instructor, walking towards the door, looking out the door into the sky…it was like walking to a death sentence!"

Jenny took a deep breath and went on, "I was so scared and terrified, Matti. Right up to the last moment I didn't think I could do it. I began to scream that I didn't want to do this over the rushing sound of the wind and before I could complete the sentence the instructor pushed me forward, out into the sky, otherwise I couldn't have done it.

"*I thought for sure I was going die.*

"The adrenalin surge through my body was the strongest I have ever experienced. But amazingly, Matti, within seconds all those thoughts and the intense feelings associated with them vanished and turned into elation! I began to enjoy each and every second immensely and intensely!"

"So, the instructor came with you?" Matti wanted to know.

"Yes, he and I jumped in tandem, so did Henry and his instructor."

"That be even worse if that parachute be openin' and not support you both? What if it didn't open or get all tangled up? Oh, Jen you be fallin' out of that sky so fast and hit the ground so hard you'd be gone in a flash! There be no way to know who was who. A little bit here and a big piece there of that big man attached to you. I can't imagine the speed you two be fallin'!"

"One hundred and twenty miles per hour, Matti! It's like sticking your head out of a car window travelling one hundred miles per hour. Your face gets distorted and you have to wear goggles to protect your eyes. You free fall for about a minute before the chute opens up but that minute seems much longer more like an hour.

"Freefalling and then flying under the parachute are two breathtakingly beautiful experiences packed into one skydive. I loved how peaceful it was when the chute opened up and you just seemed to be floating and gliding in the sky. The sight of green and brown patches of the fields, the sky, clouds and just everything from that perspective is amazing."

"Amazing or not, nobody, but nobody would ever be able to talk me into doin' somet'ing so crazy! That for sure. Tell me now, you be takin' out insurance and makin' your last will and testimony before doin' somet'ing so foolish?"

Jenny chuckled. "No, we could have taken out our own insurance but we didn't. We did however, have to sign a waiver not to hold the company responsible for any accident or absolutely anything. We literally signed our lives away!"

"Well, it be a good t'ing you landed safe and sound."

"Yes, it was a very smooth landing. The instructor flares the chute somehow just before you land which somehow puts on the brakes. In fact, my landing was so gentle it was like the way a bird spreads its wings just before landing...ever so gentle. The timing has to be just right though. If the chute is flared too late you hit the ground hard and fast. If it's flared too early, your forward speed and descent stop momentarily and then gravity brings you straight down. I now appreciate watching how a bird comes in for a landing and how it must have practiced to spread its wings at the precise time so it doesn't injure itself.

"Unfortunately, that's what happened to Henry. They came down a bit faster than they should have. He didn't lift his legs high enough in those last seconds and he sprained his right leg when it touched the ground too soon. He was wobbling yesterday after the jump and its worse today. He's going to get it x-rayed."

"They be payin' for that?"

"No, the waivers we signed remove any responsibility on their part. Perhaps that is why they have an age restriction, too. Justin wanted to come so much but you have to be eighteen or older. I think Henry said there is a company in Saskatoon that will allow younger people if an adult signs off for them, but I am not certain of that."

"Praise the Lord for that. You don't want that young child flyin' through the air. If I had my way best time to be doin' that when you be in your nineties. At least if somet'ing happens your time be up at any time and you learn how to fly before the angels come for you!"

Jenny chuckled and then said, "That reminds me, Matti. As I was free falling, I stretched my arms out and flapped them like a bird. So in a way you are right. You do get a precursor of what it is like to fly like an angel!"

"Oh Jen, you best hold on for a minute, I be getting so nervous list'nin' to all this, I have to pee. You hold on now. Don't go away."

Jenny heard the phone clanking on the counter and the sound of Matti running down the hall. A few minutes later she heard the same sounds in reverse.

"There, that feels so much better."

"I almost forgot to tell you something really good which came out of this. We had so much fun watching the videos that the two photographers took of Henry and me. We were amazed how they were able to fly all around us taking photos and videos all the while we are dropping to the earth at an incredible speed!

"Justin was rolling on the floor from laughter seeing the terror in his dad's eyes when he jumped out of the plane. Henry had a panic attack of the first order. 'Look at Dad how he's freaking out!' He kept shouting. And it was true, the expression on my face showed fear but not like Henry. His eyes were wild, his hair sticking straight up in the instructor's face and the white of his teeth were gritting together. His hands were close to his face as if he saw a fast moving train coming towards him. We should have felt sorry for him and yet we couldn't help but laugh. I have never seen Justin so excited and spirit filled. It was so good to see."

"See, there you go now how the Lord be bringin' good out of unbelievable situations. The poor man done somet'ing which helped you three unite better. That moment of fear and pain and sufferin' be all worth it if that young Justin be comin' home to his momma and daddy. That for sure!"

"Why Matti, I never thought of it that way but you are absolutely right. That was the most enjoyable evening we've had together in the three years Henry and I were married. In fact, Matti, when Justin called it a night and went to bed, he patted his dad on the back and came to me and gave me a hug. His words were encouraging too, now that I think of it. He said, "That was awesome...Jen." He hesitated just for a second or two. I think he was almost going to say 'Mom.' Oh, that would have been the icing on the cake. Why Matti, it almost makes me want to go up there again tomorrow!"

"Heaven forbid, no! Your guardian angel be keepin' you safe once; don't you be pushin' your luck now, do you hear?"

Jenny laughed, "Just teasing, Matti. Once is enough for me. All in all, we did have fun and you're right Matti, we were the closest to being a family last night than at any time before. I must say, flying the kite with Justin up on the hill was wonderful, too."

"See, how many times we don't think the man upstairs be workin' but He just waitin' for the right moment and then before you even are aware of it, He done performs a miracle right under your nose. Sometime it take a day or two like now before you see it."

"Matti! You're so insightful today."

"Livin' with Thomas for so long somet'ing has to be rubbin' off. Know what I'm sayin'?"

Jenny nodded. "Yes, I do Matti. How is everyone at the estate?"

"Oh, Thomas and the other men are fine. J.J. and Thomas growin' closer than two peas in a pod. Some days the sight of both of them sittin' on the swing in the gazebo with the Bible between them prayin' to the Lord takes my breath away. Not a day go by for as long as there's a flower in the garden, that son of yours don't be puttin' a flower in the Angel of Thanksgiving basket. He praise and thank the Lord just like his momma. You be a good example for that boy, Jenny. Yes, ma'am you done did a fine job! That's for sure."

"That brings tears to my eyes, Matti. Sweeter than the nicest music I know. Oh, I can hardly wait to see you all. Give everyone a hug for me."

'Yes, I be doin' just that, Jen and promise me not to go jumpin' out of airplanes again. You have enough excitement with them two men at the farm."

"That's for sure, Matti.That's for sure!"

CHAPTER TWENTY-FOUR

"A RE YOU SURE you don't want a courtesy car or a wheel chair, Father? The walk to where we claim our baggage is quite far."

"No, Jenny. I don't think this would be any more difficult than the hills I climb daily at the Poustinia."

Father charged ahead of Jenny and Henry,. "Come, quickly hold my hand," Father jested knowing how much his dear friends liked to hold hands. Henry and Jenny quickened their steps and each took a hold of Father's extended hands.

David's excitement was obvious. It brought back so many memories of when he and Anna attended the theatre in Vienna. How they skimped and saved to see the plays and operas. He wondered if the theatres in Toronto would reflect the beautiful architecturally designed theaters of his homeland.

Both Jenny and Henry were puffing by the time they got to the baggage claim and yet, Father didn't show any sign of fatigue whatsoever. They were amazed by his stamina and energy. Father looked handsome in his black attire. His white beard and flowing long white hair gave him a distinguished look. If it hadn't been for the white collar, he could be mistaken for a musician; a conductor perhaps.

Lauren wanted to meet them at the airport but she had a

rehearsal to attend. There were still a few glitches that had to be ironed out and she would meet them at the hotel.

They could have waited for the hotel bus to pick them up, however when a taxi drove slowly by, Henry hailed it down. He was anxious to get settled in.

A doorman promptly opened the door as soon as the taxi came to a halt at the Marriott Downtown Hotel. Father was the first to exit and headed to the trunk to retrieve his small suitcase, however a bellhop beat him to it.

"They will look after us, Father. Just relax and enjoy the next two days."

The bellhop very efficiently loaded their luggage on a cart and followed the new arrivals into the spacious lobby. While Henry went to register, Father and Jenny discussed the contemporary design of the interior.

"There are no high rise buildings in Vienna or all of Austria," said Father. "The architecture is completely different. Hotels are so ornate, they could be mistaken for a church."

"I've seen many pictures of Europe; some time Henry and I would like to explore more of it. We loved our time spent in Monaco and wished we could have explored more of the French Riviera when we were there to celebrate our first year wedding anniversary. It was so romantic."

"Okay, let's go," said Henry. "I got adjoining rooms and as high up as we could get. The lady at the desk assures me we will be able to see the CN Tower. I wanted a city view as well but she couldn't do both."

"We won't be in the rooms much, Henry. I'm sure the rooms will be fine."

The bell hop had the elevators open and the luggage cart inside. There was easily enough room for all of them.

Father went into Henry and Jenny's room and was taken aback by the spaciousness of the suite. "Oh my, Henry, this is like a small house!"

Henry smiled, "Let's see what yours looks like, Father."

Henry went to a solid door next to the elongated dresser unit and unlocked it. It opened to another door which the bellhop was just unlocking on the other side as Henry had requested him to do.

"Welcome to your room, Sir," said the bellhop as he stepped aside.

"My, my…" Father said, as he entered the room which was the same size as Henry and Jenny's. "Something smaller would have been fine Henry. Oh my, the bed is almost as big as the entire bedroom in the Poustinia. I shall be lost in it!"

They all laughed.

"You will enjoy it in no time. That's a king size bed, Father."

Father shook his head, "I'm afraid I am no king."

The bellhop placed Father's small suitcase on the luggage rack at the foot of his bed and asked if there was anything else they required, "Ice perhaps?"

"No, that will be all for now." Henry handed the young man several folded bills and he left.

They walked over to the window and at ground level was a courtyard with a European style building. "Oh yeah, the lady at the desk did mention that the view would be over a courtyard. Looks like a bit of home down there, Father; maybe it's a church."

"Ah yes, it does look like a church which reminds me Henry, can you please find out where the nearest church is, I would like to attend Mass first thing in the morning."

"I knew that would be your top priority, Father.

"There's a St. Michael's Church not too far from here that has a seven o'clock Mass. We may get back to the hotel late after the play and we lost two hours so it may be hard to get up in the morning.

"Sleep is no longer a problem in my life, Henry, two or three hours is all I need and a short nap during the day."

"Oh, look Henry, Father, I see part of the CN Tower in the distance."

Father studied it for a few minutes and said, "It's so much higher than most of the high rises."

"Actually, Father, I think it's higher than all of them. That's one of the reasons it was built so it could solve the communication problems that were developing due to all the high rises in the area. People were experiencing poor quality television reception because the existing towers were simply not high enough anymore. So they went all out to make it as high as possible."

"Well, they certainly did. It towers over any other building," observed Jenny.

Henry nodded and walked closer to the window. "They not only solved the communications problems but also created a structure that has become one of the architectural engineering wonders of the world. See that doughnut shape near the top," Henry turned to see if Father and Jenny saw what he was referring to and then continued, "Inside that dome is where all the transmitting equipment is held. I always thought the dome was made of concrete and steel but it actually is a very thin fiber glass-rayon fabric that is inflated into its balloon-like shape and kept under constant pressure to keep it blown up. It has to be made of something that not only protects all of the transmission equipment but also allows the signals coming in and going out unimpeded."

"Henry, are you ever smart; how do you know all this?"

"I was about to ask the same question." Both Jenny and Father looked at Henry who was beaming from ear to ear.

"Actually, I read up on it a few days before we left on this trip. That's why I am excited to see it if we can work it into our schedule sometime tomorrow. But I was also going to say that above the doughnut shaped radome was built a seven storey building!"

Henry's voice was rising with excitement. "Look! Above the dome is the revolving restaurant, two observation decks, a glass floor and so many other areas which I can't remember. Imagine building all this up in the sky! It's unbelievable how they lifted all that concrete and steel up the sides of the tower."

"Praise God, what gifts He has bestowed upon man to create such wonders," muttered Father.

"Who on earth would have climbed up there to build the antenna?" Jenny wondered.

"Actually, Jenny, it was built on the ground and lifted in sections—"

"But how!?"

"I would have loved to be here when they did that, Jen. They brought in this huge, special helicopter which was designed especially for a project like this. I believe there were forty four sections to the antenna. They were all lifted up there by the helicopter and set into place."

"When was this project completed, Henry?" Father wanted to know.

"It was in 1975 that the last section of the antenna was bolted into place making the Tower the amazing wonder that it is today!"

"Wow, what a commentary, Henry! They should hire you to give tour guides. I still feel the adrenalin flowing through my body. I can't imagine workers building at that height! Just thinking on it makes me dizzy."

"And me, too, Jenny. Even the thought of taking an elevator up to the top makes me jittery. Jesus, Mary and Joseph would have to help me. I have been down at ground level for all of my life. To fly in a big commercial airplane for the first time was excitement enough!"

Just then there was a knock on the door. Jenny rushed back into their room and opened the door fully expecting room service.

"Surprise! Hi, Jenny or rather, Mom!"

"Lauren!! It's so good to see you!" The two women rushed into each other's arms and warmly embraced.

Father and Henry came back into the room to see what the commotion was all about.

"Hi Dad. Hi Grandpa. Oh, you look so distinguished, Grandpa. I love your white beard and long hair. You look like a prophet. You would be perfect in the play!"

Lauren didn't know who to hug first. She opted for Father.

"My, my, Lauren, you seem to grow taller and more beautiful each time I see you."

"And you never change, Father."

She turned to Henry and they stared at one another for a long moment. Tears surfaced in their eyes. Henry opened his arms and his little girl fell into them. They just warmly embraced. Henry was too emotional for the first few moments to speak. He simply patted Lauren's shoulder and nodded.

"Oh, it's so exciting being here, Lauren, we can hardly wait to see the play and watch you perform and dance!" said Jenny.

"Yes, yes, it's been a life time since I attended a performance. Oh, how Anna and I enjoyed the operas."

"I think you will really enjoy this, Father, it's right down your alley, straight from the Bible!"

"Yes, yes, that is one of my favorite stories. Joseph has such a forgiving heart. A true soldier for the Lord and blessed unimaginably."

"How is the play going, Lauren?" Henry wanted to know.

"It's so much fun but challenging and exhausting all at the same time, if you know what I mean. We have 'clean up' rehearsals once or twice a week and also do several afternoon matinée shows along with the evening performance. So, we're quite busy!"

"Wow, that must be tiring!" Jenny said, her voice carrying a tone of compassion.

"Well, Monday is dark, meaning we get it off. Also every morning is off as well, so we do get a chance to recuperate."

"And they're all young and full of life and energy and doing what God wants of them!" Father blurted out.

"That's exactly right, Grandpa, I love what I'm doing! I couldn't be happier."

"I've read some of the reviews and they are fantastic. And Donny Osmond is making quite the hit."

"He's amazing, Dad, he plays the part of Joseph, perfectly. I can hardly wait for you all to see the play and we can talk about it." Lauren reached into her pocket and excitedly exclaimed, "Have I got a great surprise for you! I was able to work out a deal with the stage manager and I got the very best seats in the theater! Normally, we get 'house seats' which are ten rows back just off center aisle…but," by now Lauren was shaking and shimmying like Coco would on the farm and finally burst out, "I got you front row balcony seats! These are absolutely excellent seats with more of an overview of the whole stage! From there you will be able to see all the action close-up, the expression on the actors' faces and it will seem as if you are on stage with the performers."

Jenny raised her hands in excitement. "It will be wonderful being able to see you first hand like that. And thank you for the tickets!"

"Yes, Lauren, I have attended many plays but never sat in the front row of the balcony above the stage. Anna and I could never afford that."

"I thought you would enjoy being up close, Grandpa, to see the stage and orchestra. And...I would like you to come an hour and a half earlier and have a tour of the back stage! Normally we can give tours after the show, but there's a party after with the 'big wigs' and I want you to meet Donny."

Once again, Jenny raised her hands in excitement. "That's so wonderful, Lauren! It's such a bonus to have you as part of the show and get all of these extras. I feel like Matti, I'm so excited, I might be using the bathroom all night!"

They all laughed.

Father kept shaking his head slowly from side to side. Father's entire demeanor; his raised hands and the warm, tender smile on his face clearly conveying his fondness for Lauren. "Ach, mein liebes kleines Kind, Oh my dear child, the little girl who sat on my knee is now such a talented young woman. I am so proud of you, Lauren. I thank the Lord for letting me live long enough to see you live out your dream."

"I am so happy that you came along, Grandpa. I was hoping and praying that you would. You're the main reason I was able to get those seats for you all."

"That's great, Lauren. So what is our time like for the rest of the afternoon?" Henry checked his watch and it read four fifteen.

"Well, we haven't much time. The play opens at eight o'clock and you need to come in the back door of the theatre which is in the alley around six to six fifteen. A security guard will let you in. I won't be able to give you as an extensive a tour as I could after the performance but we can take about a half hour to show you around. I hope Donny is there. He's a great guy. You guys can probably have an early dinner here at the hotel and take a cab to the theatre. It's actually not too far from here, just a couple of blocks."

"Yes, we can walk. So much is missed when taking a taxi. We are here to enjoy a new city and all it has to offer tourists!"

"Grandpa, you're a party man!"

Father quickly shook his head and waved his hands, "Nein, nein, meine Liebe, Lauren!" A broad grin covered Father's blushing face.

They all laughed.

"Can you have dinner with us, Lauren?" Jenny wanted to know.

"Yes, that would be great. I can join you and have a light salad or something. It's not good dancing with too full of a stomach."

"Well, you three go along and have a visit. I would enjoy a short nap before dinner. Perhaps, fifteen minutes?"

"Yes, that's fine, Father."

Father Engelmann turned and walked into his adjoining room muttering under his breath, "I have never seen such a huge bed, its large enough for ten people!"

CHAPTER TWENTY-FIVE

THEY DECIDED TO take a cab rather than walk. The taxi cab driver knew exactly where to go. Over the years, he had driven many of the performers to the back lane entrance to the Elgin Theater. A black man was sitting on a chair beside the door making sure only authorized personnel gained entrance to the back stage.

"I'd bet my last dollar that you're Lauren's parents." Looking at Father he added, "and you're the amazing grandfather she keeps talking about."

"You're right on both accounts, I'm Henry Pederson," and gesturing to the right, "this is my wife, Jenny." Pointing his hand still further to the right, "and this is Father Engelmann."

"Nice to meet you folks, I'm Billy Bob." He smiled showing brilliant white teeth and then looked down at a clipboard he was holding. He checked off the names and then asked Henry to initial beside each one he had checked off. He reached over to the door jamb and pushed a button. A loud buzzer sounded and the door swung open. "Go right in. Lauren is waiting for you."

"Hi, Mom and Dad!" Lauren exclaimed, as she ran down the hall towards them. "Hi, Grandpa!" Lauren swung her arms around Henry and kissed him on the cheek. She did the same with Jenny and Father. "I'm so excited to show you around!"

"So are we!" responded Jenny.

"Come, follow me." Lauren took Father's hand and pulled him along down the hallway dodging crew members getting things set for the opening. Lauren tried to introduce her parents and Father to them as they passed by.

Henry couldn't get over how huge the back stage was! People were all over; props and costumes hanging from walls and ceiling.

"This is unbelievable, Lauren."

"Yeah, it's quite the set up. When the play is on and performers have to change costumes, it simply comes down and the dressers come and change them right in the wings. And look up there, all the sets for the different scenes are hoisted up into the air above us and brought down according to when the sets are needed."

"That's amazing, Lauren!" exclaimed Jenny. "I never dreamed there was this amount of space and height. Everything would have to be so well coordinated."

"Yes, many times it could be described as perfectly timed, organized confusion. All at once it's all there with the new sets in place and the show goes smoothly on."

And then Lauren said something that especially impressed Father.

"The choreography behind the scenes is as important as the choreography on stage!"

"That's well said, Lauren," commented Henry.

"Oh look, there's Donny. Donny, I want you to meet my grandpa and parents." Lauren rushed over to Donny and introduced her family.

"Very nice to meet you. Welcome to the show!"

The star of the show shook hands with Henry and Jenny and then with Father. "How do you do, Mr. Osmond?"

"Please call me, Donny." He shook Father's hand and asked, "Is this your first time in Toronto?"

Father nodded. "Yes and the first time in an airplane! Actually the second, a long time ago I did go up in a very small plane."

"That's great, Father."

"I loved watching you in your TV series. You and your sister have such wonderful voices. It was such a great family show," said Jenny.

"Marie is coming next week. If you're staying that long, please come back and you can meet her."

"Unfortunately, we are heading to Ottawa the day after tomorrow," replied Henry.

"Donny," one of the crew members hollered. "We need you over here when you're done."

"Well, I best be on my way. It was a pleasure meeting all of you."

Henry hesitated for a split second and then went for it. "Donny, would you have a minute to take a picture with us? Our friends back home will drool with envy."

Jenny had her hands touching together in front of her as if praying he would and an accompanying look that was filled with hopeful anticipation that Donny would say 'yes.'

"Sure! No problem at all."

Jenny let out a yelp and clapped her hands. Henry handed Lauren his pocket camera and they all posed with Donny. Donny offered to take one with Father Engelmann and finally a crew member took one with Lauren and her family. They all thanked Donny and waved him off.

"Oh, look at all the children coming in. Are they in the play?" Jenny wanted to know.

"Yes, we have a choir of fifty kids for every show. They have to move backstage here as well. We have wranglers, people in charge of keeping them where they are supposed to be on the stairs to the right and left of the stage. Come, I want to show you the makeup room and meet all the people who make us look gaudy yet, from a distance very glamorous!" Lauren winked and took Father's hand.

On the way, Lauren stopped at several rooms. The first one they peeked into was where all the wigs and head gear was kept. It was eerie to see row upon row of plastic shaped heads supporting one hairpiece after the other. The next room housed all the shoes. Hundreds of them! Jenny was reluctant to leave the room she was so fascinated by all the designs!

The sewing room was next. They went in to meet the seamstress. "Hi, Dorothy, I'd like you to meet my grandpa and parents. They came from Regina to see the show."

After the introductions, Henry said, "To be honest, Dorothy, we came to see Lauren dance and perform!"

"Lauren is a very good dancer, Mr. Pederson."

"Dorothy not only does repairs to the costumes but also designs them. She has a wonderful imagination and the ability to choose and select the right fabric and color and design for the part with uncanny ability. We are so fortunate to have her! If we had time, I'd love to show you some of her sketches. Very creative, Dad. You'd especially be interested being an artist yourself."

"I'm going to have to hire your daughter to be my agent, Mr. Pederson!"

"I would love to see them."

"Maybe next time, Dad, we better be moving on. Thanks Dorothy for letting us in."

Just before they went into the make-up room, Lauren had her family peek into the laundry room. "This gets pretty smelly sometimes. It's where all the performers' underwear goes. The clothes are washed daily and put out for pick up the next day," explained Lauren.

After the tour, Lauren took them down in front of the stage where the seats were. They passed some of the children already seated on the stairs and stopped to peek into the orchestra pit. Most of it was below the stage except for two rows of musicians and the conductors who stand just high enough for the conductor to see what was happening on stage.

"This is where performers' guests normally sit. They are the "house seats" but look where you are sitting." Lauren pointed straight up to the three balconies which were tiered up from one another. "Believe it or not, yours is the first one lowest to the stage."

"Wow," said Henry. "Are you sure we don't have to pay for this?"

"I agreed to do some extra work but it's just a drop in the bucket for all you did for me."

"Ah, Lauren that is so nice," Jenny remarked.

Father had both hands to the side of his face and was still gazing at the gold decorated balcony they were going to sit in, in a state of bliss, "If only my Anna could be here."

Lauren came over and gave Father a big hug. "I am so glad you are happy, Grandpa. I love you."

Tears surfaced in Father's eyes.

"Wait here, I want to see if I can find an usher to take you up to your seat so you don't have to go back outside and deal with the crowds."

While Lauren was gone, they looked around at the immense size of the theater.

"This reminds me of some of the opera houses in Vienna. The one Anna and I went to the most often was the 'The State Opera.' This one has more gold and marble gilding."

"Look at that dome, Father, it resembles a huge, gold king's crown surrounding the light," observed Henry.

"I love the plaster cherubs and the delicate gold ornamental works all over," remarked Jenny as her eyes swept the ceiling and walls.

"Yeah, you love anything to do with angels."

"You do too."

"I must admit it's beautiful and look at the crown molding and all the ornamentation. I can't begin to imagine how an architect begins to design all this and make it all come together so well. Wow!"

"There was just one time Anna and I saved enough money to sit in a balcony. It wasn't directly over the stage like this but Anna was so happy she cried through most of the opera."

"Dad, Dad, over here." Lauren shouted. "Come, I have someone that will take you up to the balcony."

They could have taken an elevator but they preferred to walk and take in the elegant staircase and pictures adorning the walls. The usher gave them each a program booklet with a colorful front cover depicting Joseph's coat and then held a curtain open for them to get to their balcony. It had four seats in the front row and four more behind that were elevated.

The view of the stage and orchestra pit was incredible. It was almost as if they would be able to touch the performers.

"Wow, what a view! It's as amazing as Joseph's Technicolor Dream Coat!" jested Henry.

Father and Jenny were in awe of it all. It was such a special privilege to be seated there. Jenny loved to watch the people coming in from this vantage point. She felt like one of the ornate cherubs who had come alive and was floating above the stage!

CHAPTER TWENTY-SIX

HENRY HELD HIS breath as the fire red curtains opened and an unseen female narrator began to introduce the Biblical story of Joseph. He could hardly wait to see his daughter dance in the scenes. What a wonderful culmination to her hard work and dedication over all those years. Henry was momentarily caught up in memories of how he and Julean drove her to dance lessons since she was seven years of age. All through elementary school and high school her love of dancing kept her committed to her talent. They were so proud to see her selected to become part of Saskatchewan Express and tour the province and country displaying their dancing talents. Lauren was blessed to be able to go on and pursue her dream.

Here she was; part of a major musical!

The narrator had finished with the prologue and the song, *Any Dream Will Do,* was coming to an end when Henry brought his full attention back to the play.

Jacob and his twelve sons were introduced.

"I love the coat Joseph is wearing; it's so colorful," whispered Jenny.

Henry nodded and reached over and held Jenny's hand. He had trouble staying focused on the play as his mind kept drifting back over time. There were moments when he wasn't sure whose hand he was holding; Jenny's or Julean's. Julean would have loved to see her daughter perform. How quickly time passes, he thought. *Lauren was twenty two years of age. She still looks like she is eighteen. Maybe that's why I don't feel my age either. Why am I thinking of this now!? The best seats in the house and here I am going down memory lane!*

"There's Lauren, Honey." Jenny exclaimed, louder than she should have.

As soon as Henry identified his daughter in the ensemble, all of the other performers simply disappeared. His focus was entirely on Lauren. He watched her every move with so much pride welling up inside, his shirt buttons could pop off at any moment. It was clear to see by anyone, Lauren was in her element. Her eyes sparkled with pure delight and her inner joy was expressed by her genuine, radiant smile. Henry tried to force his attention back to the play but it kept drifting...he wished Julean could see this. Her encouragement kept Lauren motivated so many times and all the sacrifice she made to help her daughter realize her dream. A part of Lauren was dancing for her Mom.

Another set was introduced; Henry hadn't noticed until now that Joseph was already a slave in the hands of the Egyptian millionaire Potiphar. He wondered how Lauren had changed her costume. He was sure he had kept his eyes glued on her. She was now dressed as a harem girl with several others wearing the same dress. Henry tried to imagine the new set coming down behind the scene presently going on. He visualized all the action that was taking place back stage. It fascinated him. Perhaps it would have been better if he wasn't aware of it.

Henry couldn't believe that the first act was coming to a close. The prisoners were surrounding Joseph and encouraging him to go after his dreams. The butler had been released from prison and sent to work for the Pharaoh. He will prepare the way for Joseph to interpret the Pharaoh's dream. Henry got caught up in the closing song; *Go, Go, Go, Joseph*...go Lauren... where was Lauren? Her costume had changed again!

When the first act was over they decided to stay near their seats and just stand up a bit. "You sure seemed agitated during the play, Henry. Are you okay?" inquired Jenny.

"Yeah, my mind kept wandering; I'll try to settle down a bit more in the next act."

Henry was embarrassed that he couldn't respond to many of the comments which Jenny and Father made about the play. He couldn't remember most of it.

Jenny settled into watching the crowds and Father seemed to enjoy doing that as well. It gave one a sense of omnipotence to see where people came from and where they are going. Henry was studying the architecture and how they would have built the huge, expansive dome back in 1913.

They were all delighted with the opening of Act II in which the narrator tells of changes to Joseph's fortunes. The Pharaoh orders Joseph to be brought in to interpret his re-occurring dream. After Joseph does so, the astonished Pharaoh puts him in charge of everything and thus he became the most powerful man in Egypt! The pharaoh is acted out in the style of Elvis Presley and Lauren and her accompanying dancers were in the scene right off.

Henry had finally allowed himself to glance at the other dancers and performers. He was amused by the different costumes especially the funny head pieces the wives wore. Lauren had a watering can in one scene and one of the other wives had a sewing machine on her head. He wondered if Dorothy had designed it. He enjoyed the part where Lauren pretended to be an adoring fan of Joseph's and hugged his leg during most of the number.

Henry was pleased that he had finally got more into the play during the second half. He knew Jenny and Father thoroughly enjoyed all of it. He wondered how closely the play followed the Bible story of Joseph. Father would know of any addition or deviation. Every now and then Henry would turn their way and wished he could be as free in the moment as they were. He was always thinking about something! If his thoughts weren't about Lauren and her success and how happy he was for her, his creative mind would go off on a different tangent analyzing various parts of the play.

Henry marveled over how well, the composer, Andrew Lloyd Webber worked in the various styles of music to depict the different main characters and how quickly the audience recognized and identified with the style of each one. His favorite musical selection was the Elvis inspired rock and roll for the Pharaoh. *Mind you,* Henry thought, *it would have been hard to choose between the country style singing of One More Angel in Heaven or the calypso version for Benjamin.* Henry loved Calypso music, too.

They all couldn't believe the play was nearing an end. Joseph had revealed himself to his brothers and sends for his father. As Joseph dons his colored coat once more, much to everyone's surprise, he was lifted into the air! As he was singing the closing song he flew above the audience seated in the main theatre. To Jenny, Father and Henry it seemed as if he was flying right to them! Henry was so startled and taken aback by this unexpected finale, he hadn't yet noticed that Lauren and several of the dancers jumped off the stage and ran down the aisles to sing the final note and mingle with the audience. Finally, Henry noticed Lauren wave and shout up to him. He immediately stood up and waved back and then he threw a kiss to her with the wave of his hands. Unabashed, he shouted, "I love you!"

Lauren mimicked his every gesture by throwing a kiss back to him along with the same words of affection. Lauren looked at an alarmed lady in the seat directly in front of her who had seen what she and Henry had done. Lauren smiled and said, "It's okay, he's my father." They chuckled and Lauren continued on with her number.

After much confusion, they all finally met in front of the theater and Lauren took them to a nearby restaurant.

"So, is this where you usually come after the show?" Henry asked as they sat at a table for six.

"No, the place we hang out it is a lot louder. This place would be like a library to the one we go to. We usually have a drink and shoot pool. I'm getting to be quite the shark, Dad. You taught me well how to play in the basement recreation room." She tilted her head; I think I can take you."

"No way, dream on sweetie!" Henry replied, sounding a bit like his friend, Eddy Zeigler.

"So how did you like the play?" Lauren was dying to know!

"Yes, I was just waiting to say, Lauren, it was absolutely wonderful! I enjoyed it immensely!" said Jenny.

"I can't say it any better," said Father. "To see you dance up there made me young again. I couldn't stop my feet from tapping. I am very proud of you, Lauren."

"That goes for me too, Honey. I loved the play. I have to admit, I was taken down memory lane for almost the entire first half. I kept thinking about how hard you worked all those years and here you are on stage performing as a professional dancer in a great production!"

Henry then began to portray how his analytical mind worked. "For someone not familiar with the Biblical story of Joseph in the book of Genesis, they would miss a lot if it hadn't been for the narrator."

"Yes, I agree, Henry. She told and guided us through the story of Joseph and his brothers so gently it gave meaning to the different songs and transitioned to the scenes so smoothly," observed Father.

"She did a wonderful job," concurred Jenny. And, you're right, Father, her narration helped the audience to understand the different styles of music. I found the portrayal of the pharaoh through an Elvis Presley style figure very humorous."

"Yeah, that was funny and Benjamin Calypso was great, too. Those were my two favorites," said Henry.

"Mr. Weber did a very fine job in putting this all together. His extensive musical selection mirrored so well the colorful, family-friendly storyline. It was not only most enjoyable, but may motivate people who do not read the Bible to perhaps do so. It brought out many universal themes; envy, jealousy, love, forgiveness and how God can turn all things into good within a family setting. The story depicts how God's divine providence works so perfectly. While Joseph's brothers meant evil for him, God saw it for good." And then Father asked Lauren something which startled her, "Do you attend one of the parishes near here?"

Lauren remained silent for a moment. "I have to be honest with you, Grandpa, I haven't been attending church for a while."

"What do you mean, for a while, Lauren?"

"For a year or so, maybe longer. My schedule is erratic and we are usually up till two or three in the morning and then I sleep till eleven or noon the next day and on Sundays we have a matinée." Lauren said, trying to justify her abstinence.

"The Lord has blessed you with considerable talent, Lauren; He delights in one who is grateful for what they have been given."

"I know, Father..."

"Hi, I am Susan, your server this evening, are you ready to order and would you care for a drink?"

Lauren looked very relieved and quickly picked up the menu which none of them had looked at yet. "Do your white house wines include sauvignon," Lauren asked.

"Yes, they do."

"I'll have a glass of that and a chef salad."

"And for you, Ma'am?"

"Hmm, I'll have a glass of the sauvignon too, and..." Jenny flipped back to the first page of the menu and then said, "The Mediterranean salad is fine for me."

Father just requested water and Henry ordered a glass of red wine and a mushroom and ricotta bruschetta appetizer.

As soon as the waitress left, Lauren changed the subject from what they were discussing prior to the server interrupting them and asked, "What did you think of our hats?"

"I was going to mention that earlier, Lauren. There was considerable light hearted humor throughout just from the costumes alone. I loved the way you and the other wives kept changing head gear. The watering can looked hilarious on you, Lauren."

"Sometimes they fall off, Jenny...or rather Mom. They are still working on ways to fasten the hats more securely," offered Lauren.

"Man, it sure startled me when Joseph started to rise in the closing song. It was totally unexpected. How did they do that, Lauren?" Henry wanted to know.

"Donny was attached to a flying rig, called a Foy. He would be wearing a harness under his costume that would be attached to wires that were rigged on a track. The Foy is operated from off stage by crew members."

"It was a great way to end the play. At first I thought maybe you had arranged for him to fly over to our balcony with a message of love from Lauren!"

"Oh, Dad, you're funny."

"Did you ever meet Andrew Lloyd Weber, Lauren?" Jenny wanted to know.

"Yes, I did, just once. I also met Donny's sister, Marie several times. She's great, very much like Donny."

"So, how did you like Donny's singing?"

"He's a natural for the part." Henry interjected, "But the star of the show as far as I'm concerned was you! Several times I was tempted to send a note up to the narrator to tell the audience how proud I was to see my daughter perform!"

Before Lauren could thank her father for the gesture, Jenny said, "You may not be my birth daughter, Lauren but several times I, too could have run up on stage and gave you a big hug and shouted, 'this is our daughter, isn't she wonderful!'"

"Ah, Mom, that is so nice of you to say that, thanks and thank you too, Dad."

"Well it's true," Henry said with a beaming smile. He reached over and patted Lauren's hand.

"When we attended the opera in Vienna, we usually sat so far back we had to bring binoculars to see the performers but these seats, Lauren, it was like being on stage with the performers. Oh, what a blessing it was to see the white of their teeth and sparkle in their eyes. Never would I have dreamed to have such a privilege to watch a play so close up."

"Did it take you back to the days when you and Anna attended operas?"

"Yes, yes, I had the same difficulty as Henry at times, staying focused on the play. Several times I reached out for Anna's hand, I hope you didn't think I was showing too much affection for you Jenny."

Jenny smiled, "No, not at all Father, I love holding your hand."

"I would like to see the play again." said Henry.

"Everything is sold out, Dad. You might be able to purchase some tickets from a scalper which may cost you double or more."

"Even so, it would be worth seeing you perform again and perhaps this time I can keep my mind on the play."

"Sometimes the other performers' guests do not show up due to some circumstance. I'll check around and give you call in the morning if any tickets are available."

"Okay, that would be great and I'll do some checking at the hotel. Sometimes the concierge can help out. In any case, we want to see the Art Gallery of Ontario and the CN Tower. If the Argonauts were playing it would have been fun to attend a football game at the Rogers Center."

"Wouldn't it have been something if the Saskatchewan Roughriders were playing!?"

"Yeah, I never thought of checking their schedule. We could have always coordinated our trip to when the Riders played here. You would have enjoyed that, Father. Do you recall when my dad and mom went to the Grey Cup in B.C.? That's all dad spoke of for years after."

"This trip has already been more than enough. It is all good, Henry."

"So how was the plane ride, Grandpa?" Lauren wanted to know. "I think dad said this was your first flight ever."

"No, I did go up on a small crop spraying plane when I studied for the priesthood in Gravelbourg but this was the first in a commercial plane. It seems hard to believe that a man who has lived to see one hundred has never flown more, but it is true. When Anna and I lived in Austria we never went on lengthy trips. When the war came along, travel came to a halt. When we came to Canada it was by sea and when we landed in Regina by train, we never left. We never owned a car and either walked or took the streetcar if we wanted to go somewhere in the city. Owning a store tied us down and when Anna became ill, our dream to go back to the old country faded in time. So, this is a first for me on a big plane, Lauren and one that in the remaining time I have left on this earth, I will never forget and will always be grateful to your father for."

Just then their orders came and they continued to talk about the different scenes in the play and also about how the Elgin and Winter Garden theaters are a pair of stacked theatres. Father Engelmann couldn't believe that the Winter Garden was seven stories above the theater they were seated at that evening.

"They are the last surviving Edwardian stacked theaters in the world. There is quite a history behind both theaters," said Lauren between mouthfuls and then added, "There are some brochures in the main lobby. I'll bring some to you when we meet tomorrow."

"Yes, that would be very interesting to read up on that, Lauren," said Jenny.

"Well, I hope we can get tickets so we can go again tomorrow night."

"I'll try to Dad and call you first thing in the morning."

"Not if you're still going out on the town. You will more than likely be sleeping."

"No, I promise I'll be up. I'll set my alarm and my roommate's, too."

"Oh, so what is her name? Is she in the play, too?" Henry wanted to know.

There was a long silence and then Lauren said, "It's not a girl, Dad, it's a guy. His name is Eldon."

A silence fell at the table.

"Are you living with him…?" Henry's words trailed off.

"Well, sort of…it's not what you think."

Henry gazed at his daughter not sure what to think or say. He felt embarrassed that Father was there and even Jenny. Had he failed his daughter? He wanted to look at Father and hoped he would say something. Henry would give anything to know what he was thinking. If Lauren was actually living with the boy it would be considered a sin."

"Oh, Dad. I'm sorry, I don't want to ruin your evening but...I want to be honest with you."

Henry nodded, "Yes, I would want you to be, Lauren."

Henry didn't think now was the time or place to discuss this further. He checked his watch: eleven thirty. "Well, it's getting late and we have another full day tomorrow."

"Yes, yes, and I want to be up in time to attend the parish you mentioned this afternoon, was it St. Michael's?"

"Yeah, that's it. Oh, we will be up I'm sure. So, should we hail a cab or walk?"

"Let's walk!" blurted Father. "Let's see what Toronto is like. If it's anything like Vienna, the streets will be packed."

"You can count on it, Grandpa and the hotel is just a couple of blocks away."

"Yes, we noted that when we took a taxi earlier."

Everyone hugged Lauren and thanked her again for a most delightful evening of entertainment.

"If we are out, leave a message at the hotel lobby and where you can be reached. It would be nice to have dinner together again tomorrow."

Lauren nodded, "Okay,"

"So, are you still going out? You must be exhausted, better to go home, no?"

"Oh no, it's too early and I'm still all hyped up from the show. I'll head over to where everyone hangs out and shoot some pool."

Henry wanted to say more to his daughter but decided not to. He hugged Lauren once again and watched as she walked down the crowded street. He whispered to his guardian angel to watch over and protect her. Just as he finished the prayer, Lauren stopped, turned and side stepped a few passersby to keep her gaze on her father. They waved to one another and Henry couldn't help but shout to her, "Please, go to church this Sunday..."

CHAPTER TWENTY-SEVEN

J ENNY COULD BARELY believe her eyes as she stepped through the glass sliding doors into the Ottawa Macdonald-Cartier International Airport terminal. There was her son, J.J. and Nora with Jimmy in between them holding his parents' hands. Jenny was so thankful that her relationship with J.J. was finally healed the year James died and was growing stronger by the year. Such an image of coming home to a loving family was a dream come true after so many years of coldness and strife. "Thank you sweet, Jesus," Jenny whispered as she waved back to J.J.

"Hi Mom, it's good to see you," said J.J. and Nora almost in unison.

Jenny gave J.J. a hug and kisses on his cheeks and then turned and did the same with Nora. Next she knelt down and opened her arms to Jimmy. He hadn't seen Jenny in almost seven months and was a bit shy.

"Are you going to give Grandma a hug and kiss? I missed you so much, Jimmy."

He looked up at his mother and she nodded. "Go ahead, Jimmy."

Jimmy let go of Nora's hand and went to Jenny.

"I see we just have to visit more often, don't we?" Jenny gently embraced Jimmy and tenderly hugged him. She would have loved to tickle his tummy at the same time hug him more vigorously but thought to hold off on that for now. She stood up and was going to introduce Henry and Father but they were already doing that.

"Nice to see you again, J.J., Nora," said Henry and turned to Father. "You remember Father from the wedding?"

"Yes, I do. Your hair and beard seems whiter and longer but I still remember your warm smile," remarked J.J.

"That's kind of you to say, J.J., It's nice to see you once more." The men shook hands and then Father turned to Nora, "So pleased to see you and your family, Nora."

"Same for me, Father Engelmann. You are in for one enthusiastic welcome at the estate. Matti can hardly wait for you to come. I think she is more excited to see you than for Jenny." Nora winked at Jenny.

Jenny chuckled and took hold of Jimmy's hand and together they made their way to the exit.

Just outside of the terminal door a shiny, black limousine was parked. It was one of those extended kind that looked like three cars were welded together. The chauffeur was trying to console a commissionaire who by the looks of it was asking him to move on. The driver was relieved to see J.J. and his guests. He rushed over and took the luggage and carried it to the trunk. J.J. opened several of the doors and the arrivals began to climb in.

As soon as the limo sped away, Father was the first to speak, "My, my, all this comfort and luxury is going to spoil me for sure," and then Father quickly added in jest, "Henry, you may have to renovate the Poustinia upon our return!"

Henry played right along, "Yes, I was already thinking of adding another two stories. It may not be the CN Tower, but it's a start."

"Oh, one storey will be just fine…for now, as long as it's big enough for one of those big, king sized beds!"

They all laughed.

Sitting in such a spacious interior, reminded Father of

another time he felt like a highfalutin business man. He decided to carry on with the conversation by sharing his story.

"Did I tell you of the time a similar limo, a lot smaller than this one, picked me up in front of the grocery store which I owned back in 1957? The kindly chauffeur took me to my lawyer's office which was on the eighteenth floor. At the time, the building was one of the larger high rises in the city. What a day that was. I closed the biggest deal of my life." Turning to J.J. he continued, "I know you're an important business man and close deals that go into the millions and perhaps billions but the deal I closed that day was like a million dollars."

"That's a lot of money," blurted out Jimmy.

"Yes, yes, it is Son."

Father went on to tell how he sold his small business to Safeway. How he sat in the boardroom surrounded by an entourage of lawyers and professional business men highly skilled in their field, all working together to help him get a good price for his store.

"What a day that was!"

Father had related the story so well it was almost as if he were reliving it, especially the part when the chauffeur stopped for him to buy a cigar and then toured around the city's park and waterfront.

He absently reached into his inside jacket pocket for a cigar! "Oh, my goodness, how easily one can slip back into a bad yet enjoyable habit. That was the only time since coming to Canada that I smoked a cigar."

"We can stop and get you one, Father," offered J.J.

"No, no, I was only jesting."

"I remember that day, too, Father. Mom was working for you at the time. She was so excited the day your store sold and the good price you got for it. She could hardly make supper that evening she was so happy for you."

"Yes, we had some good times in the store..." Father's words trailed off and a silence settled into the limo interior.

Once again, Father started the conversation; he asked Nora if she was working during the day.

"No, Jimmy keeps me busy and we are expecting an addition to our family!"

"Oh, Nora, that is such good news! When is the due date?" Jenny wanted to know.

"It will be another six months give or take a week or two one way or the other."

Jenny hugged little Jimmy who was seated beside her. "Soon you will have a little sister or brother to play with you."

"I hope it's a boy," said Jimmy.

"Well, time will tell."

Both Henry and Father congratulated J.J. and Nora. Suddenly everyone jerked to the left as the limo swerved to just miss another car moving into their lane on the freeway. When the car resumed its coasting speed, J.J. offered everyone a drink of their choice but all declined except for Jimmy who sipped on a Coca Cola.

Everyone sat back as the limo headed south for the two and half hour drive to the estate. While Henry and J.J. began to discuss their respective businesses, Father began to doze off. Nora, Jenny and Jimmy began to play "I spy with my little eye" trying to guess objects in the car. Soon Jimmy fell asleep on Jenny's lap. She gently stroked his head and gazed out of the window recalling the time she lived in Ottawa. Some memories were good and some sad but she made no attempt to dismiss any of them. There was one memory she wished she hadn't revived and that was of her dear friend, Tammy. She recalled several occasions when she went to the airport to greet her friend home. They had such wonderful times together. There was nothing they didn't share with other. They were closer than sisters. Jenny always thought Tammy knew her better than she knew herself. And then, there was that unforgettable day when the phone rang. It took her days to accept that her dearest friend had been shot and killed at a Pro-Life rally in front of an abortion clinic. So many years had passed since that memorable day, yet one never forgets...

Jenny's thoughts were interrupted as the limo entered the gates of the estate much sooner than she expected. She didn't recognize the security guard. The chauffeur and he exchanged words but Jenny couldn't hear as the window separating the driver from the passengers was closed. Slowly, the limo proceeded and Jenny remembered driving up the lane with James to the immense mansion. She was so nervous at that time and she still felt a twinge of it now. It was the beginning of a lonely marriage and yet it ended happy. The scripture, Romans 8:28 rang so true, God does cause all things to work together for the good. Thank You, dear Lord, were the last words running through Jenny's mind as the limo came to a halt underneath the huge canopy.

Nora came over to Jenny and lifted Jimmy off her lap. "Matti will come running any minute so you better get ready."

Jenny smiled at her daughter-in-law and looked up at the front door. Sure enough, Matti was already running down the steps to greet her guests. She was beside herself. She flung her arms around her beloved mistress before Jenny was barely out of the limo!

"Oh Jen, I be tryin' to calm myself all day, even took two sleeping pills but nothing do any good. I so excited, I put a note on the bathroom door 'out of order' so nobody be using it. You know how excited I get! Henry! You look more handsome each time I see you!" Matti gave Henry a quick hug and asked, "Where be the holy man!? I thought he be comin'?"

"He was snoozing last time I looked at him. Oh, here he comes!" said Jenny.

"Welcome, Father Engelmann! This estate be surely blessed today to have the honor of such a holy man comin' to visit. I just have to give you a hug, Father, I don't mean no disrespect."

"No, no, Matilda, I would feel totally left out if I didn't get the same affection you showed to Jenny and Henry. I could even use a little extra!"

Just as Lauren had taken Father's hand to show him the back stage, Matti took Father's hand and led him up the stairs.

Jenny and Henry followed them as the driver and J.J. retrieved their guests' luggage from the trunk.

"Ask, Charles to come help with the suitcase, Matti!" J.J. shouted just before she entered the house.

J.J. wasn't sure if Matti heard until he heard her shout to Charles, "They be needing you outside, Charles!"

Wow, Jenny thought, the atmosphere is so relaxed compared to when she first came. James would never permit such informality. Jenny was glad James had started to change it all in his last months on the estate and J.J. was following through.

Jenny hugged Charles on his way out. He welcomed Henry and Father in his crisp British accent, shook their hands and quickly disappeared outside.

Things looked much the same. The furniture hadn't changed at all in the living room. Jenny followed Matti into the kitchen and asked for some orange juice.

"Made it fresh not more than an hour ago. I knew you would want some."

Matti handed Jenny a glass of juice and as if reading Jenny's mind, she said, "Thomas be waitin' for you in the garden, Jenny."

"I was just going to ask if he was outside."

"He could hardly wait for you to come. He tried hard not to show it but he not foolin' me. He said he wants to be outside when you come out onto the patio. He said it always gave him so much joy when you were in the garden. He swore so many times that the sun be your shadow. All he be seein' is light all around you."

"Oh, Matti, Thomas is such a kindly, wise man. He reminds me so much of Father Engelmann. Their manner is very much alike."

"I agree, Jen. Many times, I visit with him and Ramon in the shed it be like we're in church."

Jenny smiled. She drank the rest of her juice and made her way to the patio doors and stepped outside. She cupped her hand above her eyes to shield the bright sun. Out of the corner of her eye, she saw a movement behind the hedge. She turned and there was Thomas, her dear friend. He was holding a pair of cutting shears; making it appear as if he were trimming the shrubbery.

He smiled, showing his white teeth. He had aged some but in a good way. He appeared more kindly if that were possible. As Jenny made her way towards him, his warm smile spread across his face; his eyes were filled with love and admiration. To Thomas, Jenny was the closest person on earth he had ever known to reflect what he imagined Jesus to be like. He never felt that he was black and she was white. They were colorless. *They were as God saw his children with perfect love.*

Thomas stepped from behind the brush and walked slowly towards his mistress. "Welcome home, Miss Jenny. The estate was never the same when you left. A little of the soul of this garden was uprooted. I felt it the moment you walked out the front door and I feel it returning the moment you come back for a visit. As much as I love to see you, it just takes what seems forever to readjust when you leave."

"Oh, Thomas you always knew how to make my heart soar. No wonder you were such a good lawyer, your words wrap around people's hearts so easily."

Jenny walked swiftly towards Thomas and gave him a warm hug. "I missed you so, Thomas. Every morning in Regina when I walked through the yard or gazed out the kitchen window at the garden, I thought of you. You have so much of the Creator within you; the flowers grow out of sheer joy to serve you."

"Now, who really is the one good with words?"

Henry watched Jenny and Thomas from the patio doors. He wondered if there could ever be a closer relationship between a white and black person. If only the entire world could know the utter joy in unconditional love. It was only through Jenny that he saw it so plainly. He didn't know if he should interrupt them or not. The thought only lingered for a moment and he stepped out onto the patio.

What an incredible garden, Henry observed as he walked down the paving stone path. He could smell the herb in the air. It was thyme. He recognized the scent from Jenny's garden stone pathway in Regina. Thomas was the first to notice Henry and waved.

"Welcome to Greystone Manor, Mr. Pederson."

"Please call me Henry, Thomas. I thought we had passed that formality." The two men shook hands.

"Thank you, Henry. I was just saying how good it is to have Miss Jenny visit us. We all miss her so when she is gone. The garden, in fact, the entire estate is just not the same. I sometimes wish there were two of her like there are two Angels of Thanksgiving."

"You can see why I liked it so much here, Henry."

Henry nodded and smiled, "I see there are still a lot of Monarchs here. Ours have thinned out at the farm."

"Perhaps it's because we are nearer to their destination."

"I think they don't want to leave the paradise you have established here for them, Thomas. Look at all the flowers blooming and I know more will bloom right up until October. I wouldn't be surprised that many simply choose to stay and die out of sheer delight."

A Monarch settled on Henry's shirt and Jenny reached over to entice it onto her hand. It flew away.

"I'm anxious to visit the gazebo." Jenny reached out for Henry and said, "Quickly, hold my hand. Come along, too, Thomas."

"I have to put the tools away and close up the shed. I will see you at dinner. It is very nice to see you again, Miss Jenny, Henry."

Henry could feel Jenny's heart race as they turned the corner by the huge lilac shrub and the white marble angel came into view. The statue was surrounded by wildflowers still in full bloom. As they neared, they could see that the Angel of Thanksgiving basket was filled with a beautiful bouquet of white daises with the gold center. They were Jenny's favorites. She knew Thomas had placed them in there for her.

Jenny turned and pulled Henry along with her to the swing inside the gazebo. Henry recalled that the last time he sat there with her was the day James had died and she had just finished reading the letter which James had left for her. Jenny had so many heartbreaks in her life and yet she survived them all. One would never know by looking at her that she had any problem at all in her life or a care in the world.

As soon as they sat down, Henry raised his arm and Jenny nestled her head into his chest. He pushed on the floor and set the swing into a gentle motion. Neither spoke; they just lived in the moment allowing each to think thoughts that floated through their minds. *They were separate and yet one, they were free and yet united, they loved one another unconditionally, they were one in Christ and that made all the difference.*

It was early the next morning when Matti came down the winding walk and saw Jenny swinging on the gazebo.

"I knew that you'd be here, Jen. I just love to see you swing there, it be like lookin' at a baby sleepin' in a crib. It take a long time to get that image out of my mind when you leave."

Matti looked at the Angel of Thanksgiving's basket. It was overflowing with wildflowers. "I see you been thanking the Lord for your blessings, Jen."

"There is just so much to be thankful for, Matti. The estate has become so peaceful and everyone has grown so close. And just look how beautiful the garden is; it just seems to go on forever. I see the butterflies have started to return to Mexico."

"Yes, I can tell that some just don't want to leave. So much nectar and flowers that bloom all the time until it freezes. It must be confusing for them, thinkin' it still be summer in October! Then again, 'spect many just figure if they goin' to die, what better place to be!?"

Jenny nodded. "We were talking about that yesterday. It's a butterfly's paradise here. Thomas is such a master landscape artist. He not only plants herbs and flowers so strategically for us to enjoy while the weather permits but also keeps all of nature in mind as well. Just look how the garden abounds with birds, bees and butterflies."

Matti sat next to Jen on the swing and patted her hand. She gazed into Jenny's eyes and said. "I can see pure happiness in your eyes Jen. That man of yours be doing all the right things."

"It couldn't be better, Matti. Every day is like heaven. I love him so much. There's only one thing that could make it all completely and utterly perfect."

"And I know what that be...you shared with me a long time ago your heart's desire. Even though your eyes be sparkling like diamonds, I still see the gem you be wantin' to give that man. It be written on your pretty face."

"Is it that obvious, Matti?"

Her dear, insightful friend nodded, a grin growing from ear to ear. "You been tryin', Honey?"

"Yes, I was so sure I had conceived the night of our third anniversary but I noticed that I am still spotting. Perhaps, I am too old. The doctor tells me that the eggs deteriorate as time goes on but when I was healed, so too were all the eggs in the ovary. When the gynecologist checked me over at that time he said the eggs were that of a younger woman. I just feel this is one of the reasons I came back. It's been such a lifelong dream, Matti. I just know it can happen."

"Well, jus' look in the Bible and read about Elizabeth, Mary's cousin. She be well on in age and she conceived a child. Good thing you not be doubtin' or you be ending up like Elizabeth's husband Zachariah. When the angel told him that Elizabeth would bear a child, he didn't think it was possible and so he was struck dumb, unable to speak until the child be born. And look at Sarah, she done give a child to Abraham who was hundred years old and she was ninety! See Jenny, anyt'ing is possible with the Lord!"

"I hope I don't have to wait until I'm ninety, Matti!"

The two women laughed.

"You jus' keep prayin' honey child, the Lord be listenin' and, I too, be prayin' everyday that a child fill that belly of yours."

"I am praying, too, Matti. It's always on my mind and I'm starting to fast as well."

"Now, that get the Lord's attention right quick, Jen. I be cutting back a bit, too, Jen. Do you notice I be shedding an ounce or two!" Matti jested.

"Why, yes, Matti you do look slimmer. Could it be for Charles? I noticed when he came for the luggage you and he seem to have a special communication going on." Jenny winked and tilted her head with a knowing smile.

"You know, at first I ask myself, what could a high, refined man like Charles possibly see in a lowly island girl? Perhaps it be my cookin' that be confusing the man, I first thought. As time go on I see somet'ing else be stirrin' inside him and me." Matti's eyes sparkled, "We be going out on occasion and he even held my hand at the movies." Matti hesitated but decided to go on, "His cottage is next to mine and at times I visit in his and sometimes in mine but no matter where we be, he gives me a hug before he retires. Now, ain't that somet'ing, Jen?"

"Ahhh, Matti that's so nice to hear. I'm so happy for you."

"I don't know what be comin' of it all but I jus' say to myself, Matti, enjoy what the good Lord gives you. If it's meant to be, somet'ing more than it is, so be it."

"That's a good way to look at it, Matti. I still recall you and Charles dancing together here in the garden the day before you left to work at James' condo."

"I have fond memories of that moment, too. It was the first time since I left the island that a man be dancing with me."

"Well, please keep me updated, Matti. That was a wonderful thing James did giving you and the other staff one of the guest houses for as long you are employed at the estate."

"Yes, that be so generous of the Master, I means Jim. It's right down in black and white that for as long as we live we can stay right here. Ain't that somet'ing? I thought when he passed on and J.J. took over there might some changes but he continues right along just like his daddy. I praise the Lord each day for that boy."

"So, he is doing well?" Jenny wanted to know.

"That son of yours couldn't be better. He turnin' out to be a fine man, father and husband. He don't work on the weekends. Why, I hear him say on the telephone all the time, "I no longer work on the weekends. Whatever it is it will have to wait until first of the week." Sometimes I think I be hearin' things. He rarely misses dinner and on Saturday he be takin' Jimmy out fishing or hiking or bike riding. On Sunday, he take the whole family to church just like the Lord be wantin' all families to do."

"That's so wonderful to hear, Matti. Was that just the result of James coming around like he did in the last year or so?"

"That be helpin' some, Jen but since his daddy passed on, J.J. and Thomas have developed a very close relationship just like Thomas and James done. But I'd say they be even closer... it be kin to a father and son relationship, know what I'm sayin'? It happened jus' like James wanted. On his death bed he say to Thomas, you look after my boy. And sure enough it turned out mighty fine. I jus' praise the Lord every day. Why it be like paradise here, Jen."

"Thomas is such a fine man, Matti. I'm so happy J.J. had the sense to see the incredible mentor in his midst. Thomas has been where both James and J.J. have been. He's very wise, just like Father Engelmann."

"That be truth, Jen. I jus' pray Thomas can keep doing what he so loves a spell longer. His arthritis be acting up somet'ing awful. Some days, he be in so much pain he can hardly pick himself off the chair. His fingers be curling so he can't hold the flower he be wantin' to plant. J.J. orders him to take it easy and have the other workers do it but his love for God's creation is so strong the poor man can't help himself."

Jenny shook her head, her face clearly reflecting such sorrow for Thomas.

"But Ramon be good for Thomas, he help out whenever he can. He knows Thomas so well that he anticipates what the man be thinkin' about doing and he quickly goes and does it before Thomas havin' an opportunity to do it! It's quite the sight to see, Jen." Matti chuckled, "The good Lord's Holy Spirit be always at work, that for sure."

A silence fell between the girls. Neither of them had noticed how many birds were chirping until now. The air was so still, there wasn't a rustle in the trees. The water fountain along the pathway near the back patio which normally couldn't be heard from the gazebo was very audible. It was soothing.

Matti noticed the sun was rising higher into the morning sky and said, "Soon, the men will be up, I best be getting breakfast on."

"Actually, Matti, Henry took one of the cars that J.J. said he could use and he and Father went to morning Mass. They probably won't be back for another hour. I think the church was about fifteen miles away. Later, we plan to take Jimmy with us for the day. I'm not sure if Father is going to come or not. So you will have an easy day until at least supper time. I'm looking forward to whatever you are going to cook. It's always so delicious."

"Nora be helpin' me. We want to make somet'ing special for you all."

"That's wonderful, Matti. How is Nora doing? She told us she was expecting again on the way home from the airport. I'm so happy for them and must admit a bit envious."

"Nora couldn't be happier, Jen. She has a golden smile on her face just as radiant as yours at times. J.J. and her be getting along as two peas in a pod."

"Matti that makes my heart soar! Everything has turned out so wonderful. It still feels like I am dreaming at times."

"Well, I be prayin' that baby of yours be coming along real quick and then all your dreams be comin' true! That's for sure."

CHAPTER TWENTY-EIGHT

JENNY SAT ON a bench alongside the Rideau Canal and watched Henry play ball with Jimmy. It had been a busy day so far. They spent over three hours at the Canadian Museum of Nature. They could have easily spent the entire day there. It was hard to get Jimmy to leave until Henry bribed him with a promise to buy him an ice cream cone. Henry never heard the end of it until he found a store that sold ice cream cones; revels or popsicles wouldn't do it.

In a way, it was a good thing as Jenny found some shops nearby to buy Jimmy some clothes; shorts, a sweater and several tee shirts, one of which was from the Museum.

Henry was very pleased he found a toy store that carried a large assortment of Tinker Toys. He bought one similar to the one Father had purchased for Joshua. He could hardly wait to get home and get Jimmy started.

It was a hot day and Jenny welcomed the cool breeze sweeping across the canal. She loved watching Henry play with Jimmy. It would have been nice had they had a child that age. Jimmy would be six in late October and she and Henry were fifty one. Neither of them looked their age, but what if she were to have a child now or in a year or so, would that still work out? By the time the baby was Jimmy's age they would be fifty seven or fifty eight. It seemed old and yet, Jenny felt it would work out. She tried to reason and justify and rationalize it all but at the same time somehow; she wanted to make it work so badly. She knew it would happen. "Oh, dear Lord, I promise to fast and pray and will dedicate the child to your service and honor and glory. She felt like Hannah did all over again. Please hear my cry, heavenly Father like you did, Hannah's."

FATHER REACHED OUT to those who sat on either side of him and the rest of the people at the table followed his lead. They had all made the sign of the cross and Father Engelmann was about to say grace.

"Dear Father, thank You for all our blessings and bringing Your children together in love and friendship to partake of Your generous bounty. I wish to thank J.J. and Nora for having us and their wonderful hospitality. I thank You for Matilda's gift to make such favorable meals. Thank You for Thomas and his workers to transform the garden into such beauty for our delight and Your glory. Thank You for Charles for looking after our rooms and every need or want. Thank You for Jimmy and the innocence of childhood. Let us always strive to remain children at heart. Bless our conversation...for this we pray through Christ our Lord, Amen."

No sooner had all the dishes Matti prepared been passed around and tasted than the accolades began flying. "Wonderful, Matti. I must get this recipe, Matti. How can you make such a variety of dishes in such a short time..." and on and on it went. Finally, Matti put a stop to it by thanking every one and then sharing a story that changed the subject and set the stage to a very enjoyable, jovial dinner.

"Now, we all know the landscape crew be doin' a fine job in keeping the grounds lookin' beautiful but it ain't so all the time. That got Thomas' attention straight off. There is a small section of lawn in front of the estate that needs cuttin' every week and frequently gets neglected. 'Spect, it's because the boys are busy keeping the garden out back in order. However, just the other week I reminded Thomas that the lawn out front needs cuttin'. He said he would get to it but another week passed by and the grass be getting taller and taller and still Thomas payin' no mind to it at all! So one day after the third week, Thomas be comin' out front and he sees me on my knees cutting the grass with a pair of scissors, one blade at a time. Surely, I thought, that be getting Thomas' attention straightaway and he be getting a lawnmower and cut the overgrown grass. Surely, he would feel sorry for me being on my knees like that and all. Well, he disappeared for about ten minutes and when he came back he not be bringing the lawn mower as I expected but carrying somet'ing small. He come up to me and he says, "Mattti, when you done cutting the grass you can sweep the driveway. Here... and he handed me a toothbrush!"

"Everyone roared and that set the mood for the next hour. Henry surprised Jenny with all the stories he had stored in that mind of his. But it was Father Engelmann's story that almost got everyone rolling on the floor.

"It was a cold winter day just after Christmas," Father started out, "when a woman came to the confessional booth and told me she just had the biggest fight ever with her mother-in law. 'She downright hit me with a broom,' the woman lamented. When I asked her what started the fight, she said, 'It was all over a gift I bought for her a year ago last Christmas.' What was the gift? I asked her. She went on to say, 'I had purchased a cemetery plot for her and this past Christmas, I decided not to get her anything. And when my mother-in-law asked me why I didn't buy her a gift, I told her it's because you still haven't used the gift I bought you last year! And that is when the ungrateful woman hit me and the fight started.'"

Once again, laughter filled the room.

Matti decided to change the subject and asked about the play they went to see in Toronto. All three, first, Jenny and then, Father and finally, Henry shared how much they enjoyed the production from their point of view. It was what Henry added at the end of his sharing that led the conversation in a totally different direction.

"I was so proud of Lauren to see her on stage using her God given talent to give such enjoyment to so many people but I have to say..." Henry hesitated at first but it had been bothering him and he just had to get it out. "I was disappointed to learn that she was not attending church anymore..." His words trailed off and a momentary silence fell over the room. It sort of put a damper on their previous sharing of anecdotes and stories and yet, it drew them all of sudden into a closer relationship. They could see Henry was hurting and each in their own way was trying to think of words that would give him hope and consolation.

Matti was the first to speak. "I met your daughters at your weddin' and both girls impressed me, Henry. Perhaps, she be searchin', finding her own way to the Lord, know what I'm sayin'?"

Henry nodded. He wasn't sure if he should have thrown this matter out there. He became aware of how the atmosphere in the room suddenly changed. Even Jimmy noticed it. "Is there something the matter, Daddy?"

"No, we are just discussing something. If you want to go play for awhile, go ahead. Bring out your Tinker Toys and we can build something together in just a little while."

"I'll get him settled," Neela offered. She left Thomas' side and pulled out Jimmy's chair and they left.

J.J. resumed the discussion. "I never went to church until after Dad, that is, James passed away. I would see Mom go from time to time but what got me thinking about going more than anything was Mom's acceptance of Dad and coming back here after all she went through touched me like nothing ever had before. Since Dad's passing, I would never have thought that I would develop such a close friendship with Thomas but I respect him and love him as my own father.

"He got me interested in reading the Bible and attending church. I was always ready to judge Thomas, to find fault in his way or if he was consistent with what he believed in the Bible." J.J. looked at Thomas and said, "You walk the talk, Thomas. You had something inside that I never saw before. Mom had that kind of inner direction but I never was allowed to relate to her during my growing up years and so I never understood it. But moving back home with my family and developing a relationship with our gardener led me to have a personal relationship with Jesus. I know He is real and alive and I look forward to receiving Him in the Holy Eucharist whenever I go to Mass. That to me is more important than anything else. No matter how good the singing or the preaching is, I believe what Jesus said, 'Unless you eat of my flesh and drink of my blood, you shall not have life within you.'" I believe that and it has changed my life."

Jenny couldn't say anything even if she wanted to. She was choked up with a deep love and respect for her son which she never felt before. She had never expected J.J. to be so bold and unafraid to share what he believed. Jenny admired his openness and honesty.

Henry was thinking along the same lines as Jenny. He, too, admired J.J. for his open sharing and felt a tinge of envy that he had developed a personal relationship with Jesus. Here he was, twice the age of J.J. and still searching to have that kind of relationship with Christ. Just the other week he had that same conversation with Father down at the Poustinia. The next person to share where they were at would give further clarity to Henry's inner thoughts.

Nora looked at Henry and said, "Perhaps your daughter is missing what J.J. has found, a personal relationship with Jesus. I can't honestly say I have that. My parents have always attended church on Sunday but during the week, there wasn't any Bible reading or mention of Jesus or God. Maybe my parents prayed privately but not openly. I often wondered if they go just because they have been brought up to go out of duty and if they miss they feel guilty or won't go to heaven. I say that because I never seemed to get anything out of going to church. I am so happy for what J.J. has found and I thank Thomas for his genuine concern and love for my husband. I guess what I am trying to say, Henry, is that so many people attend church without any real, honest engagement with God. While I'm sure many parishioners know Jesus personally, many don't and go out of duty or guilt.

"Young people today who have been brought up in a more permissive way as opposed to an authoritarian way don't buy into the guilt trip if there is nothing there for them. J.J. also mentioned how he was ready to judge Thomas and find any inconsistency in the way he lived and what he preached. That is another area that turns off young people if they see their parents or others they know go to church on Sunday and yet don't obey the teachings of Jesus during the rest of the week, they see that as hypocrisy and question why they go in the first place. When I go to church now, with J.J., I go because I see such a beautiful man in my life. He is the same at home, at work and at church and I want to thank God for this blessing. We are living out our faith daily and we see the value in it. I hope to know Jesus like J.J. some day and I pray that God will give me the grace to find Him like J.J. did..." After a momentary pause, Nora added, "I hope what I am saying makes sense..."

"Sehr gut, das war eine wundervolle gemeinsame Nutzung; that was very good, Nora, a wonderful sharing. We are attracted to the light. Jesus is the light that shines through the darkness. The darkness will never be able to extinguish it. When we allow the light to shine through us it leads others to God whether they are our children, spouse, neighbor or stranger. Both J.J. and Nora so beautifully brought this out in their sharing. In the same way Thomas was the light for J.J., J.J. is now being the light to his family, his co-workers and employees and to us! They are carrying out their greatest responsibility to themselves, their spouse and others by leading them home to the Father."

Father turned to Jenny. "We were discussing this the other week how the ladies in your group can improve their marriage and family. It is by becoming the light."

Jenny nodded; she could see what Father was saying in action through her son. "Yes, that is wonderful what J.J. is doing. He is a living example of what can be done. He is a leader in his home just like God designed it should be. He is carrying out his greatest responsibility; leading his wife and children home. I am so proud of him."

Henry was getting it too. J.J. was far wealthier than he, and yet J.J. had detached himself from his wealth and was using it and his position to advance the kingdom of God. J.J. was another example of one far from God, just like John and yet how quickly they came to see the light.

Henry wished he could, too.

Once again, Father said, "It's all about allowing the light of Jesus to shine through us; it's not enough to talk about it, we must live it. There is a wonderful scripture that summarizes this: Deuteronomy 6:5-7: You shall love the Lord your God with all your heart, with all your soul and with all your strength. And these words that I command you today shall be on your heart. You shall teach them diligently to your children, and shall talk of them when you sit in your house, when you walk by the way, and when you lie down, and when you rise up in the morning.

"This is how we allow the light to shine through us. We live it morning, noon and night. This is how we lead ourselves and others home."

Henry nodded and was feeling so glad he had shared his concern with the group. There is such a difference when we talk superficially and when we talk of things that matter to the heart. It is then that we really communicate and see firsthand how we all want to help each other.

He went on to share the differences in his children. "I may not have been the best or most consistent example of following Jesus and yet, Allison, my eldest daughter was drawn to attend a Bible College and she encouraged me to have a personal encounter with Jesus. She has what J.J. was talking about and yet, Lauren is floundering and going the other way."

Matti chimed in again, "Perhaps, Allison be touched by your example or led by someone at the College who showed the love of Jesus by their sincerity, understanding and unconditional love. No matter, the end result be what countin'. I 'spect your younger daughter will find her way. Right now, her faith may not be personal or meaningful. The church has still not touched her heart and become personal. She be going through the motions with you all them years but still the church be somet'ing that has not provin' to be of value to her like Nora be sayin. It may be in the mind of your little girl, Henry, but in time it will reach her heart. The Lord make sure of that and you be prayin' for her."

Jenny reached over and touched Henry's hand. "We just have to trust in God for Him to turn all these things into good. I can't believe how powerfully God has worked in my life. All the worrying and fretting I did was all for naught. And what did Father and you say about praising God in all circumstances?"

Henry smiled. "Rejoice always, pray constantly and give thanks in all situations, for this is the will of God for you in Christ Jesus."

"Yes, that was one and there was another, something to do with our lips praising..." asked Jenny.

"Perhaps it was Hebrews 13:15; By Him therefore let us offer the sacrifice of praise to God continually, that is, the fruit of our lips giving thanks to His name." offered Father Engelmann.

"Yes, that's the one."

"Now you be talkin'; praising the Lord be a mighty power, Henry. That be bringing results for sure and keep your mind on the Lord and not on the problem."

Father nodded and sat up in his chair, "That's a wonderful insight, Matilda. We witnessed a fine example of that in the play we saw. Look at the incredible good that came out of Joseph honoring God and doing His will. He could very well have focused on how terrible his circumstances were, dwelled on revenge, anger and hate for his brothers. Would that have impressed the rich ruler who purchased him? Certainly not, we can see how God honors not only us when we do His will but also those around us who may not have any faith at all! Recall in the play how the Potiphar saw that the Lord was with Joseph and that the Lord gave Joseph success in everything. Eventually the ruler put Joseph in charge of all he owned!

"Once again, his fortunes turned when Joseph was put into jail over the incident with the Potiphar's wife. But again,

Joseph trusted God and was once more blessed to become the Pharaoh's right hand man which eventually led him back to his family!

"So, too, is it when we show faith and trust in God in all our circumstances. Wives, through prayer and praise can change an unbelieving husband. Fathers, through prayer and praise can save their household. When we place our trust in God we will see the powerful and most wonderful influence God will have over our circumstances including our personal lives."

Thomas finally spoke. "Very well, said, Father. Looks to me like this trip not only proved to be an entertaining holiday but beneficial for the spirit as well. I must say it is most enjoyable to watch God's divine providence at work in His children, including the performers; how they minister to one another and their audience. As you said, no matter what our circumstance or where we are, we can see God's handy-work do for us what we cannot do for ourselves. It is the wise person who gives it all to God and then see it lived out through the guidance of the Holy Spirit."

"Amen." said Father.

CHAPTER TWENTY-NINE

ATHER WAS ASLEEP next to the window, while Jenny rested her head on Henry's shoulder. Henry was also dozing on and off in the aisle seat. Jenny didn't think anyone would be up to see them off as they had to leave the estate at 3:00 A.M. in order to make the long drive to the airport and be there two hours before their 7:15 boarding time. But there they were, all standing on the top step waving to see them off. Even though J.J., Nora and Jimmy were her immediate family, all of them at the estate had become family, too. What an unusual mix of people; black and white, rich and poor, educated and uneducated, employer and employee, young and old, all living together as one big family. Who would have thought that such a thing could possibly happen!?

They had only four hours of sleep and Jenny should've been tired and snoozing like Henry and Father but her mind was swirling. *What a wonderful mini holiday this was,* Jenny thought as the airplane sped smoothly, high in the cloudless sky. She was so happy that Father came along. She had hoped Justin would too, but he opted to stay at Camilla and Jeremy's place. He said he wanted to see the opening of some western movie but Jenny felt there was a more personal reason. Part of why she was fasting was in the hope God would move in

Justin's heart and accept her completely into the family. They had such a wonderful time flying the kite together. It was the first time she felt really close to Justin. But in the days which followed, he slipped back a bit. He did give her a hug when they left on this trip so, Jenny was hopeful. She would trust in God to work it out for the good. "I praise You Lord for the situation just as it is," Jenny softly whispered with confidence!

If the truth be known, however, the main reason for Jenny's inability to sleep was because of her excitement over a dream she had last night in her old bedroom at the estate. It wasn't the first time she had that dream over the years and many times she felt guilty because she enjoyed it so much that she wished she wouldn't wake up and the dream would go on forever. Perhaps it was the lonely days and nights living alone in the huge estate while James resided mainly at his city condo that brought on the dreams. It was her way of surviving in a marriage that had stalled and was going nowhere except to divorce. To dream of the summer she spent with Henry always soothed her spirit and gave her hope that one day their guardian angels would bring them back together again.

In her dreams, they would stroll up and down Broder Street holding hands. Sometimes she would chase butterflies but it was really to have Henry chase after her. She loved to play the note game where they would try to outwit one another with a note secured to the fence post with an elastic band. But the memory that would touch her heart the most was the day in early September just before high school began when they bicycled to the park. What a wonderful fall day that was. She relived that almost love scene over and over, every feeling that came and went and what might have been.

Although Jenny's dreams relived their summer together true to reality, there was one part of the dream she had altered. Perhaps it was to accept the child growing in her womb. She dreamt it was Henry who was the father of Camilla and it happened that memorable day when they went to Wascana Park the day before high school started. They had made love and it was Henry's child and not the awful boy smelling of liquor with a frenzied look in his eyes. No, she would dream that it was the tender touch of Henry, his kisses and ultimately their union in perfect love. Jenny had dreamt that dream so often she came to believe it.

Eventually however, the reality of the real truth came home to roost and Jenny finally had to let go of that misconception, but ever so reluctantly.

Still, the dreams persisted perhaps out of habit or for sheer enjoyment and temporary reprieve from being caught in an empty marriage. Eventually the dreams faded and stopped until last night. It was so real, she had to turn on the light and see if Henry was sleeping bedside her and not making love to her at the park. She turned off the lights and tried to sleep but a thought kept her awake. A plan was forming in her mind that just might make her dream true!

Was it heaven sent?

An excitement swept through her being at that moment and never left her. Even now, as tired as she was, she couldn't wait to get home and put her plan into action. She knew that this just might be the door to make her dream come true.

It did in her dream last night.

CHAPTER THIRTY

"YOU LOOK LIKE the cat that swallowed the canary, Jenny." Henry held Jenny in his arms for a moment and stepped back. "You're blushing Honey, what's going on?"

"No I'm not Henry; it's all in your imagination," said Jenny, pink tinting her cheeks.

"So, why do you want me to come into Regina today?"

"Carlos wants to make some changes to the back yard and he would like to run it by us."

"I would think your say so is more important than mine, Jenny. It's your home."

"Yes, but it's important to Carlos that he speaks to us both. It's a man thing with him."

Henry shrugged his shoulders. "I think I understand. Well, I want to change the oil in the tractor and then we can go in around eleven; would that be okay?"

"Perfect, Honey!" Jenny exclaimed with a little more enthusiasm than she should have.

"We can have lunch at the café," suggested Henry.

Jenny hesitated for a moment and excitedly replied, "I thought we would have a picnic!"

"A picnic? Where?"

"You'll see."

Henry rolled his eyes. "You're full of surprises today, aren't you?"

AS THEY PLANNED, they arrived at Jenny's home on Hill Avenue around eleven thirty. They heard Carlos whistling at the far end of the yard. For the first time, they startled Carlos. He was so engrossed in weeding a flower patch across from the gazebo that he hadn't heard Jenny and Henry come into the yard.

"Ah, Miss Jenny and Senor Henry, so good to see you. I can usually tell when you come by the agitation of the butterflies but so many have left already for Mexico."

"Yes, it's that time of the year already; my how time flies!" said Jenny.

"The garden is looking great Carlos. Why would you want to make changes?" Henry wanted to know.

Carlos wrinkled his forehead. "I plan to make no changes, Senor Henry."

Jenny giggled as she looked at Carlos, "I used that as an excuse to entice Henry to come into town this morning. I told Maria we would be here shortly before noon. She has prepared a lunch for Henry and me. We are going on a picnic!"

"You are serious, aren't you? I thought you were joking when you mentioned it earlier on."

"I have another surprise for you but first I want to show you something that perhaps we can make at the farm. Come, quickly hold my hand."

How could Henry resist? He took Jenny's hand as she led him to a narrow opening in a heavily brushed area at the very back of the yard in front of the giant fir trees. She followed a worn path in between the thick brush. She could tell they needed trimming as it was getting more difficult to pass through but once there, it opened up to a sun filled area exposing the shrine. Henry was taken aback by the scene.

"Wow, this is beautiful, Jenny. When did Carlos build this? I don't recall seeing it here before."

"He built it for Maria last fall. It's so quiet and serene here. In a way, it reminds me of the prayer house."

"Yeah, this is quite the sanctuary, alright. I love the way the rays of sun strike the Blessed Mother's face."

Jenny nodded. "Carlos studied how the light came into this area so he could erect the shrine so the sun would do exactly as you noticed. See, he's an artist, too."

"He certainly is. We should get him to build a shrine at the farm. Actually, on the island where we are planning to build a gazebo would be nice place. There is a lot of shrubbery there and it's well treed."

"That would be wonderful, Henry. I bet Father would be going there all the time to say his rosary."

Jenny turned to Henry and said, "Would you please visit with Carlos for a bit, I would like to say a prayer here before I show you my surprise."

Henry looked at Jenny thoughtfully and nodded. He kissed his dear sweet wife on the cheek and left. Jenny turned and knelt on a soft mat that Maria had put there. Jenny picked up the white rosary at the foot of the statue which Maria had given her. She made the sign of the cross and began to pray:

"Good morning, Mary," Jenny began. This was Jenny's fifth time here and was feeling more comfortable talking to Mary as a friend in the same way Maria perceived the Blessed Mother as well.

"Today is the big day, Mary. I just know it. I can just imagine how you must have felt when the Angel Gabriel told you that you were to conceive Jesus. It's such a special part of being a woman to give the gift of life. You know how much I want to bear Henry's child. God has been so good to me and showered me with so many blessings. Since He cured me, I have always felt that one of the reasons for my return was to conceive Henry's child. Would you talk to your Son and the heavenly Father to grant me one more miracle; that I become pregnant. You are a mother and I know you understand my heart's desire. Please pray for me and intercede on my behalf.

"Thank you, Mary."

When Jenny returned to the garden, Henry and Carlos were talking about the miracle of the Monarchs' trek back to Mexico. Carlos was sharing his belief that the butterflies are guided by angels when Henry noticed Jenny come out of the brush. On her way over to the men, Jenny stopped by the Angel of Thanksgiving and placed several flowers in the angel's basket. If her whispers were audible, Henry would have heard Jenny thanking the Lord for the miracle of life He was granting her.

Henry had difficulty concentrating on what Carlos was saying. The moment he saw Jenny, he could not take his eyes off her. He had never seen her looking more radiantly beautiful. He longed to hold her. Every step she took as she approached him stirred something deep in his being. It was like that unforgettable moment when he first saw Jenny walk by his house in the summer of 1956. Why such a memory would come to him now was beyond him.

Carlos, realizing Henry was no longer listening to him, turned to see what was so distracting. He thought he knew what it was. He got that same mesmerizing feeling when Maria came out into the garden as well.

"So now for the big surprise, Henry!" Jenny exclaimed.

Once again Jenny uttered those magic words, "Quickly, hold my hand." As soon as Henry did so, she led him way back behind the gazebo to where the garage was. She opened the door, flicked on the lights and there they were: two shiny new bicycles; a girl's pink bicycle and a blue boy's bike. A shiny silver carrier was mounted to the front of each bicycle.

"What on earth is this, Jen?"

"I thought we would take a bike ride. We haven't done that together since the summer of 1956, Henry."

Henry was just thinking of that summer when he first met Jenny. He shook his head and wrinkled his forehead as he gazed at his lovely wife. She was beaming with such delight; it seemed to add a glow to the old, poorly lit garage interior.

"What's that in your carrier?" inquired Henry.

A blanket to sit on while we have our lunch."

Just then Maria walked into the garage carrying a wicker picnic basket.

"I was just coming to get that, thank you so much, Maria."

"You are welcome, Jenny. I hope you enjoy what I prepared."

"It will be delicious as always." Jenny took the basket from Maria and placed it in Henry's carrier.

"So, where are we going?" Henry wanted to know.

Jenny's eyes flashed and sparkled with excitement. No sooner had Carlos opened the garage door than Jenny darted out down the lane shouting, "Come, Henry...follow me!"

It was a beautiful September day, very much like the day they rode to Wascana Park thirty six years ago. Jenny was so excited she could hardly contain herself. It felt good to cycle down the lane towards the avenue just to expend the growing adrenaline surging through her body. Henry had a hard time catching up to Jenny. He hadn't been on a bike in years and the seat was a bit low and so his legs came up too high each time the pedal rose to the top. It did impede his rhythm slightly but he quickly adjusted and got used to it. He loved the feel of the prairie wind against his face; it always gave him such a feeling of freedom. He began to pedal faster and faster as if he had wings. He soon caught up to Jenny as she turned onto Albert Street and headed north.

As soon as she crossed the Albert Street Bridge, she turned into the park. Henry began to get a sense as to where Jenny was heading.

His excitement grew and his heart began to race. If someone were ahead of both of them taking a photo, they would capture the anticipation on their faces of two youthful lovers deliriously in love. Their eyes were wild and free and sparkled with joy and happiness. Their entire beings glowed with an eagerness of two teenagers about to do something out of this world.

Henry began to relive that race back then as Jenny pedaled swiftly past the band shelter. She was in the lead back then just as she was now. She reminded him of an angel flying through the air in 1956 and again now as she sped down the winding path towards the water.

It was amazing how they retraced their paths almost as if it had been yesterday. It should really be no surprise, as both of them had re-lived the details of that journey so often and so vividly that it became a map burned indelibly in their minds and hearts. The memory was still so vivid in each of their minds it was as if the aroma of love that filled the air back then had lived 'till now for their return. Henry thought for sure he could follow Jenny blindly just by the lingering, intoxicating scent of her lilac perfume.

Henry recognized the spot where he had painted *plein air* with his art instructor. He loved painting outdoor and capturing nature before him. The flash of the sunrise over the semi-frozen lake he had painted that early morning came into his mind and then was gone. What did linger however, for a moment longer was when he had recognized that the location where he was painting was near the spot by the lake where Jenny and he had almost made love. Once again, he was heading there; he wondered if the heart he had carved into the trunk of the tree would still be visible as he peddled faster to catch up to his earthly angel.

Jenny slowed and came to a stop at the water's edge. She laid down her bicycle by the embankment. Henry did the same and came up beside her. They both gazed at a lone sail boat on the water moving ever so slowly. There was hardly a breeze in the air. The calm scene before them helped to slow their racing hearts and catch their breath.

"Looks pretty desolate here today, mind you it's a Wednesday. I didn't see anyone in the park so far. I wonder who the lucky guy is that's off from work to be out on his sail boat on this gorgeous day?"

"But then, look at the guy lucky enough to be by your side today, sweetheart."

"Ahh," said Jenny, as she leaned in towards Henry."

"I recall a sail boat being here on the day we came way back then. Do you remember the sailboat, Jenny?"

"I can't recall, Henry. You have such a good memory for detail."

Yes, he did. He recalled vividly how he oscillated back and forth like the sail boat in the water swaying this way and that, deciding whether or not to make love to Jenny.

Henry put his arm around Jenny as they stared at the reflection of the legislative buildings in the still water. He studied it for a moment and then said, "What a great plan you had today, Honey. It takes me back to the day before school when we came here in September of 1956. I recall absolutely everything about that day."

"I do too, sweetheart. It was such a wonderful memory. I don't know how many times I thought of us almost making love here..." Jenny's words trailed off.

"So did I, Jenny. I lost count after the first week when you left."

Henry pulled Jenny next to him and squeezed her tenderly. Desire was inching its way through his body. He tried to distract his thoughts, "I wonder if that's the same sail boat that was out on the lake that day we were here?"

"It could very well be, Honey. There are so many unusual coincidences in our lives."

"Yeah, and what about the heart I carved in the huge elm tree?"

They turned and just a few yards away, there it stood. There was no inner bark visible. While still keeping his arm around her, they slowly made their way to the tree.

While they moved along, Henry said, "If you were a tree, I would want to be the branches and hug you from the bottom to the very top!"

Jenny was about to come up with another saying but Henry said, "Look, there is the raised bark." The injury to the tree had grown together and sealed itself however, a deformed swollen growth was still visible. Henry always carried Julean's rosary in his left pant pocket and his small jack knife and a wad of bills in the other.

He took out his knife and said, "I wonder if the heart I carved is still hidden beneath the outer bark. I hate to scar the tree again, but I just have to know."

Henry carefully began to carve away the outer layer once again as he had done in the past when he was fifteen.

Jenny stood behind him and watched Henry whittle away the old overgrown bark. Both were amazed as the outline of the heart and inscription began to appear. He was a bit too far to the right so he worked more to the left following the line of the heart that was partially exposed as a guide. Within a few minutes there it was;

HP + JS

"And there are our guardian angels who kept their promise to keep us together!"

Henry turned and took Jenny into his arms. "I recall thinking back then that like this tree our love would withstand the storms of life…"

"And they have, sweetheart."

Thy tenderly kissed and slowly parted. Henry could feel a powerful desire for his dear wife was building once more. He wasn't sure what was going to happen. They went back to their bikes without saying anything. Henry took the wicker picnic basket out of his carrier and Jenny took the blanket from hers. It seemed as if they had lost control and were guided by some unseen force.

Still no words were spoken as they headed again towards the water's edge and strode along the embankment to the shelter of trees and shrubs. The direction of their movements was so certain and determined as if they knew exactly where they were going.

And there it was; their own private secret hideaway. It was the exact same spot where they had lain thirty six years ago. The shrubbery had grown thicker but the secluded area was still just large enough for two, maybe three blankets. Jenny held one end of the blanket and let it fall open. While still holding the one end, she took hold of the other end of the blanket and waved it gently up and forward allowing it to fall neatly open ever so softly on the grass. They both took off their shoes and sat down on the blanket.

Although it was an awkward moment, their gazes clearly revealed a powerful inner mission. The slow, determined stroll from the embankment to this secluded area was to them foreplay. Henry was mesmerized by every movement that Jenny made as he followed close behind. Their desire for one another was filled with an unexplainable passion. Perhaps, if the unseen were seen, Henry and Jenny's guardian angels could very well be imparting their heavenly energy into the gaze they were now sharing as they did that moment they first met in Engelmann's grocery store.

They lay back down on the blanket, directed by a force beyond themselves. On the surface, it seemed they were guided by instinct. Jenny was already partially beneath Henry, as he turned on his side. He propped himself up on his elbow to look down at her. Jenny never had looked more ravishing. Her blue eyes sparkled like diamonds, set off by the shimmering of her luminous skin in the sun. She glowed. He hungered for the taste of her lips. He bent down and tenderly kissed her mouth.

He had to restrain himself from moving too quickly. He followed the silver chain around her neck with his fore finger to where it disappeared underneath her blouse. He undid the first two buttons revealing the pewter angel resting just above her breast. He brushed the soft metal as he slid his hand further touching the soft warmth of her skin.

The passion was burning inside of him. He could feel it in Jenny, too, as she faintly moaned and whispered words of love. The sight, sound and lilac scent of her made the blood thunder through his veins. Her subtle movements fueling still further desire in his own body. He brought his leg over Jenny's and began to slowly press it between hers. He hadn't realized it yet that Jenny had worn a skirt much like that memorable day so long ago.

One memory after the other flashed through Henry's mind of those moments in the past and the struggle he had controlling his emotions. But he didn't have to this time. He didn't have to heed Mr. Engelmann's words of caution running through his mind; rather, thoughts of loving his first love surged throughout his being with unstoppable power. The fulfillment of what had been a fantasy for years in their minds had now become a reality.

They lay on the soft blanket for the longest time embraced in each other's arms. They had made love and were now caught in a state of ecstasy, perfect bliss and oneness. A feeling of completeness enveloped them that went beyond anything which either of them had ever known.

A sudden shadow passed over them, cooling the air. They sensed it even though their eyes were closed. Henry slid over and rolled on his back. No sooner had either of them opened their eyes than a dark cloud began to release a gentle rain fall.

"Oh, Henry, look at the dark cloud overhead." Jenny said, her voice raspy.

"It's the only one in the sky, I think it's just a light shower; shouldn't be long."

But then it began to pour. Henry thought of tossing the blanket over them but Jenny had other ideas. She moved to her knees and before Henry could too, she bent down and kissed his lips lightly and gazed longingly into his eyes. It seemed incredulous to Henry that despite the rain and a dark cloud overhead, Jenny's eyes reflected the blue of the sky and the warm radiance of the sun. She seemed to be always in the light. He could gaze into Jenny's sparkling eyes forever.

"Come on," Jenny coaxed him up. He wanted to grab her hand but instead pulled up his trousers as he rose to his knees. Jenny laughed as she ran off towards their bikes.

Henry buckled his belt and ran after her. The rain was coming down so hard he bumped into a shrub, scraping his arm. He tried to examine his bruise but couldn't see in the thick downfall. He let out a mild curse and continued in hot pursuit. The bikes were still lying on the grass near the large elm, but Jenny was nowhere in sight. He ran up the path they had earlier come down on. Elm trees were scattered here and there on the hillside. What he thought was Jenny through a curtain of rain turned out to be another elm but he heard her laughter.

"Where are you Jenny?" Henry shouted, as he swung himself around on the slippery grass.

"Over here, Henry," she hollered back, but the sound of the roaring rain was so loud, Henry couldn't tell from which direction Jenny's voice was coming from. He knew she was hiding behind a tree somewhere near; he could hear her giggle.

He would draw her out by playing their favorite game. Into the wind and rain, Henry yelled, "If you were a tree trunk, I would want to be your branches and wrap them around you from the bottom to the very top!"

Sure enough, Jenny responded, "If you were a star..." Henry turned to where he thought her voice came from but then she stopped but for only a moment and finished saying what she started from behind another tree, " ...you would be the brightest in the heavens."

Henry turned again, searching some more and then, he shouted, "If you were the wind, I would follow you to the ends of the earth!"

"If you were a song, it would be on my lips forever!"

Henry turned; he was sure she was behind that tree just to the right of him. He dashed over but she wasn't there. The rain was abating; he thought he would try one more. "If you were the moon, it would be forever full of light...I would become a sky rocket just to come to you."

The rain shower was almost over. Henry wiped away the water dripping into his eyes and listened attentively. He slowly turned and all of a sudden, it was like a monkey jumped on his back! Jenny had lunged forward and thrust her arms around Henry's neck over his shoulders and at the same time wrapped her legs around his waist and shouted, "If I were the rain, I would make you soaking wet!"

His cold clothes pressed to his body like a sheet of ice, sending a sudden chill through him. It didn't seem to have the same effect on Jenny as she laughed and slid off his back.

Henry turned, grabbed her and swung her around as she shrieked in delight. They both laughed at the excitement of it all and the way they looked. Their hair was plastered against their scalps and their clothes drooping. Henry still had his shirt tails hanging out. He stopped swinging Jenny and drew her in. He kissed her hard and then said, "Oh, Jenny, I love you with all my heart. From the day we first met, you have been the light of my heart. Your charm, playfulness, and spontaneity open me up to the fullness of life!"

"Oh, Henry I love you too. We will remember this day for the rest of our lives!"

Filled with youthful, joyous exuberance, Henry took hold of Jenny's waist and lifted her high into the clearing blue sky. She thrust her hands still higher into the air above and shouted for all to hear,

"This is the day, we are bringing a new, precious little soul into the world!"

CHAPTER THIRTY-ONE

J ENNY COULDN'T HAVE been any happier when she woke up
the next morning. She felt her belly and slowly massaged it
in anticipation of what was to come. She just knew that she was
pregnant and that a new life was growing within her womb.
She had the same thoughts the day after their third anniversary but this was different; just the way the plan unfolded
after her dream at the estate, reminding her of the months
she spent with Henry in 1956. How that one summer stood
out amongst all the summers which followed. How many
times over the months, then years, had she relived all of the
things they did together, especially the day when they went to
the park. Henry had honored her virginity that day, and she
believed with all her heart that God was honoring her desire
now to bear Henry a child.

Out of habit she reached over to touch Henry, even though
she knew he was already up. The noise from the kitchen was
drifting upstairs and the smell of burnt toast was in the air.
The clock on the night table beside her read 8:15. Justin would
already be gone. The school bus came into the yard at 7:15 a.m.
each morning without fail. There were a few days when Justin
was left behind and Henry had to drive him to school. It very
quickly cured Justin of his habit of sleeping in.

How would Justin take to his new sister? Jenny wondered. *Would that drive him further away from me? Would he accept her? Would that perhaps help Justin to accept me?*

Jenny usually was up to see Justin off but she was so excited yesterday that by day's end, she was totally exhausted. *How is Henry feeling?* She wondered. *It was quite the day for him as well. I hope he feels okay about being a father to another addition in his growing family. He's probably in the sun room saying morning prayers and thinking about it all.*

JENNY COULDN'T HAVE been more insightful. Henry was sitting next to the fireplace holding the Bible open. He started to read a chapter in the Gospel of John but quickly lost his concentration. He couldn't stop thinking about Jenny and the picnic they had yesterday.

Some picnic!

They never opened the basket, not that he cared. He relived every moment of the fun they had and the how they made love right out in the open like that. In a way, it was like painting *plien air*. Painting outdoors right in the midst of nature is exciting but nothing could compare to what had happened yesterday!

What if someone had come along?

Henry both shuddered and laughed at the thought. It was funny how neither of them even thought of someone catching them in the act. They were both so caught up in the moment that they never gave that any consideration.

It was such a beautiful moment in time; so fully lived.

Jenny was so certain she conceived; she would be heartbroken if she hadn't. They would have to take one day at a time and see where this all would lead to. He would ask Father Engelmann to pray for Jenny and the baby and for him. Henry had mixed feelings about being a father again at his age. What if Jenny's instincts were right, could he make all of the adjustments to fatherhood again?

JENNY BECAME MORE and more excited as she lay in bed thinking of yesterday at the park. She could no longer contain herself and just had to call someone.

By the time Jenny had taken a shower and dried her hair, Henry was already outside working. She made herself a cup of tea and stepped out onto the deck overlooking the valley. It was another beautiful day. She was surprised how early fall comes on the prairies. She already noticed so many trees turning golden. It came later in Ottawa.

She loved seeing the maple trees turn color. There wasn't a more beautiful sight than to gaze up high and see all that color against the blue sky. She had to admit, she missed it. How often over the years had she picked up a maple leaf and studied the veins and different colors running through it? Sometimes, she would gather dozens as one seemed to be more beautiful than the other. How was that possible amongst hundreds of leaves which had fallen? Yet each had their own story, their own pattern and color variation. She tried to preserve them, knowing it would be in vain; but she had enjoyed nature's gift for as long as she could, before it dried and shriveled up.

She looked for Father Engelmann at the prayer house but he was nowhere in sight. She could hardly wait to share the good news with him. Just before she went back into the sun room, she heard the sound of the tractor. She paused for a minute and saw Henry emerge from around the bend at the bottom of the valley. He was mowing the roadside leading to the prayer house. He'd probably stop and visit with Father when he got there.

Jenny thought of calling Camilla and talking about the baby growing in her womb and all of the details which occurred yesterday but felt too embarrassed for a mother to discuss that with her daughter. But then, Camilla was a counselor and was sure that many of the girls she dealt with would share all the intimate detail of their relationships with their boyfriends. But that seemed different somehow to a mother-daughter discussion.

If only Tammy were still alive, they could tell each other anything. Tammy lived in the secrets of her heart. Whenever Jenny had a troublesome thought, Tammy would sense it straight away; as if by some sixth sense. And even if Tammy wasn't aware of it, Jenny would share it anyway. There was nothing they would keep from one another. Tammy would be ecstatic over the news, she would be so happy for her. *Oh, Tammy, please talk to God for me to make sure my heart's desire is fulfilled. No, thank Him for it! There is no room for doubt. I just know it has! I miss you so dearly, Tammy. I will be talking with your daughter this week some time. Chloe is doing such good work.*

Besides Tammy, there was only one other person whom she felt comfortable to discuss girl things with. Jenny just had to share her news.

"This be the Hamilton residence, who do you wish to speak to?"

Feeling excited and in a playful mood, Jenny lowered her voice making it sound as gruff as possible and said, "Is the head of the household in?"

"This be as high as you be gettin', until you tell me who you are and what you be wantin'."

"This is the Prime Minister of Canada and I wish to speak with Thomas—"

"Now you listen and listen hard, 'spect you be foolin' with me—"

Jenny couldn't contain herself any longer and began to laugh.

"I recognize that laugh, I 'spect that was you right along. What a pleasant surprise. You be the only one who can make this sunny day in Ottawa seem brighter! Never expected to be hearin' from you so soon. How my dear friend be doin' this fine day?"

Jenny was so excited to share, she got right to the point of her call. "Oh Matti, I have some wonderful news to share with you. I am going to have a baby!"

There was a long silence and then Matti cautiously asked, "That be wonderful, Jen...why didn't you share the good news with me when you were here last week. Did the doctor just be tellin' you today?"

"No, Matti, Henry and I made love at the park yesterday and I just know I conceived his child."

This time it seemed as if the line went dead. Once again, Matti cautiously went on, "Now, I knows how much you be wantin' to give that man of yours a child, Jenny, but maybe you be waitin' a spell until the doctor be sayin', 'Jenny, you done got one beautiful little baby in that tummy of yours.'"

"It's hard to explain, Matti, I just know I got pregnant yesterday! And I have to share it with someone, I am so excited."

Matti put her free hand up to the side of her head and shook it back and forth, not knowing what to think or say. She never heard Jenny speak this way before. "But what if it not be the right time of month, you know what I be sayin'?"

Matti wanted to create the possibility in her dear friend's pretty little head that she just might be a little premature in this matter.

"No, I made sure everything was timed perfect. The last time I had my period, well sort of, my flow isn't that large, just spotting, was fifteen days ago. So yesterday, was day fourteen; the day the egg ovulated."

"Now, Jen, I have no reason to be concerned about these things bein' a single woman and all but if I be recallin' right, the fertile window be four or five days before your egg be coming out of the ovary and live for no more than a day, but the man's sperm be livin' for at least five days. So, most women wantin' a child be hoppin' in and out bed like a bunny getting all the sperm swimming around there to make sure one of them tiny fellows be connectin' with that lonely egg."

Jenny chuckled and said, "That's right, Matti, but I wanted only Henry's sperm from that day. I was saving it all up for that special day at the park. I had it all planned."

"You be cutting things mighty fine, Jen. Did you make love again when you came home last night to make sure?"

"No, we were both so exhausted from the day. After we made love, a sudden shower came up and we began running around like two kids playing in the rain. Later in the afternoon, we took a walk in the valley, had an early dinner and went to bed shortly after. I guess we are not as young as we used to be."

The moment those words came out of Jenny s mouth she said, "You don't think we are too old to have a baby do you, Matti!?"

"Oh, Jenny, you and that man of yours be getting on, that's for sure, but I knows many couples havin' children in their late forties. You and Henry be just a few years older and in good health and so youthful and all. And if Elizabeth and Zachariah can have a child in their old age and good Lord, look at Abraham, he be one hundred and heaven forbid the Lord fixed his plumbing so that his woman at ninety be havin' a child. Can you imagine how shocked Sarah be to see old Abe come alive like that!?"

The girls laughed.

Matti, continued, "You be as old as you feel, Jen. I can't think of anyt'ing more wonderful happenin' to you than giving birth to another baby. This time you be raisin' the child by yourself and not some nanny."

Rather than focus on Matti's last comments, Jenny responded to what Matti had said initially. "Thanks for those uplifting words, Matti."

Jenny then went on to tell Matti how much fun they had. "I purchased two bicycles for us just for that occasion. Maria prepared a picnic lunch and we rode to the park just like we did when we were teenagers. It was like reliving the entire day of our youth. We almost made love on that occasion, but didn't."

"I still recall you tellin' me that when you lived on the estate. I could see in your eyes at the time, how you wished you had. You be savin' up for this a long time, Jen."

"Yes, as soon as we got there, we were so anxious to make love that we never did have our picnic lunch!"

"No need too, you gave that man more than lunch and he be having his dessert too, I 'spect he be wantin' to go for a picnic everyday from now on."

Jenny laughed. "Oh Matti you're a card. You should be a stand-up comedian on the side."

"That for sure, I could be drawing material from here and there and all over true to life!"

"That's very true, Matti. Life can be very funny if you don't take it so seriously and you have a way of putting it all in such a humorous perspective somehow. It's a gift, Matti! Every time I talk to you, I feel more uplifted."

"Don't know how that be possible. I see you already as an angel flying around all the time just like them Monarchs!"

"See, there you go again." Jenny said and then quickly changed the subject. "So how is J.J. and everyone else?"

"We are all family, Jen."

"I was thinking of that as we left the estate last week how close we all are. It truly has become one big family!"

"It be a miracle what happenin' here. So happy I stuck it out. There be days, I want to go back to the island so bad but the good Lord be turnin' everyt'ing' into such good. There be days I jus' don't know if I'm in paradise or not. It all be so beautiful here."

"Yes, it is a beautiful estate but it's the people that gives it its heart."

"Amen, Jen, that be a kindly t'ing to say."

"And how are you and Charles getting along?" Jenny was interested to know.

"Like I be tellin' you when you were here, Charles be given me a hug before we retire and this past week I notice the embrace is a bit longer than usual. Maybe that's why I should be keepin' track of my cycle, make sure not'ing be happenin' that ain't supposed to, know what I'm sayin'?"

Jenny just laughed.

"Good, Lord, wouldn't that take all if a little black baby be running around here with a British accent! Now, that would be somet'ing, that's for sure!"

HENRY PARKED THE tractor beside the prayer house and went in to visit with Father about what had happened yesterday at the park.

"I don't exactly know how I feel, Father. I think I am happier for Jenny than for the possibility that I might be a father of another child. When I played with young Jimmy when we were in Ottawa, I enjoyed it. But if Jen is in fact pregnant, I will be six years older if I'm doing the same thing with our baby as I did with J.J.'s son. And then again there is Joshua and Noah. I can easily play with them but I have assumed the role of a grandfather and not a father. And I have to be honest, after a while, the kids get on my nerves with their constant demands and yelling and screaming. Sometimes, Father, I can't wait for them to go."

"Yes, that's true, however when it's your own, a parent is graced with more tolerance and patience. It grows gradually upon you rather than to have two or three children all of a sudden invade the peaceful environment of your home."

"I can't get over how certain Jenny feels that she has conceived. Within minutes after we made love, Father, she was beside herself that she brought another soul into the world. I think even if a doctor were there and said, 'It's impossible for you to be sure at this point, Jenny,' she would have refuted him; she was that sure."

Henry paused for a moment and then added, "I have to admit, there was something special about what happened yesterday. Jenny never looked more radiant and more beautiful. I wanted to hold her and make love to her more than anything...it did seem as if we were directed or guided to do what we did. There seemed to be a knowing presence somehow...

"I get that feeling every now and then when I feel guided by my guardian angel or the Holy Spirit."

Father simply nodded. He recalled only too well the morning Jenny came to the Poustinia and he overheard her from the bedroom praying and pleading with God that she would bear a child. It was almost an identical replay of the story in the book of Samuel; when Hannah cried out to the Lord that He grant her a child. There were so many similarities between the two ladies; Jenny's deep desire to have a child for Henry, her willingness to fast and her covenant to God to give back the child...

"Henry," Father said, startling Henry by his abrupt return to the moment, "I will pray and fast that Jenny has conceived. I will also keep you in my prayers that you accept this child graciously and lovingly into your home."

"Geez, Father, you said that with such certainty as if you believed like Jenny that she has conceived."

"I do believe, Henry. This is a special child. This child belongs to God."

CHAPTER THIRTY-TWO

SINCE THAT DAY at the park, the sparkle in Jenny's eyes just grew brighter, if that were possible. An inner happiness seemed to bubble out of her entire being; the way she held herself, walked, talked, laughed; she was filled with an unexplainable special expectancy. She uplifted everyone who came into her presence.

Henry was always amazed at Jenny's inner state. She was forever calm, centered and never seemed to have a down day. Sure, she worried about things every now and then but it was always out of concern for someone else. Never did Henry ever expect to see Jenny to be more pleasant, happy, and buoyant than she already was.

But these last two weeks, Jenny glowed.

It was as if she were just on this side of heaven. The depth of her crystal blue eyes emitted a peace and joy that surpassed all earthly understanding.

While Henry was happy for her, he was at the same time concerned over what a tremendous let down it would be if Jenny wasn't with child. Chances of her being pregnant were slim at best. Henry wanted Jenny to see Doctor Kreake and do some tests to confirm what she so firmly believed to be reality. Jenny however would not hear of it, she knew she was pregnant and didn't require a doctor to confirm it at this point.

Jenny's belief that she had conceived was centered on her firm faith that God had answered her prayer and having it confirmed by a doctor would somehow cast doubt on that conviction. While Henry didn't want to dampen Jenny's faith by injecting words of caution, he didn't want to be the doubting Thomas, either. Henry recalled only too well when Zachariah doubted the Angel Gabriel that his wife Elizabeth was pregnant in her old age; he was struck dumb, unable to speak until the day his wife gave birth.

Henry quickly said a prayer to the Holy Spirit to fill him with the same faith and expectancy as Jenny. He knew such thinking, however was all in his head and now he prayed with deep sincerity that God would grant him the grace to make his intellectual requests travel to his heart where his belief would have more conviction. To encourage this belief still more that his dear sweet wife was indeed, with child, he began to convince himself that at fifty one, he would be a great father! Yes, the child would keep him active and young. It may be the best thing that ever happened to him...to both of them!

Shortly after noon, Jenny came home. Henry had lunch ready and the two of them sat down at the table in the sun room and discussed Jenny's meeting with the ladies. It was the first meeting of the fall season since they had shut down early last summer.

"So, how did your first meeting go, Honey? Any new members?"

"This is the first time all the same women are back. Two more wanted to join but I had to refer them to another group. It doesn't give all the ladies enough time to express themselves and share if the groups get too large. Anyway, it was a great meeting. Susan was present and shared that she and her children were at home and that her husband willingly agreed to live on his own while seeking counseling for his anger management and communication skills."

"That's a good way of smoothing over verbal and physical abuse."

"It's a way of preserving one's dignity and yet her husband is very aware of his behavior and acknowledges it. The good thing is, he is the one that moved out of the home rather than Susan and the children having to find shelter. He has agreed to respect Susan's wishes and terms as to when and if they should come back together again, which is their ultimate goal. The counselor in the case also confirmed that he feels Susan's husband is sincere in his efforts to make things work which is also a good sign."

"That's great, Jenny. It seemed like such a scary thing to bring this out in the open and deal with it and here it is."

"Yes, we are almost always apprehensive about the unknown and how people will react. The other ladies are making progress, too. The nice thing about the groups is that they are Christian based and all of the ladies agree that putting Jesus at the center of their marriage and family is vital. Three of the ladies shared that their husbands are cooperating towards that end and two others say their husbands don't want to have anything to do with it."

"So, what are you doing?" Henry wanted to know.

"Leading by example like Father Engelmann shared. We also started to pray over some of the ladies to give them strength and wisdom. Laying on of hands expresses an outpouring of love and concern for others. Camilla told me several weeks ago, that is what Jeremy and she do every now and then. I thought I would suggest we try it and it was well received at this morning's meeting."

"Hmm, that's good to hear," said Henry, with a nod.

"One of the ladies suggested that it would be good if the men were involved somehow in the group discussions. I told them that you were a counselor at one time and that you might speak to the men or at a couples' night later in the fall or next winter. They all thought that was a great idea. Are you still open to doing that?"

Henry nodded. "Yeah, I have been thinking about it actually. I have an exhibition to get ready for and several commissions that I have to complete. Next winter, closer to spring, would work best for me. In the meantime, however, I could start lining up guest speakers to talk to the men and women about topics related to marriage and family. When you meet again with your group leaders, plan a schedule for the entire fall and next winter with times and dates when you would like to have a speaker come in and I will try to fill those spots with someone."

"That would be wonderful, Henry!"

Henry nodded and said, "And by the way, Matti called earlier this morning. I told her you would be back shortly after noon so you can expect a call any time now."

MATTI COULDN'T WAIT another day. She had to know if Jenny was indeed pregnant. She had called earlier that morning but Henry informed her that Jenny had gone into the city to meet with her ladies' group. When Matti congratulated Henry on being a father once again, he was surprised that Jenny had told Matti she was pregnant and he seemed to accept Jenny's conviction that she was pregnant with the same degree of caution that Matti was feeling. Henry advised Matti to call back around one o'clock, as Jenny usually got back to the farm a little past noon. At precisely three o'clock, which was two hours ahead of Saskatchewan time, Matti dialed the number to Henry's acreage.

"Hello," Jenny said.

Matti thought she would play the same game Jenny had played on her two weeks ago, by lowering her voice and pretending she was the Regina City Police trying to collect a speeding ticket. Just the thought of her doing that, however, made her laugh so hard, Jenny knew in an instant it was her dear friend.

"Matti, so nice to hear from you. Henry said you had called earlier."

"Jen, tell me straight away, are you with child or be it a false alarm?"

"Of course, I am pregnant, Matti. It will be two weeks today.!"

"So, you be tested?"

"No, I haven't seen a doctor to be tested, if that's what you're asking."

"Yes, and no and well, did you test yourself? There be ways to test the urine but who am I to tell you that."

"Oh, that's fine, Matti, but no, I haven't done that either. I just know I'm pregnant and in nine months from now, give or take a week or two, the baby will be born."

Matti didn't know what to say. She was just as concerned as Henry. What if Jenny didn't conceive? Oh, what a letdown that will be for her sweet mistress. Matti dared to ask one more question, "What has been your average menstrual cycle, Jen?" Matti quickly added, "Now, it's none of my business…"

Jenny knew where this was heading and decided to just go with the flow. Jenny appreciated her friend's concern and desire to be helpful even though it wasn't necessary. "It's been pretty consistent at 28 days."

"So have you had any spottin' and bleedin' in the last few days?"

Jenny laughed. "Oh, Matti, you are such a dear. I know you're concerned about me and I did spot a bit yesterday. Now, I know what you are going to say; that if I was pregnant my period would have stopped."

"That's it, Jen, the hormones be tellin' the blood rich tissue to stay intact to support the growing baby and you should stop any shedding, know what I'm sayin'?"

"Yes, Matti, but at times, there can still be bleeding or spotting. It could be due to implantation bleeding."

"What's that Jen? You got me there."

"Well, the fertilized egg could be burrowing into the blood rich lining of the uterus and cause a little bleeding which could account for the spotting. In any case, Matti, rest assured that you are going to be an adopted auntie!"

"Oh, Jen, I be wantin' this so bad for you, I be visitin' the bathroom more often than I should. Please, forgive me for doubting but…oh, dear Lord, I be prayin' for you and that baby of yours. I be counting the days until you lets me know that doctor of yours tests positive…see, now there I be goin' again. Sorry Jen."

"No need to be, Matti. You are a dear friend who wants the best for me but I know I am with child… my guardian angel as well as the Holy Spirit have looked after it all."

"So, what Camilla and Chloe be thinkin' of all this?" Matti wanted to know.

"You are the only one I have shared this with so far, Matti. I'm having lunch with Camilla next week and then I will share the news with her in person. I want to see the expression on her face when I tell her. Then I will call Chloe and tell her the news as well."

"Oh, Jen, they all be so happy for you!"

CHAPTER THIRTY-THREE

EVEN THOUGH THE noon hour rush was over, the dining room at the Hotel Saskatchewan was still full. The ladies had placed their order and were discussing one of the girls Camilla was counseling at the Tutorial School for Unwed Mothers.

"I feel so sorry for Sandra, Mom. It's similar to a case I was telling you a while back about Marcia who went ahead with an abortion and Jeremy prayed over me to help me get over it."

"Yes, I recall that and I still keep her in my prayers."

"Well, Sandra is one week into her second trimester and is seriously considering abortion. At first, she was going to keep the child and then it was adoption and now under increasing pressure from her boyfriend and even family, she has decided to terminate her pregnancy."

"Oh, Camilla, that is so sad. At any stage, it is such a tragedy but at thirteen weeks, all the major organs have been formed. It is a tiny human being clearly identifiable as a member of the human race. Even at three or four weeks, the nervous system has begun to form along with the heart. One can see the arms and legs budding. It's amazing how quickly the baby develops."

"It truly is. We view videos and slides all the time with the girls and I am always awed by it all."

"How does Sandra feel about seeing what is going on inside of her?" Jenny wanted to know.

"That's one of the reasons she has not terminated her pregnancy. She loves the baby growing in her womb but can't deal with all the pressure. She has also had a rough pregnancy so far; extreme fatigue, morning sickness. She throws up regularly at class and complains of swollen, tender breasts. Her mother keeps telling her that will be all over with as soon as she gets rid of the baby."

"But that usually goes away in the second trimester and as uncomfortable as it is the end reward far outweigh these symptoms."

"She is aware of that. I think she is just using that as another reason to have an abortion."

"How do you help girls struggling with that decision? It may haunt them for the rest of their lives."

"I know; so many girls who have aborted their child come regularly to talk to the girls and let them know just how huge the decision is and how it affects them. I try to get them to look at all the options and also all the consequences of their decision. I also encourage them to watch a video of an ultrasound film that has recorded an actual abortion and how the doctor inserts various instruments to open up the uterus, puncture the water sac and use a suction machine to tear the baby apart. Sometimes, like in Sandra's case, the head is too large to be sucked up by the tube and so another instrument like a pair of tongs is used to crush the head in order to get it out of the uterus. A lot of girls will not watch the video but those that do usually decide not to go through with it. They see how the baby reacts so fearfully, as its sanctuary is violated with such aggression. How a doctor can do this day in and day out and not feel anything is difficult to understand."

"I recall speaking with Chloe about this and she made a point I will never forget. It is impossible to harm the baby without harming the mother. Similarly, you cannot harm the mother without harming the child."

"That's so true, Mom. I wish we could find another solution

to all this that protects both the child and the mother. It's a terrible law that allows this to go on. When I read the staggering statistics of the thousands upon thousands being killed each year it breaks my heart."

"How on earth can this be stopped?"

Camilla shook her head. "It's an overwhelming challenge, Mom. TV, movies, magazines all portray sex outside of marriage. In many cases, it's glorified. Boy meets girl at a bar and before the night out, they're in bed. And guys have to be more responsible too. Look at Sandra, the same guy that has her pregnant believe it or not got another girl pregnant two years ago. She, too, had an abortion. Even if Sandra opts for an abortion, more than likely, he will leave her and find someone else. They want sex with no responsibility or commitment. It will complicate their life too much and the list goes on.

"We have had a girl come in pregnant three years in a row and each time has an abortion. Last week, I heard that she is pregnant again. In all too many instances, abortion can become just another method of contraception. Somehow, the message has to get out there to abstain and keep your standards high. Have a set of values that mean something. Will power and self discipline for many is simply not in their life.

"So, how are your ladies' group sessions coming along--?"

"Here is your order, ladies. The Mediterranean salad was for you I believe, Ma'am."

"No, mine was the chicken Caesar salad."

"Sorry, Ma'am."

"Would you care for some wine with your meal?"

"No, this is fine."

Camilla shook her head as well, "No thank you."

"You asked about the ladies' group; it's coming along great. Henry and I had some terrific conversations with Father Engelmann and he gave me several ideas to share with the ladies one of which is our most important responsibility to our spouses."

"What is that?" Camilla wanted to know.

"To see to it that your spouse comes safely home to our

heavenly Father. The more one thinks of it, if that is your main goal in the marriage, it has many implications; not to be a stumbling block, submitting to the other, dying to oneself, accepting the other, putting into action the biblical meaning of love in Corinthians. And then there's the practice of living out a strong Christian life; praying together, reading the Bible, attending church, praying at meals, night prayers. It's not just about attending church on Sunday. To be a Christian is a committed way of life."

Camilla nodded and swallowed her food, "Yes, I agree. Having Christ at the center of your marriage is so critical. He is the Teacher, Mentor, and perfect example of picking up one's cross daily and following Him."

"Father Engelmann really stresses the Holy spirit in all this. I have to admit, I never thought of the third Person in the Holy Trinity that much until Father started to talk so much about Him. And it's true, Jesus said several times before He ascended into heaven that He will send the Comforter, the Helper, the Holy Spirit to dwell within us, to give us the grace and strength to follow Jesus' teachings and to remind us and convict us of all that Jesus said and did when He was on earth. You know, it's just like our guardian angel; the more I acknowledge that I have one to guide and protect me, the more I become aware of my angel. Now that I am beginning to pray to the Holy Spirit, I am becoming so aware of Him in my life, too. And, I do feel strengthening in a more obvious way. Before when I thought I was gaining strength through nature and God's creation, it really is the Spirit of God that I am drawing from."

"You're beginning to sound more and more like Father Engelmann, Mom!"

Jenny chuckled. Her face began to light up and her eyes sparkled with delight, "Anyway, Camilla, I am dying to tell you some news!"

Camilla was holding a fork full of salad, ready to put it into her mouth and she stopped mid-air and slowly let her hand fall back to the table. Her eyes grew big, she had an idea of what her mother was going to say and hoped with all her might that she was right...

"Camilla, I am pregnant!"

"No way...!"

Jenny nodded with a huge smile covering her pretty face that glowed radiantly.

"It happened the day after we came home from Ottawa. Henry and I..." Jenny hesitated not sure if she should go into the details but she couldn't help herself.

"Henry and I went to Wascana Park for a picnic and made love!"

"To the park during the day and made love!?" Camilla retorted in disbelief.

Jenny nodded hardly able to hold back a laugh that was dying to come out.

"Weren't there people around?"

Jenny shook her head smiling from ear to ear. "No, it was a Wednesday afternoon and we went to a very secluded place that we had gone to when we first met in 1956. We almost made love then but we didn't...until last week!"

Camilla shook her head back and forth. "If you made love just last week, how do you know you're pregnant, Mom? Have you seen a doctor? Is it confirmed?"

"No, I haven't seen anyone yet, but I know, I'm pregnant....I just know."

"When was you last period, Mom?" Camilla had to know.

"Honey, you're asking the same questions that Matti asked when I told her. Don't be concerned about that, Honey; I just know I'm with child."

"Did you test your urine?"

Again, Jenny shook her head negative. "It's okay, Sweetie; it's just one of those things, you will have to trust me."

"But Mom, I've counseled many girls over the years that have felt after they had sex with a boy that they were pregnant only to find out after a doctor visit that they weren't. I don't want to let you down or put doubt in your mind, Mom, but you have to have it confirmed."

"I plan to, Camilla, not for my sake but for Henry, Matti and now you and when I call Chloe later today, I'm sure she will give me the same drill."

"Oh, Mom, I'm sorry. I am certain you are but…okay! You are! I'm going to totally and completely accept it." Camilla got up, dashed to her mother's side, and hugged her in her chair. "I'm so happy that you're pregnant, Mom," Camilla said louder than perhaps she should have and at least half of the restaurant heard her comment and saw the huge show of affection.

Jenny noticed and turned redder than the roses in Carlos' garden. Camilla jumped up and down and could hardly contain herself as she returned to her seat.

"So, if you're two weeks pregnant, then your due date will be sometime in…"

"May!" said Jenny. "I'm already counting the days."

"Okay, now that we have that established, I still think you need to see Doctor Kreake right away. At your age, he may refer you to a gynecologist. They will probably do an ultrasound to make sure the placenta is well attached to the uterus and check how the embryo is coming along."

"Well, maybe I am relying on my firm belief that everything is fine and don't need medical attention at this point."

"Oh, Mom, why do you suppose God's plan for some people to become doctors and nurses and care givers is? The same with me and the talents God gave me to help girls. If everyone exercised their faith like you, we wouldn't need any helping services."

"Yes, that's true, Camilla, you are right. I will make an appointment as soon as I get home."

"And further, maybe you need certain supplements, vitamins, exercises and a whole host of things that can be done to help the embryo along and get a good start."

Jenny nodded.

"And you actually made love in the park?"

Jenny beamed and nodded.

"And it was during the day, like in the afternoon?"

Again, Jenny grinned from ear to ear, her eyes sparkling with a daring look.

"Oh, Mom and you weren't self-conscious or anything!?"

Jenny shrugged her shoulders and began to chuckle. "Daring isn't it? A bit crazy…we just let it happen!"

Camilla smiled and shook her head from side to side. "Oh, my gosh, Mom…I can't believe it…at your age?"

Jenny kept laughing, reveling in doing something so out of character and yet it was something that was meant to be.

The two ladies gazed at one another for the longest time each in their own thoughts. Every now and then they would burst out in laughter as thoughts of what happened at the park during broad daylight struck their imaginations!

This time it was Camilla's eyes that began to light up as she was about to share something, too! "I'm so happy for you, Mom and it's such a relief for me…" Camilla's words trailed off and Jenny studied her daughter for a moment…

"Since I know how much you want a child, I was holding back on some news that I have been dying to share with you, too, but was reluctant as…"

Jenny's eyes grew wide, "Camilla, don't tell me you're pregnant, again?"

Camilla lit up with a huge grin just like her mother did moments ago and nodded her head. "Yup!"

"Oh, Camilla," Jenny said and thrust both hands across the table taking her daughter's waiting hands in hers. They shook each other's hands so hard that the water glass spilled over. A waiter nearby saw the mishap and rushed over and mopped up the spilled water. "I will be right back and refill your glasses.

"Now I know why you didn't order wine earlier, Camilla," and looking at the server, Jenny continued, "No, since we can't have wine, perhaps bring us some sparkling water with cranberry juice. We have to celebrate!"

Unbeknownst to Jenny and Camilla, by now, patrons of several tables around them were drawn into their conversation. It was like a soap opera. A mother and daughter who almost looked like twins, discovering that each was having a baby at the same time! How unbelievably, uncanny was that!?

One of the tables began to clap and was immediately joined

by several other tables. The girls blushed and nodded to the patrons in appreciation.

"So, Honey, for how long have you been pregnant?"

"I am just going into my third month."

"Oh, Camilla, you've been holding back all this time. Oh, Honey, I'm so sorry I indirectly caused you to withhold your news."

"No, Mom this couldn't be better because now I feel the joy inside whereas before I was thinking more of you and your dilemma. Now, we can really celebrate!"

Just then, the waiter returned with two tall fluted glasses that looked like they were filled with a bubbly red wine and set the glasses on the table. Just before the ladies made a toast, Jenny couldn't resist giving her daughter the third degree like she did to her.

"So, Camilla, are you sure you are pregnant? Did the doctor confirm…"

"Oh, Mom!"

And just as the ladies raised their glasses to toast the great news they shared to one another, the patrons within earshot raised a glass too and toasted along with Jenny and Camilla. Once again, the ladies turned beet red and laughed.

A lady just a few tables from them got up and as she was leaving she stopped at their table. She looked directly at Camilla and winked.

"From across the room, it was difficult to see who the mother was or who the daughter was as you both look so much alike. But now that I am up close I can easily see that you're the mom!"

They all laughed and then the lady went on to say, "I came along late in my mother's life, she was close to sixty when she became pregnant with me. She is now in her eighties and she looks sixty! If it's any consolation to you, my mom swears that her youth is due to me coming along." The lady smiled and added with pride, "Mom always says I keep her young at heart, active and not her age at all even if I'm a pain sometimes! I just want to congratulate you both and wish you all the best!"

"Oh, thank you so much," said Jenny. They held each other's hand for a brief moment and the young lady left.

"What a nice thing for her to stop and extend her wishes," said Camilla.

"But she did bring up something that I have been thinking of lately. I am fifty one and by the time the baby is twenty, I will be in my seventies and so will Henry."

"Oh, you and Dad will be fine, Mom. It will all work out just great. That's the message I think the young lady wanted to convey to you. So, what are you hoping for? A boy or a girl?"

"Well, it really wouldn't have mattered but I know the sex of the baby."

Camilla titled her head and wrinkled her brow, "You do…?"

Jenny nodded, once again a huge smile covering her happy face. "It's a girl!"

"Did you have an ultr…no, of course not, it's too early to tell…." Camilla gazed at her mom who looked so certain and confident.

Jenny shrugged her shoulders, tilted her pretty head and said, "I just know!"

CHAPTER THIRTY-FOUR

Ever since Jenny was miraculously healed of her cancer in the spring of 1989, her monthly medical checkups which followed for the next year, showed no signs of any re-occurrence of the disease. In fact, Dr Kreake was astounded by Jenny's health. Her weight, heart, blood pressure and all vital signs checked out perfectly. Ultra sounds, x-rays, MRI's, and CT scans showed no signs of any tumors. This was also the case for the next two years when Jenny went for a complete physical check up at six month intervals. Each time, she was in excellent health and had no need to see a doctor otherwise.

For this reason, Dr. Kreake was surprised to see Jenny after only two months since her last six month checkup. As soon as Dr. Kreake stepped in to the examination room, Jenny stood and gave the doctor a hug.

"Hi, Doctor Kreake, it's nice to see you again."

He smiled and said, "You are the only patient of mine that gives me a warm hug. I must say, it makes my day!"

"You are the best doctor, ever. I will never forget how well you looked after me when I was in the hospital fighting for my life."

"Thanks, Jenny," said Doctor Kreake as they both sat down.

Jenny smiled at her doctor. "You must be surprised to see me?"

Doctor Kreake nodded. "Yes, you look great, in fact, radiant as ever." He wrinkled his brow and continued, "Is there anything troubling you?"

"Doctor Kreake, you are not going to believe this…" Jenny's eyes widened and sparkled with an effervescent joy and exclaimed, "I'm pregnant!"

At first, a look of shock covered Doctor Keake's face. Could this be possible? The chance of her conceiving a baby at this point in her life was extremely slim and yet she was completely healed of cancer defying all medical explanation and restored to perfect health. Could this be another miracle in her life?

"That's wonderful, Jenny. I recall you expressing your desire to bear a child and I have to be honest, I never thought that would be one dream of yours that would come true. So, you must have done a home pregnancy test?"

"No."

"Have you seen another doctor, then…"

"No, I just know, Doctor Kreake that I am with child!" Jenny once again exclaimed."

Doctor Kreake wrinkled his forehead, "Have you missed a period or two?"

"Oh, Doctor Kreake, I did spot last week, but I'm definitely pregnant. It happened three weeks ago. I just know that the good Lord has blessed me with another miracle."

Doctor Kreake smiled. "The good Lord has blessed us with ways of confirming His blessings, Jenny. I need you to go to the lab on the second floor and have you tested. Then come back and I'll go over the results with you. We need to confirm this right away."

"Well, okay, have it your way." Jenny smiled and winked at the same time.

Doctor Kreake filled out a lab request form and wrote a note to the lab technician and then handed it to Jenny. "Have the test done and I'll see you in a bit."

Doctor Kreake didn't say anything else. He wanted to respond as positively as Jenny looked yet, he had to be cautious. Over the years, he had seen many disappointments of women who thought they were pregnant. The fact that she spotted may be an indication that Jenny may be jumping the gun. But then, one never can be sure until all tests are done and confirmed.

FOR THE FIRST time since that memorable day at the park, Jenny felt a twinge of doubt. She was so certain the moment they had made love that she had conceived. It was so real, that it all happened just perfectly the way God had designed it to work. She knew however, that as certain as she was, it had to be confirmed.

On the way down to the lab, Jenny read the note which Doctor Kreake had written on the form:

Please notify me of results ASAP. Will see patient following test.

Jenny was so absorbed in what Doctor Kreake had written, she hadn't noticed the elevator had stopped and the doors had opened to the second floor of the Medical Arts Building. Just down the hall, a sign over the doorway read:

LABORATORY

There were two other people seated in the reception area. A young girl behind the counter smiled at Jenny and took Doctor Kreake's form. She read the instructions and looked up at Jenny with a knowing smile. She put Jenny's name on a small test tube with a stopper on top. She handed it to Jenny and said, "Please take this to the washroom and fill half way with a urine sample and then put it into a rack in the small closet above the toilet tank. When you are finished, you can return to your doctor's office. He wants to see you."

Jenny waited almost an hour before the receptionist showed Jenny to Doctor Kreake's office instead of the examination room. It felt strange that she would be seeing him there. She recalled a similar time when she was called in early after tests had revealed tumors in her body. She was filled with fear as the receptionist opened the door and she stepped inside. Doctor Kreake was writing something at his desk.

"Please sit down, Jenny. I'll just be a moment." Jenny could feel heat surge through her body. She studied the doctor sitting before her looking for a clue, any sign...*please dear God, let the results be positive.*

No sooner had the words left Jenny's thoughts than Doctor Kreake laid down his pen and looked up at Jenny. A broad, happy smile began to grow on her dear, sweet, doctor's face and instantly she knew what she had already known. Before Doctor Kreake could begin to tell her the good news, Jenny looked up and lifted her hands in a prayerful pose and said, *"Oh thank you dear Lord, please forgive my moments of doubt."*

CHAPTER THIRTY-FIVE

HENRY HEARD THE garage door close; Jenny was home. His heart began to pound. He hoped with all of his might that for Jenny's sake the doctor had confirmed her instincts; she was indeed pregnant. He would know as soon as he saw her if the news was positive. Henry had to admit he felt ambivalent about it all. On the one hand, he wanted whatever made Jenny happy and yet, on the other hand, he was fearful of bringing another child into the world at his stage in life. *Would he be able to handle being a father once again?*

Henry heard the laundry door open that led to the garage. Ginger had snuck in with Jenny and was the first to find Henry standing in the foyer. She was wagging her tail excitedly but Henry ignored his pet, keeping his gaze at the doorway.

If the news was good she would already be shouting it out, wouldn't she? Oh please God, let her be with child.

When Jenny stepped into the foyer, she was smiling through her tears. She was so excitedly happy, she couldn't speak. She just rushed to Henry and thrust her arms around his neck and began to sob out of sheer happiness. Without knowing the reason for his dear wife's emotional state but more out of sympathy for her, tears immediately surfaced in Henry's eyes. Jenny's chest heaved uncontrollably against Henry's. It was another one of those many moments in their relationship that he felt so deeply united with Jenny. He was hopeful Jenny was pregnant and yet, so far, were her tears of happiness or sadness…he wished she would say so.

Slowly, he pulled inches away from his beloved and looked into tear filled eyes…

"Are you pregnant, Honey?"

Jenny simply nodded, still unable to speak.

"Oh, Jenny…my dear, sweet, Jenny…"

Once again, Henry pulled Jenny in to his chest and stroked his hand soothingly on her back.

Wrapped in each other's arms, they stood there and wept. They might have stayed there longer if it hadn't been for Ginger nudging between them and brushing her tail against their legs. Finally, they parted and gazed into each other's eyes. Henry brushed away the tears on Jenny's cheeks and then on his own.

"I'm very happy for you, Jenny and so relieved that it turned out as you believed. I have to admit I'm both excited and nervous to be a father again."

"It's our special child, Henry. It's been my heart's desire and prayer for so long… *It's my gift to you.*"

Henry gazed into Jenny's happy, blue eyes and kissed her tenderly.

"I love you so dearly, Honey," said, Jenny tenderly.

And ever so softly, Henry whispered, "I love you, too, Jenny and our little baby."

After making some refreshments, they made it out to the deck and stood at the railing overlooking the valley. They looked to see if Father Engelmann was out and about but there was no one there.

"I can't wait to tell Father the good news. He will be so pleased to know that my pregnancy has been confirmed."

"I think he was more like you in that regard, Jenny. Last time I spoke with him, he felt certain you were with child. However, besides myself there are a few others who are dying to know if your pregnancy has been confirmed. Matti called three times this morning to see if you came back from the doctor yet. Chloe and Camilla also called. You're going to be busy today just returning calls."

"Oh, yea of little faith," Jenny laughed, knowing she was guilty of doubting, too.

"So, was Doctor Kreake surprised to see you so soon after your last check up?"

"Yes, he was. He was also surprised to learn that I was pregnant primarily because of my age and medical history. Although, he knew when I was healed of cancer, I was thoroughly checked over by a gynecologist, he still found it difficult to believe my healing was so complete in all respects. He did want to know about my previous pregnancies."

"Oh yes, you had Camilla and J.J. which goes back a long time."

"J.J. was born January 29, 1969 and Camilla in 1957."

"Wow, twenty three years ago. That's a lot of years between pregnancies."

"He wants to do some more blood tests which require that I fast before going. I think I will do that tomorrow before my ladies' group meets. Oh, they will be so excited to hear my news."

"So, when do you see Doctor Kreake again?" Henry wanted to know.

"I will see him next week to go over the blood tests but after that, he referred me to see a gynecologist to look after my pregnancy. His name is Doctor Webster. His office will call me when I'm to see him. Probably in about three to four weeks."

"Did Doctor Kreake prescribe any vitamins or supplements?"

"No. When I told him what I'm presently taking and eating and after checking me over, he said to continue on as everything looks fine."

Just then the phone rang.

"It's probably one of the girls calling." Jenny ran into the house and got to the phone on the fourth ring. It was Matti.

"Oh, hi Matti, Henry said you called this morning."

"I just have to know, Jen, what the doctor be sayin...?"

"See, Matti, he just confirmed what I have been saying for the last three weeks—"

"Then you must be expectin'…isn't that so?"

"Yes, Matti I am pregnant! And Doctor Kreake said that everything is fine."

"Oh, Jenny, I be prayin' so hard my knees are sore, you'd think I be the one in labour wantin' the baby."

Jenny chuckled. "You are such a dear, Matti."

"So, when be the due date, did the doctor figure it out?"

"Yes, he did. He calculated it to be in May sometime. I will still have an ultrasound which will help to confirm the date."

"When they do that, they can tell if its goin' to be a boy or girl, isn't that so?"

"Yes, an ultra sound can tell towards the end of the first trimester; around twelve weeks. But…I will share a secret with you Matti, I already know what the sex of the baby is."

"Now, Jen do you have 'in' on that too?"

"I do, Matti, a little baby girl is growing in my womb!"

There was a momentary silence. Matti didn't know how to respond. "Now, how can you be so sure? You say it with the same confidence that you be pregnant and sure enough, you know even before the doctor tellin' you it's so."

"Well, it's just something between me and the good Lord, Matti. You are the only person I will share that with for now, except Henry."

"Here I be doubtin' again, but what if…now, just what if, it be a boy would you be upset?"

"Oh no, Matti, I would love either sex but in this case, I know it's a baby girl."

"Well, I'll be…'spect you have the name all picked out already too."

"Yes, I do, Matti…" Jenny hesitated not knowing if she should share it with Matti before telling Henry.

"Oh, Jenny, you got me so curious, now, I just have to be knowin' what that beautiful girl be called. I don't know if I can wait…I promise I won't be sayin' a word until you decide to let everyone know."

"Oh, Matti, her name is going to be Hannah."

There was a long silence, "Hannah, oh, Jen, that be such a

beautiful name and it's in the Bible, that for sure!"

"Yes it is, Matti. There's a beautiful story about Hannah who wanted a child just like I did...well, instead of telling you about it, read Samuel 1, and you will see the similarities between Hannah in the story and me. But another reason I want to call her Hannah...and I hope Henry likes the name too, is because my guardian angel's name is Hannah!"

"Now, that's what you be tellin' me a long time ago. Father Engelmann met your and Henry's angels...now, ain't that somet'ing. So, in a way, you be makin' your unseen angel, Hannah for real that you can see by giving birth to your little angel Hannah!"

"That's right, Matti. I never thought of it that way but they will both be my angels; one to look after me in the unseen and one to love in the seen."

"*Seems to me, Jen, this child be heaven sent. That's for sure!*"

WHEN JENNY RETURNED to the deck, Henry was still at the railing looking down into the valley. They both saw Father Engelmann emerge from the prayer house. He must have sensed that Henry and Jenny were out on the deck as he stopped and looked up their way.

Henry looked at his dear friend and mentor who was also waiting for the news. At the top of his lungs, he shouted, "Jenny is pregnant!" The message echoed through the valley.

He took Jenny's hand and raised their arms upwards. They couldn't see Father's face from that distance but obviously, he heard the good news.

He, too, raised his hands upwards and shouted back,
"*Praise to the Lord!*"

Chapter Thirty-Six

THE MOMENT MATTI got off the phone, she ran outside and called for Thomas. He was way on the north end of the estate, directing the planting of more milkweed and flowers that would bloom until the end of September and weather permitting, into October. Matti's shrill voice alarmed him and he came running up the path as she was running towards him.

Thomas stopped, trying to figure out what Matti was so excited about. Perhaps there had been an accident or some urgent matter had come up.

"What's the matter, Matti...?"

"Oh, Thomas, I can't wait to tell you the news and the rest of the family when they come home. Jenny's pregnant! She went to the doctor this morning and he be confirmin' it. Our mistress be with child!"

"That is good news, Matti. Now we know for sure."

Matti stopped just short of Thomas and took several deep breaths of air trying, to catch her breath.

"For the first time, she be havin' a child in a normal, happy setting. It be takin' a long time but the good Lord be blessing our dear, Miss Jenny."

Thomas thought over Matti's words and he had to agree, Camilla was born out of wedlock and not the best of circumstances and J.J., he recalled only too well, the hell that James put her through in trying to raise the boy.

"My only concern for Miss Jenny is her age. She is getting on and the eggs in the ovary deteriorate over time which could affect the development of the embryo and fetus."

"Now, how you be knowing of such things, Thomas. You soundin' more like a doctor than a gardener."

"I handled a case once where I had to become informed in such matters. I represented a woman whose husband divorced her because she got pregnant and wouldn't abort the child. She was in her mid-fifties and the husband was eight or nine years older."

"What happened, Thomas?"

"The divorce went through, but it cost the husband big time in support—"

"I don't be carin' about that, Thomas; did the lady have the child?"

"Yes, she did and—"

"And… was it a healthy baby?" Matti was anxious to know.

Thomas hesitated for a moment, trying to choose his words. He could see Matti's concern wasn't necessarily for the woman he was talking about but her dear mistress and the child she was carrying.

"I was about to say, Matti, it was a complicated case…"

Matti sensed this might take some explaining. She approached Thomas and took his hand. "Come, let us sit a spell in the gazebo and you be explainin' it to me. I may not have your knowledge, Thomas but I'm not too old to learn."

When they sat on the swing inside of the gazebo, Matti said, "Now tell me about this case and why you be concerned about Jenny bein' along in her age."

Thomas took off his cap and wiped his brow with the back of his hand at the same time. He now regretted saying what he did.

"Problems can happen to pregnant women at any age as you well know, Matti. I don't want you to jump to conclusions; all I'm saying is that in older women the risk of pregnancy complications increase not only for herself but also for her child."

"Okay, I be with you so far."

"Well, in this case the woman's egg which she ovulated had an extra chromosome."

Matti wrinkled her brow. "Chromosomes be makin' up the body and contain all the information about us. Ain't that so?"

"That's right, the chromosomes are contained within all of the cells in our body including the egg and sperm which as you said contain the genetic information passed on from parent to baby."

Thomas paused and then continued, "In many cases, a woman carrying a fetus with an abnormal number of chromosomes miscarries, or, if they carry on as normal, the fetus can have any one of a number of physical abnormalities."

"You not sayin', Jenny may be havin' a problem?"

"No, not at all, Matti, all I'm saying is that in older women the incidence of abnormalities developing increases."

"So, what happened to the woman in your case?"

"In the eighteenth week of her pregnancy, she was tested for detecting chromosome problems and it was discovered that there was an abnormal number of chromosomes as I mentioned earlier. The baby had forty seven chromosomes in each cell instead of the normal forty six which each of us carries."

"I'm not sure I be understanding all this but I needs to know what kind of problem be comin'."

"Well, in this case, she and her husband were informed that the most common condition associated with an abnormal chromosome number is Down's Syndrome and they were given the option to terminate the pregnancy."

"Oh, my...so what be happenin', Thomas?"

"That is when the problem began. The husband wanted his wife to abort the child and she refused."

Matti shook her head and asked cautiously, "When the baby be born, did the child have Down Syndrome?"

Thomas nodded. "Yes, the child did."

THE ANGELIC LETTERS SERIES: THE HOUSE WHERE ANGELS DWELL

A silence fell between them. Matti got up and picked a few of the late blooming wildflowers surrounding the glistening Angel of Thanksgiving and placed them in her basket. She muttered a prayer which Thomas couldn't make out.

"You be takin' these pretty flowers to Jesus with our thanks for Miss Jenny and her baby."

She returned to the swing and sat down. She took Thomas' hand in both of hers and said, "From today on we be prayin' for Jenny that she be havin' a healthy baby girl."

Matti suddenly realized that she had promised to keep the sex of the child a secret and quickly corrected herself. "Or a healthy boy, if the good Lord willin'."

Thomas nodded. "Yes, Lord, we lift up Miss Jenny to You and ask You to bless her and Henry and the child growing within her womb. We ask that the child be healthy and strong in every way. We ask this through Jesus Christ, Amen."

Matti nodded and tightened her lips. "Amen, and I be sayin' it again, Amen."

LATER, AT DINNER time, Matti had to share the good news with everyone. They were all so excited but most of all it was J.J. who couldn't get over it. Right after dinner, he called his mother.

Jenny was just preparing dinner when the phone rang at the farm.

"Oh, hi J.J., what a pleasant surprise, I was going to call you and Nora later this evening."

"I think I know what you were going to call about...Matti spilled the beans, she couldn't help herself."

"Isn't it exciting?" Jenny said cautiously. She wondered how J.J. had taken the news.

"I'm really happy for you, Mom." J.J. said with an emotional tone in his voice. He paused for a moment and then continued, "I wasn't the easiest child to raise and I hope this baby fills your life with all the joy and happiness that you didn't have much of when I was growing up."

"Oh, J.J., we did have our challenges, but I loved watching you grow and develop. It was such a blessing to have you."

"You are being too kind, Mom, I know what a brat I was especially in my teen years. Both Dad and I gave you such a rough time." There was a pause and then J.J. said, "I know I apologized to you when Dad was ill in the hospital but I want you to know, I fully realize how blessed both Dad and I were to have you. I am very sorry for hurting you in so many ways; I love you and wish the best for you."

J.J.'s comments were so unexpected! She thought he might be against her being pregnant. His words touched Jenny's heart and tears were surfacing from deep within. Once again, she found herself unable to speak; the emotions erupting were so strong. Jenny just kept praising the Lord for His goodness in turning so many things in her life into such good.

Finally, in an incoherent, tear-filled burst of gratitude, Jenny said, "Oh, J.J. your words touch my heart. Thank you so much. Your words mean so much to me."

There was a silence on the other end. If Jenny was overjoyed and found it difficult to speak, J.J. was doubly so. He was immersed in the midst of experiencing love in all its fullness.

It's a gift the Lord gives us when we repent from the heart and soul.

Finally, J.J. said, "Nora and the rest of the gang here all want to talk to you and extend their best wishes, Mom. Before I go, when is the due date? Has that been determined yet?"

"Yes, a rough estimate was made today by my doctor. He thinks the baby will be born sometime in May."

"That's great, Mom. I know how much you love spring and all the new life it brings. It will coincide perfectly with the season you love so much."

CHAPTER THIRTY-SEVEN

J ENNY WAS FEELING guiltier with each passing day for not telling Henry about the sex of the child she was carrying and also the name she wanted to give their little girl. Since he had doubted that she was even pregnant, how would he react to the rest of the story? She was mainly concerned about him being worried for her if it didn't turn out to be the way she expected and she would be disappointed. Henry was a scientist in his own way and he wanted facts to be confirmed and not based upon some woman's intuition.

Yet, Jenny felt she just had to discuss this with him. Their relationship had to be based upon full disclosure. She already felt a bit uneasy sharing more about the baby with Matti than him. In a few days, she would have her first appointment with Doctor Webster and this entire matter may very well come up again. She just had to share with Henry all that was on her heart.

They had just finished dinner and decided to sit out on the deck and enjoy a cup of tea. Although it was mid November, there wasn't a sign of snow on the ground and the warm, balmy weather of September had extended itself all through October and threatened to do the same in November. Also, unusual for the prairies was that the wind had hardly made its presence known. As a result, many of the trees nestled in the valley were still able to show off their beautiful fall colored leaves.

Henry and Jenny loved to watch how the bright rays of the sun sinking in the western sky revealed the richness of the yellows, golds, oranges and browns in those dying moments before the long shadows swept across the valley floor turning it all into darkness. It was as if a dimmer light switch was slowly turned off in the valley.

Jenny brought tea out to the deck on a tray for both Henry and herself and sat it on the table between them. Henry didn't notice as his full attention was still studying the changing light in the valley. Twilight always fascinated him and Jenny knew what he would say next.

"One of these days, I am going to do a series of paintings that capture this peaceful time of day." He looked at Jenny as she sat next to him. "Thanks for the tea. I was just going to warm water and make some for us."

"See, how much our minds think together," Jenny observed. "Not only our enjoyment of tea after dinner but also of this special time of the day. I wish I had your talent as I, too, would love to capture on canvas the serene mood created by the backlighting of the setting sun before it is completely gone to another part of the world."

"Yeah, it's best captured down in the valley by the water. Ponds and streams give life to the land. I love how the hills and the light that is still caught on the tips of tall grass surrounding the water's edge reflect in the still pond. Such a peaceful atmosphere is created...the earth coming to rest for the day."

"Oh, Honey, you will just have to set up an easel on the deck by the prayer house and capture what your heart tells you to. You have always said how much you love painting outdoors."

Henry nodded and began to take notice of a dim light inside the prayer house growing brighter as the valley grew darker. His thoughts changed from his painting to what his mentor might be doing at this time. "Father must be at his desk writing or reading the Bible. He loves to do both by candle light. He said to me once that just having a light on the paper before him helps him focus more on what he is doing. He and his work become enveloped by the light."

"What a lovely thought, Henry. I can just picture Father in the bedroom by the table writing in the light of the candle beside the paper while the rest of the room is in shadow or semi-darkness. It would be so cozy and focused as you just described."

"Almost like having the twilight in the bedroom; so still, quiet and peaceful; a perfect atmosphere for creative writing."

"I wonder how Father is coming along with the story?" asked Jenny.

"I know he is working on the last book. The last time we talked about it, he said that I would have to finish it if the good Lord called him home before he did. I can't imagine all that he would have written about us. He certainly wouldn't be at a loss to write about life and how to live with purpose and meaning with eternity ever in mind."

"But then he did say when he was on the other side, he was allowed to see into our lives and all that went before right up until the moment he was returned back to life," Jenny offered.

"Yeah, that's right. He remembered everything about his stint on the other side and he even was allowed to see into some future event which prompted him to agree to come back. It had to do with some second mission which the Lord wanted him to carry out."

"I wonder what it is?" Jenny asked.

"He doesn't even know, Jenny. Apparently, it was removed from his memory. He will only know what it was when the present eventually catches up to it."

"Wow, it gives me goose bumps just thinking on it."

"Yeah, I guess we'll know soon enough, Honey."

Henry reached over to the cup of tea and brought it to his mouth. He blew on the steaming brew and took a cautious sip. "That sure hits the spot, Sweetheart. Thanks for making it."

Jenny waited for Henry to set his tea down and then reached over and took his hand and placed it on her tummy. "Do you feel the little bump, Honey?"

He rubbed his hand slowly and lightly. "Yes, I think I do!" Henry said excitedly. "Imagine a little life growing in there."

"Yes, I'm sure I felt her quicken this morning in the shower but not definite. It's about this time that they do start to move and kick. I can hardly wait."

"You said, *she quickened*, does that mean you might think we have a little girl?"

Jenny knew her observant husband would pick up on her comment. The door opened and Jenny walked in and said what lay heavy on her heart in one fell swoop. "Oh, Henry, I know it's a little girl and I do want to name her Hannah."

Henry gazed at his dear wife for a moment and said, "You are that certain, are you?"

Jenny beamed and simply nodded.

"So, we are going to go through that again, are we? First, you knew you were pregnant and the day you conceived and you were right on both accounts and now you know for certain you are carrying our little daughter…an ultra sound would confirm that, you know."

"Yes, I know but there is no need and I don't want an ultra sound…

Henry looked at Jenny quizzically and then said, "Well, let's take this one step at a time. You're certain that the baby is a girl and you want to call her Hannah. Has this got anything to do with your guardian angel's name? Or, what you called the Angel of Thanksgiving?"

"In a way that's true, Henry, but there is more to it or rather more to the story…"

"Okay, now you have my full attention, Honey. But before you begin, I want to get a blanket; I don't think the heavy sweater you are wearing is enough to keep you warm. I want to get my jacket, too."

Henry got up, rushed inside, and quickly returned. He wrapped a blanket around Jenny's shoulders and gave her a kiss on the cheek. He put on a jacket over his sweater, turned his chair slightly towards her and sat down.

"Okay, Sweetheart, tell me what that beautiful mind of yours is thinking."

"It's going to be a long story, are you sure you want to hear it?'

"I have all the time in the world for you, Honey. I was going to go up and work on my painting but that can wait. I'm all ears…"

"Well, you know I always wanted to have a baby of yours. Ever since that day in the park when we first met, I envisioned one day carrying your child. Not just during my teenage years but also through my marriage with James. It is what I wished for more than anything. When we finally came together and married it was still in my mind but even more so."

"And why is that?" asked Henry.

"When I was a librarian at the high school I worked at in Ottawa, a teacher there had commissioned you to do a prairie scene for him and his wife. I learned about it and went to his home to see the painting. I remember when I read the biography on the back it mentioned that you and your wife and family lived in the valley near Lumsden."

"Geez, Jenny that was a long time ago. I do recall the teacher, but go on."

"Well, I often thought about you and your children and have to admit, I was envious of Julean. She had given you four wonderful children, and I, too, want to at least carry one of yours. My dream has finally come true!"

"But Honey, I've told you before that I couldn't possibly love you anymore than I already do, regardless if you carry a child of mine or not."

"Yes, I know, but to me it's a lifelong dream and I can't help myself. But there is more to this story."

Henry smiled and reached over and squeezed Jenny's hand. "Okay Sweetheart, go on."

"Last summer before we went to Toronto to see Lauren in Joseph, I went to the Poustinia to talk to Father Engelmann in the hope he would pray for my desire to get pregnant. When I came to the prayer house that morning, Father wasn't there. I didn't know that he was in the bedroom and I began to pray out loud to God pleading that He answer my prayer. I expressed my wish to give you a child just like Julean did."

"When Father came into the chapel, he was astounded how similar my plea was to that of Hannah in the Old Testament in the book of 1 Samuel. When he told me the biblical story, I, too, was amazed over the similarity. And just like you tried to reassure me of your love regardless if I bear a child for you or not, Hannah's husband, Elkanah, did the same. You may want to read about it if you're not familiar with that book in the Old Testament."

Henry remained silent, obviously fascinated by Jenny's sharing. He was however beginning to see how Hannah was connected to this and where this story was going.

"Anyway, Sweetheart, when Father told me that Hannah made a covenant with God that she would give the child back to Him if He answered her prayer, I did too."

"You what!?"

Jenny sat up in her chair and moved closer to the edge. She took hold of both Henry's hands and stared into his eyes, "Honey, I promised God that if He gives me a child, then I will give the child back to Him. I just know Henry that the infant within my womb is a girl and she will be a nun and her name will be—"

This time Henry sat up. "What!?"

"I know it may take some time for you to take this all in but so far everything is working out just as God and I agreed it would."

Henry couldn't believe what his dear wife was saying. He was momentarily speechless. "But, Jenny, making a covenant with God is serious stuff. Are you serious? Isn't this just like any other pregnancy?"

"Well, I am pregnant at age fifty one, which is rare, and I knew exactly the day and time I would conceive and I know that the child in my womb is a female which I so dearly want to name Hannah. If you want me to take an ultra sound it would be only for your benefit, Henry. Maybe God has some special plan for Hannah."

A SILENCE FELL between them as the first star of the east brightly shone its loving rays down on the three of them; Henry, Jenny and their dear, sweet little baby budding in the womb. Once again, Henry didn't know what to say to his wife. She was so unwavering in her faith and trust in God. He was amazed how certain she was and her belief in what was and still is to come to pass. Her relationship with the Lord was every bit as deep and strong as Father Engelmann's.

Jenny was gazing at the stars when he turned towards her. The light of the full moon hanging low in the sky glistened in her happy eyes. He could sense his wife's love for the Lord over the miracle of life in her womb which He had granted her. Henry had to admit that at their age and all Jenny's body had gone through, it was truly a miracle.

He followed Jenny's gaze into the heavens in awe of it all and wondered, too, what was the plan which God had in store for each of them since the beginning of time.

CHAPTER THIRTY-EIGHT

IT'S TRUE WHAT they say about pregnant women; they never look more radiant. Their skin seems to exude a special luminosity during this time more than at any other time in a woman's life. Doctor Webster noticed that special glow in Jenny the moment she was escorted into his office by the attending nurse. He was seated behind his desk about to finish writing a sentence into his file when Jenny walked in. He was spellbound by her beauty and youthful appearance. Never would he have guessed that the stunning woman in front of him was in her fifties. He continued to look up at Jenny and smiled.

For some reason she couldn't explain, she liked her new doctor instantly. He appeared to be in his late forties, wore round, rimless glasses and donned a mustache and goatee. His hair was black with grey growing out the sides near the temples, giving him a very distinguished look. It was the dark pointed beard on his chin which reminded Jenny of Freud, that the doctor looked more like a psychiatrist than an obstetrician.

The image of a tall, dark, handsome doctor however had to be slightly modified when he stood up and extended his hand to Jenny. His height surprised her; he was almost a head shorter than she was.

"Pleased to meet you, Mrs. Pederson, have a chair." He then directed his attention to the nurse and added, "I'll call for your assistance when we go into the examination room, Sandra."

Sandra nodded and left.

For the next half hour, Doctor Webster took Jenny's history. At certain times, he referred to three thick files which Doctor Kreake had sent over that had to do with Jenny's bout with cancer and her subsequent healing. Jenny felt very comfortable the entire time. She liked the doctor's friendly demeanor and his thoroughness.

"It's hard to believe that a woman who was so ravaged by cancer is perfectly healed and seated across from me. There's no other explanation than a miracle has occurred in your life, Mrs. Pederson.

"I would have to agree, Doctor Webster and please call me Jenny."

The doctor nodded and then went on, "I would further add, it is rare for a woman of your age to be pregnant."

Doctor Webster shook his head and said in jest, "Perhaps this is another miracle in your life!"

But Jenny didn't take it that way at all. "Oh, yes, it's truly a miracle! Every day I thank God for all the blessings He keeps giving me. Trust me, Doctor Webster, I could go on for some time telling you all that has occurred in my life over the past few years. But I will tell you, this pregnancy is something I hoped and prayed for, for most of my life and it's finally come true! I am so happy!"

"So I see, Jenny. So I see…"

WITH THE ASSISTANCE of the nurse in the examination room, Doctor Webster did a pelvic exam to assess the size of Jenny's uterus, a pap smear and breast exam.

"Everything seems fine. I am going to order an ultra-sound for you. With your past history, I don't have to tell you what that's all about."

Jenny nodded. "Yes, I am familiar with ultra-sounds. It's a bit too early to find out what sex the child is though, isn't it?"

"Yes, it is. I will order another ultra-sound at twenty weeks. For now, I want to see how the fetus is developing; if we can detect a heartbeat and determine more accurately the due date. I also want to make sure the placenta is well attached to the uterine wall and see the location of the umbilical cord. Are you experiencing any morning sickness, headaches, pain or anything out of the ordinary?"

Jenny thought for a minute. "No, everything seems fine. My appetite may be increasing, though."

The doctor nodded and then asked Jenny to sit up. He took Jenny's blood pressure and then said, "It's up slightly but that is to be expected during the first visit or two until we get to know one another better."

"The white coat syndrome?" Jenny asked with a smile.

The doctor nodded and returned her smile. "I would like more lab tests done in the next week or so."

The doctor took out a form and checked off all the tests which he wanted including a urine analysis. He handed the form to Jenny and then without looking at his nurse, he added, "Sandra will measure your weight and height before you leave. I would like to see you in a month and we can go over the test results and ultra sound. You will have to wait a bit longer before we can determine the sex of your baby."

"Oh, I know what it is already."

"How is that Mrs. Ped... or rather, Jenny?"

"Oh, I just know it's a little girl growing in my tummy."

The doctor studied Jenny for a moment and smiled. "See you mid-December, Jenny."

Chapter Thirty-Nine

THE AUDIENCE IN the church hall consisted of the husbands and wives from Jenny's groups that met across the city as well as others who had heard that Father Engelmann was to be the guest speaker. He was perfect to kick off six scheduled social events for speakers to talk on different topics related to marriage and family. Since Henry was working on an art exhibition, his presentation on the role of men in the family was postponed until next spring.

Brenda Oakley, the Leader Post reporter, was also present to interview Father after his presentation and write a report on his message and hopefully as much of his life that she could get the holy man to talk about.

After Jenny introduced Father, he was greeted with a standing ovation as he made his way to the podium. His long, flowing white hair and beard only added to the wisdom he was about to share. Henry sat in the front row and savored every move the holy man made, burning the image of his beloved friend in his memory to draw upon when he was no longer here. Just the thought of his teacher passing on stung his heart.

In his usual style, Father surveyed the group before him, attempting to connect with each and every person there, and then he began.

"In Genesis, we learn that the good Lord was very pleased with everything He created, but when He saw Adam alone in the Garden of Eden, He could see it was not good for man to be alone. So, God created Eve as a mate for Adam. How true this is; without a mate or others in our lives, we would be very alone. We were made out of love and for love; to love our heavenly Father and to love others. When we obey Jesus' two commands to do this, our lives are fulfilled. When we don't, we soon run into trouble, emotionally, physically and spiritually.

"From the moment we are born, an infant who is not nurtured and loved and held close to the heart is quick to manifest symptoms of being deprived of this basic human need. It is further compounded in countless homes in which children grow up in families where love is thwarted and held back or simply incapable of being given. Many times, it is due to the parents themselves who have not been loved or shown how to love in their upbringing. So many of us are emotionally scarred; not able to love or receive love, unable to show affection, anxious in the presence of others, lacking a wholesome love of self, unable to relate in a meaningful way with their spouse or their children...the results are crippling and devastating. It is as if we are like Adam, alone in the garden even though God has blessed us with a mate. One has only to see the statistics showing the rise in divorce and separation, not to mention the loneliness, psychological problems and needless struggle that so many endure as they journey through life.

"To show love and affection towards one's spouse and children should be the most natural and easy thing to do and yet it is alien to many. One of the great dangers in a marriage is when the honeymoon is over and couples lapse into the dangerous state of taking each other for granted. Couples immerse themselves so deeply in the challenges of daily living that they become unaware of the needs of their spouse and children! They neglect to use the basic gifts that all of us have been blessed with.

"Very briefly then, my message to you this evening is simply to remind all of us of some of the more basic ways to show others we care and love them.

"Listening. So many wives have expressed this to me over the years, 'Father, my husband doesn't listen to me half the time, if not most of the time. He doesn't seem to care or feel that what I have to say is important. He is just not interested and yet, when he is around his colleagues, his boss or friends, he is all ears. Am I less than them? Am I valued as an equal? I am around the children all day and sometimes I can't wait until he gets home so that I can have some adult conversation.'

"Perhaps to some of you this may sound all too familiar. The underlying message is clear, is it not? You don't care about me.

"Now, I know after working all day, many men are tired and many times not in the mood to come home and listen to problems about the children or things your wife may have to say but if we care, really care for our spouse, we listen and we listen with our hearts. We stop and look at our spouse and try to reflect her emotions. If she is happy about something, smile and be glad for her. If she is feeling sorrow, let your eyes and expression show it and be sincere. Why? Because we love our spouse and are willing to sacrifice ourselves and our immediate needs for hers. Yes, that's right, we care and should be concerned about her feelings and welfare as much as your own.

"Ask yourself, if you did this as much as you can would it make your wife happy? Would she feel you cared for her and that what she says is important?"

Many of the women in the audience chuckled and Henry surmised that many of the ladies probably gave their husbands the elbow.

"In the same way, wives have to listen with their eyes and ears. When your husband comes home, study him for a moment. Is he okay? Is he worried about something or troubled? Sometimes, his needs are more important and his need to share what is going on in his life takes priority. At times, wives have to hold back on their news until they help clear what bothers their husband.

"Listening, observing and communicating with sensitivity is always required. Listening from the heart can't be hurried and requires our full attention. The key is to always be willing to sacrifice our needs for the needs of the other.

"Touch. As I said from the beginning, we are touched and caressed by our mother in her womb all the while we are getting ready to come into the world. We are then immediately nurtured and loved all through our early years but it doesn't stop then either. All through life, we hunger to be touched in ways that convey that we are loved. Touch is critically important and one of the most powerful ways of sending out the message that we care about you. At times, it has to be shown with discretion but when done appropriately it is vital to uplifting our spirits and filling us with joy.

"There is nothing sweeter than to receive a kiss, a hug or pat on the back. When you walk by your spouse or one of your children, a gentle touch or rub on the shoulder conveys such a warm message. Touch is love in action; it requires such little effort and should be done daily. Don't be stingy with something that makes others happy and secure. It confounds me why something so easy and effortless to give is so often withheld or not in one's awareness to do! Never hesitate to show care and affection for another. Each moment we hold back is a precious moment lost in time which could have done so much good. Often, just a smile is needed to lift someone out of the doldrums.

"When I was a parish priest, I loved it when a couple would come into church holding hands or sitting in a pew with their fingers entwined. It was wonderful to see a father with his arm around his son or daughter. What a wonderful beacon of light parents are to others when they show affection to one another. I firmly believe that families, who give hugs, pat one another on the back, show affection, express care and concern through gestures of touch have a greater bond with one another than those who don't.

"How we respond to signs of affection is equally important. If someone rests their hand on your shoulder reach back and pat their hand. Show appreciation with a smile, a thank you or return the affection. We need to encourage this constantly and never give the cold shoulder as this immediately closes the door to the present experience but also instills a hesitancy to repeat such actions in the future.

"There are times when it is difficult for a person to receive love by way of words, touch or affection. It is important for both the giver and recipient to be sensitive to this. Sometimes, this can lead to a heart to heart discussion or a self examination as to why this is so. In any case, expressions of love must always be acknowledged.

"A most beautiful practice when someone is going through a trial or challenge is to pray with them. Holding their hands or resting your hands on their head or shoulders shows concern and that they are not alone in this; that they are in your thoughts and prayers. Touching others in this way gives more power to the caring words you express. We are lifting them to the highest level; the Great Healer.

"There are many families who carry out a practice similar to this which was very common by Christians in the early church. It was the act of laying hands on others to bless them, offering them up to the Lord and inviting the Holy Spirit to fill their hearts and strengthen them.

"I would like to demonstrate this in the hope of encouraging all of you to revive this beautiful way of showing care, concern and love for another."

Father paused and surveyed the large hall, "Is there someone here that has a need or illness or a concern that they would like prayers for?"

Several hands went up. Father selected a man who had just learned that he had prostate cancer. Father directed Bryan to sit on a chair next to the podium. He then asked several people to come up, surround Bryan, and place their hands on him. Next, Father invited everyone to join him in prayer as he too, placed his hands on Bryan's head.

"Dear Father, You have promised that where two or three are gathered in Your name that You will be here with us.

We lift our brother, Bryan, up to You with all his fears and concerns and ask You to fill him with trust and peace. You have promised that if we bring our burdens to You that You will make them light and easy. That You will help us to deal with the challenges and trials which come our way. Send your Holy Spirit into Bryan's heart so he gives this illness to You to deal with. If it is Your will, heal Bryan and restore his health to fullness better than before. We know that You can do this directly with Bryan or work through the doctors and the medication they prescribe. Guide these medical healers of Yours with wisdom and insight to do the best for Bryan. We praise and thank You Lord for the gift of life and healing. We thank You for Bryan and his family and pray for them to trust in You and Your goodness to turn all things into good."

Then Father led everyone to say the Lord's prayer after which a peaceful silence filled the room. It was obvious to all those present the wonderful emotional healing and support Bryan received from the group's prayer. After several minutes, Father Engelmann thanked everyone and Bryan and his prayer partners returned to their seats.

"What you have just seen is what can be done within your family. We love one another and wish the best for them. As I said earlier, there is nothing higher than to touch someone and pray for God to heal and bless them. It transmits our deep care and that we are here for them. We help the person we pray for to carry their trial or illness and in many cases, speeds up the healing process and even a miracle results!

"I have already alluded to words and how powerful they are to express love and affection. Words can touch one's heart in an instant both positively and negatively. Always use the power of what you say to uplift and when possible combine your words with a tender, warm embrace.

"Give all to one another.

"Next to bread, words of simple kindness, respect, tenderness, affection are the food we all hunger for. Honest, open communication from the heart is the secret of friendship and closeness in a marriage.

"Men are often criticized for not showing affection both verbally and physically. To be fair and to a lesser extent, I have noticed this with women as well. This happens to a large degree when we are raised in homes that were not demonstrative in giving affection, touch, verbal praise or embrace. So many men have learned from their fathers to withhold affection or tears as this is a sign of toughness and masculinity but oh, that is so lacking in truth. Men have feelings too that need expression. Men need to be loved and to give love. All humans do. Unfortunately, as I said earlier, our life experiences have handicapped many of us in this regard. In so many relationships, a spouse is longing for affection and the other makes no effort or is handicapped to meet the needs of the other.

"Many wives in an effort to accept their spouse's handicap rationalize it away as 'that's just the way Bill is', but no, Bill is not an island. He needs to grow in those areas and die to the ego and wrong thinking, otherwise the spouse will suffer and children will perpetuate what they see and live. It is a man's responsibility to overcome these incorrect perceptions. Every effort must be made to change; to show affection and verbalize it even if it feels unnatural at first.

"Just ask your spouse if they don't appreciate a hug, an unexpected kiss or a phone call during the day to say hello or a whisper that says, 'I love you.' Yes, soft words of affection over the phone can touch your spouse's heart in an instant! I repeat because it is so important; when we are loved, appreciated, listened to, respected, accepted, given affection, shown kindness and consideration, it is indeed uplifting and encouraging but even more so, our hearts are filled with joy!

"Sometimes, I pray that I could come into a family and shake the husband and wife into realizing that the days are passing and how unsatisfying it is to take one another for granted! This is what happens when we fail to use the wonderful gifts we are blessed with; all the senses of touch, smell, sound, sight, our emotions, tears, smiles, understanding, compassion and on and on. They are free and can be given so easily and can give such happiness to others!

"God made men and women for this very reason to give each other life!

"Sadly, so often we feel alone; only half alive to the fullness of life! There is so much stress and anxiety from day to day that could be eased if not eliminated by a soft touch or tender word and yet, all too often we remain silent; self absorbed in our own world.

"Ironically, it is when we reach out to others, we help ourselves!
"Meine lieben Kinder, think of your spouse as a flower that has just begun to bud. We know that in a day or so if the flower receives the warmth of the sun and is watered it will bloom into a beautiful flower. If it doesn't receive the light or is cared for with water and fertilizer, it begins to wilt and die.

"We all are like that.

"We all have the potential to bloom, too! But we must be tended to daily or else we too, will wilt and die. Watch the petals of your spouse unfold and see the beauty inside as you keep it watered and warmed by your love. See it sprout up when given a little fertilizer by enjoying an evening out together or an unexpected gift or bouquet of flowers. With just a little effort and awareness, life can be taken to a more beautiful level...is that not so?"

"Begin tomorrow morning! Arise early before the others, and begin the ritual of praying to the Lord. Without Jesus at the center of your life this simple message will not take root in your mind and heart. Ask the Holy Spirit to convict you and open you to Jesus' teachings so we grow to love Him and follow in His footsteps and His sacrifice. This is how we prepare for the day; filled with the light of Christ's Word, you are ready to make sacrifices as well and to implement all the gifts we talked about and shower others with blessings!

When we are tired, we love anyway. If we are afraid or feel uncomfortable to show affection, give your spouse a warm embrace anyway. When we are upset, we hold back anger and critical comments. When we don't feel like listening to our children or our spouse, we especially listen even more so from the heart. Your spouse and your children see that you are trying to care for them over yourself. Believe me, that says how much you love them a hundred times more than when you say it verbally.

"Actions speak louder than words.

"Yes, it is not good for man to be alone, so no longer get up each day as if you were alone! Don't waste these gifts any longer, not even for a moment. Reach out to your family and see the joy and sparkle in their eyes come alive! See the happiness and pride in your own eyes as you see yourself grow and become all that God made you to be!

As beautiful and incredible the world is that God has created when shared with others becomes even more-so. How many times have we noticed a sunrise or sunset become even more spectacular and heartfelt when shared with another? How much more do the stars in the meadow of heaven twinkle and sparkle when viewed with the warmth of a loved one's hand in yours? How much more does a full moon on a warm summer evening shine more brightly when viewed in the arms of a loved one? Without others in our lives we wouldn't appreciate the gift of touch, a tender embrace or the soft words of love and care by a friend, a spouse or a child.

"Can you not see how much we need each other!?

"The gift of life with all of its possibilities and ways to love and receive love is endless and there for your pleasure. Jesus said, 'I have come that you may have life and have it abundantly,' did He not!? These heavenly gifts are free, so use them lavishly and often, never to be taken for granted again. Each moment we live is a moment that we can bring the love of Jesus into the heart of someone in our family or a stranger we cross paths with during our day. Keep in mind, if these precious moments of life are not used to bring love and hope into the lives of others, they are wasted, gone and never to come your way again. How often do I think of my Anna when we were married and wish that I had embraced her more, kissed her more, loved her more so that I would have more memories to hold onto which made her happy.

"In closing, my dear brothers and sisters in Christ, choose to live the way the good Lord intended for you to live. When you fully appreciate all the Lord has blessed you with and begin to use the gifts you have been given, you will truly live a life of joy and gratitude! When you begin to live with praise and thanksgiving, it is a sign that you have begun to see that everything is a miracle; you begin to truly see the wonder of God's creation. You no longer think with lack, but abundance. You are living in the moment and the fullness of life! You are now living with trust in God and a heartfelt appreciation for everything our heavenly Father has done.

"Our life becomes a prayer of thankfulness!

"What a wonderful example we become when we shower others with our light. They will want to return it and spread it out to others too, out of gratitude! So, light up your spouse's life, teach your children how to lovingly use God's gifts. And most of all, meine lieben Kinder, continue to be a witness of what Jesus did all of His life right up to the end; He sacrificed His life for you and all of us. We are called to do the same. That is what we ultimately want to instill in others; our deep gratitude to Him; our love for Him and why we want to follow Him!

"May God bless you all, in the name of the Father, the Son and the Holy Spirit. Amen"

No sooner had Father Engelmann's last words left his lips than Jenny ran towards him and gave him a big hug.

When they parted, Father winked at everyone and admitted, "This is why I accepted the invitation to come here this evening, I knew one of God's heavenly gifts would be in store for me!"

Everyone laughed and stood to give Father a standing ovation. When the large group sat down again, Jenny made another announcement.

"Before we conclude our meeting and enjoy refreshments and fellowship, there is a brief prayer that Henry and I made up that we say every morning together. As Father David pointed out, it is so important to get your day off to good start; not only to read, meditate and pray by yourself but also to pray together as a married couple and family if you have children. I would like to share it with you and if you are interested in a copy of the prayer, we have printed a supply of them on the table at the back.

Jenny adjusted the microphone and began to read:

MORNING PRAYER

Dear Jesus, You are my Lord and Savior. Forgive me of all my sins. I place You at the center of my life and our home. Fill me with Your Holy Spirit so I might have the grace and strength to do Your will by being obedient to Your Word in all my thoughts, words, and actions.

As I journey through this day, let Your example of love and sacrifice be my guide to love, honor and serve my spouse and to be a light to my children which leads them in the Christian faith.

Protect me, oh Lord, from the wickedness and snares of the evil one so I do not become preoccupied with worry, unforgiveness, anger, concerns and self-centeredness. Rather, help me to be glad and rejoice in this day trusting completely in our heavenly Father's divine providence to turn everything which comes my way into good.

Free me from myself so I can live in the moment so I can serve You fully; to bring You to others not so much by words but by example. Let Your Light shine in my heart so that everyone I meet today will encounter kindness, compassion, understanding, patience and a friendly smile.

Thank You, too, dear Father, for my guardian angel to protect me from all dangers to my body and soul. To continuously prompt me to do good. O My God; Father, Son and Holy Spirit, thank You for all Your blessings and the gift of life and another day to love and serve You with the ultimate purpose of bringing my spouse, my children and me safely home into Your loving arms.

Amen.

CHAPTER FORTY

"D R. WEBSTER'S OFFICE, how may I help you?"

"Hi, this is Jenny Pederson, I have an appointment for ten o'clock this morning and I won't be able to make it. The storm on the farm is very severe and visibility is almost zero."

"Hello, Mrs. Pederson, it's not much better in the city either. Several other patients have called in to cancel this morning as well."

"Is there another opening available on Friday or early next week?"

"I'm sorry, we are fully booked and the doctor is travelling home to Wisconsin over the Christmas season and won't be back until the fourth of January. How are you feeling? I can book you in with someone else."

"No, that's fine. I'm feeling very good, actually. When do you have an opening in January?"

There was a momentary pause, "Would Monday, January 18th, at nine thirty work for you?"

Jenny checked the calendar and then said, "Yes, that works for me just fine."

HENRY WAS READING by the fireplace in the sun room when Jenny walked in. "The doctor is going home for Christmas and so my next appointment has been deferred until the third week in the New Year."

"Is it okay to wait that long?" Henry asked.

"Oh yes, I'm feeling fine and if I have any problems, I can always see Dr. Kreake. My only concern now is what to do for the next three days. You were going to cut down a fir tree but I guess in this weather it would be impossible."

Jenny gazed out and barely could see the railing not more than five feet in front of the window she was looking through. "I wonder how Father Engelmann is doing at the prayer house?"

"He will be fine. Over the years, he has been snowed in up to four days. He likes to turn on the wood burning stove and read the Bible or write the story he was assigned. I'm sure he and Coco are just fine. Perhaps, I will go down with the skidoo later this afternoon and see how he is doing and if he needs any supplies."

"How can you go there in such low visibility? You won't be able to see the Poustinia until you're right there. What if you get lost?"

"I know my way pretty good, Jen. I'll be okay." Henry got up and went over to Jenny and put his arm around her waist. "We could also do something else for awhile..." Henry said in a soft tone, as he drew her closer.

Just then, Justin came into the sun room carrying a book he was reading in his bedroom. "The storm is still pretty strong. Too bad its Friday and not Thursday, I might have gotten out of two days of school."

"You just might get out of a day's work tomorrow too if this keeps up."

"Are we going to cut down a Christmas tree today or is it too stormy out?"

"Yeah, Jenny was mentioning that earlier. We could fire up the skidoos and just go to the top of the hill. There are two that were planted out of the straight line that the others follow. Either one of them are the right size for the family room."

"Yeah, I remember them. One is on the north side and the other one is down a way on the south side. They do get in the way of grass cutting with the big tractor. Can we take out both sleds if we go?"

Henry thought a moment. He could see Justin's excitement and didn't want to dampen it. "Well, we could as long as we stay together. We can easily get lost up in the open field area."

"I'll stay close behind you. And it's just above the hill."

Jenny came up to Henry and gave him a kiss on the cheek, "Perhaps we can work on your other plan later on when you come back out of the cold."

"Love the idea, Jen."

Jenny was going to give Justin a hug but he was already gone.

Henry met up with Justin in the mud room. They both put on their snowsuits and carried their helmets out into the garage. There hadn't been too much snow right up until the end of November and so the skidoos were not used since last winter. Henry hoped they both would start. Henry's snowmobile fired up right away but Justin's had to be started manually by pulling on the cord. After about ten pulls, it started but idled poorly.

"Probably flooded, let's run them both a bit until they're warm." As soon as Henry packed two saws, an axe and a compass in the storage compartment, he opened the garage door and sped out. Henry waited until Justin was clear of the garage and pressed the door closer. He waved to Justin to follow him.

As Henry sped out of the drive way, he recalled the day of Julean's burial in the cemetery. A winter storm raged that day as well. Memories of barely seeing Father go over the last rites at the other end of the coffin flashed across his mind. Today was almost a repeat, except worse, Henry thought as he sped along cautiously.

HENRY COULD HARDLY see in front of him. There was a complete white out wherever he looked. He turned and could just make out a translucent image of Justin no more than ten feet behind him.

Henry turned off the road leading up to the house to begin climbing the hill to where the evergreens were. Because he was going so slow the rubber treads of the skidoo began to spin and sink at the base of the slope when all at once it caught and thrust forward and upward. Afraid to slow down and lose momentum, Henry continued his climb at a steady rate. He hoped Justin was close behind.

When Henry got to the top of the hill, he turned slightly north towards the row of trees he was going to select their Christmas tree from. Feeling he was on level solid snow, he stopped and turned around to see if Justin was behind him.

He wasn't there.

After a few minutes, uneasiness began to crawl from the pit of his stomach to the top of his head. Despite the bitterly cold temperature, he felt beads of perspiration form on his forehead under the helmet. He slightly opened the front visor of the helmet to let in fresh air as the clear plastic front was beginning to fog up.

Henry began looking in all directions and strained to hear the motor of the other skidoo. All he could see was thousands of swirling snowflakes creating a solid sheet of white in front of him and the steady roar of the wind. He bent over and looked down for his snow tracks which he made coming up the hill but they had vanished. Even if they were still there, the visibility was so bad he wouldn't be able to see them anyway.

Keep calm, he said to himself, trying to fight the growing concern and what to do. Should he just wait or start to look for him? They should only have taken out the one skidoo, being swayed by Justin's excitement to have his own sled had gone against his better judgment. He shook his head, it was too late to go there, he could only hope and pray Justin would implement survival safety measures.

Henry was certain he knew where he was and he had the compass with him if he needed it. He turned his skidoo around to what he thought was 360 degrees and slowly went forward. He didn't want to run into Justin and yet, he had to go down the hill to see if his son could have gotten stuck either at the base like he did for that split moment or perhaps he veered off the trail he established when he first went up the hill.

The skidoo began to tilt forward, a good sign that he was beginning to head down the slope, hopefully in the direction he had come up. Cautiously he descended. He strained to see in front of him but there was nothing except swirling white snow.

When he came to the bottom he turned left towards where his instincts told him the house was. He was relieved to see the shadow of a huge structure emerge like a ghost. The house blocked and slowed the swirling snow allowing Henry some thankful visibility. The fact he could find his way home so easily gave Henry hope that Justin may have gone home. He could visualize his son inside by the warmth of the fireplace with Jenny. The only problem disrupting that image was that Justin's skidoo was nowhere in sight. It could however, be inside the garage.

Henry ran to the front door but it was locked. He pressed the doorbell repeatedly and saw Jenny rushing to the door through the side light window beside the door. The wind pushed Jenny back as a rush of cold air swept inside the foyer along with Henry. Jenny leaned forward with all her might to close the door. Henry took off his helmet and asked hopefully, "Is Justin here?"

Instantly, fear and concern covered Jenny's face. She brought her hands up to her mouth and softly she answered, "No, Henry, he's not here...what happened?"

"When we left, we drove to the end of the lane and then I turned to go up the hill to where the evergreens are. I got momentarily stuck at the base of the hill where the snow was high and within moments I was free and sped up the hill. When I got to the top, Justin wasn't behind me. The snow storm is so heavy, I couldn't see anything. I was hoping he came back home. Oh, Jenny..."

"Should I call for help? Perhaps, the RCMP or fire station?"

"They would never make it out here. The visibility is virtually nil, Jen." Henry shook his head. "I should have waited until the storm abated or only taken one sled like I originally wanted to."

Jenny had just heard on the radio the announcer warning citizens not to go out and that the storm might last for several more hours but she didn't want to worry Henry any more than he already was.

Henry interrupted Jen's thoughts. "Have you heard what the temperature is at?"

"Last I heard it was forty below and with the wind chill over 70 below. I've never heard of such cold temperatures, Henry."

"It can get pretty cold on the prairies. The wind picks up and can freeze exposed skin in seconds."

Jenny rushed to Henry. "Oh, Honey, things will turn out. Have you been in snow storms before?" Jenny wanted to know.

"Yes, quite a few over the years but not one this bad. The children have been instructed to always stay with their vehicle. All of our cars have survival kits but I can't recall what I had in the skidoo which Justin took. I think there was a blanket, flare, candle and chocolate bar. Let's pray the supplies are there and that Justin uses his common sense."

"I have to go out to look for him, Jen. I'll check back every hour."

"Make sure you have all the supplies you need in your snow-mobile, in case you get stuck."

Jenny and Henry held hands and said a prayer for guidance and their son.

Henry kissed Jenny, put his helmet back on and rushed outside. Jenny could just make out Henry checking the compartment behind the sled to make sure all the supplies were there which he would need in case of an emergency.

The sled was still warm and fired up instantly. Within moments, Jenny saw Henry disappear into the swirling snow.

Henry tried to mimic the moves they made when they initially left the garage. About three quarters of an hour passed since then. Henry stopped at the base of the hill to where he thought he originally turned up before. He paused for but a moment and then pressed hard on the accelerator control on the handle. Instantly, the sled shot forward and up the hill. Henry had to keep the sled at a certain speed so as not to get stuck on the hill-side and hoped that he wouldn't run into Justin or his sled.

So far, Henry just penetrated the blinding snow. He knew that the evergreens were further ahead and off to the right. He was certain that Justin knew which trees Henry was considering to cut down. Henry slowed the vehicle's speed and turned slightly to the left towards the trees. Perhaps, Justin was already there and waiting for him.

Within a few minutes, Henry came to the trees but neither Justin nor his sled were anywhere in sight. He began to feel panic. The cold wind was beginning to penetrate his snowsuit adding to the chill he was feeling. "Where would Justin be?" He tried to think like his son. "What would he do?"

Suddenly, a hopeful thought entered his mind. He wondered if Ginger had heard the skidoos leave the garage. If she did, she would have come out and followed them. Since she wasn't with him, she might be with Justin. Perhaps, the dog would help his son, even lead him home. Henry recalled the stories on the farm where horses led many farmers home during a snow storm. Henry hoped Ginger was with his son and not cocooned in the dog house. The wind was howling so loudly however it was likely that Ginger didn't hear them. Henry tried to hear the sound of the motor of his sled.

He couldn't.

Henry decided to follow the tree line and head in an easterly direction. He tried to read the compass on his dash but couldn't make it out. He went as slowly as he could lest the sled begin to sink in the soft piling snow and get stuck. He followed the tree line. At times, he went too close to the trees and the branches struck hard across his helmet and chest. Soon, he hoped he would bump into the one tree that was planted out from the straight line of the others. It wasn't there! Somehow, he missed it as he started to descend down the hill. He was at the end of the tree line and would now start to go down towards the house.

He could visualize the layout of the land perfectly in his mind and yet seemed confused. Why hadn't he hit that tree that was out of the line of the row of trees?

He slowly turned the sled and once again followed the tree line going west. He prayed to find his son. The storm wasn't letting up any and he could feel himself getting colder. He was wearing a good snowsuit but it was the growing nervousness that was dropping his temperature.

Suddenly he hit a tree. How was that possible? This tree should have been the one that stuck out on the other side of the row of trees. Instantly, he realized his mistake! The reason he didn't come into contact with the tree when he headed towards the house was because the tree was out of line on the other side of the row of evergreens. He got mixed up. Since Justin wasn't at this tree, he could very well have gone to the other one nearest the house. His concern over Justin and his whereabouts were distracting him!

Henry put the sled in reverse and just skidded and began to sink. He stopped immediately. He knew the sled would bury quickly and then never be able to get out. He had to feel around the sled to survey what had happened rather than visually see what was going on. He felt a large branch which had caught itself under the handle bars and the sled had dipped forward towards the base of the tree where the snow was low.

He got a saw from the compartment and cut off the big branch and then went behind the sled and tried to scrape away the snow so the snow mobile could back straight out rather than have to climb. He wanted to avoid at all costs having the sled sink in the deep snow surrounding the base of the tree.

Henry could feel heat return to his body as he dug the snow away behind the sled with his hands. He was actually beginning to sweat. He slowed and tried to work more calmly as he didn't want to get wet. That would only make him colder once he stopped working.

Yet, every moment counted. "Dear God, please protect my son."

Henry got back on the sled and held his breath. He prayed the sled would start. He pressed the starter and instantly the motor came to life. He put it into reverse and pressed the accelerator. The sled began to sink, he pressed harder and the sled began to move backwards but not fast enough and began to sink again. He panicked and pressed the accelerator all the way in. The engine roared over the wind but the treads turned in the same spot and wouldn't propel the sled backwards. Within seconds the skidoo buried itself in the deep snow.

Henry was stuck and he knew it.

He would never get the sled out unless pulled by a truck or another skidoo that was on firmer ground with a tow rope. He now faced the dilemma of making the choice to walk home or stay with his sled how he always instructed his children to do.

However, this was different.

Justin might be in serious trouble. He simply could not lay there waiting for the storm to clear which could take hours. He had to keep searching or at the very least get back to the house and call for help.

Total panic swept through Henry as he stood there. He removed his helmet to see if he could see further and get his bearings better, but it was worse. The swirling snow immediately blinded him and the freezing cold wind bit instantly into his exposed skin. He quickly put the helmet back on. But in that instant, it took him back again to the memory standing exactly like that the day they had buried Julean. The snow storm raged on the prairies that day, too; it was the same bitter cold and the same degree of visibility. He recalled how he had just stood there like a frozen statue feeling the cold spread throughout his being. He remembered how Father Engelmann stood at the edge of the grave shouting into the wind as if he were just moving his lips without sound. His image fading in and out with each gust of wind.

But there was something else Henry sensed along with those memories; he felt the presence of his dear former wife. A calm assurance began to inch its way up his spine and slowly spread throughout his being. He hadn't thought of Julean for some time but he should have known her spirit would always be with him and her children, especially Justin; they were so close.

Why was he recalling this now…was Julean, perhaps trying to tell him something or lead him to their son? The eerie feeling he just felt came back only stronger. Maybe, she was here in spirit along with his guardian angel to find Justin.

"Thank you for coming, Julean. Please, help me find Justin." He also whispered a prayer to his guardian angel to guide him, too.

Henry wiped the snow building up on the outside of his helmet, stared ahead, and saw snow swirling. He wasn't sure now if he had seen an image of Julean or was it just his imagination. He stepped forward but quickly sank into the deep snow; it came up to his thighs. With great effort, he pulled his other foot out and up to make another step but this time stumbling forward. He managed to get up and noticed his breathing was growing heavier. He didn't know how far he could make it through the deep snow. One thing in his favor was that the snow was soft and hadn't hardened yet. Rather than lift his foot up, he just slightly began to push one foot forward and then the next. It seemed better but his forward progress would be slower.

After gaining five or six feet, he was puffing so hard, he had to stop and catch his breath. He felt the cold radiate through his suit. He felt chilled. Just when he thought he could go no further, the wind seemed to abate for just a split second but during that time he was certain he saw Julean up ahead. It spurred him forward. He was getting tired and was no longer sure if he was heading in the right direction.

He prayed it was homeward.

Once again, just when he felt he could go no further, Julean would appear suddenly just ahead and beckon him, "Come, Hank."

"Oh, dear God, let this not be some kind of mirage…" surely, he was being led home.

After about twenty minutes, Henry felt exhausted. Trudging through the deep snow was taking its toll. He knew he couldn't go much further. He began to worry that he might collapse and freeze with no one there to search for his son. "Please, dear Lord, help me. Saint Anthony, please help me find Justin."

Henry's focus was so much on his son, he didn't realize how utterly exhausted and cold he was getting. His finger tips and toes were beginning to get frost bitten. He felt he wanted to just lie down and sleep.

Another five minutes had passed and Henry found himself literally crawling in the deep snow. Thoughts of dying and not seeing Jenny again or their baby tugged deeply at his heart. How would Jenny deal with this? Would they find Justin in time? As tired as Henry was, panic swept through him in waves.

He thought of being eaten by coyotes. He recalled a few years back when one of his quarter horse mares fell through the ice in the creek at the bottom of the valley. She couldn't get out and died standing up in the creek to her shoulders. When they found her, the coyotes had eaten her head off. Would Henry suffer the same fate? The last couple of weeks had seen winter at its worst. Probably making up for the late fall. But with all of the snow since then, it had been hard for both the deer and coyotes to find food. Just a couple of days ago, Henry and Justin put out extra bales of hay for the deer.

"Oh God, please help me find Justin before it's too late." With all of the energy he had left, he stood up in the deep snow. If he was going to freeze to death, he would die standing rather than lying down. The snow would cover him and it would take days to find him. Chances are coyotes would discover him sooner than a search party. He wobbled back and forth in the tempestuous wind. He moved his feet inches forward, still trying to make any kind of progress.

"There she is again!" Henry cried.

Julean was just up ahead waving for him to come forward. Adrenalin gushed through his body and unbelievably, he gained his second wind. He thrust up one foot and then the other. He raised his visor exposing his eyes, nose and mouth and at the top of his lungs he shouted, "Julean, wait for me!" Henry stepped forward again and once more, he frantically shouted, "Julean, Julean, where are you!?"

Suddenly out of nowhere, he was hit hard by a lunging animal. The wind was knocked out of him as he fell backwards.

He quickly moved his legs to stay upright. He thrust his right hand in a sharp downward motion causing his skidoo glove to shoot off. He reached into his pocket and searched for his pocket knife. He hoped he could open it up in time. How many of them were there? The animal thrust forward again at his face and Henry fell backwards. He jabbed repeatedly at the animal with his knife.

The last thought Henry had before passing out was being eaten alive by a pack of coyotes.

CHAPTER FORTY-ONE

S HORTLY AFTER HENRY left to go back out to look for Justin, Jenny called the Lumsden RCMP detachment. She told them what had happened and was very concerned for Henry and Justin. She pleaded with them to come as soon as the storm let up.

Jenny didn't know that the RCMP hooked up a trailer on the back of one of their SUVs holding two skidoos and headed towards Henry's farm. They didn't know how far they could get in the storm but they would venture as far as possible and then go on their skidoos and be guided by a special compass instrument. They got as far as the first acreage off the main highway and decided to travel by sled across the open field. One of the officers knew where Henry's acreage was as he and his wife had purchased a painting from him, two years ago.

Jenny was looking outside the front door window when she saw two headlights pull up on the driveway. She opened the front door and waved the police in.

"Oh, I am so happy to see you. Thank you for risking yourselves to come. Henry still hasn't returned. He has been gone for well over an hour and half and Justin is nowhere in sight."

"Do you know which direction they went?"

Jenny told the officer what Henry had mentioned earlier; that they went to the end of the driveway and then turned right to go up the hill to where the evergreen trees were situated. That's all she could tell them.

Between the two officers, they decided to head out together to go up the hill and systematically go back and forth at the top in the hope of running into Henry or Justin.

Jenny saw the men hurry to their skidoos and quickly disappeared into the storm that showed no signs of letting up.

She wished she could phone Father Engelmann to pray for Henry and Justin but there was no phone in the Poustinia. She called Camilla and Matti and asked both women to pray and to tell the others in the family that prayers were needed. Jen placed a chair by the front door and prayed as she stared out into the swirling snow.

As Henry drove up the hill when they first started out, Justin moved forward and tried to mimic his dad's every move. But just like Henry, Justin got stuck at the base of the hill in the deep accumulating snow. It took a couple of minutes to get free and then Justin's sled shot up the hill as well. However, instead of going straight up the hill it went off at an angle. Justin wasn't aware that he had veered off course as the blinding snow had disorientated him. When he got to the top, Henry was nowhere to be seen. In actuality though, Henry was no more than ten yards away, shielded by the wall of blinding snow.

Justin assumed that his father would go to the nearest tree that was off line from the main row. Justin headed towards the tree line and as soon as he came to the row of trees, he knew that the one they were going to cut down would be on the other side of this tree line or the one further west. Justin hoped his dad would have chosen this one. Although the visibility was almost nil, Justin found the tree in question. It was just on the other side of the tree line but Henry was not there. He must be at the other one. Justin tried to back up but he went too slow and the skidoo began to sink in the deep snow.

He was stuck.

He thought he could easily walk home but Henry had drilled it into them how easily one can lost in a storm and to stay put. Set up a shelter and ride out the storm.

Justin couldn't believe his eyes to see Ginger behind his sled. The dog was struggling in the deep snow and was nearing exhaustion. He patted his friend and made his way to the back of the sled and took out the survival kit. It was a blanket and rolled inside was a candle, matches, flashlight, a bottle of water and two chocolate bars. Although it was cold, Justin still felt warm and easily maneuvered his way around the tree. He dug out a hole near the base of the evergreen tree and placed the blanket over top of the low branches creating an igloo of sorts under the tree by piling snow up on all four sides. He crawled inside with the candle and matches and bars and beckoned Ginger to come in. He lit the ten-hour candle and he and Ginger snuggled up together. Remarkably, the light from the candle, body heat from the dog and shelter from the wind, the temperature remained just below freezing inside the makeshift snow hut.

Justin wondered what happened to his dad. He was certain his dad would have found him by now. It was either this tree that he was snuggled under or the other about fifty yards west of the tree line. Justin assumed that if Henry didn't find him at the other tree, surely, he would make his way to this one.

And that was exactly what was happening!

Once Henry realized that he was on the wrong side of the tree line, he got back on track. He was at the tree at the west end but Justin wasn't there and that's when his skidoo got stuck. Henry was working himself back to the tree Justin was under but was nearing exhaustion trudging through the deep snow.

Ginger was quietly sleeping next to Justin in the hut he had constructed and Justin found himself dozing off like Ginger when all of a sudden the wind seemed to abate and he heard someone shouting. Ginger heard it too and she immediately raised her head. Justin found it hard to believe when he heard someone shout the name of his mother, Julean. He raised himself up and rested on his elbow. *Was he dreaming?*

When the shout came again, Ginger jumped up toppling the candle and burst outside of the hut. The blanket that formed the top of the hut followed Ginger for a few feet, exposing Justin to the full blast of the storm which was raging again.

Ginger quickly disappeared. Justin felt for the flashlight and got up being very careful not to stray too far from the hut that he was prepared to rebuild. However, he had to see what the shout was all about and where Ginger had gone to. Within seconds, Justin found Ginger wrestling with his dad. It almost seemed as if Henry was trying to defend himself against Ginger. Justin didn't realize right away that Henry had thought the farm dog was a coyote!

When Justin shone the light on Henry's face, he could see his father wasn't conscious. He prayed that he wasn't dead. Justin took off his glove and slid his hand inside Henry's snow suit and pressed it against his chest where his heart was.

He felt a beat.

He looked for the skidoo but there was none in sight. Slowly, Justin pieced together what happened. His dad must have been searching for him on foot and didn't recognize Ginger.

Justin tried to pull his dad to the base of the tree where the hut was but he was dead weight and he couldn't budge him. Justin went back to the tree and gathered what he could and came back. He laid the branches over the walls of the trench Henry had carved in the snow as he worked his way down the tree line. He put the blanket above the branches and then laid more branches down. He crawled in one end of top cover and pushed snow up the ends to keep the wind out as much as he could. He called Ginger into the hut and she snuggled up in between Henry and Justin. Justin tried to light the candle which immediately went out as too much wind was coming in from the end where their feet were. Justin kicked and scraped his feet trying to build up a wall of snow at that end to keep out the wind. Luckily, one of the branches blew down carrying some snow with it and sealed the end almost completely of the cold air.

Justin turned on the flashlight, lit the candle and stuck it into the snow just above their heads. There was just enough room for him to see Henry was missing a glove. He hoped his hand wasn't frozen; a knife was clutched in his hand. He quickly took off his mitts and began warming his dad's hand. He opened his snow suit and stuck Henry's hand inside. Like Ginger, he got as close to his dad as possible trying to keep him warm. Justin was scared.

He began to pray.

When Henry regained his consciousness, he wasn't sure if he was dead or not. He heard someone praying for him. It was Justin. Henry opened his eyes and there in the dim candlelight he saw Ginger next to his stomach and Justin with his arms wrapped around him praying and weeping at the same time.

He felt warm. His one hand was stinging. He wasn't sure which one it was, the right or left. Justin was relieved to see his dad was awake.

"Dad, are you okay?"

"Where are we, Justin?"

"We're next to the tree that we wanted to cut down, the one nearest the house."

Henry nodded, "So, I made it back to you. I was at the other end and when I saw you weren't there, I assumed you would be here but the sled got stuck and I tried to walk through the snow when I was attacked by a coyote."

"No, that was Ginger. She heard you shouting mom's name and so did I."

"Oh, I didn't hurt Ginger, did I? I was stabbing at her with my knife."

"It's a good thing it wasn't open and that she heard you."

Henry remained silent for a moment and then he said, "I saw Julean, Son. She led me back here and if I hadn't called her name and you and Ginger heard me, I would have died out there. Isn't that something, Son?"

"Yeah, I'm glad I found you and had the blanket to cover you."

"You did a good job, Justin. Between Mom, you and Ginger, my life was saved. I might very well have frozen to death."

"How is your hand and are your feet okay?"

"My hands and feet are stinging. That's a good sign that they are thawing. We might have to wait here till the storm stops and then you can get some help and come back for me. I don't think I can make it through the deep snow."

Justin searched for the two bars and could only find one. He took the wrapper off and gave it to his dad lying that he had eaten one already. Henry didn't want any water.

Henry was so exhausted physically and emotionally, he fell back to sleep. Justin was too excited to sleep and was so thankful that he and Ginger had heard his dad. He wondered if his mom was there in spirit.

Finally, Justin dozed off and just before nightfall he was the first to be awakened by the sound of snow-mobiles. He couldn't hear the roar of the wind and assumed the storm must be over. The sound of motors was getting louder so he decided to break their shelter and see if someone was looking for them. He peeked his head out from the blanket cover and saw the clear sky above. In the distance, he saw two sleds not more than fifty feet from where he and his dad were. He jumped out of the hut and waved. Within moments, two RCMP officers on sleds pulled up beside them. They helped lift Henry on the back of one of the sleds and Justin climbed on back of the other. He called for Ginger to come. She hopped in his lap and the sleds headed down the hill towards the house.

Jenny was in tears when Henry and Justin came into the house accompanied by the officers. She thrust her arms around Henry and hugged him for dear life. She then did the same with Justin. The officers helped Henry and Justin take off their snowsuits and checked them over for frost bite. Amazingly, Henry's fingers and toes were okay. They were red but not seriously frost bitten. Had Justin not realized one of Henry's gloves had fallen off, it might have froze and have to be amputated.

Jenny made coffee and hot chocolate for the men and warmed up some soup. The RCMP officers were thanked profusely for their heroic efforts. They kindly declined an offer for supper and headed back to their SUV and returned to their headquarters.

As Henry and Justin ate their soup and toast, Jenny began crying. She was so worried that something had happened. When Henry told Jenny what Justin had done and how he saved his life, she was so proud of her step son. He was happy to see Justin accept Jenny's sincere compliment for his maturity in a crisis situation. Ever since Justin had helped Jenny try out the kite, things had been steadily improving.

They all agreed that perhaps this year they would buy a tree from the Kinsmen rather than venture up the hill again. This was one adventure they didn't want to replay!

Chapter Forty-Two

"THE HEIGHT OF the tree is just perfect, Dad," said Justin as they positioned it in the corner of the living room next to the fireplace.

"Yup, there is just enough room to put the star on."

"What about the angel? Mom liked to put it on top of the tree."

"That's a great idea," said Jenny as she walked into the living room. "I can see why Julean preferred the angel too. From that vantage point, our angel can have a good view of all of us as we gather around the tree and help to remind us of our protector."

Jenny walked closer to the tree and continued, "I'm glad you decided to cut the tree from on top of the hill rather than go into the city and get one. Its shape is so nice and the fresh smell of pine fills the room.

Henry came next to Jenny and put his arm around her. "Yeah, it is a nice fragrance and also a reminder of how fortunate Justin and I were during that storm."

"I was so worried about you both. I sat at the front door for hours and cried. I can't remember ever praying so much."

Justin reached into the Christmas storage box, took out a small pewter angel, and hung it up as high as he could reach to the cone shaped gown of the angel which now decorated the top of the tree. The pewter angel instantly caught the light and sparkled as it rotated at the end of the string.

"What a beautiful angel. I don't recall seeing it last year," said Jenny.

"Yeah, it was there but it was covered over with angel hair and Christmas balls," said Justin with a note of disappointment in his voice.

Henry remained silent, hesitant to share a memory which was growing in his mind. He looked at Justin for a moment and then decided to go ahead and say it. "Julean bought that angel for me the year Jeremy was born. She surprised me by hanging it up high just like you did, Son. She told me how she happened to come across it. She saw a dressed up Santa ringing a bell in front of a Salvation Army Christmas pot. When she stopped to put some money into the pot, she noticed a pewter angel sparkling high on a Christmas tree inside a display window at Eaton's. The tree was covered with ornaments but it was that one which she wanted to give to me; she knew how much I loved my guardian angel. She went into the store to buy one but all the angels were sold except the one on the tree in the window. The cashier said that it wasn't for sale only for display.

Just then the manager of that department came by and Julean asked (almost pleading) if she could buy the pewter angel ornament in the window. When he saw that she was almost in tears, he agreed to sell it to her. When she came out of the store, she wanted to thank the Santa for ringing the bell because if she hadn't stopped to put some money into the pot she wouldn't have noticed the angel in the window right behind him. But he was gone; just disappeared into the falling snow."

"That's amazing, Henry," blurted out Jenny. "Isn't that exactly what happened to you when ..."

Jenny stopped short of revealing to Justin that the same thing happened to Henry when he went to buy her the pewter angel she was wearing.

Without looking at Justin or Henry, Jenny walked over to the tree, took the pewter angel hanging around her neck, and hung it just beside Julean's angel.

"Your mom and I would have been very good friends, Justin."

The sight of the two angels dancing in the light touched both Henry and Justin. Henry felt blessed to have two such beautiful women in his life and Justin knew that Jenny wanted to show him that she wasn't there to replace Julean nor shut her out; that Julean was still as much a part of the family as she was.

Henry shook his head as his mind was suddenly flooded with memories of how Julean knew about the pewter angel he had sent to Jenny from his dreams. Incredibly, Henry had revealed so much of what was hidden in the recesses of his heart to his dear, sweet, understanding wife at that time. In a way, he wasn't hiding anything from Julean and perhaps that is why she was so accepting of it.

"Well, Honey," Henry began, "if you want to finish decorating the tree, Justin and I will finish what we have been working on all week in the garage."

"Is it still a secret project?" Jenny wanted to know.

"You will soon find out. But I will give you a hint. It has to do with Rudolf the red nosed reindeer!"

"It's really neat ... Jenny," added Justin.

Jenny smiled at the two men before her. "If it's anything like the nativity scene you men put up outside the patio doors to the prayer house, it will be quite something. I can't wait to see what you men have made!"

"Well, there are only a few more days left to get everything done before the kids from all over start coming home to the farm. Come on, Son, let's get back to work."

"OH LAUREN, IT'S so good to see you. We thought maybe you would be performing right through the Christmas season and not get home."

"It's a crazy time of year. Everyone is off except us! People want to come and see the show during the holidays and so we get very few days off. Next week between Christmas and New Years it's going to be crazy! As they say, the show must go on!"

Jeremy came in and brushed by the two ladies carrying a

suitcase and backpack. "Thanks Jeremy and thanks for picking me up at the airport."

"No problem, Sis. It worked out great. I closed the store early and your flight worked perfectly into the schedule."

Jeremy took off his coat, shook Henry's hand, kissed Jenny on the cheek and went inside.

Henry came over and gave his daughter a hug. "It's good to see you, Honey. Have a good flight?"

"Yes, the plane was only half full. I guess with it being Christmas Eve, most people must already be here that are coming to Regina. Anyway, I'm so happy to be home. It looks so Christmassy. The lights on the trees coming down the lane, the lights outlining the roof and the angel at the front door looks great! And, I am soooo hungry; can't wait to have some good food! So, who is here and where are they?"

"Alison and Camilla are in the kitchen helping me with dinner, thank God. I would be lost without them. Justin and Father are in the family room looking over photos of the grocery store and Noah and Joshua are downstairs in the game room playing with the pile of toys and games Henry keeps bringing home for them."

"I'm so glad the show shut down for three days. Christmas wouldn't be the same without you."

"Thanks Mom. Geez, it's still funny calling you Mom ... but I love it!"

"I love it, too! Come in, everyone is waiting to see you!"

Jenny put her arm around Lauren and led her into the kitchen.

"Hi, Lauren!" said Camilla as she rushed towards her step sister to give her a hug.

"Oh, Camilla, I see you're expecting. When is the big day?"

"Just a few months away and you know Jenny is expecting too?"

"Yes, oh it's going to be a blast having two little ones running around here! Hi Allison ...."

Henry smiled as he stood at the front door listening to the kids welcoming each other. He was so happy that they got along so well.

I don't think we could squeeze another person into the dining room, observed Henry as everyone was seated.

"This reminds me of Sunday dinners at home when company came and everyone squished together in the small kitchen on Broder Street."

Father Engelmann nodded. "Somehow, Mary always managed to make do. Henry and I loved it. I often wished my parishioners would sit closer together!"

"The fire looks so cozy and oh, the tree is decorated so nice. Did you do that Mom?" Lauren wanted to know.

"Yes, with the help of the men. They got it set up and Justin put the angel on top instead of the star this year."

"I like the angel, too," said Alison. "Which reminds me to say the guardian angel prayer. I forgot to say it this morning."

"Do you still say that prayer?" asked Lauren.

"Yes, everyday. The more we acknowledge our angel that God gives each of us the moment we are conceived, the more we are aware of their presence in our lives."

"I'll say Amen to that," interjected Jenny. "Not a day goes by without greeting my protector! Okay, we best get started …Father would you please say grace."

"Yes, yes, of course, Jenny. Oh, what a wonderful gathering and feast you have prepared … In the name of the Father and the Son and the Holy Spirit. Thank You, Father for bringing us together to celebrate the birth of your Son! It is His life, sacrifice, death and resurrection that have made the gift of family possible. It is truly out of your Your boundless love that You have created us, that Your Son has saved us and the Holy Spirit who came to empower us to live as Jesus so we all come home to heaven. We thank You for the gift of each other, for this beautiful Christmas feast that Jenny and her daughters have prepared. Thank You for bringing Alison's boyfriend, Carson to the Pederson home. And I must thank You Father for the gift of yet another year to serve You and be a part of this wonderful family. The Pederson's have accepted me as one of their own. I am filled with memory after memory of happiness; good times and sad times, kindness, warm smiles, laughter and love! Thank you to all! Amen."

"Everything looks so nice, Mom …the candles, the silverware, china, the fire, the tree …oh, it's so good to be home! And I can hardly wait to start this delicious looking meal!"

"Here you are Lauren, start with the potatoes," offered Jeremy.

"And here is the turkey," offered Justin.

"Are you ready for the gravy?" asked Alison.

"Whoa!" exclaimed Lauren.

Everyone laughed as Lauren's eyes were growing too big for her stomach.

"Can we open some of the presents tonight, Mom?" asked Joshua.

"Yes, can we please!?" echoed, Noah.

"I think we can after we come back from the prayer house. Father is going to say Mass later after dinner at the Poustinia. You can open some gifts when we come back and the rest tomorrow morning on Christmas day."

"Oh, the joy of Christmas," remarked Jeremy. "Where did the idea of giving gifts at Christmas come from anyway, Grandpa?"

Father swallowed what he was eating and then said, "Over two thousand years ago, God gave the world the greatest gift …Jesus. The Gospel of John in 3:16, says it best of all, 'For God so loved the world, that He gave his only begotten Son, that whosoever believeth in Him should not perish, but have everlasting life.'

"But it was the Wise Men who started it when they gave baby Jesus the presents of Frankincense, Gold and Myrrh. So, when we give gifts to each other, it is to remind us of His birth. The customs and traditions of this celebration vary from country to country but the theme is the same; to celebrate the birth of the King of Kings. But here is the important thing; that we receive Him. Imagine, God offering the gift of His Son to each and every one of us. Only the very unwise would not receive Him in their life today or any day throughout the year. The gift of His life gives us freedom and the promise of eternity."

Henry expected Lauren to perhaps rebut Father but she respectfully remained quiet and continued eating. Perhaps, it was the food that kept her silent.

"So, is the show still getting good reviews, Lauren?" Alison wanted to know.

"Yes, they are. In fact, next spring when the production of Joseph runs out at the Elgin Theatre, there is talk of the show going on the road."

"Will it come to Regina!?" Justin asked excitedly.

"I don't think it would as it requires a huge stage and back scene area. But, it would go to larger centers and into the United States."

"That sounds great, Lauren." Jeremy said. "Camilla and I would love to see the show. Mom and Dad said it was excellent."

"Yes, and don't forget about me," interjected Father. "I can't remember when I enjoyed a play more or had such a delightful outing, especially having a member of the family in the cast! Perhaps you and Camilla can work it in before the baby comes along."

"I'm afraid that is out of the question for now, Father. I am busy enough just keeping up with the girls at the Tutorial School and the men in my life are a real handful. And another man is on the way!"

Jenny was about to ask Carson about his work in Alberta, when Justin asked Father a question which surprised everyone.

"I was thinking about what you said Grandpa, that Jesus' birth is celebrated all over the world. How can God be everywhere at the same time?"

"Isn't that something!?" blurted Henry. "I asked that very same question of Father or rather he was Mr. Engelmann at that time. I, too, was fifteen. We were sitting out back of the store on the old grey crates. I still remember our conversation to this day because what Mr. Engelmann said about God being everywhere helped me to understand something which is a mystery."

"What did Grandpa say to you, Dad?"

"Well, he used the idea of electricity. It's something we don't understand and yet it can be available to everyone at the same time. Father used Regina as an example; the entire city can receive the power of electricity at any time. Everyone in the city can heat their homes or turn on the stove or radio at the push of a button or flick of a switch. I have to admit, I still don't understand how electricity works. It's a mystery to me and yet I can tap into it.

"Now take God and His Holy Spirit as a source of power not just for the city but for the entire world! He is available to everyone's home but the home he gives Himself to is our minds and hearts. At any time, His love, His 'electricity' is available to anyone. We can turn Him off if we want to and be in the darkness of life or we can flick on the switch to our mind or heart or soul and enter the light. Through His Holy Spirit, He is always available to hear our prayer, petitions and to work His divine providence."

"That's cool, Dad," remarked Lauren.

The same type of comment came from the other children as well. And then Henry added something else.

"I also recall at the time, Mr. Engelmann reminding me of my guardian angel who can report to God what is going in our lives. Angels always see the face of God while they are watching over us; that is another way God can be everywhere at the same time. This really hits home when you realize that you should always be on your best behavior as it makes your angel sad when you turn your back on God and He sees it through your angel."

Father Engelmann broke a momentary silence that suddenly fell at the dinner table. "You have an excellent memory of our discussion, Henry. The example of electricity helps to explain how God can be with everyone at the same time but a few weeks ago, I came across another analogy that perhaps helps us understand a bit more of this mystery."

Henry always loved it when Father would share an insight he had and always took him back to the time he was seated on the old grey crate out back of the store with his beloved mentor. Henry slid to the edge of his chair. Henry didn't notice but Father suddenly had everyone else's attention, too.

"It was just under a month or so ago when a friend of mine who lived in the town of Silton asked me to come and minister the last rites to his mother who was quite ill. As we were driving across country, Adam turned on the radio and kept pushing buttons until he found a station which he liked. It made me think, here we are driving in the country in the middle of nowhere and simply by turning the radio on, we were able to hear the news or messages or music from not only one radio station but other ones too.

The thing is that not only Adam and I could receive the radio stations but thousands upon thousands of other people in homes, other cars, trucks and offices could hear it too, all at the same time. Imagine, Justin, in the same way that there are billions of unseen radio waves in the air that we can tap into if we have a receiver, God's Holy Spirit also permeates the universe which we can tap into. He has created us in such a way that we too can be receivers of His unseen Spirit. Not only are we able to receive Him and His strength, grace and power in our lives but so can people all over in the world!

"Where radio stations are limited by the power and height of their transmission towers, there is no limit to God's power. Just a few months ago, we were in Toronto and saw the CN Tower; an amazing feat to build such a high tower with a powerful transmitter that can send signals unobstructed further and further."

Father Engelmann paused and raised his hands. "But God is in the heavens. How high is heaven and how much more power does the Creator of the universe have? There is no limit to the height of heaven. There is no limit to how far God can transmit his Holy Spirit! It can go to infinity! At any time, you or I, or someone in Russia or France or anyone or all of them in London can tap into the Holy Spirit of God. Imagine the God of creation loves us so much that He makes Himself personally available to us.

"This is not all, Justin, His system goes way beyond that of the very impressive feat of the CN Tower. In God's system, He not only transmits Himself so he is available to us but we can transmit back to Him or call upon Him at any time. It's much like a two-way telephone conversation between two people but in God's case, He can do this all at the same time with everyone in the world! Imagine, Justin, talking heart to heart with God. He is on call at any moment. He is never too busy and loves when you come to Him."

"Wow! That's an excellent way to describe it, Grandpa."

This time Lauren stopped eating and just nodded.

Once again Henry blurted, "Geez, Justin that was exactly my response too, back in 1959!"

Jenny also chimed in, "That sure helps me too Father. What a great way to explain something which is so mysterious and incomprehensible."

Father nodded excitedly and added, "Now here is the thing we must remember. Because we have free will, God always gives us all the choices we can make for good or bad. He allows Satan to prowl around the world ready to influence us to his way, too. In the same way, there are all those radio waves in the air of different frequencies carrying different messages from different stations that we can tune into, it is the same in the unseen spiritual world. God is right there waiting for you to tune into Him. You have the choice to tune into Satan too. If you face a temptation, he is quick to urge you on. But God is right there too, ready to give you the strength of the Holy Spirit to overcome or deal with life's challenges. The choice is yours as it is for everyone in the entire world. No matter where you are we can tune into God or the evil one.

"Amazing, isn't it?

"That's why we are so grateful at Christmas time that Jesus was born into the world and eventually taught us how to live and follow Him. If we put Him at the center of our lives and always stay tuned into God's frequency, we will always make the right choices!

"When you see the big picture of God's plan, it all makes sense, doesn't it?"

Father winked at Justin. "Trust me, my son, the one who stays tuned into the Holy Spirit of God is the one who lives at peace and experiences much joy in their life."

"You sure have a knack of explaining things, Father," said Alison.

Jenny went on to ask Carson about his work like she wanted to before this discussion came up but Father did something which he rarely does. His mind faded into the background and he no longer was listening to the conversation. He knew that his time to go to the Lord would soon be at hand. He tried to tune into the discussion but memories kept pulling him away; thoughts of how he came to know the Pederson's and when Henry started to work in the store. The photos he had looked at earlier that afternoon with Justin and Carson brought back so many happy and sad thoughts. The years of happiness he spent with Anna, the joy that Henry brought into their lives and even though he was so young, he was the answer to their prayer to restore the business. The death of Anna led him to his final vocation; to sell the store and become a priest.

Occasionally a loud voice or laughter would break him from his reverie but the pull of memories was too strong.

He wondered if this would be his last Christmas with the family.

CHAPTER FORTY-THREE

I T WAS ALMOST eight o'clock when Henry said, "This is the holy night and the stars are brightly shinning. The moon is full and I hear the angels singing over the Poustinia. While the kids are still wide awake, let's all get dressed and head down to the prayer house for Mass."

"But how are going to go in the dark Grandpa?" asked Joshua.

"Justin and I have a surprise for you. Our neighbor couldn't give us the hay ride like he did last year. One of his horses hurt its leg and the other one can't pull the wagon alone. But when one door closes, the Pederson's always find another door to open."

"What is it?" Joshua asked continuing to probe on behalf of his brother and his own growing curiosity.

"You'll soon see, Josh."

After everyone got dressed and began congesting under the front door canopy, the sound of motors starting up behind the garage could be heard. A minute later there appeared what looked like a team of reindeer coming towards the front of the house. Henry was dressed like Santa and his own grey beard magically had added another three inches. Behind Henry, was Justin disguised as Santa's helper driving the second skidoo and also pulling a large sled.

What Henry and Justin had done was cut out almost life size reindeer on plywood and painted them. Somehow, they attached the four deer; two on one side and two to the other side literally hiding the skidoo Henry was driving. Henry had painted the nose of one of the lead reindeer red and attached a light to it which glowed. Noah immediately recognized it as Rudolf the red nosed Reindeer!

As Henry and his son pulled up to the front door, he kept shouting "Ho, ho, ho, merry Christmas everyone!"

It was like Santa himself had landed and personally came to the Pederson residence! Everyone clapped and cheered as the men came to a stop.

"Okay, all aboard everyone!" Santa shouted.

Noah went up to touch Rudolf's red nose.

"Come on, Noah! You can sit up here with Santa and help steer the reindeer down to the prayer house."

Noah ran to Henry and said, "You are not Santa, you're Grandpa!"

Henry scooped the young boy off his feet and sat him in front of him.

Jenny climbed on the skidoo behind Henry and after everyone had boarded on the two sleds, off they went.

The moon was full and bright; snow clouds had not yet covered it. Between the light of the moon and the stars sparkling in the heavens, it was almost unnecessary to have the lights of the skidoo on. However, Henry decided to leave them on as they cautiously travelled down the road winding precariously around the side of the hill to the bottom of the valley.

Everyone held their breath as they turned the bend, exposing the prayer house all lit up with Christmas lights of all colors. Henry and Justin had strung lights right up to the cross on top of the cupola. The sparkling lights outlining the Poustinia reflected colorfully on the ice of the pond where it was cleared of snow that afternoon for skating.

As they pulled up to the house, the nativity scene on the deck next to the patio windows came into view. It was as if they were like the shepherds and wise men coming to pay homage to the newborn King.

"Oh, this is so beautiful, it brings tears to my eyes," commented Alison. "Imagine the Son of God being born in a stable and the humble life He lived."

"Yeah," said Henry. "One would think that He would have come in all His glory as King of the universe and lived in a palace and yet, He chose to live a life of poverty, sacrifice and humility."

"And look!" as Alison pointed through the patio doors to the large cross hanging above the altar. "Here He is a baby being born and there He hangs at age thirty three, His mission that He came into the world for was accomplished. He was born to save us ..."

The deck grew silent as each of them contemplated the immense sacrifice and love that Jesus has for us to lay down His life.

Father broke the silence and said, "Yes, just like Jesus had a mission, God has a plan for each of us too. No matter what work we are called to do it should be in service to others so as to continue the redemption that Jesus started. We have to be willing to say 'yes' to God's will just like Blessed Mary said to the angel Gabriel when he told her that she would conceive the Son of God; 'I am the Lord's servant. Let everything you've said happen to me.'"

Father paused and then added, "The children which both Jenny and Camilla are carrying and soon to be born, will be like Jesus laying here in the manger. They will have a mission in life just like all of us have."

And then Lauren said something which was hopeful, "It's really quite amazing what Jesus did and the impact He had on the world to be remembered and celebrated like this over all of the centuries."

"That is a good observation, Lauren. When Jesus began His ministry at age thirty, He was baptized not only with water but also the Holy Spirit descended upon Him. It is the Spirit of God which gave Him the power and strength as a man to do all He did for the next three years upon the earth. Shortly, we will be going inside the house and reliving those last days leading up to His death. But here is the answer to your observation, Lauren. Before Jesus ascended into heaven, He told His disciples that the Father would send His Holy Spirit to guide and strengthen them and remind them of His teachings. He would not be physically present with them anymore but He would indwell in them through the Holy Spirit. It was through the Holy Spirit who inspired some of the apostles to write Gospels in the Bible and He also continues, urges, prompts, and leads all of us to Jesus. So, you see, Lauren, it is the Holy Spirit who keeps convicting all of us from the days of the apostles right up to the present. That is why we should always tune into this immense power which God has given to us."

Henry nodded in agreement to Father Engelmann's comments and added, "The entire drama of God's plan for the world is right here before us; the creation of the world by God the Father; His Son coming into the world to save us from our sins and reconcile us with God and the Holy Spirit coming to help us to live like Jesus and follow Him. All three persons in the Holy Trinity; each playing their part in the entire scheme of things."

"I never thought of it that way before, Dad," said Jeremy. "But when you see the big picture, it all falls into place, doesn't it?"

Once again, a silence and peace fell over them as they pondered over the love that God has for all mankind.

"It always feels so holy to be down here. I can almost feel the flutter of angels flying all about us."

"Yes, Jenny," responded Father. "There are many angels that watch over the chapels in the world. I feel their presence all the time, too."

"I feel the peace here, too, Mom," said Alison. "It's so silent and holy."

Suddenly Camilla chimed in. "Oh, I was just thinking of the same thing and the Christmas song of Silent Night came into my mind. I wonder if the person who wrote that song was inspired on a night such as this?"

Father Engelmann said, "It is an interesting story how that song was written, Camilla. Silent Night actually originated from my homeland in Austria. It was Christmas Eve, December 24th, 1818 in a small village called Oberndorf, just hours before Christmas Mass and Pastor Joseph Mohr needed new musical plans for the upcoming church service. I'm certain it was the inspiration of the Holy Spirit who prompted Joseph to take the Christmas poem he had written two years earlier to his friend Franz Gruber, the church organist, to set his poem to music. Once again, I'm sure that the Holy Spirit helped Franz too! Amazingly, in the few short hours on that evening of December 24, 1818, Franz composed the 'Stille Nacht' melody. That evening, Joseph and his good friend Franz stood before the altar of the St. Nicholas Church in Oberndorf to perform their own work!"

"Do you still remember how to sing the song in German, Grandpa?" asked Justin.

"Yes, I do. The words of the original poem are slightly different from the song that is sung today in the western world."

"Would you please sing the hymn for us?" asked Alison.

Father smiled and nodded. Let us hold hands and silently say a prayer of thanks to those two fine musicians who were inspired to create such a beautiful melody that has captured the hearts and minds of the entire world in countless languages. See, what I said earlier, how each of us has a purpose for the Lord. When you are ready to begin, hum the melody and I will surprise all of you with my outstanding voice!" Father winked and bowed his head.

Huge snowflakes began falling from the sky, filling the valley with even more peace than already existed if that were possible. Every now and then the howl of coyotes broke the silence. It was as if they wanted to participate in the impending performance. Justin noticed a deer across the pond but didn't want to disturb the others from their thoughts.

The aura around the Pederson clan brightened as they took hold of each other's hands and softly began to hum the melody of Silent Night. The light around them grew to envelope the prayer house as angels on high joined in. After humming the first verse, they started again, this time Father joined in. To many people, Father's voice may only have had the quality of a mediocre singer but that evening standing with his family on the deck when Fathers voice chimed in, it sounded like the finest tenor that ever performed.

It was truly a song sung from the heart for his King and his homeland:

Stille Nacht, heilige Nacht! Alles schlafft, einsam wacht
Nur des traute hochhelige Paar. Holder Knabe im
      lockigen Haar,
Schlaf in himmlischer Ruh, Schlaf in himmlescher Ruh.

Stlle Nacht, Helilige Nacht! Hirten est kund gemacht.
Surch der Engel Halleluja Tont es laut …

CHAPTER FORTY-FOUR

O N CHRISTMAS MORNING, Henry and Jenny were surprised that they were up before the children. However, it was to be expected the kids would sleep in; they were so tired after the Mass was over and coming back up to the house to open some of the presents. In any case, they appreciated the quiet time as they reminisced over the happenings of yesterday and last evening at the prayer house.

"I can't seem to get the lyrics to Oh Holy Night out of my mind. The way Alison sung it at Mass last night was so beautiful and haunting."

"Yeah it touched me too, Honey. The words are so appropriate:

O Holy night, the stars are brightly shining
It is the night of our dear Savior's birth
Long lay the world in sin and error pining
Til He appeared and the soul felt it's worth
A thrill of hope the weary world rejoices
For yonder breaks a new and glorious morn
Fall on your knees
O hear the angel voices
O night divine!
O night when Christ was born

O night divine!
O night, o night divine!
And in His Name, all oppression shall cease
Sweet hymns...

"Oh, my gosh, Honey, you sing it so nicely too! The words tell the story so beautifully."

Henry nodded. "Yeah they sure do. I was thinking about how Father sang *Silent Night*. He did such a wonderful job of it. It must have recalled many fond memories of Austria just the way he sang it so much from the heart."

"I had tears in my eyes the entire time. It sounded so beautiful when sung in German as if it was always meant to be sung that way."

"And it was, Sweetheart. It's the rest of the world that was so taken by it that we adopted it."

A silence permeated the sun room as both Henry and Jenny gazed out over the valley covered in freshly fallen snow. It exuded a peace that captured the wonder of the season.

"I'm expecting Father to come out of the prayer house any moment with Coco. He was up for hours I'm sure."

"Like clockwork, Jen. He's up before the sun every day. He probably has read his breviary, celebrated Mass and may have written a bit more in the epic story he is writing."

"I would love to start reading it. He keeps saying it's a story about us and about how God intended for us to live our lives. He's already on book five. I can't imagine what on earth he has written that takes up so many books!"

"Well, he is a very insightful man and has the ability to explain things so clearly. But what I was thinking about was how he took us through the prayer house after Mass and told each of us our inheritance. To Lauren he would leave the Bible he received when he was ordained into the priesthood. Alison couldn't get over receiving Anna's rosary. He treasured that so much ..."

"And I love the framed photo of him and Anna. I will treasure that always."

"Yeah, that is a treasure, Jen. The happiness in their eyes as newlyweds is very obvious."

"She was a very attractive, sophisticated looking woman. They both look so handsome together. Father's tan suit looks so distinguished on him."

"Yeah, he said that he wants to be buried in that suit just like Anna was buried in her wedding gown."

"Really!? Was she really buried in her marriage attire?"

"Yes, I was 17 at the time when she passed away; I couldn't believe it either as I approached her coffin. Her face was covered slightly with the veil and I pushed it aside to give her a kiss on the cheek. It was so unusual to see her lying there wearing her wedding gown. The idea was that it was the gown she wore when marrying David and now she was wearing it to be wed to Jesus. We always loved when she came into the store; she gave it a special ambiance. She was such an elegant woman."

"I would have loved to know her. It will be so sad when Father passes on. The painting you did of Father holding her hand the day Anna died in their bedroom is so special. I guess it will come back to you. Father didn't say who he wanted to give that to."

"That's right. He gave the cross that was hanging in their bedroom to Jeremy and Camilla so all the kids including us received something of his to remember him and Anna by."

"I assume the cross hanging over his bed in the prayer house is the one that was in his and Anna's bedroom."

"Yes, it's the same one. Did you notice all the manuscripts on the desk?"

Jenny nodded. "I saw them when I peeked into the bedroom. Oh, Henry, I would give anything to be able to read them. I can't imagine all those books telling of our love story. Surely, it must have a lot of other material."

"Well, Father Engelmann has lived a long and amazing life. As I mentioned before, he is filled with wisdom and closer to the Lord than any other person I know. Almost every time he speaks, some insight or other is revealed. I'm sure his books will reflect the teachings of Jesus applied to real life situations."

After a long silence, Henry said, "He was so emotional when he assigned his earthly possessions to the various members of the family. It was almost as if he was thinking that this may be his last Christmas with us. In a way, he was living out his last will and testament. I hope not. I will miss him dearly."

"He seems so healthy. One would never know he is one hundred and three years of age. And yes, it will be such a devastating loss when he passes on."

"He lived a worry free life and one of total detachment to the world. I recall vividly driving him from the grocery store to the church, all he had was one suitcase; filled with the cross, his tan suit, the Bible, photo and Anna's rosary.

"Over all those years he never added anything to his possessions. Any money he received that wasn't used in his humble life style he gave to charity. Imagine, he has absolutely nothing in the way of materialism and yet he owns the world. He is richer and freer than all of us. His entire life was always aimed at storing treasures in heaven and not on earth."

Jenny nodded again showing full agreement.

"He is a rare person indeed and yet, just a simple man who decided to live like His Lord. St. Frances and Father Engelmann are much alike. They both aspired to live a life of poverty, chastity and charity. St. Francis' prayer describes perfectly the life which they both chose to live."

"Well, Honey, I better get the turkey in. Camilla helped me with the stuffing yesterday. She is such a good cook. She suggested covering the turkey breast with strips of bacon. It looks very good. It's a large turkey and will take most of the day to cook. And I hear little feet scampering about upstairs. Noah and Joshua will be down any minute to see what Santa got them. They will probably ask you to go tobogganing right after they open the gifts, so you better get dressed too. Let's say morning prayers and thank God for all our blessings before the house comes alive once again with the Pederson's."

Henry got up and went to Jenny. "Merry Christmas, Jenny. I love you so much. To me, you are the best gift ever!"

Chapter Forty-Five

WHEN THE RECEPTIONIST showed Jenny to the doctor's office, he and the attending nurse were discussing her file.

"Yes, come in, Mrs ...ah, Jenny and have a seat. I was just going over the test results and ultra-sound and noticed they are from last November."

"I missed my December appointment with you due to a snow storm and couldn't re-schedule as you were going home for Christmas."

"I remember that now; however, we need updated test results. They do indicate everything looked fine at that time; the embryo is developing and a heartbeat was detected. It was too early to determine the sex but then...you already know, don't you?"

The doctor smiled as he looked up at Jenny.

"That's right, my little girl, Hannah, is growing just fine."

"I see you have already given her a name?"

Jenny nodded. "Yes, it's a beautiful name, don't you think?"

Doctor Webster smiled, "Yes, very nice, Jenny, indeed." He paused a moment and then said, "According to the ultra-sound, it does confirm the gestational age which Doctor Kreake determined when you first saw him. You are now into your seventeenth week, about one third into your second trimester."

"Oh my, time is going so quickly."

"Yes, before you know it, you will be up all hours feeding Hannah."

"I love what you just said. I can just picture it. Oh, I can't wait to hold my little girl!"

Doctor Webster smiled and said, "Let's go into the other room and complete the examination."

"So, HOW DID everything go today, Honey?" Henry asked no sooner than he gave his dear wife a hug and tender kiss.

"Well, everything seems fine. My blood pressure was a little high and I gained three pounds. He gave me another requisition for lab tests and a prescription for the hypertension. Other than that, the pregnancy is moving along as expected."

"Did he order another ultra-sound to check the baby's well-being?"

Jenny suspected Henry was more interested in confirming the sex scientifically. "No, he didn't but I can ask him to at my next appointment. It will show the sex of the child. I don't need to know because I believe I already know. However, if another one is done, you can come along and the technician can whisper to you what the scan shows."

"Actually, Honey, I don't think I need to confirm what you already know in your heart. So, I am going to pass on that."

"Wow! That's quite a leap of faith you're making."

"Sweetheart, if I can't refuse you anything your little heart desires, how possibly could the good Lord?"

Jenny beamed, "Oh, I think I felt her kick!" Jenny rushed to Henry's side and took his hand to her tummy.

"There, she did it again. Do you feel it!?"

"Yeah, I did!" Henry said excitedly. "She's sure starting to grow. The bump seems larger than two days ago."

"Yes, I think so, too."

"When you were gone to the city, I read Samuel 1 and Samuel 2 in the Old Testament and I have to admit, there is quite a similarity between you and Hannah. I can see why

Father Engelmann would have been surprised by your prayer that morning."

"Samuel turned out to be such a special child and man and prophet. I think God has something special for Hannah as well. I can just picture her in her nun's habit."

"Now, Honey, let's not put the cart before the horse. Hannah may have other ideas or something else entirely in mind."

Jenny simply smiled and slowly shook her head, "She belongs to God, Henry. I gave her back to Him."

Henry tenderly gazed at his dear wife, words failing to come to him.

Her faith was simple, yet so deep. She reminded him of his mother in that regard. Mary, too, accepted people the way they were; she loved unconditionally and fully trusted in God. Often, she would say, "You think too much and complicate it all; just accept, Henry." Henry shook his head and almost audibly muttered, "I'm working on it, Mom."

THE NEXT MORNING, both Henry and Jenny were up early. When they came downstairs, Justin was eating his breakfast and going over his history lesson at the same time.

"Morning, Justin. All set for school?" inquired Jenny, as she passed by him and gently rubbed his shoulder. There wasn't the usual negative flinch. He seemed to be more accepting of her since the time they tried out the kite but especially after that outdoor adventure he and Henry had before Christmas. He was continuing to be open to Jenny's care and love for him.

"Yeah, just about. We are having a history quiz this morning. I forgot to study last night."

"I'm sure you will do well. History was one of my favorite subjects besides English. Sometimes, I find it hard to believe that all those things happened in the past. All the wars and how people treated one another down through the ages."

"Nothing too much has changed in a lot of countries," Henry chimed in.

"It's all about greed and some dictator at the top always wanting more land or power," offered Justin.

"That about sums it up. I think I saw the headlights of the bus, Justin."

"Geez, she gave me heck yesterday for not being out there on time." Justin closed his book and dashed to the front door. Jenny grabbed his lunch from the fridge and hurried to the foyer. Justin grabbed his bag and tossed his note book and history text book inside and made his way to the door.

"Here's your lunch, Justin."

"Yeah, thanks, Mom...er, I mean, Jenny."

Jenny looked neutral and pretended she didn't hear his remarks. She wanted desperately to go over and give him a hug and kiss but thought the time wasn't just right.

"Have a nice day, Son," Henry yelled as Justin ran out the door. Jenny remained in the foyer and watched as Justin climbed into the bus and it drove off. She rushed into the kitchen and exclaimed, "Did you hear Justin call me Mom...he changed back to Jenny but it was so good to hear him say that, Henry!"

Henry came over to Jenny and hugged her. "See, the Pederson's basically have a soft heart. He'll come around."

"Oh, Henry, that makes my day. Why don't we walk down to the prayer house and attend Mass with Father this morning? I noticed the temperature is just a few degrees below freezing on the gauge hanging outside when I watched Justin leave for the bus. It stopped snowing; I would love to stroll in the snow. What do you say, Honey?"

"How can I refuse when you say it so romantically?"

No sooner were Henry and Jenny outside when Ginger emerged from the dog house. It was still dark out, although, the winter sun was beginning to light and tint with color, the wispy clouds just above the horizon over the eastern sky. The dawning of a new day was at hand.

When they got to the Poustinia, it was evident that neither Father nor Coco had been out yet, as the deck was covered with at least four inches of fresh fallen snow.

"The deck looks like a white canvas, Henry."

"Yeah, and the sun is toning it with a warm golden color."

"You are so good at seeing even the slightest of color caused by the light. To me the snow is still white. Anyway, I just have to do this." Jenny took two gentle steps and lay back down on the snow. "I recall one day when I lived on the estate during the winter time, when I made an angel in the snow and then I did it again just beside it and pretended it was your angel. Come, Honey, lie beside me and let's make our angels together!"

Henry gazed at his playful wife. He actually wanted to get inside as he felt a bit chilled but how could he refuse her? He stepped forward, turned and lay on his back beside her. "Okay, Henry, on the count of three let's move our legs and arms like car wipers. And so, they did.

Coco must have heard the commotion and was scratching at the door. Father came and opened the front door and was shocked to see Henry and Jenny lying on the deck. "Jesus, Mary and Joseph, pray for me. Is that you, Henry and Jenny?"

They laughed. "Yes, it's us Father," replied, Jenny. "Come join us, Father!"

"Oh, I will just watch."

Careful not to damage the angels they made in the snow, Henry got up and took hold of Jenny's hand and pulled her up. They stepped towards Father and then all three looked at the images of two angels in the snow.

"We have just made the unseen visible, Father."

"Yes, yes, I can just see Hannah and Gabriel lying on the deck!"

"You know, Father, every now and then I see so many angels flying around the Poustinia at night. Did you know that or ever see them?" Henry wanted to know.

"Yes, I think I mentioned it to you at one time; it has to do with the chapel inside. Wherever Mass is being offered up to the Lord, choirs of angels are always present. Many times, I feel their presence and on occasion, I do see them."

"I do too!" Henry blurted. "Every now and then in the evening when I am out on the deck, just for split seconds, I see flashes of brightness and angels all around the prayer house."

Father nodded. "The Lord is blessing you, Henry with

visions of His heavenly spirits. Perhaps, the angels are beckoning you to come for a retreat."

Henry remained silent.

"Did you say Mass yet, Father?" Jenny wanted to know.

"I was just reading the gospel. Come in and I will begin again. It's wonderful to celebrate the Mass with others."

"Henry and Jenny brushed the snow off their clothes and went into the foyer. Ginger had already gone in, the heavy coat of snow on her fur and paws had melted, and water was on the floor. As soon as Jenny took her outer garments off, she got a cloth and wiped the hardwood. She smiled as she saw the two dogs already lying together beside the stove. "Aaah, look at Coco and Ginger, isn't that so cute?"

The men nodded in agreement.

After Mass, they sat by the window and chatted. Jenny was still receiving feedback from her ladies groups about the speech Father gave at the social event they had last November.

"Your talk about using the gifts God gave us to show affection and care for their spouse and children continues to have a very positive effect in many homes, Father. Some of the women whose husbands rarely show their emotions were touched by your words and are making great effort to meet their spouse' needs."

Father nodded, "That is good to hear, Jenny. Sometimes a reminder is all that is needed to spark an awareness of how important it is to touch, embrace and say words of care. Such easy simple acts and yet mean so much."

"Yeah," Henry chimed in, "When we show effort and that we are trying it makes such a great difference in a relationship. All too often at marriage ceremonies, Saint Paul's scripture on love is read. Soon however, the words become hollow and when one doesn't show love the other becomes resentful, grows silent, or withholds affection and love. It's difficult when one tries and the other doesn't. It's difficult to accept."

"Yes, that is true and yet, if one can love unconditionally, to accept where the partner is at and pray and seek strength from the Holy Spirit, miracles can happen as we are seeing in Jenny's group."

Henry nodded, "That's what happened in Jenny's marriage. No matter how rude and irritable James could be, his disposition was not able to drive the sun out of Jenny's spirit and soul."

Jenny took the compliment in stride. She remained silent and listened to the two men.

"Nor could my disposition and character do the same to Anna. There is great power and strength in loving others unconditionally. It is being Christ like and eventually it overcomes all obstacles in the end. One must always be willing to rise above the challenges of marriage. The blind cannot lead the blind lest both fall in the ditch!"

Henry turned to Father and said, "Imagine when two people learn to love one another unconditionally; how fully alive their relationship must be. Imagine two people actualizing their lives as well as their partners. They are both growing and becoming all that God intended for them and their marriage to be."

"Yes, that is so wonderful when two people are bent on serving one another," Said Jenny.

Father nodded and added, "Such a match may seem like it is made in heaven but really, it just requires sacrifice and the wisdom and strength of the Holy Spirit. My case is a good example. As I matured and began to see the light, I strived to make Anna happy. No longer did I want to be an obstacle in her personal growth or drawing closer to her Lord. I loved to see the joy in her eyes and the gratitude flowing like sweet honey from her lips."

"That's beautiful! Father," said Jenny, her eyes sparkling.

Father nodded, pondering Jenny's words thoughtfully. "Anything is possible when--"

"Jesus is at the center of your life and marriage," Henry interjected.

Father nodded.

Jenny chimed in, "And He is, Henry, and that is what makes the difference in our marriage."

Henry smiled at his dear wife. He saw in Jenny what Father saw in Anna. She had become like the flowers she so loved. Her radiance and inner beauty was unstoppable. She shone like the morning sun rising above the eastern hills and streaming through the patio doors. The beams struck Father's face revealing the wrinkles of joy around his eyes. It seemed as if each furrow curled up at the ends as if smiling.

"I love the early morning sun. It's not hot enough to be stifling but so warm and cheery. The rays almost sing a song of praise to the new day."

"That was well said, Jenny. How many days of my life have I watched the sun begin another day the Lord hath made? I never fail to rejoice and be glad in it."

Henry shook his head; the Holy Spirit was continuously whispering words to Father. "See, how beautifully you always tie things into the Lord's word? And speaking about words, how are you coming along with the story Father? Jenny and I are so anxious to read the books."

"I am working on the fifth book. It may be the last in the series. It now consists of what is happening in our present moments from day to day. I have some catching up to do as I have spent the last week working on a homily which I wanted to give when I was the parish priest at St Mary's. I will now have that opportunity to do so. Father Knuka wants to go home for a visit now that the Christmas season is over and I said I would cover for him."

"What is the sermon going to be about, Father?" Jenny asked.

"Abortion. I was astounded when I read an article at the care home how it's increasing. So many infants whose lives are taken before they've begun. It breaks my heart to see that in today's day and age, we are carrying out such a horrific practice."

Jenny nodded. "It's so sad, Father. I pray that your words touch the hearts of all parishioners. It has always bothered me that most people see it as such a wrong but don't step out and try to put a stop to it. If we see someone harm a child, we would be the first to report it and have it halted immediately and yet, women are terminating the life of their own child and we remain silent."

Father nodded. "Many terrible acts are done in the darkness. We may know what is happening behind closed doors, but if we saw an abortion being carried out it would have a more serious effect on people."

"I think that's correct, Father. Camilla told me that an ultra-sound was done filming an actual abortion procedure. Pregnant mothers who see it usually don't go ahead with the abortion. They can see how the infant tries to escape the instruments of death and the pain inflicted upon the infant when it is torn apart by the suction tube. I would give my life for Hannah before I would allow anything to ever happen to her."

Jenny put her hand on her tummy and gently massaged it. Henry gazed at his dear, sweet wife; her love of life written clearly on her pretty face.

CHAPTER FORTY-SIX

As FATHER ENGELMANN made his way to the podium, not a sound could be heard. He looked like a wise old sage; a prophet in his own time leading his people home. At one hundred and three, he looked frail because of how lean and slim he had become due to regular fasting. Yet, he was still spry and had a lively spring to his step. Although there was always a welcoming twinkle in his gaze, one could also detect fervor there as well; his mission and purpose in life was written all over his demeanor. He was a soldier for Christ and until his dying breath, he would completely devote every moment either praying for the sins of the world or bringing each person he came into contact with to salvation.

Unbidden tears surfaced in Henry's eyes as he gazed at his beloved teacher. How many more days, weeks and if possible, years, would Father still be here? He loved his mentor deeply and knew his heart would surely break when his dear friend went home to the Lord. Daily, Henry thanked Jesus for being so blessed as to have been led by such a holy man all of his life. Many times, Henry felt as though Jesus was walking beside him.

Father surveyed the seated parishioners in his usual manner. He swept his eyes slowly from one side of the congregation to the other making contact with each and every parishioner trying in earnest to reach not just their minds but their hearts as well. Father knew if his words were not guided by the Holy Spirit flowing through him, the message would not touch the souls of those in front of him and his message would be lost.

The church was packed from front to back including the large entrance foyer of St. Mary's Parish. Father Engelmann was dearly loved by all the parishioners and like Henry; they too, found each of these occasions to hear him speak a true blessing. They knew their highly revered priest's days on earth were coming to an end and felt so fortunate to just be in the presence of their holy shepherd, who many already believed would be nominated for sainthood. He was already considered "Blessed" because of the several miracles which had occurred through his intercession.

Almost simultaneously, Henry and Jenny squeezed each other's hands conveying the similar thoughts they were having about their beloved servant of God. They knew of the topic Father was going to speak about today and especially, Jenny could hardly wait to hear what he was going to say. She wished Chloe and her dearly departed mother, Tammy were here. They would have loved to hear Father speak on this subject that was so close to their hearts.

Softly, Father Engelmann began. "It always gives my heart such great joy to come back to this parish and fill in for Father Knuka while he is visiting his family in the Maritimes. In so many ways it is for me the same; to come home to visit my family. It's a wonderful opportunity to reunite with friends and see so many of you whom I baptized as an infant and whose parents I was honored to officiate at their passing.

"My, my, how the years have passed since Anna and I came to Canada in the forties and opened up Engelmann's Grocery and Confectionary just a few blocks from here on Victoria Avenue. The store has long been torn down but the memories of a loving, close knit community will be forever in my mind and heart. So many dear friends and how we helped one another through good times and bad. When the Lord took my dear, loving wife, Anna home in 1957, He asked me to marry another bride; the church."

Father spread open his arms towards the people and said, "What a wonderful way to end my journey on earth by being a part of your family."

A thunderous response was immediate! The congregation stood and clapped for over five minutes; tears of love for their shepherd permeated the air in the church like an electric charge.

Father beamed with tears of joy. His attempts to speak were drowned out by more cheers and clapping. Finally, Father raised both arms and stretched them up and forward. He moved his hands gently up and down gesturing for them to be seated. Reluctantly the applause and appreciation for their beloved Father Engelmann subsided and they sat down.

"Thank you...thank you from the bottom of my heart." Father brushed away a tear and composed himself and then said, "Family is the building block of community and society at large. What a wonderful plan God had when He created the world. How beautiful it is how God instituted marriage whereby a man and woman come together and become one flesh to produce another life and yet, the beginning of another family. And since we are all created by God, we are all His children here to love and worship our Lord and to love one another so we all return home to our Father; such a beautiful design for life on earth.

"Prior to the Second World War and after, life was simpler then; the values and morals were different than what they are today. Families prayed together, stayed together, worshiped together, movies were wholesome and what I remember and still cherish, was how deserted the city became on Sunday. All the stores were closed and it was truly a day of rest for family and relatives to come together and celebrate life.

"Just a cursory glance at me and it's easy to see I have lived a long life. Unfortunately, I have seen this wonderful plan of family begin to break down over the years. Even though I have been retired from running a parish for some time, I am still in touch and help out in many parishes in the city. What concerns me and my fellow colleagues in Christ is the direction in which society is heading. Slowly, insidiously over the years, many changes have been made that have adversely affected the family. Stores opened all hours of the day and night, the pursuit of materialism, the relaxation of sexual content on the movie screen and television, pornography, drugs, violence and on and on.

"In turn, attendance at Sunday Mass is declining especially amongst young people, prayer in the home is declining and in many homes completely absent, couples increasingly are living together outside of marriage, there is an increase in the number of families torn apart through divorce and separation. And finally, there is a silent, growing *evil* that is attacking the core of our family and society and has grown into epidemic proportions; the plague of abortion.

"These are signs of a society that has lost its way and is wandering through life aimlessly without guidelines, principles and solid moral values and standards to live by. It is little wonder that society is growing more and more ill by the day. While it may appear that the ills of society are separate ailments and dilemmas in our world, I believe that they are in a large part symptomatic of the breakdown of the family unit as God designed it. I could speak on any one of these ailments or dilemmas, this morning however, I would like to center upon abortion.

"Abortion is an intentional choice to destroy a life; it goes against God's design of creation. None of us would be here if our mother had chosen to terminate our life. The very thought of it as the words come out of my mouth tastes and sounds like something which couldn't be possible; unthinkable. How could a mother make such a choice? What possible justification could there be for turning the womb of a mother, supposedly the safest place for a fragile, defenseless infant to grow into a death chamber?

"Does the baby not have the same right to life as we do? How can one say a woman has the right to kill her child as long as it's in the womb but the moment it is born and takes its first breath of air its now illegal and indictable as a murderous act under the law."

Father Engelmann threw his hands up in the air. "Tell me, what am I not seeing or understanding?

"When I hear or read of the reasons why many abort their child, they can't possibly justify the termination of their baby within their womb; it's inconvenient at this point in my life, they say, it will affect my happiness and future, I will lose my boyfriend and on and on go the feeble excuses in an attempt to rationalize the killing of another human being! Oh, more sophisticated arguments in favor of this atrocious act are presented under the guise that it is a woman's right to choose what she does with her body but it's all semantics; the twisting of words to hide the truth like a clever lawyer who crafts his argument to get a murderer off who is as guilty as sin!

"Meine lieben Kinder, there is nothing, absolutely nothing that can justify the killing of the child within the womb of a mother.

"Although abortion was legalized in 1973 by a decision made by the Supreme Court which opened the door to this holocaust, the killing of over one and a half million infants in the United States this past year alone has occurred. Unfortunately, their decision is further compounded by the breakdown of the family. Abortion should not just be looked at in isolation; it is part of a bigger concern.

"At the beginning of this sermon, I described how God designed the family where a man and woman come together and become one flesh. A holy covenant is made between them; to honor and cherish, to love in sickness and in health until death do they part. That is a powerful binding vow between two people; I am now committed and come hell or high water, I am going to do whatever it takes to make this work.

"Under the umbrella and security of a marriage, the home is now a safe, loving, secure environment to carry out God's plan of procreation. This is fair to the wife, the husband and the children they bring into the world. Within this family unit, we live and grow and love each other and God our heavenly Father. This is also according to His design as laid out in Ephesians 5:18-33. This, my dear friends, is God's design for marriage for His children."

Father paused and at the same time spread his hands and thrust his shoulders towards the congregation, "Does this not make clear sense and a wise way to begin a family?" Father stopped again and looked from side to side giving anyone opportunity to refute him.

"Many people today, especially the young, reject God's plan and engage in sex outside of marriage when dating or deciding to live together in common law.

"First let me say, this is a sin. Second, where is the security and responsibility for the consequences of such a choice? It's as if they are saying, I may love you but not enough to be committed to you in a marriage. I want to play house and have the pleasure of sex but with the backdoor always open; if things don't go my way, I'm out of here.

"This is where most abortions take place; outside the umbrella of marriage. In many instances, abortion is no more than another method of contraception. I am certain when the learned judges of the Supreme Court said that it is the woman's right to abort the child within her womb, they could never have conceived that they had passed a law which would result in the killing of millions upon millions of infants. Unbelievably, this can be done through all nine months of a woman's pregnancy! I dare to say, this has become big business in the medical industry. Doctors who once vowed to save lives are now making a lucrative business out of killing lives.

"This, my dear people, is what happens when we go against God's design and plan for His children."

Father shook his head and paused letting out a long sigh. He took a deep breath and then went on, "Imagine a woman making an appointment with a doctor, say, for next Wednesday or Thursday when there is an opening so she can have the doctor terminate the child within her womb. Now, I don't mean to make light of this, I know how painful it must be for so many women to make the decision to terminate the life of their child but according to the unbelievable statics, abortions run into the millions each year! For all too many, it's as if we have so accepted such an evil practice as no different than going to a doctor for a checkup or a dentist to have a tooth extracted.

"Imagine this woman going into a room, lying on a table and prepared for an abortion. One can only imagine the fear, and anxiety that a woman must be going through as the sanctuary of her womb is suddenly invaded by instruments designed to efficiently kill the child she is carrying? And what about the fetus? Ultra-sound videos show how the infant tries to escape from the invasion, as the instruments are inserted but the baby has no place to go! It is totally defenseless and at the mercy of their mother!

"Imagine, the sac filled with fluid that nature designed to protect the infant, is broken and then a long tube connected to a suction device is inserted, powerful enough to pull the baby apart into pieces. When it comes to the head, another instrument like a pair of tongs is used to crush it so that it can be removed from the woman's uterus. All that's left are shards; bits and pieces of what was once a living human being; a member of the human race. The body parts are thrown away into a pail or jar and then discarded by other means. The woman sees none of this but can only imagine what has taken place. The infant is nameless, is not buried in a cemetery to visit, instead tossed away as trash having no value.

"This is the mother's memory of the abortion."

As Father paused and took a deep breath, Henry immediately brought to mind the death of his son, Michael. His son's life was not even for a day and caused unimaginable grief and yet Julean and Henry had memories, took photos, buried the infant and visited his gravesite. But Father was correct, with an abortion there was none of that. There was nothing wholesome to hold onto only emptiness and thoughts of what was done. Surely, there must be grave consequences for the mother.

It was as if Father had read Henry's mind.

"After the operation, the woman gets off the operating table, dresses and goes about her daily chores. She has been told she is now rid of her problem and free to go on with her life as if nothing has ever happened."

Father Engelmann paused and shook his right hand back and forth, "Nein, nein, no, my children, it is impossible for a woman not to be affected by what she has done. We know better; we know right from wrong. We grieve whether the child dies outside the womb or inside. The grave difference is that when the infant is terminated inside our grief is compounded with guilt. To do evil and think that it gives some kind of benefit is a lie of the first order. The mother will realize, although too late, that she has been misled by friends, doctors, and even parents.

"Think on this? How can a woman who is given the gift of motherhood by God to love the child with a mother's love not be affected by what she has done?

"Tell me, how?

"God blessed women to bring in the miracle of life. Mary, the mother of God was most blessed amongst all women. Jesus chose to come through the womb of a woman to enter this world, He could have come in other ways but women are blessed by God to perform this miracle of life and God honored it. Jesus, the King of the universe, our Lord and Savior humbled Himself by becoming man and entered the world just as you and I have. He too, grew in the womb as an embryo, fetus, new born infant, child, teen adolescent, adult; all the stages from conception to death that a human goes through. At no point was Jesus not Jesus. At no point is an infant not a human being, a member of the human race. His or her rights to life is the same as ours.

"How grateful we must all be to God for this wonderful gift of life that brings such joy to the whole world in a family. Yet, this gift of motherhood can be rejected, attacked, and destroyed by the evil of abortion.

"Women who terminate the life of their child are seriously affected and wounded by this action. Thousands upon thousands of women are suffering emotionally, spiritually and mentally. Healing centers are springing up across North America to help women overcome the effects of abortion.

"When we sin and do wrong, God has designed us to feel the remorse of our deeds. I have lived a long life and fully understand how our heavenly Father has created us to be. I have listened to thousands upon thousands of confessions of people who were troubled by dishonesty, lying, and the lack of forgiveness; look within your own life to see if this is not true? But imagine, for a mother to terminate the life of her child, surely, she cannot go unscathed as if nothing has happened. It is a sin to intentionally kill another human being and goes against God's other commandment to love one another...not to kill! It goes contrary to a woman's instinct and nature to love and nourish and care for the baby in her womb. The emotional, psychological, and spiritual post traumatic effects of abortion are widespread and clearly show the deep wounds to the mother!

"There can be no justification for abortion!

"This I know, God did not give the gift of motherhood to women to give birth to daughters that would chose to kill the child within their womb. For the daughter to deny the right to life that she was entitled to by her mother goes against the will of God and is a rejection of His creation.

"This brings us back to the family. Abortion is both the result of the breakdown of the family as God designed it and also the greatest destroyer of the family. The legalization of abortion has opened the door so wide that it not only threatens the woman's peace and well-being but affects relationships with her mate and her own family; grieving parents, grandparents, siblings and relatives. Those affected can either be supportive or opposed to the abortion.

"Most abortions involve women outside of marriage as I have already mentioned. In most cases, too, the boyfriend has input and it's usually to pressure the girl to have an abortion. This shows no sense of responsibility for his actions. It lacks love and compassion and care because it was more a sexual act outside of a secure loving atmosphere. The man has little or no concern how the woman suffers with the decision to kill her child or the aftermath of an abortion. He wants his pleasure, but don't bother him with the consequences.

"Where is the restraint, the discipline, the moral guidelines and the maturity to do what is right?

"Here is my point!" Father cried as he pounded his fists against the podium. "Where are all the men in this battle!?" How a frail man could raise his voice like a giant startled the congregation.

"If more fathers take it upon themselves to operate a home that instills godly values, perhaps more young people wouldn't find themselves in this predicament. The most influential member of the family is the father as he is at the headship of the home. I appeal to the men, as leaders you must step up to the plate each and every day and face the challenges to restore the family and values we once held dear to our hearts. A man's goal must be to become like Christ in his thoughts, words and deeds; to live by example; to be a role model. I will even go as far as to say; a father wants to be not only a leader and hero to his family but a saint! A man whose family looks up to and follows. A man like this must know the word of God so he knows where he is going. A man who will be unwavering; who is not afraid to go against the pressures and standards of the world. A man who is tough and bold to engage in spiritual combat to defend women, children and unborn defenseless infants. A man who sits down with his wife and decides to put Jesus at the center of their lives and marriage. Men can no longer be silent and sit back.

"Based upon Christ's teachings, the man and his wife establish solid and firm guidelines which they agree upon and implement for the raising of their children. Without Christ, the task is impossible. Without the grace and strength of the Holy Spirit, it cannot be done. Without beginning the day to pray, reflect and meditate on the state of your life and family, and what you need to do to guide and protect your family safely and securely on the journey home, you will live aimlessly.

"Tell me, how else can this be achieved? Search your hearts and tell me if this is not so! Show me any other way that offers a sure path to safety and inner peace and a healthy family and society.

"It's all in the Bible how we should live and be within the family. Introduce prayer upon rising. Let your children see their parents turn to God. Let them see how their parents submit to one another, dying to themselves and expressing kindness, love and forgiveness. Together as a family, say morning prayers to begin the day. Pray before meals and after dinner. Sunday must be a day of family worship. Children must see the value and importance of prayer and how we communicate to the Holy Trinity.

"The family that prays together stays together is so true.

"The Holy Spirit blesses such a family and showers it with the grace, strength and wisdom to live for each other and God!

"Fathers and mothers, if you don't want to see your daughter one day facing abortion then you must teach her the importance of chastity and abstinence and the gift of her pure body to her husband on the evening of their marriage. You must teach her the sacredness and miracle of life. Curfews must be followed and modest dress must be practiced.

"So many young girls as well as mothers must understand the importance of dressing modestly. A man is easily aroused and tempted into sin. We want our daughters to be respected for who they are and not desired because of the exposure of their skin. Mothers must lead by example. How a young girl dresses sends out a message to boys. Does she want to attract men for who she is as a person or that she is available for other means?

"It is the same with your sons. If you do not want him to be pressuring some girl to abort her child which is one of the leading causes of abortion, you must teach and instill in him the sacredness of life and respect for women and that their bodies are not to be used simply for his pleasure.

"Perhaps one of the greatest character traits you can instill within your children is will power, discipline, restraint and the reasons why the development of these gifts from God are so important. In today's instant society where we want all our needs gratified right away, to be able to deny self and put sex off until marriage is indeed a blessing.

"It is not an impossible task. Many parents have chosen such an approach for their children. Men must be strong role models for their children. Children imitate their parents for better or worse. Children come to know God through their parents, especially the father.

"Never before is there such a strong need for men who have thought things out and become saints within their home. The more men put Jesus at the center of their lives and their marriage and strive to become like Him the more they are building their home on a rock. They are not aimless and tossed about like some leaf in the prairie wind. They can withstand the storms of life. We either live as a model family that fights to defeat the ills of society or we become part of the problem!

"Women must follow the lead of their husbands and if their husbands are not taking on their responsibility they must be encouraged to do so. The women must pray for guidance and help and support. God is the God of the impossible. I have seen miracles over and over in marriages and family through coming to the Father in daily prayer and thanksgiving. One of the greatest things parents can do for their children is to love one another as Jesus would have them love. Jesus is the example of sacrifice and submission to one another. This is how we bring each other home.

"Can you not see if we begin to live the way God intended how much simpler life would be? We have direction and purpose and as a bonus the wisdom and strength of the Holy Spirit to live this way comes into our lives. Amazing, miraculous things happen when we turn our lives over to Jesus. Can you not see how divorce would decline; abortion, unfaithfulness and the ailments of society would subside.

"Fathers too, must practice abstinence if they want to limit their family and expect their children to do so prior to marriage. It has been shown that abstinence followed by the husband and wife during that time when the woman is fertile has the effect of extending their courting relationship. There is something beautiful and beneficial about practicing discipline and will power. We appreciate more what we have in all respects. If you eat chocolate cake every morning, noon and night it soon loses flavor and appeal. So, it is with all aspects of life. Fasting, praying and denial to self, reap huge benefits and rewards and is wonderful for children to see and participate in. Children identify with their parents consciously and unconsciously; for better or for worse, children perpetuate what they have seen their parents do."

Father paused and grew silent. One could feel the weight of what he was preaching upon his shoulders. "The family, my dear children, is the key to resolving many of the ills and evils of society. One family may feel that they cannot do much but they are wrong. A model family within the community spreads quickly and encourages other families to do the same. People need to see the light in the darkness. When we choose to become beacons, we attract others to the light. They will want what we have."

Father shook his head and held his hands in a prayerful pleading manner as he said, "Please, please don't remain silent any longer on the issue of abortion. Please do not sit on the sidelines and remain inactive and passive in the face of evil. We must become the voice of the unborn and stop the holocaust which is going on. Let your politician know that he or she too must take a stand against this issue or you will find someone who will. Especially when the next election comes up, make this a number one priority on your list. Votes count and if enough voice their objection to this holocaust, it will stop.

"If a friend or relative comes into your life that is considering abortion, there too, we must speak. These mothers need guidance and support and input into all aspects of abortion. Pray for them, be there for them, explain the alternatives and love them. There are so many adoptive parents out there who would love to have a child. There is financial support available and so many support agencies are available that will help the mother get her through her pregnancy and beyond.

"And for the mother who has aborted her child, I am not here to judge or to condemn. Yes, it is a sin and a horrific act. In the majority of cases, abortion is done under duress with no insight into other options. Most important of all is to see that we are all sinners but we are not the sin. It may always be a part of you but it is not who you are, you are a beautiful child of God who loves you from all eternity and His love is boundless and endless. There is no sin that God will not forgive.

"Christ has opened the door for us to the Father. He died for us so we may have eternal life. Let His death and suffering be not in vain. Don't be defeated by your sin when Jesus has already defeated it for you. He is waiting for you; the door is open, trust Him. Don't suffer a moment longer! Come with a sorrowful repentant heart and know the mercy, forgiveness and love of God and His Son and the Holy Spirit."

Father Engelmann could no longer go on. He shook his head from side to side and began to weep. "There is so much needless suffering..."

Father tried to compose himself but the holy man felt such compassion for others, he couldn't stop wanting to convince others of Jesus' endless sea of mercy. He wanted to heal...

After several minutes, a tall figure stood up eight rows from the front of the church. At first, he looked like an East Indian by his apparel. Henry gasped as his friend, John McBryne, passed by him and walked to the podium and put his arms around Father Engelmann. While holding him, comforting him, John slowly guided Father to his chair.

John returned to the podium and said, "Father Engelmann saved my life. He was the first man to show kindness, love, mercy and unconditional love. It was through Father Engelmann that I saw the light that shines in the darkness. I was a sinner in the gutter of life; a drug addict and dealer, a liar, thief; I was dishonest, cheated and committed every sin imaginable and eventually I was responsible for the death of another person.

"While in this state in my life, Father came to me and showed me God's mercy and forgiveness by reflecting Jesus. Short of Jesus Himself coming to me, Father was there in His place. It was through Father that I came to know and trust in God. Father Engelmann was the first real image of a loving father. What I have learned from this is that our heavenly Father works through us by His divine providence to minister to others.

"In Father Engelmann's sermon, he mentioned the importance of fathers in a home. Believe me, we need role models, heroes, saintly people in our lives who can influence us. Dads don't ever fully realize how critically important they are to their children. I can only imagine how my life might have been had my father been like Father Engelmann. I can only imagine how many years of my life were wasted and how much good I could have done. I thank the Lord every day for this holy man to have come into my life.

"This is the same for mothers. If it hadn't been for my mother's love through my childhood to overshadow all the abuse which occurred in our home, I think I might very well have been a suicide statistic.

"God works through his people.

"Just as Father was a powerful influence in my life, I in turn try to be an example to others and become the light for them. I am now a missionary in India bringing Jesus' love to the people.

"*Of all truths, I know, that has to be at the top of the list.*

"Our thoughts, words, deeds, attitudes, emotions and moods affect those around us deeply. They either become closer to Christ or we can drive them even further away. Before Father came into my life, I was the latter. I despised myself and others did too. But after receiving the mercy and forgiveness of Jesus, I am quick to pass it on. I see hundreds of abortions. If I am there before it happens, I immediately become the voice for the infant. Many times, I am able to save the child's life. And for those which have aborted their child or are suffering from the trauma, I am the first to forgive.

"Abortion is a sin, but like me, if God can forgive me, He

can forgive you. I am living proof of what Father Engelmann was saying. The mercy, love and forgiveness of Jesus is endless."

John lowered the microphone again and returned to his seat.

Father Engelmann came back up to the podium once again composed to go on.

"Thank you, John, for sharing your love for Jesus Christ. If only we knew how much we are loved, how much Jesus desires for us to come to Him. He wants so deeply to forgive us and bring us home to our heavenly Father. He wants to give you the Holy Spirit so you can come to know Him intimately. Come to Him just as you are with an open, repentant heart ready to give your all for Him. In return, 'Rivers of living water will flow out of you.'

"We need families to become beacons of light. Please come to Him and accept the challenge. Bitte meine lieben Kinder, please do not sit idly by any longer. Do not let the ills of society continue.

"*We must change to make the world change.*

"If we want a strong family, you know what needs to be done. It won't happen by itself. Imagine in six months from now or a year from now how your family, your relationships, your community will be if you turn your life to Jesus and be obedient to His teachings.

"*Every change for the better goes into the world to spread its healing love.*

"Come, fathers and mothers, let us raise children who respect and honor the gift of life God has given us.

"Become the voice for all of the injustices in the world, especially for the defenseless infant in a mother's womb. Their voice is silent and can only be heard if we stand up and speak for the child. He or she has just as much right to live as us.

"For mothers who have been wounded, as John said, the love and mercy of Jesus is endless. There is a wonderful weekend healing retreat called Rachel's Vineyard proven to have miraculous results in healing victims of abortion. It's for mothers, husbands, boyfriends, couples, parents, grandparents, all who have been adversely affected by this terrible act.

"In closing, I would like to say a prayer;

"Dear heavenly Father, enlighten our minds and hearts to see the dreadful wrong in terminating the life of an infant growing in a mother's womb. Help all women who are considering abortion today to see the many other choices available to them. Give the men who are the fathers to these babies the fortitude to accept their responsibilities for their actions. Illuminate the minds and hearts of both men and women to be supportive of one another and together find solutions which protect the life of the baby and welfare of the mother. Remove their fears and anxieties and help them to trust in You and see that You are the God of all possibilities to bring such great good out of this. Give foresight, dear Lord, to both the men and women to fully realize the devastating effects that abortion has especially on women who choose to terminate the child in her womb.

"Give courage to all those bystanders who see the evil of abortion to be silent no more and to be a voice for life in this culture of death.

"Dear Lord, help us to prevent these situations from arising in the first place. Grant men and women the wisdom to see the beauty in chastity before marriage. Give men the strength to control their desires for the greater good; to respect women and be conscious of the consequences of their urges. Help men and women to see the beauty, wholesomeness and enjoyment of sex within the security of marriage where it belongs and was intended to be. And even here, help married couples to practice abstinence and witness for themselves the tremendous love that grows for one another and how the example of this affection touches their children's hearts.

"Father, help us to fully appreciate and understand the depth of love that Jesus has for each of us that He gave his very life so that we may live. Help us to love each other with His love, to see the gift of life through His eyes and how precious it is and not something to be destroyed and discarded as worthless and having no value.

"And finally, dear Jesus, give fathers the wisdom, commitment and brave-heartedness to put You at the head of their lives to lead their family in these truths and become a warrior for the Lord and restore the values that once again protect life and give honor and glory to You.

"I ask this in Christ's Holy name. Amen."

CHAPTER FORTY-SEVEN

H ENRY KNEW INSTANTLY that it was Eddy Zeigler on the other end of the phone even before he spoke. It was both his distinctive voice and cough that gave him away.

"Geez Eddy, it's good to hear from you."

"*Cough, cough...cough. Cough, cough,* It is foolish of me, *cough*, to ask you how you knew it was me. I, *cough*, tried to hold off coughing but can't control it anymore, *cough*, at all. So, how, *cough*, are you doing Mon?"

"Great Eddy! Jenny and I are doing fine and couldn't be happier. You will never believe that I am going to be a father again."

"No way, Mon. Still, *cough*, able to contribute to, *cough*, *cough*, the population. That's great, Hank. *Cough...*"

"How are you doing, beside the cough and how is Coreena?"

"Yah Mon, Coreena is fine, *cough*, still in the restaurant business and, *cough , cough*, I'm still restoring old boats, *cough*, and selling them for others to enjoy but, *cough, cough,* my health ain't so good, Hank. *Cough, cough.* Doc's say the big 'C' finally caught up with me. One of, my lungs is shot and they can't replace it. Geez Mon, *cough cough, cough,* they can send a man up to the moon and can't, *cough,* fix a lung."

Henry would have loved to say that Eddy had no one to

blame but himself but bit his tongue. In fact, his heart went out to his friend.

"How serious is it, Eddy?"

"The doc's recommend I go back, *cough, cough*, to Canada and have the doctors assess the situation. Maybe try to remove part of the lung that's shot but I don', *cough, cough*, don't know if I want to bother with it. I've had a good life and the extra few months or year that the, *cough*, treatment will give and all the, *cough*, suffering that goes along with it may not be for me, Hank."

"Well, you have stopped smoking right, Eddy?"

"Na' Mon, what's the use at this point, right? Still enjoy the weed, *cough*, in my mouth and inhaling the smoke is a feeling I, *cough*, don't want to give up. I know better, Mon, yet, *cough, cough,* what can I say?"

Henry didn't know what to say. "Well, at least it may stop irritating the lungs and cancer from developing in the other lung. I'd give it up in a heartbeat, Eddy."

Once again, Eddy didn't answer right away. He went into a coughing spell. Henry noticed that Eddy didn't call him 'ole buddy like he used to but now it was 'Mon'.

"I see you have picked up the island slogan, 'Yah Mon'. I recall when Jenny and I went to Jamaica for our honeymoon that was a phrase we heard over and over again. As soon as we arrived at the airport in Montego Bay, the customs lady, taxi driver, bell hop and receptionist at the hotel all said the phrase over and over. Almost the first day, Jenny and I started using it in our conversation, too," Henry said with a chuckle.

"Ya' Mon, with all the tourists, *cough*, coming in, they seem to enjoy the phrase and like, *cough, cough,* you just said, soon they start saying it themselves during their stay here."

"Well, we sure enjoyed our vacation there and the resort we stayed at was fantastic. Great beach. But I have to admit, the Jerk Chicken at Coreena's restaurant was much better than at the resort. So, are you thinking of coming home?" Henry asked.

"Yah, Mom ain't doing so hot either. She, *cough, cough,* moved into a care home last spring but we need to move, *cough,* her up to another level of care. She had a mild stroke a week ago."

"That's too bad, Eddy. What care home is she in, maybe I can visit her?"

"They are just looking into it. Should know by next week and then, *cough, cough, cough,* I'll let you know."

"Do you know yet when you are coming home?" Henry wanted to know.

"Coreena wants to come, too. As soon, *cough,* as we make arrangements for someone to look after the cafe…"

Eddy began to cough again and couldn't stop. Finally Henry heard the click of a lighter and he knew Eddy was lighting up. He heard his friend take a deep drag. Henry was waiting for Eddy to start coughing again but he didn't.

"That's better, Mon. Seems when I light up the cough goes away. So, how's the wife, Mon?"

"Jenny couldn't be better, Eddy. She is so elated to be pregnant and can't wait for the baby to be born."

"That's swell, Hank. So, when's the kid gonna pop?"

"It's still a ways off. She is over five months in, so I guess another four months? Have you and Coreena decided not to have a baby? I think you mentioned to me before that you can't…something to do with the polio you had. "

"Yah Mon, we tried, but it's not in the cards for some reason. Docs can't find anything wrong with the reproductive equipment. Maybe it's me and the polio I had as a kid. It would have been good to have a son or daughter but that's the way the chips fall, Mon, and we have to make do with the cards life deals us."

"Yeah, you're right Eddy. You have always had a good way of dealing with life's challenges."

"Ain't no other way, Mon. Doesn't do any good, right?"

"You're right, Eddy. Have you thought of adoption?"

"Yeah, we did but we are getting up there, cough, and with my health not being so hot it's best to just let things be, know what I'm saying?"

"Yes, I understand Eddy. Geez, your cough seems to have gotten better."

"Yah Mon, crazy ain't it? Smoking another weed seems to, *cough*, calm it down. Have you heard from Gary and John and how they're doing, *cough, cough*, in India?"

"Actually, Eddy, John is home for another week. His mother passed away. I saw him at church last Sunday. They are doing great. John has sure become a soldier for Christ."

"Yah Mon, never would have figured John to turn religious like that and become a missionary, *cough, cough, cough*, damn cough."

Henry paused for a minute until *Eddy* stopped coughing and then went on, "Yeah, I've felt that way too, Eddy. But, you can never tell what God has in store for us. I am going to keep you in my prayers and have Father Engelmann say a Mass for you."

"That's cool, Mon. You have always been big on prayers, ole' buddy. So, how is the Padre doing these days? Geez, he must be getting up there."

"Amazing Eddy, is all I can say. He's one hundred and three and still going strong. Says Mass every day, walks the hills and valleys at the acreage, and hears confessions at the care home at least once a month for hours on end. The line ups are incredible. Anyway, I love Father and am so grateful for his lifelong friendship."

"Yeah, *cough, cough*, that's something that a grocery store owner enters the priesthood late in life like that. But he, *cough, cough* was a natural. He and the missus were quite, *cough, cough*...the pair in the store. Real church goers, know what I'm saying, Hank?"

"Yes, I do. I know exactly what you mean. They were both more interested in serving the community than selling groceries. It was the perfect vocation for Mr. Engelmann to go into after Anna died."

Henry didn't know if Eddy heard him as he went into another coughing spell. Eddy's lighter clicked again. Henry will never forget that sound of Eddy lighting up a smoke. Henry could hear him wheeze as he took in a drag and let the smoke out. Henry could visualize every move Eddy made as if he were right next to him. Henry sent up a prayer for him.

"Well ask the Padre to pray for me, Hank. Maybe he can ask the Lord to heal my lungs if it's in the cards. If anyone can get through to the Boss it's the Padre."

"I'll let him know, Eddy. I am seeing him later on today and I will be taking John to the airport to see him off next week when he returns to India. I'll mention to him that I spoke to you."

"Yah Mon, give him my best, tell him I'm proud of him and that he's doing a good thing."

"I will, Eddy. So let me know when you and Coreena are coming home and I'll pick you up at the airport. Where will you be staying? You and Coreena are welcome at our home."

"Thanks, ole buddy. That means a lot to me that you would do that. You're a good man, Hank. We'll see. We just might rent a condo, depends on how long we are staying and if I'm hospitalized right away. I know Coreena wants to see her sister, Matilda in Ottawa, too. As soon as we, *cough*, know our plans I will let you know. Give my best to the missus…good to talk to you ole' buddy."

"It's great to talk to you, too, Eddy. I must say, I like when you call me 'ole' buddy', it carries our friendship, somehow… know what I'm saying?"

There was a long pause over the phone as tears surfaced in both men's eyes. Their relationship had a shaky beginning but over the years grew into a deep affection for one another.

Finally, with a tone that came from his heart Eddy said, "Yah Mon."

CHAPTER FORTY-EIGHT

IT WAS ALMOST a replay of the month of December when Jenny had to re-schedule her doctor's appointment.

"Good morning, Dr. Webster's office, how may I help you?"

"Hi, this is Jenny Pederson, I have an appointment for nine thirty this morning and I won't be able to make it. The highways have been closed from Davidson to Regina due to icy conditions."

"Yes, the freezing rain is causing a lot of accidents in the city as well, Mrs. Pederson. Let me see when we can re-schedule. Oh, I see Valentine's Day is two days away. Happy Valentines!"

"Yes, Happy Valentines to you, too! It would have been nice to have my baby then."

"Once in awhile, it happens. Now, let me see, I can work you in next Wednesday morning, February 24th at ten thirty."

Jenny checked the calendar and replied, "I have a ladies' group meeting that morning and it's also Ash Wednesday and church to attend…would there be another time available?"

The receptionist checked again and after a few minutes came back. "The only other opening is the third week of March, Friday, the 19th, at 2:00 p.m."

"Oh my, that's a long time. Well, I do feel fine and should I have reason to call back, I will. I did all the lab tests the doctor wanted me to do, so if anything shows up, I'm sure he will be in touch with me."

"I can also put you down for any cancelation."

"Yes, that would be great. I'm sure that I will be fine."

"Living out on an acreage doesn't always work to get into the city for appointments, does it?" Jenny said as she walked into the sun room.

Henry looked up from a book he was reading and said, "Yeah, we are more under the control of nature if that's what you mean. Were you able to re-schedule your doctor's appointment?"

"Yes, but not until next month, March 19th."

"You haven't seen the doctor since January."

"Actually, I have only seen the doctor twice. The first time was in November. I had to cancel December's appointment when we had that severe winter storm."

"Yeah, I won't forget that one for a long time."

"I did see him January 18th. And now here we are once more that I have to cancel today's February appointment, too! But, I really am feeling okay. I am glad we cancelled our trip to Mexico though, my headaches seem more frequent and a little swelling in my ankles would have made it difficult to trek up the mountain."

"Well, we can visit where the Monarchs spend the winter in another year or so."

"Yes, but it would have been nice to participate in the festivals and celebrations that go on in late February. J.J. said it's an amazing thing to see how the Monarchs hibernate during the winter."

"Well, Honey, it's more important to keep you healthy and fit. I suppose if you needed to see a doctor before your next appointment you can always get in to see Doctor Kreake if you have to. Does he still deliver babies?" Henry was interested to know.

"Yes, he still does in straightforward cases. But at my age and with history of cancer, he wanted me to see a doctor who is both an obstetrician and gynecologist."

"I think you did mention that before. What is the difference between the two?"

"Well, my understanding is that gynecologists look after preventive reproductive health care, fertility issues, and treat diseases, while obstetricians deliver babies and care for the mother and baby during post delivery."

"So, in other words, you get the full deal. A doctor who is capable of handling anything that might come up during a pregnancy."

"Yes, that's a good way of putting it."

Jenny made her way to Henry, unbidden tears surfacing in her eyes, "Oh, Henry, I am so happy. It will be wonderful to hold Hannah." She took Henry's hand and put it on her tummy and rubbed the enlarged abdomen.

"Yeah, I think she's grown since last week. How does it feel to have a little baby live and move inside of you?"

"It's wonderful, Honey. God's plan for procreation is so amazing. Just think how the two of us came together to create another life. What an incredible miracle and..." looking at Henry ever so tenderly she added, "What a beautiful expression of love!"

Henry nodded and smiled thanking God for blessing them with a child but also for this wonderful woman.

Just then the phone rang. Jenny picked up the extension phone next to Henry, "Hello."

"Hi, Jenny. This is John McBryne. How are you doing?"

"Oh, hi John. I'm doing fine. I'm so sorry to hear of your mother's passing. We wanted to attend the funeral but the highways were closed yesterday, too."

"It was a small funeral, only a few people there. Most of her family and friends have passed away, too. But I am thankful she is with the Lord and at peace. She was a good mother, Jenny; very warm, compassionate and caring."

"That is so beautiful to have such thoughts of your mother. You will miss her, John."

"Yeah, I will. There is no-one to really come back to in Regina for except Hank and Father Engelmann. Father is such a saintly man and I love him like my father."

"Henry does, too. He is quite the man. Hopefully, next time you are back to Regina, we can spend more time together and have you here for supper. I would love to hear more about your work in India."

"It's very rewarding, Jenny. I receive more from the people I serve than I give."

"Well, we will keep you in our prayers John, and have a safe flight back. Say hello to Gary for me, too. Here is Henry."

"Hi John, it looks like I may not be able to take you to the airport this afternoon. The forecast is for freezing rain until late into the evening. Father Engelmann will be disappointed as he was looking so forward to seeing you before you left."

"Yeah, I wanted to see him, too. You never know when the Lord will call us."

"I was here listening to your conversation with Jenny. It would be great when you come back to Regina to have you out here. In fact, you're welcome to stay with us the entire time. We have an extra car you can use too. Perhaps, Father Engelmann will want you to spend some time with him as well at the prayer house."

"That would be great, Hank. What a beautiful spot you have there. Last time Gary and I were there I burned the image of the Poustinia and the surrounding setting into my mind. When I walk in the scorching heat of India, I will be able to soothe myself with that scene. God has blessed you, Hank."

"That's for sure, John. Oh, by the way, I was talking to Eddy last week and he says 'hi' to you and wishes you all the best."

"How is Eddy doing, Hank?"

"Well, he's hanging in there. He has a bad cough and also cancer in one of his lungs. He may come back to Regina and have one of his lungs removed."

"Yeah, he was always quite the smoker; a cigarette was constantly dangling from his mouth. It was bound to catch up to him. I will keep him in my prayers."

"Well, John. It was great seeing you and by the way, that was a nice thing you did for Father Engelmann at the Mass a couple of weeks ago. He needed support at that time."

"He's one of kind, Hank. He's like Mother Teresa; it's not them who lives but Jesus within them that lives. Both are very holy people. I best be on my way, take care and God bless you and...yeah, all the best with your new addition to the family coming up. Tell Jenny I'll be praying for her."

"Thanks John. Blessings to you, too and give our love to Gary."

Henry hung up the phone and turned to Jenny. "He's turned out to be such a nice guy. I can honestly say I really like him, Jenny. I was so filled with hate for him at one time for being the cause of Julean's death."

"Love conquers all, Honey and it's a good thing. Imagine the prison you would be in now if you hadn't."

Henry nodded. Jenny sat in the chair next to Henry's in the sun room and got the conversation back to their upcoming little baby.

"When I go into the city, I want to go through some of the cedar chests in the basement on Hill Avenue. There were so many blankets, outfits and little toys that I had purchased for Camilla. Even though I had given her up for adoption, it was my way of keeping in touch in 'spirit' with her. By buying outfits according to age, I could imagine her size and how she looked playing and..." Jenny's words trailed off as tears surfaced once more. "I will share a secret with you...I even bought the largest doll I could and dressed it with some of the outfits I bought. That way I could imagine better how adorable she looked. Oh, I just knew in my heart that one day we would find one another.

Henry nodded. "Yeah, it's really amazing how she came into our lives by way of Jeremy and how your searching for her led us eventually back together."

He gazed at his lovely wife in awe of it all; yet, it must have been so painful for her to go through all those years not seeing her daughter in real life but only in her imagination. Henry also knew Jenny's time with James wasn't the easiest and how J.J. was raised mainly by a nanny. Henry's heart went out to Jenny as he imagined and felt deeply the gamut of emotions his dear, sweet wife had endured. Yet, as he stared at her, she came through it all as if she were on top of the world.

Joy and happiness swept through Henry at the sight of his dear, sweet Jenny. He had to stand up and embrace her; he was so overcome with emotion. He understood now what Father Engelmann said about Anna and how he wanted to make her happy. Hopefully the birth of this baby and raising it would make up for all the challenges Jenny endured with Camilla and J.J. The thought and sight of the immense joy Hannah would give Jenny uplifted Henry's spirits. He gazed lovingly into his dear wife's sparkling eyes and softly whispered, "I love you so much, Jenny. I can hardly wait to see our little angel, too."

CHAPTER FORTY-NINE

TWO DAYS BEFORE Valentine's Day, Henry had locked himself up in his studio and didn't allow anyone to come in. Jenny was wondering what the secret project was because she usually went in to visit with Henry several times a day as he worked on the next exhibition.

Jenny was trying to guess what was going on and if it had anything to do with Valentine's Day as she, too, was busy planning for the event herself. She had sent Valentine cards to Lauren and Alison and planned to take in a card for Camilla and a special package of treats for Noah and Joshua.

As soon as Jenny opened her eyes that morning she thought she might see a card dangling above her like the day of her anniversary but there wasn't. She turned to Henry's side and he was already up. Perhaps she would find something in the washroom like last year. Henry had bought red heart shaped soap bars and all the towels had several heart cut outs pinned to them each one saying "I love you."

Jenny got up and made her way to the washroom. Once again however, there wasn't anything different from the days before. Could it be possible that Henry had forgotten this special romantic day? It's not like him to forget and he always came up with such creative ideas on anniversaries, birthdays or sometimes gifts out of blue.

A look of disappointment began to form on Jenny's pretty face, but just for a second. She was certain that something was waiting for her downstairs and even if Henry forgot, it would be okay. There was the rest of day to quickly make plans.

Justin was just leaving for school when Jenny came down. "Good morning, Justin. Happy Valentine's Day!"

"Oh, geez, is it Valentine's Day today? No way...is it really?"

"Did you forget? And is Henry in the kitchen?"

"He left about a half hour ago. I think he went down to see Father Engelmann. He said for you to come down for Mass when you get up. They will wait for you. I better go; I just heard the bus honk."

"Your hearing is better than mine; I didn't hear anything. Jenny made her way to Justin and gave him a peck on the cheek. "Have a nice day, Justin and don't forget to give the pretty girls at school a wink and a happy Valentine's Day wish."

"Yeah, for sure," he said with a bashful grin and made his way to the front door.

Jenny looked all around in the kitchen for flowers or anything to suggest that Henry had remembered what day it was, but there was nothing. She was very surprised that her dear husband had completely forgotten...but, had he really?

Jenny went from one room to the other just to be certain. The sun room was the same as was the living room and family room. Every room was just as the day before. Well, she would put out her cards. Jenny went to the closet and got the cards she had purchased last week. She put one on the counter for Henry, another beside it for Justin for when he came home from school. She would also put another one for Justin in the secret hiding place in the roll top desk and a second one for Henry under his pillow.

Jenny had her breakfast and got dressed to head down to the prayer house with Ginger. The temperature was so mild for that time of the year. A chinook from Calgary came in last week. For the last three days it had just been below freezing. It would be a pleasant walk and she was looking forward to it.

Ginger was already waiting for her when she came out the front door. Jenny tried to take a deep breath of fresh air but her jacket was too tight from the growing baby in her womb. She would have to buy another winter coat before the winter was out.

"Hi Ginger, ready to go for a walk?"

Ginger wagged her tail excitedly and they were off. If Jenny had listened more carefully, she might have heard Justin and Henry peering out of the garage window waiting for her to leave the house. Justin had played hooky from school to help his dad set up a valentine surprise for Jenny when she returned from the Poustinia.

As soon as Jenny was out of sight, the men began to work. Henry brought in the dozen red roses he stored in the cool garage since yesterday and set them in a vase on the pass-through counter between the kitchen and sun room. Justin brought several packages of streamers with little red cardboard hearts dangling. They planned to hang them in the foyer and kitchen.

Henry ran up to his studio and brought down a Valentine's card made of two full 3 foot by 4 foot sheets of mat boards taped together. The one on the front was red which he had cut into the shape of a heart and the inside was white. He read the message on the front and the message on the inside as he placed it on end slightly opened on the table in the sun room where he planned to have a romantic dinner later on.

"Wow, Dad, that's some card!" Justin commented as he peeked through the kitchen opening to the sun room.

"Yeah, it looks so much larger here than it did in the studio. Jenny will get a kick out of it."

"Yeah, she'll think it's cool to see a teddy bear in the fridge, too," Justin said as he placed a small brown teddy bear wearing a white tee shirt with a heart in the middle of the chest area in the fridge. 'Be my Valentine' was written on the heart. He smiled as he pictured Jenny opening the door and seeing the bear there.

While Justin was hiding and placing little cinnamon hearts all over the family room and sun room, Henry went upstairs to their bedroom and began bringing out the heart shaped soap, white towels with red hearts on it and this year he picked up something a little different. A medicine bottle with a label on it that read, 'A Prescription for Love. Take one nightly before bedtime.' It was filled with hot cinnamon hearts.

When he placed a rose and two heart shaped chocolate covered peppermint candies on Jenny's pillow, he noticed part of the card under his pillow which Jenny had placed there earlier. He was tempted to open it up but thought he would wait and act surprised later that evening. He got out the candles and set them on the chest of drawers next to their bed. He was all set for a romantic evening.

The big surprise was still in his studio. He would save that for last. He dashed downstairs just as Justin was finishing up too. With the streamers, balloons all over, and roses in the kitchen, the house had taken on a huge transformation since earlier that morning.

"Thanks for helping me, Justin. The house looks great!"

"Yeah, i wish i could be home to see her face when she comes in. I could see she was a little disappointed that we had forgotten all about valentine's day. Did you get her a gift, dad?"

"Yes, I did. It's a surprise for Jenny and the entire family. I think you all will like it?"

"What is it, Dad? You can tell me."

"Sorry, it's a surprise. Come on, let's get you off to school."

HENRY DROVE JUSTIN to school and then headed back to the farm. He went directly to the Poustinia.

Jenny and Father were sitting in the two chairs in front of the patio window.

"Hi, Jenny, Father, sorry I'm late for Mass. Have you said it already?"

Jenny got up, came to Henry, and put her arms around his neck. "Do you know what day it is today?"

Henry wrinkled his forehead. "Did I forget someone's birthday?"

Jenny smiled and studied him closely. She wondered if

he was kidding with her or not. He seemed sincere. "Honey, today is Valentine's Day! I can't believe that you forgot such a romantic day. And where were you? Father was expecting you first thing this morning and Justin said you came down here."

"Oh, no. That's right, today is February 14th! I did recall the date today because I had to run in to the gallery and drop off a painting that a client wanted to look at later this morning. I tried to get back as fast as I could. Ice is melting on the highway and it's a bit slippery."

Henry gazed lovingly into Jenny's eyes with a look of true sorrow, "I'm so sorry Jenny." He shook his head, "I completely forgot."

Once again Jenny studied her husband. So far his story seemed to be true. She relaxed and accepted the fact that Henry had really forgotten this special day!

"You are not the only one who has forgotten this day, Henry. I didn't know either until Jenny gave me this wonderful card. And no, I haven't started Mass yet. We had a nice chat about little Hannah soon to come into the world and you to be a father again!"

"Yes, it is exciting. If it wasn't for Jenny's stomach growing I would think that this is all a dream."

Father got up and said, "Well you two just sit here while I put on my Mass garments. I won't be but five minutes."

It was just before noon when Henry and Jenny came back up the house. After parking the truck in the garage, they entered through the laundry area and made their way to the foyer. All the way up from the prayer house, Henry kept apologizing for forgetting Valentine's Day and that he would quickly go to Lumsden and pick up a card at the drug store. Jenny told him that wouldn't be necessary as he more than made up for it in all he had done during the previous years.

As soon as Jenny entered the foyer and saw all the streamers and balloons, she almost keeled over. She wondered if she was in the same house. Just a couple of hours ago, there was nothing! How could this possibly be!? She quickly turned to

Henry with an astonished look on her face, "Henry, what on earth has happened here? How did this happen? Where did these streamers come from?"

She turned and walked into the kitchen and it was even more decorated. Streamers, balloons, cards taped to the cupboard doors, roses on the counter. Jenny let out a loud squeal! Once again, she turned to Henry and thrust her arms around him.

"Honey, you are amazing! How could you do all this in that short of time? It's impossible! This is all too wonderful!"

Henry had a huge smile on his face. "Anything is possible when you have an angel helping you!"

"Yes, you must have!"

Jenny twirled around and took it all in again. She went over to the kitchen sink to smell the roses on the pass-through counter to the sun room. She took in a deep whiff of the wonderful fragrance of roses. When she opened her eyes and gazed out into the sun room, she immediately noticed the huge card standing partially open on the table.

"What on earth is that, Henry?"

Jenny quickly turned and ran down the hallway to the doorway opening to the sun room. She stopped about five feet before the table to take in this humongous card. She had never seen anything like it before. Henry had outlined with black paint on the red heart shaped cover a sketch of an attractive woman that was obviously pregnant. On the top was written in large curvy letters:

'Will You Both Be My Valentine?'

Tears surfaced in Jenny's eyes as she slightly opened the card a bit more so she could read the romantic message inside.

> *My dear Jenny and Little Hannah,*
> *As I look at the miracle before me I am*
> *overwhelmed with gratitude and thanksgiving.*
> *How much closer can a mother and daughter be*
> *for me to love at the same time in this incredible way!*
> *What a Valentine's gift of love the Lord has given*

us. This will be the only time I can send you both a Valentine's card in this special way!

Jenny, you have made my life complete. The joy you give me each day makes my heart smile and my spirit soar. You are my inspiration and light to all my days!

You are my comfort and joy, my lover and best friend.

But most of all I love you because you are you!
Henry

Jenny turned and once again, she flung her arms around his neck, "Oh, Honey, there are no words to tell you how much I love you."

Tears filled both their eyes as they warmly embraced and tenderly kissed.

When they parted, Henry took Jenny's hand and led her back through the house and up the stairs. Jenny thought he was going to take her into the bedroom but she was wrong. At the top of the stairs instead of going straight ahead they turned around the open stairwell and went into Henry's studio.

"I thought the large card must have been the reason you had closed the studio for a day or two. Is there something else… Oh, Henry, not another surprise!?"

Henry nodded, "I was able to finish it in the last two days."

Henry's easel was covered with a bed sheet. It was clear that a painting was underneath by the shape of the draped cloth. Henry positioned Jenny directly in front of the easel and then he slowly removed the sheet.

Jenny brought her hands to her mouth as the framed canvas with a heavy gold molding revealed the half portrait of her sitting on the chair. The day or two she had posed for Henry, the background was very dark, almost black but now it was light sky blue with butterflies flitting all about. Rather than sitting on a stool in his studio, she was now sitting on a large rock on a hillside with a look of wonder and gratitude for life. She was wearing the same blouse but opened to show the pewter angel as she did that day he re-sketched it. Her skirt was rucked up showing her knees touching together. Her hands were intertwined resting just above her knees.

It was the beauty Henry had caught in Jenny's face that was so breathtaking. Henry had gazed at his dear, sweet wife so lovingly that he not only saw Jenny's fair skin color but the undertone; the color that comes through from underneath the skin's surface to affect the overall tonal quality. The warmth, the softness, the inner luminosity, the hints of blue, yellow, peachy and golden hues were so delicately captured on the canvas the portrait came alive!

Her cerulean blue eyes were painted with a light that carried depth and clarity and the tiny speck of white placed so perfectly as to catch Jenny's perpetual sparkle. Henry often said he was so drawn to Jenny's eyes that he could swim in them.

Indeed, he did.

Jenny began to shake almost uncontrollably. She was overtaken by what Henry had done. She kept shaking her head from side to side still unable to speak.

The entire piece spoke of Jenny; her spontaneity and charm. Her vivaciousness, her cheerful effervescent personality. Her freedom and love of life and nature.

With tears of happiness streaming from her eyes, Jenny approached the master painter of her life. She wiped the tears away with the tips of her fingers of both her hands and fell into Henry's waiting arms.

"I love you so much, Henry," was all she could say as they tenderly kissed each other again. When they parted, Henry scooped Jenny off her feet and carried her into the bedroom. It had been prepared for that evening but neither could wait to express their love for one another.

Jenny removed her clothes as her romantic husband lit the candles. As Henry undressed he saw Jenny smelling the rose he had placed on her pillow. The profile of Jenny's beautiful body in the warm light overwhelmed him; how absolutely lovely she looked as a mother with child. The form and smoothness of her abdomen revealing the result of another time when they had made love. There it was in all its mystery; a new life which they had created through the love of God and His purpose.

Thank you, dear Father, for this wondrous gift of love...thank you, for Jenny!

CHAPTER FIFTY

J ENNY'S DOCTOR APPOINTMENT couldn't have come soon enough for Henry and Jenny. It was two months since Jenny's last appointment in January.

When Doctor Webster realized it was that long since he had seen his patient, he expressed surprise and concern.

"It's unfortunate how you somehow managed to evade my examination last month. I will have to check to see how that happened."

"I was unable to keep my February appointment due to weather conditions. Your receptionist tried to re-schedule, but either I couldn't make it at the time she had an opening or there were no openings available until today."

The doctor shook his head. "Well, I'll have to check into that. I like to see my patients at the start, every month and perhaps now, we could schedule appointments every two weeks. Let's see how things are developing."

Jenny lay on the table in the examination room as Doctor Webster examined her. He asked the attending nurse to check the gestation date.

"Mrs. Pederson would be at her twenty-seventh week."

The doctor nodded and then said, "Everything seems to be coming along. The fetus seems small. I'd like to have another ultra sound done."

When Jenny sat up, the nurse handed the doctor the cuff to measure her blood pressure. When Doctor Webster finished, he expressed some concern, "It's high; 160/90. Are you dealing with any stress in your life at the present time?"

Jenny thought for a moment and then said. "No, there is nothing bothering me. Oh yes, there was a major concern a while back. My husband and his son went out on skidoos during a blizzard just before Christmas and lost one another. Actually, it was the day I was supposed to come in and see you. Anyway, they both were missing for almost a day. I was extremely anxious at the time but in the days ahead, I regained my composure."

"Well, something like that can be traumatic and trigger hypertension. Are there any other symptoms you are experiencing since your pregnancy?"

"I am having mild headaches and notice a little swelling in my ankles. My shoes seem to fit tighter."

The doctor asked the nurse how the urine analysis turned out in the last lab test as he bent down to feel Jenny's ankles.

"I was just checking that for you, Doctor. As of seven weeks ago, there was no evidence of proteinuria."

The doctor nodded and said, "Good." He then turned to Jenny and continued, "From now on, I want to see you once a week rather than the two I said earlier. Also, I'm going to increase the strength of the beta blockers to get the blood pressure down." He then filled out another lab form requesting blood tests, urine test and an ultra sound to see how the fetus was developing.

"When you have the ultra-sound done, you will be able to confirm the sex of the child."

"No, I don't need to know the sex. I already know."

The same expression that covered Henry's face when Jenny said those words now was visible on the doctor's face.

"You are certainly confident about Hannah, aren't you?"

"You remember her name!"

"It's a nice name, Jenny. A name which is hard to forget."

When Jenny arrived home, she had difficulty locating where Henry was in the large house. She knew he was home as his SUV was in the garage. She finally found him upstairs in his studio working on a landscape. He immediately put down his paint brush as he was anxious to know all about the doctor appointment.

Jenny related pretty much everything that happened. The doctor was concerned about her hypertension and also some of the symptoms she was having; the swelling in her feet and headaches. He ordered more lab tests and that she was also scheduled for another ultra-sound.

Henry recalled the time when he accompanied Julean to the clinic and they both found out that their last child was a boy; Justin.

It was as if Jenny had read Henry's thoughts. "If you would like to accompany me for the ultra sound that's okay if you want to confirm that it's a girl."

"No, I believe you that it's a girl and I'll honor the agreement you made with the good Lord, too"

"Oh, Honey, you are always so supportive. Thank you. Let's pray that the test results are okay. The doctor wants to see me every week from now on so I will have to get the tests done by next Monday or Tuesday."

"I am going down to see Father later this afternoon; I will have him say a Mass for you, too."

"I see you are finally doing a twilight scene of the valley. It's coming along so beautifully. It already has the peaceful, serene feeling of that time of the day. Oh, Honey, I wish I could capture God's creation like that." After a long pause, Jenny added, "Is that a beaver swimming down the stream?"

"Yeah, they start to come out at night. I love the way they silently cut through the water detected only by the light of the moon. In fact, I was going to put a reflection of the moon near the Poustinia to draw attention to the prayer house and the peace which seems to surround it."

"Yes, that would be wonderful to do that. Looks difficult but I know you can do it."

"I'll stop in a few minutes and we can have lunch."

"How about tuna melts and tomato soup?"

"One of my favorites, Jenny. Call me when you and Hannah are ready."

Jenny giggled and left the studio.

JENNY RESTED FOR most of the afternoon which surprised Henry as she was always full of energy. But then she was now feeding two persons and all the hormonal changes going on must be very draining.

After dinner, Camilla called and wanted to know how everything went at the doctor that day.

"How did the check up go, Mom?"

"It went well. The doctor was concerned that he hadn't seen me in over two months. He ordered a bunch of tests and wants me to see him weekly from now on."

"That's good. I'm glad everything is checking out so far. Did he indicate how many weeks you are into your pregnancy?"

"Yes, I believe the attending nurse said I am in the twenty-seventh week; Just about three-quarters of the way there. I can hardly wait!"

"And is he going to order an ultra-sound for you?"

"Henry asked the same question."

"He probably wants to know the sex of the child just like I am. I'm dying to know if I have a brother or sister, that's why I'm asking!"

"Oh, Camilla in all the excitement and busyness of all this and the group meetings I may not have mentioned that I am having a little girl. I'm surprised I didn't tell you when we had lunch shortly after I knew I had conceived."

Camilla remained silent for a moment and then said, "Yes, that's right, Mom. You did say at the time you were certain you had a girl. But the ultra-sound you had at that time was too early to identify the sex of the baby? How do you know Mom?"

This time Jenny remained silent for a few moments, "Oh, it's just something that I know for sure, Camilla."

Jenny wanted to change the subject and asked, "How are Noah and Joshua doing?"

"They're fine. Joshua is turning out to be a big help with Noah, He's really taken his little brother under his wing. When I was growing up I always wished I had a baby sister. In a way, I am living out my dream vicariously through my own children. Isn't that something?"

"I understand what you're saying. I had that same wish. In a way, my wish came true when I started high school and became very good friends with Chloe's mother, Tammy. She was just like a sister to me. There wasn't anything we wouldn't share with one another nor hide from one another. Sometimes, I thought Tammy knew me better than I did myself."

"I wish I had met someone like that. I have friends but not really ones that close. I think that's why I enjoy my work at the tutorial school so much. I get to know the girls so well. There isn't anything that most of them don't share with me. The only problem is, I can't share my life with them."

"Well Honey, if it's any consolation, I hope you and I can continue that kind of relationship."

"Yes, I do too. I just love sharing my life with you. And you were about to tell me how you are so certain that you are carrying a little girl. You were that certain about being pregnant, too. Do you have some kind of an 'in' with God?"

"Well, you might say that, Honey!"

"Are you going to share it with me?"

"Well, it's a long story, camilla. It mainly has to do with having faith and trust in god. During my prayer times with him in the early morning we have a way of communicating with one another. The more one draws near to him the more he in turn draws near to you. There is such a knowing in my heart that he has answered my prayers. She is going to be a special child, camilla and i have already named her too; hannah."

There was a long silence. Camilla didn't want to dampen her mother's faith and said, "Oh, Mom, that's a beautiful name, biblical, too, I think, but aren't you rushing it a bit? What if it turns out to be a boy, are you going to be okay with that?"

"Yes, I would be, Honey, but I know it's little Hannah growing in my womb."

Once again, the phone went silent. "Well, the ultra-sound will confirm it. When are you scheduled to take it?" asked Camilla.

"Next Wednesday, a day before my next doctor appointment."

"Well, please let me know what the technician says."

"I am not going to ask, Camilla. It's a trust thing between me and God. As far as I am concerned it's a done deal. Hannah is on the way!"

Camilla reacted much like Henry did. Words failed to come; Camilla remained speechless.

"If you want to come and see the ultra sound you can. Just keep it to yourself."

"Oh, Mom, I want so much to believe that you are right but I have to see. So many girls have been disappointed over the years and I don't want to see you hurt. Which clinic are you going to for the ultra-sound?"

"The one on Albert north. It's next Wednesday at ten thirty if you want to attend, I don't mind. Just keep it a secret."

"So, how are your checkups coming along, Camilla? We haven't seen one another for over two weeks; your tummy must be growing!"

"Yes, it sure is, Mom. It's about this time it always looks like it's ready to pop but I still have another month or so to go."

"So, everything is going fine?" Jenny wanted to know.

"Yes, my blood pressure is higher than it should be and so I am taking some medicine for that."

"I am too. In fact, the doctor increased the strength of the beta blocker in the prescription he gave me today."

"What was your blood pressure at?"

"It was 160/90; a bit higher than it was in January. Actually I don't feel like my blood pressure is high; it's more the headaches and swelling that are beginning to bother me."

Camilla remained silent and then asked, "Did he do a urine analysis, Mom?"

"Yes, the one in January seemed okay, I recall the attending nurse say that it was free of protein or something like that."

"That's good—"

"That's exactly what the doctor said. Why is that so important?"

"Well, I don't want to jump to conclusions or concern you but several of the girls over the years have developed a condition known as preeclampsia. It's when the blood pressure gets out of control and accompanied by symptoms some of which you mentioned; the headache and swelling feet. I'm glad they didn't find protein in the urine as that could affect your kidneys. Like I said, over the years we had several cases in which the babies didn't make it and one mother didn't either."

"So, it's a serious condition…"

Camilla tried to avoid answering that question directly. "Like I said, Mom we have to wait for the next lab results. Since you haven't been checked for a couple of months we need to get an update."

"Yes, I now understand why Doctor Webster wanted me to do all the lab tests and also another ultra sound to check on the well-being of the fetus."

"Exactly, Mom. Perhaps take Dad with you when you go to your next appointment. And if you don't mind, I would like to attend the ultra-sound; I just have to know what's growing in that tummy of yours. Are you sure you don't want to see the baby, Mom? It's quite a sight to see inside your womb."

"Camilla, I told you already, it's a little girl and her name is—"

And almost in unison the two ladies said,

"Hannah."

CHAPTER FIFTY-ONE

CAMILLA WAS WAITING in the reception area when Henry and Jenny walked into the clinic.

"Hi, Mom, Dad. I came a bit early. I'm glad you are here, too, Dad. I am so excited to see my sibling and what she looks like. I hope the baby is in a good viewing position."

"Yeah, I must admit, I am excited, too. I already know what the sex is and so it won't tell me anything new, however, I would love to see what the little girl looks like," said Henry.

"I see you have the same faith as Mom. I sure hope you two are right. With three boys in my family, we could use a little feminine touch in the family."

"Jenny Pederson, you're next."

"Oh, my, that didn't take long. Jenny took off her coat and hung it in the closet by the front door. Henry did the same and the three of them followed the technician waiting for them at the door to the examination room.

"Now which one is Mrs. Pederson?"

Almost in unison, Jenny and Camilla replied, "I am."

The two ladies laughed, "We are mother and daughter and both have the last name." said Jenny.

"Yes, and I see you are both pregnant and so which one do I do the ultrasound on?"

"It's, me," said Jenny.

Henry and Camilla were seated on one side of the table near a screen monitor while Jenny was directed to lie down on the table.

"I am going to lift your sweater and lower your skirt."

Jenny lay down and watched what the technician said he was going to do. In a few minutes, Jenny's tummy was fully exposed from the rib cage down to almost the pubic area. The technician then began to rub a warm gel on Jenny's tummy and said, "This gel allows the transducer to slide more easily on your abdomen. It also improves the transmission of sound waves into your body. And in case you're concerned, an ultrasound causes no risk to your baby.

The technician turned on the monitor and placed the transducer on Jenny's tummy and began to move it around at first at random and then systematically making measurements and notations.

"I see the baby!" exclaimed Camilla. It's beautiful Mom. Why don't you watch the screen?"

"Oh, I might, I'll see."

The technician moved the hand-held device back and then forward, exposing the sex of the baby.

"Oh, Mom, I know what sex the baby is, do you want to know?"

"I already know, Camilla. Did you see it too, Henry?"

"Yup, I did Honey…you won't be disappointed, that's all I'll say."

Henry beamed from ear to ear, as a proud father would. He was even more proud of Jenny and her faith and trust in God. Little Hannah was in fact growing inside his dear precious wife's tummy just as Jenny expected her to be.

"How does the baby look? Is she developing nicely?" Camilla asked the technician.

"The doctor will go over all of that with you when your Mom goes for her next appointment. I should mention to you that we can check for any abnormalities if you wish—"

Jenny immediately replied, "No that will not be necessary.

However the baby is born is completely immaterial to me. I will love the child all the more."

The technician removed the transducer and wiped Jenny's belly. Jenny pulled up her skirt, lowered her sweater, and sat up. Camilla got up, went over to her mom, and kissed her cheek. "The baby looks beautiful, Mom."

As Camilla stood next to her mother, it was clear to everyone present that there was a huge difference between the size of Jenny's belly and Camilla's. And yet, there was less than two months' difference in gestation dates.

Henry wondered if it was because Camilla's baby was a boy and Jenny was carrying a girl.

CHAPTER FIFTY-TWO

F OR THE FIRST time since her pregnancy began, Jenny felt
nervous as she and Henry walked into the Medical Arts
Building. As soon as the elevator doors opened, Jenny said
the magical words which lifted some of the building tension.

"Quickly, hold my hand."

Over the last few days, Jenny began to piece together various
bits of questions and information she had picked up from her
last appointment with Doctor Webster and then the conversation she had with Camilla sort of put the puzzle together. Was
her pregnancy in some kind of trouble? Although Henry didn't
verbalize any specific concern, Jenny could sense his anxiety
especially when they said their morning prayers, "Please, dear
Jesus, protect Jenny and Hannah and keep them healthy in
every way..."

Two other ladies were seated in the reception area when
they walked into the doctor's office. Surprisingly, they had
no sooner sat down than Doctor Webster's attending nurse
emerged from down the hallway to greet Jenny and asked her
to come. Henry got up and followed his wife. He hoped the
doctor wouldn't mind his presence. He wanted to be supportive of Jenny and thought that the doctor would understand.

Henry's reasoning was correct.

"Nice to meet you, Mr. Pederson. It's always a pleasure to see husbands come with their wives. I must add, I am especially glad to see you with your wife this morning. Please have a chair.

Sandra pushed another chair in front of the doctor's desk beside the one that was already there.

"Before I go over Jenny's lab results, I want to do an examination of her first in the other room. We will then come back and discuss her results.

No sooner had Jenny gone into the examination room when Doctor Webster asked if she was still having headaches or blurred vision.

"You must be physic, Doctor, my vision is fine but I was going to say the headaches are more frequent and getting stronger. Normally, I never have them and I was wondering if it's related to my pregnancy."

"Yes, they might be. And you say your vision is fine?"

Jenny nodded and smiled.

He asked Jenny to lie on the examination table. He began by feeling around her abdomen concentrating more in the upper right side, "Do you feel any pain in this area?"

"No," Jenny said.

From there he went down to her feet and felt her ankles and asked, "

Has the swelling in your ankles and feet increased and what about your hands?"

"Yes, my shoes do seem tighter and I can't remove my wedding band anymore." Jenny studied the doctor for a moment and then asked, "Is something wrong with that?"

"I am just coming to that but first I would like to take your blood pressure." He lifted the cuff off a hook hanging beside the table and wrapped it around Jenny's arm so that the gauge that would read her blood pressure faced him. He inflated the cuff and also placed his stethoscope on her wrist to listen to her pulse and watch the gauge as he slowly released the pressure. Half way into the procedure he inflated the cuff again and let the air out. He removed the strap folded it and placed it back on the hook

"Your blood pressure is high; 175/95. Normal is 120/80. The beta blockers I prescribed last week haven't helped reduce the hypertension. The nurse will help you get dressed and come back into my office. We will go over all the results to date."

Jenny didn't like the sounds of what the doctor was saying. She instantly prayed that it was nothing serious and that she wouldn't faint which she was in the habit of doing.

Jenny sat next to Henry when she returned to the office and reached for Henry's hand.

The doctor was reviewing the lab results and then he looked up at the concerned couple in front of him.

"Your pregnancy is developing a condition known as preeclampsia."

"My daughter, Camilla, mentioned that to me the other evening when we spoke. She is a counselor for unwed mothers and some of the girls in her care have had that condition. How serious is this, Doctor?" Jenny was anxious to know. She felt Henry's hand squeeze hers.

"It can be serious if not treated and brought under control. It is often seen in first time pregnancies. That is why your daughter runs into it frequently with the girls in her care. However, it is also common in women over forty."

"Is high blood pressure the only symptom?"

"That is the main one as well as swelling and protein in the urine. We also have to watch for headaches, blurred vision, abdominal pain and rapid weight gain."

"Well, I have a few of those you mentioned but so far I am free of having protein in my urine based on the tests I had in the past."

"Yes, your first urine test was clear but the one you had this past week showed a significant amount of protein. You definitely have preeclampsia."

"What causes preeclampsia?' inquired Jenny, nervously.

"It's the result of a placenta that doesn't function properly. The exact cause as to why is not known. Some researchers suspect poor nutrition, high body fat or insufficient blood flow to the uterus. In your case, it's probably the latter. Genetics can play a role as well."

"So, how can we get rid of it or treat it?" Henry wanted to know.

"The main thing we have to do is get the blood pressure down and under control. I am going to prescribe both beta blockers and calcium channel blockers to see what that does. It should help to lower the hypertension. We want to keep a good enough supply of blood into the placenta for the baby. We will do the same lab tests this week."

Jenny felt faint. "Oh, dear Lord, this sounds so serious."

"Is there no cure?" Henry blurted out, obviously frustrated by the developing news of Jenny's condition.

The doctor nodded, "The only cure for preeclampsia is to deliver the baby. However, at this stage the infant is not developed sufficiently to be born. The ultrasound shows its development is smaller than it should be. It's not receiving enough blood and nutrients. The lungs are not developed enough either to support the life of the child and could lead to other complications. I don't want to get into that at this point. Let's take one day at a time."

Henry didn't want to ask another question that immediately concerned him when the doctor mentioned the condition preeclampsia. The 'pre' in the beginning of the condition must be only the start of something more serious. They might as well know now what the worst-case scenario might be.

Henry asked cautiously, "Doctor...the condition, preeclampsia must be the precursor to something that might be more serious, is that a correct assumption?"

The doctor studied Henry and then Jenny. He nodded and said, "Your observation is correct, Mr. Pederson. Preeclampsia can lead to eclampsia with the onset of seizures."

The word seizures instantly sent shock waves of anxiety through Henry's being. Seizures were what Julean had at the end which caused her eventual death.

"So, if it reached that stage, it could put Jenny and the baby at serious risk..." Henry's words trailed off. He didn't want to alarm Jenny and yet the words just came out.

Doctor Webster nodded. "Yes, it can be serious, however,

we now know what we are dealing with and will do everything we can to treat this condition and get it under control."

The doctor filled out the lab form, more prescriptions and handed them to Jenny. "Try to rest as much as possible, Jenny. Drink lots of water and elevate your feet several times during the day. Avoid salt in your meals."

Jenny reached out for the forms; her hand was trembling.

Henry was glad he woke around 3:30 in the morning. He was dreaming of those last days before Julean died when she had convulsions. The doctors tried everything but to no avail. He shuddered as the images still played across the screen of his mind.

He wasn't sure if Jenny was sleeping or not. He reached under his pillow for Julean's rosary and began to pray. What was happening to Jenny was so similar to the disease Julean had. Headaches, high blood pressure and blurred vision were symptoms that his former wife experienced as well before leading up to the seizures. Anxiety began to sweep through him. Just the other day, they couldn't have been happier and within twenty four hours, Jenny's dream of giving birth to her dear, little Hannah was threatened.

How would Jenny go on should the baby not make it? He couldn't say die; it sounded too final. "Oh, Jesus, please send your Holy Spirit to help us bear under all the pressure in the days ahead. Jenny needs strength and guidance.

"Please help us."

Henry began to say the rosary for the Blessed Mother Mary to intercede. She was a mother and understood.

"Please ask your Son to heal Jenny.

"Hail Mary, full of grace, the Lord is with you. Blessed are you among women and blessed is the fruit of thy womb, Jesus..."

Henry didn't realize he was softly whispering the prayer out loud. Suddenly, Jenny completed the prayer.

"Holy Mary, Mother of God, pray for us, now and at the hour of our death. Amen."

Unbelievably, Jenny was holding the other end of Julean's rosary in her hand and was saying the rosary as well. Without saying a word, Henry moved closer to his wife, raised his arm and she snuggled under his shoulder. Henry brought his hand holding the sparkling beads on top of Jenny's tummy. Jenny's hands were already there. Together, they said the remainder of the rosary and then ever so softly they said the Guardian Angel Prayer:

> *Angel of God, my guardian dear,*
> *To whom His love commits me here,*
> *Ever this day be at my side*
> *To light and guard, to rule and guide*
> *My life…and Jenny's and Hannah's and Henry's*
> *Forever and ever,*
> *Amen*

A peace began to settle in the room as they slowly drifted off to sleep.

CHAPTER FIFTY-THREE

ALTHOUGH SNOW HAD fallen, it wasn't enough to prevent Henry from driving his SUV to the Poustinia. They both wanted to let Father Engelmann know of the prognosis of Jenny's condition and have him pray over her and the baby.

The SUV skidded in places as Henry cautiously maneuvered the vehicle on the winding slippery road leading down into the valley. They were just turning around the bend which exposed the prayer house nestled serenely by the frozen pond. Smoke from the chimney drifted lazily up into the sky and quickly disappeared into the large falling snowflakes. It would make a perfect Christmas card. If only the peaceful scene in front of them could somehow be transplanted into their agitated minds. Deep concern over the future of Jenny and Hannah rested heavily on their hearts.

Father was just finishing Mass when they entered the prayer house. He was startled momentarily; the peace of the chapel was threatened. He felt the weight of their hearts before they could tell him. He quickly made his way towards Henry and Jenny. He stopped short of hugging them.

"What is troubling you, Jenny?"

Tears were already flowing and Jenny found it difficult to speak. She stepped forward and fell into Father's arms. He patted her back and rubbed her shoulder. "Trust in God, Jenny. Whatever it is, trust in Him."

"We were at the doctor yesterday, Father and Jenny was informed that she has a serious condition which is affecting her health and that of the baby. We need your prayers, Father."

Father nodded slightly and slowly let go of Jenny. "Come, let us sit down in the presence of the Lord and invite Him to talk about this."

Henry and Jenny sat in the new two seat couch which he purchased a week ago, for just this purpose. The couch faced the wicker arm chairs next to the patio doors and directly out to the pond. Father was already seated in one of the chairs leaving the other chair empty...for Jesus. Rather than begin discussing their concerns, Father turned to the glass patio doors and stared outside. Henry and Jenny followed his gaze to the frozen pond just beyond the snow covered deck. The foot prints they made when they came in were already filled by the glistening, falling snow.

The pond seemed so still, so different from the summer time when the stream flowed steadily along the valley floor. Not all of the ice was covered. There were bare places where the wind swept the snow up into drifts of different sizes and shapes like carved sculptures on the pond.

Henry was about to speak, when a deer came out of the brush at the edge of the frozen stream and caught their attention. Its back was covered with a blanket of snow and its winter coat blended in with the grey bark of the shrubbery and trees. The deer stepped cautiously on the ice testing it for safety. Its front legs skidded and quickly adjusted to get a firm footing. It started to come across the pond towards them and then stopped suddenly. The deer raised its head, listening and then turned and went back to the brush and quickly disappeared.

Jenny, feeling calmer, was the first to break into the peaceful silence. "I never knew that I was prone to high blood pressure and that it can have such a serious effect on a baby..." With each word Jenny uttered, her anxiety quickly returned. She was so emotionally distraught, she couldn't go on. Henry reached over and put his hand on hers.

"Jenny has a serious condition known as preeclampsia. It's already affecting the growth and health of the baby and also her own health. Jenny's blood pressure is way too high and she is now taking medicine to get it down and under control. The news came so suddenly, we are still reeling from it all."

"Will the medication get it under control?" Father wanted to know.

"So far it hasn't. The doctor increased the strength and gave Jenny other medicine as well to see if the blood pressure can be controlled. I think it constricts the blood flow to the baby reducing the oxygen and nutrients it receives. It's something like that."

"Is there any cure for this, Henry?"

"I asked the doctor that same question. The only way is to deliver the baby and the condition goes away."

"But it is way too soon. Jenny still has a long way to go."

Jenny, feeling more composed, said, "I am only in my twenty eighth week of pregnancy, a good two months yet to go before the baby is ready to be delivered. At this point that is not an option, Father."

"Yeah, the only thing we can do for now, Father, is to pray for healing and that everything turns out for the good."

"Yes, yes, we must pray and be filled with trust, praise and gratitude."

Father got up, went over to his dearly beloved friends, put his hands on each of their heads, and began to pray in tongues. Every now and then Henry would catch Father expressing his prayers with such deep yearning and pleading, it had to be done through the Holy Spirit. It was a soothing language. He loved it when Gary, John, and Father prayed that way last summer. Father went on for some time until he seemed spent.

He paused for the longest time as if saying a private prayer and then said, "Dear heavenly Father, we know that you are present among us. We know Your caring love overflows for us. Fill us with peace and help us to understand Your will. Help us to accept the challenges that confront us as we journey through life. These are all part of the natural consequences of life on earth. We know if it is Your will, You sometimes choose to intervene. We know of the many miraculous healings You have performed in our lives. We ask You to heal Jenny and her child and restore them to full health.We ask You to give wisdom and guidance to the doctors as they treat Jenny and her baby. We ask You to fill Henry and Jenny and Hannah's hearts with your Holy Spirit and give them the strength and courage to face these challenges. We ask You to fill them with peace, trust and faith in You. We ask You to help them accept Your divine will. We ask this in Jesus' name, Amen."

When Jenny and Henry returned to the house, Jenny rested until lunch time. When she came downstairs, Henry told her that Camilla called and wanted to know if she could do lunch tomorrow.

"Yes, that would be nice."

CHAPTER FIFTY-FOUR

IT WAS THURSDAY morning, April 1, 1993. Henry also knew that this was April Fool's Day. He had thought about playing a prank on Jenny but she was so nervous about her doctor appointment, he thought it best to just treat the day as any other. He did however stop off at the florist on his way home last night and picked up a bouquet of white and yellow daisies. He put them in a vase and kept them in his SUV overnight. He set them on the island kitchen counter along with a note. She noticed the flowers as soon as she entered the kitchen and quickly walked to the counter.

"Oh, Honey, the flowers are beautiful. They're like a ray of sun peeking through the overcast winter sky." She smelled the flowers, taking in a deep breath of the scented air as she looked down and saw the note:

> *Dear Jenny,*
> *Just a note to let you know how much I love you.*
> *You make my days feel like I'm in heaven.*
> *You are the light of my life!*
> *With all of my heart and soul and very being, I*
> *love you!*
>
> *Henry*

She turned and gazed lovingly into Henry's eyes. "Thank you, darling. That was so thoughtful of you." They tenderly kissed one another and warmly embraced for several moments.

Just then, Justin came into the kitchen. He already had his breakfast and was putting on his coat getting ready for the bus to take him to school. They had told Justin of Jenny's condition last evening at dinner time. Henry could see straight off his concern for Jenny. Henry could see that same look in the boy's eyes as he did for his mother.

"How are you feeling...M..." Justin's words trailed off. He was trying to call her 'Mom' but the words caught in his throat; but not in his heart. He repeated Mom several times in his mind and wished he could express his love and care more openly.

"Good morning, Justin," Henry and Jenny almost said simultaneously. Henry added, "We are about to say morning prayers, please join us."

Justin nodded with no objection or hesitation. Henry and Jenny parted and went to the concerned young man and hugged him. They all made their way to the kitchen sink which overlooked the sun room through a large opening. Their gaze extended beyond the glass windows of the room to see the outside view of the snow falling ever so slightly. The snow seemed suspended as each flake danced merrily in the still air as it slowly descended to the earth.

The view was peaceful and calming.

Justin stood in the middle, his shoulders covered by Henry and Jenny's arms. Henry made the sign of the cross and they said their morning prayer to which Henry added, "Dear Jesus, we place this day in your hands. Please help us to accept the news which the doctor is going to give us this morning. Fill us with the grace, peace and light of the Holy Spirit."

THEY DELAYED GETTING the lab tests done until just two days ago. They wanted the report to be as close to Jenny's appointment as possible in the hope the medication had kicked in and the results were more positive. As soon as they entered the reception room the attending nurse showed the nervous couple to the doctor's office.

"You can wait here, Mr. Pederson, while I take Mrs. Pederson into the examination room. The doctor wants to do his examination first before he talks to both of you."

Jenny followed the nurse to the next room and sat on the examination table. Her headaches were about the same as last week, however she did think the swelling went down some. She wished she could sense if her blood pressure was better. It was something one can't feel and so one never knows if the condition is improving or worsening. It's so silent and yet it would soon be brought to light. The thought sent shivers up her spine.

"Hi Jenny," said the doctor as he entered the room. His buoyant demeanor lifted her spirits, it gave her hope...but not for long.

"So how are the headaches and swelling, Jenny?" he asked as he strapped the cuff around her arm.

"My headaches are still there but I do think the swelling is not as bad as last week."

He started pumping air into the cuff and placed his stethoscope on her blood vessel just below her elbow. She watched the doctor as he listened and studied the gauge on the cuff. He pumped it up again and slowly let out the air. He tightened his lips as he removed the cuff.

He shook his head, "It's increased, Jenny. It's too high...it's reached 195/95."

Jenny's heart sank, not so much for herself but for Hannah. She wanted to give her little girl all she needed and more to grow and flourish!

"Oh Doctor, what are we going to do!?"

Jenny followed the doctor back to his office in the adjoining room. Henry first studied the doctor but was unable to guess what the prognosis might be. When he looked at Jenny however, he knew the news was not good. Like Jenny, his heart sank.

Doctor Webster sat down behind the desk and opened the file in front of him.

Henry couldn't wait a second longer. "How is her blood pressure, Doctor Webster?"

"I'm afraid it's gone up since last week. It's too high and not responding to the medication. The urine analysis is no better. There are significant amounts of protein in her urine and I'm concerned about kidney damage. I am going to do a complete blood count; renal panel, liver tests and urine analysis for kidney function. I will also increase the dosage of the calcium channel blockers. I am surprised that it's not dilating the blood vessels more than it has. It's a strong muscle relaxant and should be treating the hypertension by now. Hopefully the meds will kick in this week. Avoid all activity and rest in bed as much as possible. There is also one other treatment I would like to start before you leave today and that is to inject you with betamethasone, it's a steroid to help accelerate lung maturity in the fetus. If we have to deliver baby preterm, she can have trouble breathing because the lungs are not fully developed. It also reduces the risk of the newborn having serious complications or dying."

Jenny stared directly at the doctor and cautiously asked, "So, the longer the baby stays in the womb the better the chance for survival...?"

Doctor Webster nodded, "Yes, but with this condition, if we don't get it under control, there is further risk to your health and to the fetus. You will have to stay in bed as much as possible and we may have to admit you into the hospital."

A silence fell over the room as hope dimmed in the light of the results so far. It was what the doctor eluded to next that caused what seemed like an explosion in the room.

"I am going to suggest something for you to consider in the days ahead...We may have to deliver the baby preterm and take a chance on its survival but it also may come to..."

He hesitated for a moment and Jenny sensed where this might be going.

"If you are about to suggest that I terminate the pregnancy, I would never do that!"

"But Jenny, there may already be damage to the fetus and your own health and life is at risk," countered the doctor.

"No! No! I would never abort my child, Doctor." Jenny covered her face with both of her hands and burst into tears. She shook her head and began trembling. Henry got up to console her but she got up at the same time and ran out of the room.

"We will do all we can," Doctor Webster said.

His hopeful words fell on deaf ears.

NOT A WORD was exchanged between Henry and Jenny as they drove back to the acreage. So many mixed emotions and images crossed the screen of Henry's mind. He recalled feeling similar emotions when Julean and he drove home empty handed when their first son died. He knew he should reach out to Julean at that time but he was so spent he had nothing to give. He found these same emotions blocking his love and support for Jenny. Perhaps he was angry with God for allowing another one of life's curves to come his way or rather their way. The doctor's words resonated in his mind; *the baby's life was not only at risk but Jenny's was too. Could it be possible that could happen?* It did with Julean and he couldn't get over how similar his former wife's symptoms were to what Jenny was experiencing. The thought of Hannah dying would be terrible blow to their life but for Jenny to die... *it would be the end of his life.*

Silence still prevailed in the SUV as Henry turned down the lane to his farm. In the distance, Ginger was running towards them. The sight of dogs coming to greet them always lifted his spirits but it only lasted a second before his thoughts returned to their dilemma.

If only Father Engelmann had been there in the office with them. He always knew what to say and was able to bring peace to any situation. Just his very presence exuded calm. He remembered when he brought Julean home from the hospital without their baby, how their heavy hearts were instantly lifted when they saw Father Engelmann sitting on the front steps to their apartment to greet them home. What could have been a night of dread and sorrow turned into one of hope and renewed faith.

Suddenly, in front of him, Henry saw a sight he hadn't seen in several years. There was Coco standing in the lane to the house not more than thirty yards in front of him not knowing what to do. When she heard the truck, her instinct was to come and greet the vehicle, but ever since she attached to Father, she gave up that routine. For a moment there, Henry thought Coco would come to greet him but her love for her new master was too strong and she headed back to the house. Could Father Engelmann possibly be there waiting for them in their moment of need?

Henry could barely believe his eyes when he pulled up to the driveway, there was Father sitting under the front door canopy wearing his usual benevolent smile. In the same way the angel statue stood by the door to greet visitors, Father Engelmann mimicked God's messenger. His arms too, were outstretched towards them.

Henry shook his head. How Father could still walk up that steep hill was one thing but he just seemed to have an uncanny sense to know where and when he was needed. Henry stopped the SUV and Jenny jumped out and ran to him. It was as if she saw Jesus and wanted to be loved by the Lord and to learn why her dear child was about to be taken away from her.

Yes, Father Engelmann would have the answer or be able to comfort her. He would be able to give Jenny hope and keep her from falling into the deep dark abyss that was swirling all around her.

Afterwards, Henry parked the truck in the garage and hit the button to close the doors. He walked through the mud room into the foyer and looked outside through the front door window. Father and Jenny were sitting facing one another. Jenny was holding Father's hands, pouring her heart out to the holy man. Compassion dripped from his face. Henry just remained there silently and prayed. He thought it best not to interrupt them. Jenny needed to be with Father. He was with her all through her struggle with cancer and they had developed such a close relationship. Jenny needed Father now and Henry didn't want his presence to restrict in any way Jenny's expression of her deepest thoughts and emotions.

"OH, FATHER, MY condition isn't getting better, it's worsening and affecting Hannah's growth and development. Please pray to God to do what He wants with me but please let Hannah be healthy. She is such a special baby and destined to do so much good. She needs to be healthy and strong. Let us pray now, Father," Jenny urgently cried out.

Father squeezed Jenny's hands and gazed calmly into her sorrowful blue eyes. His heart reached out to her. So many trials had come her way during her lifetime but he could see this trial went deep, very deep; he could hear the depths of her soul crying out.

"My dear Jenny, don't lose hope or faith in God. His arms are open and He wants to comfort you. At this hour of your great need, you must trust Him to turn this all into good. As we travel in the darkness of life, God is there. I am an old man and I have seen and personally lived through life's challenges. There is only one way to deal with them no matter how big or small. Bring your cares and burdens to Him, He will give you rest. His yoke is light. You are very wise to bring this heartache to Jesus.

"Life on earth is not easy, Jenny. When Jesus came, His life was filled with trials and challenges all along the way. Yet, through it all, He was obedient to the Father unto death. There are many times we can question God's will and why He allows sorrows to come our way but He will turn them all into good just like He did the death of His Beloved Son. Jenny, so many times, I have seen you pick up your cross and follow Him. Don't stop now. Give praise and thanks to God and trust Him. I do not have an easy answer for you but above all else, we must continue to trust in Him. He is the God of all possibilities.

"Dear heavenly Father, take Jenny's anxiousness away and give her the wisdom and grace to continue to come to You in prayer and supplication and let her needs and requests be known to You. Let the state of her heart be filled with peace amidst the outward circumstances of life. To never allow evil forces to have dominion over her but to be ever quick to cast her cares, burdens and sorrows upon the Lord to receive Your peace which surpasses all understanding. Grant Jenny, to be a light in the midst of this trial so all those around her can see the rock upon which she has built her life. We ask this through Jesus Christ, our Lord and Savior, amen."

SHORTLY, HENRY JOINED Father and Jenny by the front door. Jenny made tea and sandwiches and they chatted some more about their appointment with the doctor that morning. After lunch, Henry offered to drive Father back down to the prayer house.

"That was very kind of you to be there to greet us when we got home, Father. I know it was on Jenny's mind to come and see you. I could sense her spirits lift as soon as she saw you sitting by the front door. You are such a dear friend, Father. I am amazed that you are able to climb this hill and it's icy in places, too," Henry added as the SUV skidded a bit on the steep slope.

Father simply nodded. "And how are you holding out in all of this, Henry?"

"I was very saddened to learn that the medication is not working and that both Jenny and baby's health is deteriorating. If something happened to Jenny, I don't know what I would do. The doctor this morning suggested we think about terminating the pregnancy. Did Jenny tell you?"

"No, she didn't mention that. Only that the medication is not working and that the baby is not growing as it should and would not survive a delivery at this point.

"See, it's not worth discussing as she won't even consider that option for a second. I would never have thought that I would ever either, but if they can't deliver pre-term and Jenny's life is threatened, isn't that something we should consider? That seems to be the only cure for this condition. Just a few weeks ago, your homily so accurately described the evil of terminating the life of a defenseless baby and here I am considering such an option to reduce the risk to Jenny. What is the Church's view on that, Father?"

Henry was reluctant to use the word abortion but that is what this would amount to.

"The Church is very firm on the sanctity and sacredness of human life. It is a gift from God, the sole creator from the beginning to the end. It is directly contrary to the fifth commandment, "You shall not kill.'"

"But if the mother's life is at risk—"

Father shook his head. "Under no circumstance, can anyone have the right to destroy another innocent human being. Only in certain cases such as aggressive uterine cancer for example, where the cancerous uterus has to be removed, as it is a direct threat to the mother's life. The operation is necessary even though the child will die as an indirect and unintended attack against the infant's life. Abortion, however is a direct, intentional act to kill the infant growing in the womb."

Father paused and then said, "Here is the point, Henry; the unborn child and the mother have equal human dignity and have the same right to life. When a medical crisis arises during a pregnancy such as has now occurred with Jenny and Hannah, there are two patients involved. The doctors must do whatever they can to save both lives, never attacking the one through drugs, surgery or other means to save the other."

Henry let out a long sigh as he recalled Doctor Webster's suggestion to abort Jenny's pregnancy was definitely not an option should it come to that. Henry knew that Jenny was in perfect agreement with all of what Father said.

CHAPTER FIFTY-FIVE

J ENNY HAD JUST come downstairs from an afternoon nap when the phone rang.

"Hello."

"Hi Mom, this is Jeremy. I tried to reach you this morning. I took Camilla in around nine thirty as her labor started and she just delivered an eight pound, three ounce, healthy baby boy!"

"Oh, Jeremy, that is wonderful news! How is Camilla?"

"She is fine. The labor wasn't too long but she is tired. The doctor had to put stitches in as there was a tear during the delivery due to size of the baby. She will have to stay in the hospital for a week or so."

"Congratulations, Jeremy. So, is the baby's name going to Jacob?"

"Yes, another boy and named after another biblical name."

"I love the names of all your children. They carry such strength."

"Yeah, but some had their weaknesses, too."

"Just a moment while I get Henry on the phone."

Jenny covered the receiver and called for Henry. He was in the sun room reading. He rushed to Jenny's side. "What's up, Honey?"

"Camilla had a baby boy!"

Henry instantly studied, Jenny. She was aglow with joy for her daughter and yet the news of a baby couldn't come in a more untimely manner. "That's great, Jenny. Is that Jeremy on the phone?"

Jenny nodded and handed the receiver to Henry. "Jeremy! Congratulations Son! Three boys! You are well on your way to baseball team."

"Whoa, Dad. Three boys are going to be a challenge."

"How is Camilla?" Henry wanted to know.

"She's doing great, Dad. She needed some stitches; other than that, she is happy it's over. Her back pains were something else with this one. He's the biggest of the three boys so far."

"Well, I'm glad it's over and Mom and baby are doing fine. Can we come up in the morning?"

"Yeah, she's pretty tired right now but the morning would be great. I'm having the assistant manager come in to cover for me tomorrow."

"That's a good idea. The boys will need you at home for the next few days. Have you got someone coming in to help you?"

"Yeah, Gertrude from next door is looking after the boys. She is very good with them."

"Well, if Mom and I can help in any way, let us know."

"Yeah, and how is Mom doing? Camilla asked if I knew how her appointment with the doctor went this morning."

Henry didn't know what to say. He didn't want to put a damper on the good news. "The doctor is still trying to get the right combination of medicine working. Tell Camilla, Mom will tell her all about it when she sees her tomorrow."

Jenny whispered from the side, "Tell Jeremy I can hardly wait to see and hold the baby!"

"Yeah, Jeremy, Mom and I are anxious to see your new addition. Jenny wants to hold him, that's for sure. Are you still up at the hospital?"

"Yeah, I'm using a payphone. I tried to reach you this morning but I guess you were in town at the doctor's office. Anyway, Camilla wanted to make sure you knew that she delivered her baby or rather our baby!"

"Very happy for you, Son. Give our love to Camilla and tell her we will be up around ten or so tomorrow morning."

"Sure thing, Dad."

When Henry hung up the phone, he approached Jenny and embraced her lovingly. He held her close to his heart and whispered, "Don't forget, Honey, Camilla is much younger than you. Getting pregnant at your age is open to complications and we will have to deal with them."

"Yes, I know, Henry, I am trusting in the Lord to work everything out...that's all we can do. In a way, the birth of Camilla's baby gives me hope that Hannah will be fine too."

Henry nodded. "Come, I made your favorite Caesar dressing with a little garlic in it. Then, after lunch let's take a walk down the winter lane. It's a beautiful day and we can pray as we walk and celebrate another new addition to the Pederson clan!"

CHAPTER FIFTY-SIX

J UST AS THEY were about to leave for the city, the phone
rang. Henry knew right away who it was by the sound of
the cough.

"Eddy, Eddy Ziegler, is that you?"

"*Cough*, yah Mon, it's me. Just calling to see how you're
doing, Mon."

"My son, Jeremy and his wife, Camilla just had another
son. Jenny and I were just on our way to the city to see our
new grandson!"

"That's, *cough*, great, Hank. Give them my re...*cough, cough*,
regards."

"Yeah, I sure will Eddy. Your cough isn't getting any better.
Have you been in contact with the doctors in Regina? Are they
going to be able to help you?"

"Yeah Mon, *cough, cough*, that's what I'm calling, *cough*...
about. The lung cancer seems to be responding to, *cough*...
cough, to radiation treatments. Decided to give it, *cough*
...a try..."

There was a pause. Henry knew Eddy was going for a smoke.
He was right. Henry heard the sound of the lighter clicking
shut with a distinct metal sound. It was followed by a long,
slow exhale.

Coreena and me decided to go to the Mayo Clinic, *cough*, to see what they can do and recommend. We, *cough,* may come to Regina after that."

"That sounds like a good idea to go there. I hear they have very good doctors and are up on all the latest techniques and that. So how is Coreena?" Henry wanted to know.

"She's good. *Cough,* still running the best restaurant on the, *cough, cough,* island. So, has Jen delivered the new bambino yet?"

"No, she is still a couple of months away… but we are having some complications and so she might have the baby earlier."

"Hope it's not too serious, Mon. *Cough,* have the Padre pray for her. That's why I'm calling, *cough,* Mom keeps telling me to have Father Engelmann pray for me. *Cough, cough,* says he has healed a lot of people. *Cough,* tried getting him at the care home but they said, *cough,* that he's with you at the farm."

"Yeah, I might have mentioned it to you last time we spoke. He is here but he lives down in the valley in the prayer house. He's become sort of monk. He prays and writes these days."

"That's cool, Hank. Tell him to pray for me and Coreena. I'd sure like to beat this damn disease."

"Are you still smoking?"

"Yeah, can't seem to, *cough, cough,* shake it."

"Seems to me we need to pray for that too, Eddy. You have to throw that weed away. And Father will be the first to tell you that it's not him that heals but he prays to God on your behalf to heal you."

"*Cough,* yah Mon, he's got an 'in' with God, Mom keeps telling me."

"Well, I can't disagree with you there; he's a very holy man, Eddy. He's completely devoted to Jesus and to bringing as many people he can to the Lord."

"Well, if it wasn't, *cough,* for him, I wouldn't be thinking about God. He's the only one that ever made an impression on me that he has something that's cool, Mon."

"He will be excited to know you called, Eddy. I hope you and Coreena will make it to Regina and like I said our home is open to you."

"You're a good man, Hank. I appreciate your friendship, Mon."

"And I do yours, too, Eddy."

"I'll be in touch. Hope things go well for you and the missus, ole' buddy. "

"Thanks Eddy,

"And, yeah, Camilla, that's Peter's daughter too, *cough, cough*, isn't it?"

"Yes, in fact, Peter and his wife will probably come down for the baptism of the baby when that happens. We have all become good friends."

"Cool, Hank. That's really, *cough, cough*, really cool. Give them all my best, Hank."

"I sure will, Eddy and say hello to Coreena. Hope you make it here soon and I'll tell Father to pray and say Mass for you. Jenny and I will pray for you as well."

"Thanks, Hank. Appreciate, *cough, cough* it."

"Please give up the weed, Eddy. We will all pray that you quit."

"Thanks ole buddy. *Cough*, take care, Mon."

"See you, Eddy."

When Henry and Jenny got to the Grey Nuns Hospital they had to check in at the nurse's station. A nurse took them into a room where they had to sign in, put on a gown, gloves, and mask before they were permitted to see the baby. Camilla was nursing the baby and since they were the grandparents they were allowed to go into her room. Camilla was sharing the space with another mother who had also given birth within hours of Camilla.

A curtain was drawn between the two mothers when Henry and Jenny walked into the room. Camilla was just burping the baby when the nurse pulled the curtain aside and said, "You have visitors!"

"Camilla took a second look as her parents both had masks on. "Oh, hi Mom, Dad, it's so good to see you."

Tears came into Jenny's eyes at the sight of the baby. "Ah, Camilla, he's adorable." Jenny came over and had a close look at her new grandson. "Hi, Jacob." She put her finger to his cheek. "Ah, Jacob you look so strong and big."

"Do you want to hold him, Mom?"

"Oh, I would love to, Camilla." Jenny reached out, took the baby while supporting his head, and gently brought the infant to her chest. She tenderly cuddled it and shook her head in awe back and forth. "Oh, I love you to bits, Jacob. I love your little wrinkles and dark hair. I think you are going to look like your daddy. Yes, I do."

"Oh, Camilla, he's so cute and adorable."

The baby started fussing and wrinkling its face ready to cry. "I think he wants to continue to nurse, Honey." Jenny returned the baby to her daughter. Camilla put the infant to her chest and began to breast feed the baby once more.

"Was it a difficult labor, Camilla?"

"No, not really, around seven hours and then the baby came very quickly. It's the third one and so it seemed easier than Noah. Joshua was long and difficult; I remember that one for sure, as Matti would say."

They chuckled.

"How did your doctor appointment go yesterday, Mom?"

Jenny didn't want to worry her daughter and so she said, "The medicine hasn't been very effective yet. The doctor prescribed a stronger dose of medicine for my blood pressure. It's still too high."

"Is there protein in the urine, Mom?"

Jenny nodded, she couldn't conceal her concern anymore and unbidden tears surfaced.

"Oh, Mom, it will be okay. You will have to rest a lot. The doctor might suggest you remain in bed much of the time. That seemed to help some of the girls who had preeclampsia. How is your vision?"

"You sound like my doctor," Jenny smiled as she wiped away a tear rolling down her check. Henry came to her side and put his arm around her shoulder.

"My vision seems fine but the headaches seem to be more frequent and stronger. My feet are swollen, too."

"Yup, that all fits the condition. How is the fetus doing? What did the ultrasound report say?"

"Well. The baby is smaller than it should be and the doctor is concerned about its overall health and development. The nurse gave me a steroid injection to speed up the development of the baby's lungs in case they have to deliver preterm."

Camilla remained silent however, her concern wasn't easily concealed either. Her continuing silence said a lot.

Henry decided to chime in, "We are very hopeful that everything will turn out, Camilla. Father is praying and we'd like you and Jeremy to pray as well. That's about all we can do and hope what the doctor does helps. I guess the big thing is to get Jenny's blood pressure down."

Camilla nodded, "Yes---"

The nurse walked into the room and pulled aside the curtain. "So, how are we doing here? Is that little guy done nursing, yet?"

"Yes, I think so; he's content and sound asleep."

The nurse came over and took the baby from Camilla, "Try to get some rest as the next feeding will come soon enough."

The nurse looked at Henry and Jenny sort of hinting not to stay too long.

Henry picked up the cue. "Yes, we will be leaving shortly." "Come here and sit down beside me, Mom," said Camilla.

As soon as Jenny sat, she leaned into Camilla's waiting arms. "Oh, Mom, I will pray for you. Things will turn out. I've seen this condition several times and in most cases the mother and baby get through it all with flying colors. I know how upsetting this can be." Jenny was softly weeping and Camilla was too. Henry couldn't hold back his tears either. He felt helpless and wished there was more he could do.

"When do you go back to the doctor, Mom?" Camilla wanted to know.

"Next Wednesday. I will have the lab tests done on Monday and so that will be the most updated report of where things are at."

"How far are you into your term, Mom?"

"I think the nurse said, I was into the twenty ninth week. It's still a bit too early for delivery, isn't it?"

Camilla nodded, "Yes, but in a pinch, a delivery can be made. The lungs are a concern but one never knows. The longer the baby can stay in the womb, the better but I've seen many premature babies come through and develop into strong healthy babies. They have to live in an incubator for awhile."

Camilla tried to express words that were hopeful but they all knew how easily complications can set in. The first trimester was critical to the growth and development of the fetus. The blood flow to the placenta had to be strong; otherwise the baby could be affected by the lack of oxygen and nutrients. The fetus could have already developed any number of conditions. And Jenny too, could have already suffered complications or damage to several of her organs. They would have to pray hard that the blood pressure came down soon.

Camilla gazed at her mom with love and compassion. Her life had not been easy, yet there she stood next to the love of her life; her eyes sparkling with hope.

CHAPTER FIFTY-SEVEN

WHEN HENRY WOKE up Saturday morning, he was surprised to see Jenny was already up. Justin went to Jeremy's house to help watch the boys and so there was no need for her to be up that early.

Jenny was on the phone when he came down. She was talking with Matti. Henry thought it was a bit early but then realized they were two hours behind Ottawa. Henry could tell Jenny was crying. He just stood at the base of the stairs and quietly listened. He didn't mean to eavesdrop; he was more concerned with allowing Jenny to talk to her friend freely.

"I'm afraid to go back to the doctor next week in case my blood pressure hasn't gone down. Every day that it's out of control can be harmful to the child."

"And what about you, Jenny?"

"I am not so much concerned about myself as I am of Hannah. I want her to be healthy and strong."

"And you be sayin' the only remedy is to deliver the child?"

"That's right, Matti but Hannah needs to develop more. The big concern is that the baby's lungs may not be developed enough and she would have difficulty breathing. She may not survive and if she does, the lack of oxygen could cause many complications."

"But you sayin' the longer the baby be stayin' in your belly, the worse it gets for you too, isn't that so?"

Jenny paused for a moment, "Yes, that's true, Matti. At my last appointment the doctor suggested we may have to deliver pre-term but I want to wait as long as possible to help the fetus to develop. But then If I wait too long and complications set in the doctor said I might have to terminate the pregnancy as the risk to my health is growing too great. Matti, I could never end the baby's life growing in my womb. It is Henry's child too and the baby is the answer to my hopes and dreams for us. It is a gift from God and has just as much right to live as I do. I would never consider abortion."

"Oh, Jen, what can you do? The Lord be placin' a heavy trial on your heart. We be prayin' for you everyday already, but now we be doublin' our efforts. I have a talk with the Lord as soon as we done chattin'. I be tellin' Him to get busy and do His healin'. There ain't be a more deserving mother nor a better and more loving mother and He knows it."

Jenny was silent for a moment not sure how to respond to Matti's kind words. "Yes, for now that's all we can do. That is one of the reasons for my call, Matti that you all pray for Hannah and that I can deliver her in the normal way. I need to lower my blood pressure so I can keep her inside for a while longer."

"We be doin' just that, Jen. You can count on it."

"There is another reason why I'm calling. Camilla had her baby boy at over eight pounds a couple of days ago and everything is fine."

"Whoopee! That be a big boy, Jen! So, you be a grandma again. How many is that now?" Matti wanted to know.

"That's a good question. Well, Camilla has three children now and J.J. has one and another on the way, I think."

"No, that be a false alarm. Nora missed her period twice but it was due to something else. She be on track again but so far no other little Hamilton be comin' along any time soon. But Camilla bein' J.J.'s step sister be making him another uncle to her new baby, isn't that so?"

"That's right, Matti. Please tell him Camilla and Jeremy have named the new little boy Jacob."

"Ah, that be a fine name, Jen."

"Yes, I like it too."

"Well, I like the name, Hannah, too, Jen. We just have to work on makin' that little girl just a wee bit bigger and stronger and then, look out world, she be doin' wonderful t'ings, I just knows it!"

"I do too, Matti, I do too!"

Just as Matti got off the phone, Thomas came into the kitchen. He was clearing the overnight snow off the front steps.

"Brrrr, that's a bitter wind out there Matti, It blew considerable snow on the steps. The canopy doesn't do much good when the wind is blowing that hard. We'll have to check for drifts on the road later. J.J.'s limo must have made it through to the gate okay."

"He be leaving at five thirty this morning, Thomas. Some big meetin' with folks from Japan. Still some hot coffee in the urn, Thomas, I can make a fresh batch in just a few minutes."

"No, the coffee in the urn is just fine. I need something to warm me up more than anything."

"Jenny be callin' not more than five minutes ago."

"Is that so, how is she doing, Matti?"

"Not so good. Her blood pressure is very high and affectin' her and the baby. The medicine they be givin' her not much good so far. We have to pray hard to the Lord, Thomas, to heal our dear friend."

Thomas nodded, "High blood pressure restricts the flow of the mother's blood to the baby and can have all sorts of complications, even brain damage."

"Oh, Thomas, I don't like what you be sayin'."

"My aunt Jessie had some kind of condition with high blood pressure, too when she was with child. This goes back a spell but she suffered from kidney damage and the baby was born with Cerebral Palsy."

Matti shook her head and raised her hands and shook them

in front of Thomas and said, "Now I don't want you to be sayin' anyt'ing anymore. Jenny's baby is goin' to turn out just fine. What we need be more prayer, Thomas."

"Yes, you're right, Matti. I didn't mean to upset you. Did you tell Jenny that Neela and I are coming to Regina to visit Carlos and Maria in two weeks?"

Matti threw her hands up in the air and brought them to rest on top of her head, "I done forgot, Thomas. That news be cheering her up. I be phoning her back right a way to let her know, that for sure."

"We're hoping the prairies have an early spring to melt most of the snow. I would love to have a look at the backyard layout. Carlos sent me pictures last year but there's nothing like seeing the garden first hand."

"The yard, front and back is beautiful, Thomas."

"Yes, I remember when we went to their wedding. Jenny did a fine job. I don't think I could suggest any better layout than they already have. I think Carlos wanted to know if there were some different flowers he could start. In any case, it's more to visit with Carlos and Maria and to see Henry and Jenny."

"And don't forget about the preacher man, Father Engelmann. You give him a big hug for me. Never seen such a holy man filled with the Spirit…" Matti paused for a moment and then added, "You know, Thomas, in many ways you be a lot like him; you be kind, know the Holy Book from back to front, there ain't anyt'ing you don't seem to know, you be ready to help anyone out, you—"

"Whoa Matti, don't give me a swelled head now. You know how hard it is to be humble."

"Oh Thomas, there be no danger of that ever happenin'. I knows how them words be passin' through that head of yours like a barn with the front and back doors wide open. The reason you like gardenin' so much is because it allows you to be down on your knees so you can thank the Lord for His beautiful creation."

Chapter Fifty-Eight

MARCH CAME IN like a lamb and out like a lion. Unfortunately, the lion was still raging into April as Henry and Jenny drove cautiously to the city for Jenny's doctor appointment. Although the blizzard had dissipated overnight, it left wet snow on the highway which froze as the temperature on the prairies was dropping. The icy condition of the road complimented the icy tension which hung over the car.

"I pray the medication lowered my blood pressure, I'm so worried about Hannah getting enough nutrients. I'll try to carry her as long as I can to make sure her chances of survival are good."

Henry didn't want to take his hands off the steering wheel for fear of getting caught in a skid and so he said with as much compassion as words can convey, "I'm worried too, honey. I want so much for our little girl to be healthy. We just have to trust that everything works out."

Henry couldn't help himself but take a chance and quickly reached over to his sweet wife and pat her hands. For the rest of the way, they began to pray and praise God for all their blessings and by the time they reached the city, their moods were filled with hope and optimism. As they made their way to the doctor's office however, nervousness returned and began to rage inside Jenny like the lion that refused to go away from blustering on the prairies.

Jenny was so nervous when the nurse called her into the doctor's office that she had to lean on Henry for support. As soon as Jenny got into the exam room she collapsed on a chair; her legs were so rubbery and weak. Henry and the nurse noticed Jenny's hands tremble and her knees bounce.

"Oh, Honey, it will be okay. I love you so much, please try to relax."

"You will have to go into the doctor's office and wait for us until Doctor Webster exams your wife and then we will all come into the office and go over the results of the examination and last week's test results."

"I understand," said Henry. He didn't need to be shown his way to the adjoining office. He bent over, kissed Jenny, and made his way to the other room.

Jenny tried to calm herself as the nurse prepared her for the examination. It reminded her so much of the time she went to the doctor to find out if she was pregnant as a result of the rape which occurred in the park when she was a teenager. The experience was so traumatic for Jenny; it was forever printed in her mind's emotional bank. *Please,* she silently prayed, *don't let me faint. Give me strength dear Jesus, to endure this.*

The door suddenly opened and startled Jenny. Doctor Webster sounded buoyant but that was his manner. He was hard to read, he was good at hiding his prognosis. Jenny wished he wasn't so but rather more revealing to better prepare the patient for the news rather than hit them hard.

"I don't have to ask how you are, Jenny. I feel your tension and it's written all over you. Take some deep breaths and try to relax. I hope we can see some improvement over last time."

After the doctor checked her internally, he asked Jenny to sit up and then proceeded to take her blood pressure. This was the crucial test and dictated what the future had in store for Jenny and Henry.

He strapped the cuff to Jenny's arm and pumped the empty chamber applying pressure against Jenny's arm. She thought she would faint with each movement the doctor made. The release of the air felt good on Jenny's arm but then the cuff was inflated again. Jenny wobbled on the table not sure if she could take another moment. She felt relieved when the doctor released the air once more and let it completely dissipate. He removed the cuff but as skilled as he was in concealing his emotions, Jenny knew the news was not good.

The doctor could see Jenny growing faint and he quickly took hold of her shoulders and said, "Just relax, Jenny and lie back on the table for a minute. Sandra, run a wash cloth under cold water and put it on her forehead."

Henry was becoming more and more agitated by the length of time it was taking for the examination. At least twice the normal time had elapsed. He was about to get up and knock at the door to the examination room when Jenny followed by the doctor and his attending nurse walked into the office. Jenny looked white as a candle.

Henry expected the worst.

Doctor Webster looked more serious than usual as he began. "I wish I could have good news for you both but the prognosis isn't very favorable." Turning to Jenny he continued, "Jenny, your blood pressure read 200/100. It may have been exacerbated by your nervousness but regardless; it's simply way too high.

"The lab tests show the protein in your urine has increased and is beginning to damage your kidneys. The liver is also being affected and when I felt the upper right area of your abdomen where the liver is located you flinched with pain. Although you didn't say, I assume you still have severe headaches and if you haven't as yet experienced blurred vision you soon will." He looked at Henry and then Jenny and said, "I don't like to add to all of this but the complete blood cell count we did indicated the platelet count has exceeded the normal count and there is a danger of blood clots developing."

Doctor Webster paused and tightened his lips, "Jenny, I understand that you are adamantly against terminating the pregnancy, at least at this point, so the next option is to admit you into the hospital. We need to monitor your blood pressure, your blood count and make sure it doesn't lead to DIC. This is a condition known as disseminated intravascular coagulation which basically means that your blood could clot excessively reducing blood flow or block blood from flowing to bodily organs. And then there is the fetus of course, whose wellbeing we want to closely keep an eye on."

Both Henry and Jenny's eyes were filled with tears. Neither of them could speak. They were in a state of shock. The nurse walked slowly over to Jenny and rubbed her shoulder.

"How soon can we admit you into the hospital, Jenny?" asked the doctor.

Jenny shook her head. "This is Easter weekend coming up, we were going to have a family dinner."

"Jenny, I cannot stress the seriousness of your state of health nor the baby. You must be admitted as soon as possible."

Henry finally spoke, "Would Saturday or Sunday be soon enough? That will give us a day or two to get ready."

"Mr. Pederson, I'd try to get your wife into the hospital first thing tomorrow morning, there is the danger that her condition could escalate into eclampsia at any time. In the hospital, we can better monitor her condition and control the medication. She is much better looked after under our care."

"Yes, of course, Doctor, I understand."

Henry knew only too well what that could mean if Jenny started to have seizures; the same is what happened to Julean. He shook his head and muttered, *"How on earth could this be happening?"*

WHEN THEY LEFT the doctor's office, they decided to go straight back to the farm. They had intended to stop by the Grey Nun's Hospital on the way but both Henry and Jenny were emotionally exhausted, distressed and totally distraught. What initially appeared to be such a blessing and answer to prayer, the pregnancy was turning out to be one of deep concern, agitation and conflict. The options available to them were so limited and growing even more slim by the minute. The only solution seemed to be delivering the child one way or the other.

Jenny for all her life had a positive outlook and was able to accept intolerable situations and difficult people. She was able to remain centered because she always stayed close to her Creator. She saw God in nature and daily received spiritual sustenance to cope with all situations. This was just another such circumstance but only much closer to her heart. It challenged her faith and trust in the very thing that always gave her hope or so he thought ...

"You know, Honey," Jenny said as they drove down the highway, "Today is Holy Thursday. The day before Christ gave up His life for us. Can you imagine the agony He was going through knowing what lay ahead? All the pain, torture, suffering and ending with the actual crucifixion. And to think, God the Father allowing it to all happen seems so unthinkable and unfair. And here we are in a similar circumstance. Life on earth is not always good or fair or to our liking. This is the way the world is and comes with the gift of free will. There has to be consequences for everything.

"More than anything, my heart's desire since the day we met in the summer of 1956 has always been to bear your child. God has answered that prayer but it comes with consequences. I am older and thus more prone to complications. It's the natural order of things and not God's fault or wish for us. If He started interfering with every situation we wouldn't have free will, we wouldn't grow in faith and trust and we wouldn't know joy without despair or light if there were no darkness. This is the world God created. At times, He interferes with the natural order of things but in most cases, Henry, we have to accept our trials and challenges whatever they are.

Jenny reached over and touched Henry's shoulder. "But this I know, God is always there for us no matter what to help us see it through even if it is unto death. He has done no less for his Son. He refused to take the chalice away from His own Son but look at the good that came out of it. Look at how Jesus was glorified."

"But Honey, what good can come out of your being so sick and Hannah's life endangered with so many complications and possible death?" Henry wanted to know.

Jenny shook her head, "First of all, Henry this is life and we have to face it. All of us eventually die. Many die peacefully in their sleep but many die after months and years of suffering. It was what life dealt them. Sure, we may say as parents to those suffering, I would do anything to save you or help you but we can't. Life goes on. Yes, God has the power to interfere and heal and He has for us in the past but it's not the way He created the world. We are free to live and to die according to all the choices we have made. When we have free will, the world becomes imperfect and unfair because of the choices that are made not only by us but all those around us which can affect us for better or worse."

Henry turned and took a quick cursory glance at Jenny. A tear was sliding down her cheek. Jenny took a deep breath and went on. "But all of this is temporary and if we live with eternity in mind our lives change because we see life on earth for what it is and our eternal hope is where our real hope lies. In the end, Henry, it always comes down to how we lived and how we respond to life's trials.

"If we choose to trust and have faith in Him, our lives are made easier despite our difficulties because if we turn to Him, He will comfort us. He will give us the grace and strength to get through what we are facing. He will help us in a world which He knows is unfair and can be cruel and so He offers Himself to us to help us through these difficult times. Somehow, Henry, if we trust in Him, He will turn it into good or bring good out of it."

Henry shook his head and couldn't respond. How could she be so accepting? And yet, what good does the alternative do? To be un-accepting, cold hearted and angry only compounds the situation and closes us off from receiving the comfort, grace and strength of the Holy Spirit to cope with life that is not perfect and fair. He further noticed that where he was focused on himself, she was more concerned for Hannah's health and his well-being rather than herself. She was trying to prepare him for the worst and to be accepting of what life may bring. His dear Jenny had the heart of an angel and the mind of Jesus.

She is full of Truth and Grace.

Her trust was so deep and strong in God. Henry couldn't get over how her life was so similar to that of Father Engelmann. Henry knew Jenny was right, yet he wanted more from God. He wanted to control the situation. He wanted to be God. He did many things for God and now wanted some return for his earned efforts. He wanted his dear wife healed and expected God to do so.

Isn't that how life works?

CHAPTER FIFTY-NINE

$\qquad$ ◆◆◆ $\qquad$

J ENNY SPENT PART of the afternoon getting ready to go to the hospital and the rest of day calling the girls and her dear friends for prayer support. Alison offered to come home and help at the farm but Jenny didn't think it was necessary at this time. Alison did say she would have the Bible College say prayers for her and Dad and the family. Lauren, too, was allowed compassionate leave from the show but once again Jenny said that everything would be fine and to let her know if more was needed from her.

Matti was devastated by the news and promised that the entire family at the estate would pray morning to night for her and the baby. Jenny asked for J.J. to call but he was in Japan with Nora on both a business trip and holiday. Matti told Jenny that Thomas and Neela were coming in the following week to Regina to visit with Carlos and Maria and also with them, too. Matti's last bit of news was that James' mother, Nancy was admitted into the hospital yesterday and so J.J.'s trip may be shortened depending on his grandma's condition.

Matti and Jenny's conversation did end on an upbeat note. "How are you and Charles coming along?" Jenny asked.

"Whoopee, Jenny! That man like more than my cookies, that for sure!" We be talkin' about taking a trip back home to Jamaica this summer. He wants to see the island I keep talking about and my next of kin. All I have to say, Jen, there be love in the air!"

"That's for sure!" exclaimed Jenny.

NEXT, JENNY CALLED Chloe and Robbie to see how they were doing and also ask for their prayer support.

"Hello," said a male voice.

"Hi, Robbie, is that you!?"

"Yeah, is this Jenny?"

"Yes, it is. Oh, it's so good to talk to you Robbie! How are you keeping?"

"I'm fine. Still involved with the Campus Crusade and getting ready for another spring conference in Chicago. So how are you and Henry doing?"

"Well, we are fine...I have some news, I am pregnant with a little girl."

"Hey, that's great! Chloe mentioned that to me a while back. So when is the due date?" Robbie wanted to know.

"Well, it was supposed to be in another couple of months but complications have set in and I'm going into the hospital tomorrow. The doctor wants to closely monitor me and the baby's health from here on in."

"I'm sorry to hear that, Jen. I'll get our team to pray for you right away. What's the problem?"

"It's mainly my high blood pressure. It won't go down and it's creating so many negative side effects on my organs and also restricting the growth and development of the baby."

"Praise the Lord, Jenny. We have to do some serious praying for you. Oh, I just heard the door slam; I think Chloe just came in. Perhaps talk to her about your condition, she deals with so many different problems, she might have some suggestions for you."

"So, things are going well for you?

"Yeah, I started dating a Christian girl. After all these years, I never thought I would find anyone like Tammy but April is a very nice lady and we have been going out for about a year now."

"Oh, how wonderful, Robbie. I'm so happy for you."

"We are quite a sight, Jen. You know how tall I am."

"Yes, I remember how you have to bend over when you walk through a door way. Tammy was at least two heads shorter than you were."

"Yeah, that's right. Well, April is still shorter yet. She's also ten years younger than I am and many times she gets confused as being my daughter! Talk about robbing the cradle!"

Jenny laughed at the sight of it in her mind's eye. "The main thing is that you're happy with one another."

"And that we are, Jenny. Well, here is Chloe, she's chomping at the bit to talk to you. I wish you and Henry all the best and we'll all get praying for you straight-away, Jenny."

"Thanks, Robbie."

"Hi Auntie, it's so good of you to call!"

"Hi Chloe, I've been meaning to for over a week now and with doctor appointments and all that's been happening around here, I keep putting it off."

"So how are things progressing with your pregnancy?"

"Well, that's part of the reason for my calling but first I must tell you that Camilla had her baby boy two days ago. He was a big eight pound, three ounce baby."

"Wow! That is big. How is she doing?"

"Just fine. There was some tearing during the delivery which required stitches, but the baby is healthy and Camilla is in great spirits and relieved that it's over. Her back pain was quite an ordeal for her."

"Yes, that seems to be a big complaint with the girls. So how are you doing, Auntie?" Chloe wanted to know.

"Well, not so good, Honey. I am being admitted into the hospital tomorrow…"

"Oh, Auntie, you still have two months or so to go! What's happening!?"

"I have a condition called preeclampsia."

"Yes, I am quite aware of that condition. They should be able to get it under control before it leads to eclampsia."

"That's what they are concerned about for one thing but

the medication I have been taking hasn't been able to get my blood pressure down. It's causing many other complications and I am so worried that Hannah isn't getting enough oxygen and nutrients."

"Oh, Auntie, it is a bit pre-mature to deliver now…if only you were a month further along the baby would be developed so much more and things would straighten out very quickly."

"The doctor has suggested an early delivery but is concerned about the baby's lungs and I, too, want to wait as long as possible for the baby to develop. The doctor did allude to terminating the pregnancy because of the complications which are developing."

There was a long silence. Jenny knew what Chloe was thinking. She reassured her adopted niece however that abortion was not an option. "I would never terminate the pregnancy, Chloe. Hannah and I are in this together."

"I have seen so many pregnancies especially amongst young girls develop that condition. In most cases Auntie, the mother and baby turn out fine and quickly get back to normal. I must admit that is not the case with all such cases. Serious damage to both the mother and child can happen." Chloe wanted to add that death was also very possible.

"I am aware of that and am going to trust in God to turn it all for the good."

"I will pray for you Auntie and I know Robbie will be on his knees pleading on your behalf."

"I am so thankful for your and Robbie's support. I will get a phone in my room at the hospital right away so we can keep in touch."

"It's good for you to be in the hospital. The medication can be controlled and monitored intravenously. Bed rest is excellent, your diet is controlled and you're in the best place to be in case of an emergency. Oh, I recall one thing a doctor did was to give a girl in my care a steroid injection to speed up the development of the baby's lungs."

"Yes, my doctor has started that a couple of weeks ago, in case he wants to deliver the baby sooner."

"That would be the best option, Auntie. The sooner little Hannah comes into the world the better."

NOT FIVE MINUTES passed when Henry picked up the extension phone to check if Jenny wasn't using the main phone. He wanted to call his father–in-law, Doctor Carter.

"Hello, this is the Carter residence."

"Hello, Vera. It's Henry, or rather Hank calling."

"I thought that was you. Jeremy called the other day and told us Camilla had her baby. Jack was up to see her yesterday when doing his rounds at the hospital. He said that's a fine boy she delivered and we love the name Jacob."

"I like the name, too. I am very happy for the kids and glad everything has turned out fine."

"And how is Jenny's pregnancy coming along? It must be getting soon to be delivered."

"Well, another two months is close to full term but she is having a lot of complications. She has a condition called preeclampsia."

"Oh, dear, I am aware of that. In fact, I had that when I was pregnant with Julean. I was confined to bed for almost two months."

"Well, they can't seem to get her blood pressure down..."

"Yes, I remember that very same thing, Hank. In my case, too, it was hard to control. Jack had me admitted to the hospital and that seemed to help."

"That's what I was calling about. Is Jack around? I would like to speak to him about Jenny."

"You know, I think he just came in. I heard the garage door close a minute or so ago. Let me check, Hank and give my love to Jenny."

"Yes, I will, thanks, Vera."

"Hello, Hank, how are you keeping?"

"Hi Jack, to be honest, things could be better. As you know, Jenny is pregnant but she has been battling high blood pressure for the last month and it's developed into a condition—"

"Pre-eclampsia?"

"Yes, Jack—"

"Has she got proteinuria, headaches, swelling and blurred vision?"

"Well, she has protein in her urine, swollen ankles and her headaches are getting worse but her vision is still okay."

"So, no seizures, yet?"

"No, thank God. Anyway, Jack, Jenny is going to be admitted into the Grey Nuns tomorrow and if you have time when you're doing the rounds, can you check in on her?"

"Of course, I will. Is Doctor Kreake her doctor?"

"He is our family doctor but he referred Jenny to an obstetrician by the name of Webster—."

"Oh, yes, Adam Webster, a good man, Hank. He is from the States and we are fortunate to have him."

"That's good to hear, Jack. I want Jenny to be in the best care possible."

"Doctor Kreake couldn't have recommended a better doctor. He's both an obstetrician and gynecologist, so he is very capable to deal with any emergency that comes along."

"The thing is, so far nothing Doctor Webster prescribed has worked yet and that's why he is admitting her."

"Pre-eclampsia is a very difficult condition to deal with. Vera had it too, with Julean. Bed rest and careful monitoring of the condition is the best thing short of terminating the pregnancy. What is her gestation date?"

"If you mean how many weeks she is pregnant I heard the attending nurse in the doctor's office say Jenny was in her thirtieth week."

"The fetus needs more time to develop, especially the lungs. And Jenny's condition is more than likely affecting the growth of the baby."

"That's exactly what is happening, Jack. The baby is small and the doctor is worried that the lungs are not sufficiently developed to deliver at this time. He did start giving Jenny some injections to speed up the development of the baby's lungs."

"Sounds to me like he's on top of things, Hank. The only thing I could suggest but he's probably going to start as soon as Jenny is admitted is to give her magnesium sulfate to ward off seizures."

"Geez, Jack I remember that's what they gave Julean."

"Yes, they did but didn't do much good in her case. Like I said, Hank, it's a tough condition to deal with. Now that she is going into the hospital, she will be in better care and medical staff to deal with any emergency. Hopefully, the doctors are able to ward off eclampsia and deal with other complications such as liver and kidney function."

"Well, talking to you does make me feel more confident in Doctor Webster. I thought perhaps there was more he could be doing."

"Like I said, Hank, Jenny is in good care. I'll drop by and see her later tomorrow and check the charts. If there is anything I can do or suggest, I will."

"Thanks, Jack, much appreciated."

Chapter Sixty

THE CANDLE FLICKERED quietly between them, as they sat eating their dinner in the sun room. Their silence seemed to echo the candle. Usually, Justin excused himself immediately after dinner but tonight, he sat there. He was told that Jenny was going into the hospital tomorrow and it suddenly hit him how critical his step mother was and that he may not see her for awhile or ever. Although he was only five at the time, he would never forget that day in the hospital when his birth mother died. How he tried to bring her back to life but it was not to be.

Unbidden tears surfaced in the young man's eyes as he gazed at his father and Jenny across from him. Justin had grown to love his step mother but had trouble showing it. Somehow, he felt he wasn't being loyal to Julean. He knew his coldness hurt his father and Jenny but he just couldn't let it go. He was ready now; but he struggled with his feelings. When he looked at Jenny trying to speak it was as if he saw Julean. Jenny would never be able to replace his mom but Jenny now was his mother and she tried so hard to love him as her own. He sensed his pride, his resistance, his non-accepting attitude and the weight of the hurt he had inflicted on his dad and Jenny rested heavily on his heart. He somehow knew this was a defining moment when he could reveal his true feelings for the lady his father had chosen to be his wife and mother for his children. They all had accepted Jenny except him.

Justin stared at Jenny with tears in his eyes. He was feeling the release of feelings which had imprisoned him. So many emotions; anger at God for taking his mom, anger at Julean for leaving him, resentment of Jenny for coming into their lives and replacing his mother and stealing away his dad's love which should be for Julean, his struggle with his loneliness, his pride and all the other useless, self-defeating rationalizations he held to justify his coldness were finally unraveling and losing their strangle hold on him. That's what happens when we choose to love. Our hearts overflow with rivers of living water to quench the thirst of both our self-inflicted desert and how we projected it onto others.

Both Henry and Jenny gazed at Justin not knowing the inner turmoil he was going through. Suddenly, however, they knew where his heart was at as Justin blurted out his sorrow. "Jenny, I want to say I'm sorry for not being there for you and am really going to miss not seeing you here for awhile..."

In a split second, an act of love washed away all the days, weeks, months and years of coldness Jenny felt. Instantly, their relationship blossomed. *It had been budding for so long and just needed a drop of humility to open it up in all its beauty.* Justin's words flooded the desert Jenny was in like a cooling balm watering her heart.

It lifted her spirits to see how good was already being brought out of this circumstance.

Tears swiftly filled Jenny's eyes and she reached across the table for Justin's hand. "Oh, Justin, I understand the struggle you have been going through and how much you miss your mom. I just want to be here for you and what you just said means more to me than words can say."

Henry reached across the table and with tears in his eyes as well said, "That was a very good thing you just did, Son."

Jenny wanted to go over and hug him to pieces. She studied him for any sign that he was ready for her love but Justin just sat there unable to say anything more. He just wept.

Jenny followed her heart.

She got up, moved her chair next to Justin, put her arm around him, and softly said, "I know how much you miss your mom, Justin. Henry told me many times how close you were. I will never be able to replace her for you Justin but I do want to love you in my own way if you let me. You have such a beautiful, tender heart Justin and I want to be part of it. Your care for me in what you just said, are words I will always cherish."

An awkward silence fell over the sun room and yet streams of messages and healing were permeating the air. *Like the very oxygen we breathe to live, love is needed to make us heal and grow.*

"I really hope everything turns out okay and you have the baby. It would be so cool to have a little sister..." Justin's words trailed off but continued to penetrate deeply into Jenny and Henry's hearts. What seemed such a solemn evening was turning into one of joy and family unity.

This time, Henry got up and was unable to speak but patted his son's shoulder with a warmth and touch that conveyed more than words could say.

Henry and Jenny had difficulty sleeping that night, knowing how uncertain the future was. In so many ways, Jenny's complications mimicked those of Julean's. Meningitis may be called a different illness than preeclampsia but the end result was the same. If it couldn't be controlled, it could have mortal consequences. It was when Henry got up to go to the bathroom and turned on the lights the full impact of Julean's disease was being replayed in Jenny.

"Honey, please turn off the lights, they are so bright and blinding." Although the words may not have been the same that Julean spoke that night so many years ago, Henry had never forgotten how he and Jeremy managed to get Julean to the station wagon and lay her in the back area. Here again, Henry was confronted with the same horrific scene and he began to panic. Doctor Webster was correct in his prediction that blurred vision and sensitivity to light would be another symptom in the chain leading to eclampsia.

Jenny was one step away from having a seizure.

Although it was only four thirty in the morning, Henry thought it best to get Jenny to hospital. They had planned on spending the morning on the farm and taking a nice ride in to the city after lunch and visit Father Engelmann at the care home. He had gone there for Holy Week to celebrate the death and resurrection of Jesus with the residents. The risk, however of keeping Jenny at home was now too dangerous.

Henry turned on the bathroom light and partially closed the door to dim the light in the bedroom. He got dressed and Jenny managed to dress herself. Her suitcase was all ready as she had packed it yesterday. They made their way to kitchen and had a light breakfast thinking it more for the baby to receive nutrients than for her.

Henry went back upstairs to tell Justin that they were going. Justin came down with his dad and came into the kitchen. Just the under counter lights were on and it momentarily shocked Justin to see Jenny in the semi-darkness. Guided more for a deep sense of concern for his step-mother than for self-pride, he went quickly over to Jenny and hugged her. He couldn't hold back the tears. "Oh, Mom," he started out…he took a deep breath to release the rest of the words choking within and said, "I love you. Please hurry and have the baby and come home."

Jenny got up and they embraced. Henry came to them and put his arms around both of them. When composure began to settle in, Henry whispered a prayer to God.

"Dear Jesus, please help us pick up our cross like you did on this very day. Give us your strength and peace and healing. Thank You for the gift of each other and uniting us as a family. Please heal Jenny and make her strong to deliver Hannah as a healthy baby. Amen."

As THEY DROVE to the city, Henry couldn't get over Jenny's concern for others despite her serious medical condition.

"I was so looking forward to my ladies' group at this time of the year. Holy week is such a perfect time for married couples to see why it's so important to have Jesus at the center of their marriage. Yesterday, which was Holy Thursday during the last supper, Jesus washed the feet of his apostles and told them to do as He did and become servants to one another. And as Father Engelmann so beautifully explained to us that day at the Poustinia, Jesus laid down his life for us. What a perfect example to married couples of love, humility, forgiveness and sacrifice."

"That's beautiful, Jenny. I am amazed that as dire as your health is at this time that you could be thinking of your women's group."

"But, Honey, it's such a good time to show that if we place Jesus at the center of our lives and marriages, He becomes our example, teacher and guide in our daily lives and how we too must die to ourselves for the growth and betterment of the other."

"Oh, Jen, you're something else. You are so much like Father Engelmann. The next event you will wait for and use in your groups is the Pentecost, when the Holy Spirit descended upon the apostles and many other disciples and empowered them to overcome their fears, concerns and live boldly for Christ.—"

"Yes, Honey, that would have been perfect! Without the Holy Spirit in our lives, we can't do it! We need His strength, wisdom and conviction."

Henry just shook his head and sped to Regina.

WHEN THEY GOT to the hospital emergency entrance, Henry went inside and quickly returned with an attendant pushing a wheel chair. Although Jenny was capable of walking, she was now in the care of the hospital. As soon as they got inside, it was unusually quiet. There was only one other person waiting in emergency. They were immediately attended to and began to fill out the necessary documents and sign permission for the doctors to administer medication. Jenny also signed the right for Henry to sign on her behalf or make decisions should emergency attention be required and Jenny was not conscious or able to on her own.

"Okay, Honey, I'll park the SUV and come up to see you shortly." He bent over, kissed Jenny, and watched as she was whisked away to the maternity ward.

Around four thirty in the afternoon, Father Engelmann came into Jenny's room. Henry was sitting on a chair by her bedside holding her hand. Jenny's eyes lit up as soon as she saw Father.

"Oh, Father, how did you know I was here?"

"My guardian angel keeps me informed, Jenny." He winked and then added, "Henry left a message for me at the care home. I was watching for you at the three o'clock service. I suspected that something may have come up. It's good that you are here Jenny and directly under the care of medical staff."

"Yes, I suppose so but there's no place like home."

Father nodded. "So, how are you feeling, Jenny?"

Jenny shrugged her shoulders, "I wish the headaches would go away. This morning my vision was slightly blurred but that has gone away. My eyes are still a bit sensitive to the light, that's why the blinds are closed."

Henry got up and said, "Please, sit here Father, I need to stand for awhile."

Father made his way to Jenny and sat down. He reached for her hand and pressed it between his.

"Seems just like old times, Father when I was in the Santa Maria Care Home."

"Yes, but this time it's to give life! I am just as anxious to see Hannah as you and Henry are. What are the latest reports on the baby's progress?"

"No doctor has been—"

Jenny barely finished her sentence when Doctor Carter came into the room.

"Jack!" said Henry. "It's good of you to drop by. You remember Father Engelmann?"

Father answered for him, "Yes, yes, of course we remember each other. We had many fine discussions and you and Mrs. Carter were always present for the baptism of all the Pederson children."

Doctor Carter came over and shook Father's hand and then turned to Jenny.

"How are you doing, Jenny?"

"I was just telling Father my headaches are still there but my blurred vision seems to be improving."

"I called Doctor Webster. He is not coming in today but will see you first thing Saturday morning. I ordered a complete blood count, urine analysis and also instructed the nurse to begin administering magnesium sulfate. It has a depressant effect on the central nervous system to prevent or ward off seizures. It does not adversely affect you or the fetus. I noticed on the chart your blood pressure was still high. We will try to get that down. I'm sure Doctor Webster will want to do another ultrasound tomorrow to check on the baby."

"Thank you for coming in, Doctor Carter, that's very kind of you," said Jenny.

He just waved it off. "Vera had the same condition and we managed to get her through it. It is more prevalent amongst young girls or women over forty. I'm sure you will do fine. I best finish my rounds." He reached down and patted Jenny's hand. "I wish you all the best. Vera and I will keep you in our prayers."

"Thank you, Doctor Carter," said Jenny with a smile.

"So, were there many residents at the service today, Father?"

"Yes, the chapel was full and then some. Many people from the neighborhood are still attending. Most days, Father Philips from the Cathedral says Mass for the residents. He is busy with Holy Week so this has worked out fine."

"Do you want a ride home? Justin or I can drive you down to the prayer house."

"No, I plan to stay at the care home from now on until Jenny has the baby and comes home. Since you will be here daily, I will come to visit with you and bring Holy Communion and we can pray together."

"Oh, Father, thank you so much. It makes me feel better knowing that you will be here."

"We are family, Jenny. *A family sticks together and prays together.*"

CHAPTER SIXTY-ONE

HENRY WAS IN the room when Doctor Webster walked in around ten o'clock Saturday morning. Jenny already had an ultrasound done earlier that morning and the doctor was there to go over the results.

"I'm glad you are here, Mr. Pederson. The results are not good. The urine shows high levels of protein and there is liver and kidney damage. I am not sure of the damage the fetus has incurred due to lack of oxygen but the growth and estimated weight of the fetus is small for the gestational age of the baby. I see on the charts that you are experiencing blurred vision and sensitivity to light. You have all the symptoms for the onset of eclampsia, I am very concerned not only for your health but your very life, Jenny."

He paused for a moment to let what he said sink in and then the doctor continued, "I know how much you want this baby but the risk of carrying the fetus is just too high. Under normal circumstances, I would not suggest that you consider abortion, Jenny. In this case, however, I strongly recommend you consider terminating the pregnancy. It could only be a matter of days when that option may no longer be available to you."

Jenny shook her head and was about to speak when a nurse

rushed into the room, "Doctor Webster you are needed right away in the nursery."

"Please discuss what I have said with your husband and I will be back later to go over this further and answer any questions you might have."

"I don't like the focus Doctor Webster has. Ever since my last appointment with him at the office he seems bent on terminating the pregnancy."

"I want the child more than anything, Jenny, but you must not risk your life. Doctor Webster has your best interests at heart."

"Henry, I cannot deny giving birth to this child in my womb. We created Hannah together and for me to deny her life is unthinkable."

"But Sweetheart, the risk is too high. What if you should die, I could not bear to lose you."

"I cannot choose my life over Hannah's, Henry. She has as much right to life as I do. We're in this together…"

A heavy tension and silence fell over the room. Not even the hustling and bustling in the hallway drifting into the room came into their awareness. Henry was panicking at the thought of Jenny dying. How could this suddenly be such a real possibility? It all seemed surreal.

Jenny read Henry's fears and heart and brought them out into the open, "I love you so much, Henry. The last three years have been wonderful, the happiest of my life. My wish would be for it to go on forever, but our life on earth is only temporary. One day sooner or later, we all will return to God—"

"Please, Jenny, I can't think of this happening…" Henry's words trailed off as fear swept through him.

Jenny knew Henry's heart and continued, "We have to view death not as a frightening thing. Death is a part of life. It's not an end but the beginning of our real life in heaven."

Henry was not taking in any of what Jenny was saying. To him it was unfair that she should sacrifice her life for a child that may die too or be still born or have so many complications that its life span may only be days or months. This entire matter was getting out of hand and no longer making sense to him. If Jenny were to die then he would want to, too.

There was a tap at the door. It was Camilla. She had wheeled herself from the fourth floor.

"Hi Mom, Dad, thought I would come down and visit for awhile. I just fed Jacob and he should sleep for at least two hours. Who would ever have thought my mom and I would be in the same hospital, pregnant and delivering babies! I can't wait for yours to be born so we can share our experiences."

As she spoke, Camilla sensed that she had interrupted something. She felt tension in the air. Worry was written all over Henry's face.

"Is everything okay?" Camilla wanted to know.

Jenny didn't answer directly. "Oh it's good to see you, Camilla. Come here! I need a hug and so does Dad."

Camilla wheeled over and warmly greeted her parents and then she looked at Jenny once more and said, "Well?"

"Well, I don't want to concern you, Camilla. This should be a happy occasion for you."

"Oh, Mom, I can handle things, I'm a counselor, remember? What's the latest prognosis? Has the doctor been around to see you?"

"Yes, Doctor Webster was here this morning and all the test results are the same or worsening. He recommends terminating the pregnancy."

"He's very concerned over Jenny's health and risk to her life and so am I..." chimed in Henry.

"So, you're at thirty weeks, right?"

Jenny nodded, "Yes, just past thirty."

"Has he suggested delivering the baby? It can survive at thirty weeks."

"I am hoping to hold off as long as I can, so the baby grows and develops more."

"But, Mom, your condition may be causing more damage than good."

Just then, Doctor Webster returned.

"That was good timing, our daughter was just asking a

question which you can answer...this is Camilla, she just delivered an eight pound, healthy baby boy."

"Congratulations, Camilla! You and your mother look very much alike! The resemblance is remarkable. If it were not for the age difference you would be considered as twins."

"Yes, a lot of people say that. There's quite a story behind this which I can share with you some other time. But Camilla was just asking about delivering the baby preterm. Is that still a possibility?" Jenny asked the doctor.

Dr. Webster turned to Camilla and said, "The baby's lungs at this stage are not developed enough and will have difficulty breathing and could cause other serious complications due to lack of oxygen. Fetal intrauterine hypoxia which can lead to cerebral palsy is very possible in this case. A C-section could work in case of an emergency but the blood count indicated that severe clotting could occur. The latest count however indicates the platelets are being used up and now there is the danger of Jenny bleeding to death."

The doctor was about to explain that with her high blood pressure and developing complications, the stress of inducing labor may be too hard on her and the baby when Jenny began to feel an aura around her. She had felt that strange feeling yesterday morning when her vision was beginning to blur.

"I think I am going to throw up," Jenny suddenly said. She put her hand to her head and added, "Oh, my head aches and feel so light headed, so str ....."

Jenny's eyes began to blink and move to one side and then upward...she was losing consciousness. Her face began to twitch.

"Oh, God, no, please don't let Jenny die!!!" cried Henry. He instantly recognized the onset of a seizure. The memory of seeing Julean having convulsions was forever burned into his mind.

Doctor Webster went quickly to the headboard and hit the emergency button. A nurse came immediately. "The patient is beginning to convulse and needs magnesium sulfate." Turning his attention to Henry and Camilla, you will have to go to the waiting room. We will let you know when Jenny is stabilized."

After five minutes, the twitching began to spread. Jenny's body, arms and legs began twitching and making jerking movements. Jenny was not responding to the magnesium sulfate. The doctor then administered Valium to induce a coma. Shortly, the seizure stopped as Jenny fell into a deep sleep.

When Doctor Webster came out to see Henry in the waiting room, Camilla had returned to her floor for the next feeding of her baby. He could barely believe what the doctor was saying; Jenny was in a comatose state. Would he ever see her awake again? Panic began to sweep through him. He was relieved with the doctor's next words.

"She is heavily sedated and will be asleep for a day or so. We have to make a decision about terminating Jenny's pregnancy. That would quickly put an end to the eclampsia. Her blood pressure is not responding to the medication and is now over 200/100. The longer we leave it the more organ damage is being done. It may already be too late for the fetus."

What the doctor said next went straight to his heart.

"Mr. Pederson, if your wife doesn't wake up soon, you will have to decide whether or not to abort the baby. Did Jenny give you authority to make decisions on her behalf when she was admitted?"

Henry stared at the doctor in disbelief. How could he possibly make such a decision?

CHAPTER ONE

HENRY CALLED FATHER Engelmann at the care home. He didn't recognize the person answering the phone but she knew of him. She informed Henry that Father had left for the hospital to see Mrs. Pederson.

When Father came into the dimly lit room, Henry was seated at Jenny's bedside holding her hand. Father rushed to their side. Henry had to take a second look; he wasn't used to seeing Father in his black suit and white collar rather than his brown Franciscan habit. The concerned priest placed his hand on Henry's shoulder and asked, "How is she doing, Henry?"

Tears were sitting at the edge of his eyelids and began to spill over. He wiped the rolling tear off his cheek and said, "Jenny had a seizure and somehow they stopped it by inducing a coma. Hopefully, she will awaken in a day or so."

Henry shook his head, "It's like reliving the same nightmare when Julean was in the hospital with meningitis. I don't know if I could cope if Jenny died too."

"What do the doctors recommend?"

"That's the thing, Father. The doctor is adamant about terminating the pregnancy. He maintains that is the safest and best option at this point and would quickly restore Jenny's blood pressure to normal and end the condition she is suffering from."

Henry paused and then said, "I am inclined to agree with him, Father. I don't want Jenny to die. He said to me this morning that time is running out and a decision has to be made. If Jenny doesn't wake up, the doctor wants me to decide...to go ahead with the abortion or not."

Father shook his head, "Oh, mein lieber Gott. Such a decision, Henry. What would Jenny want?"

"We both know Jenny's heart, Father, but should we just let her die without doing anything?"

Father nodded and kept shaking his head.

"If we don't terminate the pregnancy, both Jenny and the baby are at risk of dying. If we do, we can save Jenny..." Henry's words trailed off.

"Can they possibly deliver the child without aborting it?" Father wanted to know.

"Yeah, we discussed that. The doctor thinks the baby is too underdeveloped and won't be able to breathe. And to bring on the labor will be too stressful. It might kill Jenny."

"Yet, it might deliver the baby."

"Yes, that is a possibility, I suppose. I'm not sure even the doctor can predict that. Jenny is extremely ill and becoming more so. If Jenny doesn't wake up soon, I'll have to make a decision."

"I brought communion for you and Jenny." Father reached into his jacket pocket and pulled out a small gold Pyx. He unscrewed the lid and took out one of the consecrated hosts. He turned to Henry and said, "The Body of Christ."

Henry replied, "Amen" and made the sign of the cross. He bowed his head and said a private prayer. Father stepped in between Henry and Jenny so he could put one hand on Henry's head and the other on Jenny's forehead and prayed, "Oh, heavenly Father, creator of life, if it is Your divine will, restore Jenny's health and that of the child within her womb. In the same way Your Son on this day lay in the darkness, let Jenny, Henry and their daughter, Hannah resurrect with the

Lord into new life. Through the power of Your Holy Spirit give Henry the wisdom to know Your Will in this situation and the trust, strength and courage to carry it out. Fill their hearts with peace, praise and thanksgiving for all of Your blessings. We ask this in Jesus' name, Amen."

HENRY WENT HOME shortly after six, had a light dinner and was on the phone continuously for over two hours. He called Lauren and Alison to give them an update on Jenny's condition. He told the girls that he was struggling with the decision whether or not to terminate the pregnancy. Matti and Chloe were also surprised to learn that Jenny's condition was worsening. In all cases, he asked for their prayer support.

He did however, ask Chloe about the decision he was faced with and asked for her opinion. All she said was that she has seen many cases where the mother's life was at risk yet, when the mother went ahead with the pregnancy it all turned out and both baby and mother quickly recovered. In the end, the decision was his and that she and Robbie would pray for him and his loved ones.

Early, Easter Sunday morning, Henry, along with Justin travelled into the city. Henry hoped he would see his dear wife awake but she was still in a coma. The similarities between Jenny's situation and that of Julean's were eerie to Henry. So many memories flooded his mind. Just as Henry and his son sat down on either side of Jenny's bed, a nurse came in and took Jenny's blood pressure. It had come down a tad but still way too high; it was at 190/95. Henry asked if Jenny had woken up at all.

"No, she hasn't."

"Is there a danger that she might not?" Henry was anxious to know and needed reassurance.

"She was given a very strong tranquilizer yesterday. The drug has a half-life of a day or so. She may not wake up until tomorrow."

"Was Doctor Webster around yet?"

"No, he doesn't usually come in on Sunday unless there is an emergency."

For most of the morning it was just Henry and Justin in the room other than nurses coming in periodically to check Jenny's vitals. Henry was surprised to see Justin just sitting quietly for all that time. Occasionally, Henry noticed his son wipe away a tear or two. He wasn't much good at hiding it. In many ways, Justin was like him; his son wore his emotions on his sleeve.

Henry knew Father wouldn't be in until after lunch as he celebrated two Masses that day at the care home. He knew there would be too many people coming for Easter Sunday.

At one point in the afternoon, the room was filled; Jeremy and his son Joshua, Camilla, Father, Carlos and Maria and several of Jenny's friends were there. For almost an hour, a prayer vigil was held for Jenny and Hannah. There were tears and hugs and well wishes floating around. Even the attending nurses left with tears in their eyes.

Around four thirty everyone had left except Henry. Justin went home with Jeremy and Father caught a ride back to the care home with Carlos and Maria. Henry was glad to learn from Carlos that Thomas and Neela were coming to Regina for a visit. In the few days he had spent in Ottawa, before James' passing and again just that past summer, Henry had observed Thomas to be a godly man and who in many respects possessed wisdom similar to that of Father Engelmann. He looked forward to the support of Thomas and his wife.

Despite all the prayers and discussion that day about what to do in Jenny's critical situation, Henry was still struggling with the decision of whether or not to abort the baby. If Jenny didn't come out of her coma by tomorrow morning, he had to make up his mind what to do. Every passing minute was having its toll on Jenny and the baby.

Just as he was praying deeply to God to know His will in the matter, Doctor Carter walked into the room. He could see the tears of worry and sorrow in his son-in-law's eyes. He had read in Jenny's charts that she had a seizure and was put in an induced comatose state. He was concerned over the woman who had taken his daughter's place in Henry's life but just as worried about Henry's state of mind and well-being too. He got one of the chairs, pushed it beside Henry, and sat down.

"When Vera was pregnant with Julean, I was just as worried as you, Hank. Sometimes life throws us a curve that's too much for us to handle. I know you're a man of God and so I don't need to tell you to go to Him. I was on my knees more than once when Vera was struggling with the same condition. High blood pressure can be the cause of many serious complications."

Henry nodded. "I am struggling with the decision to abort the child, Jack. Jenny is getting worse by the minute. She wanted to hold off as long as possible so the baby grows and develops more but we have run out of time. Doctor Webster feels the best option at this point is to terminate the pregnancy. He feels the risks to do a C-section or induce labor is too risky."

"And what do you and Jenny think?" Doctor Carter wanted to know.

"Jenny is absolutely against aborting the child. She would never agree to do that. I am the same but I don't want to lose Jenny. I thought my world would end when Julean died and here again is almost the exact replay of what happened. What good is it to try and save the baby if Jenny dies? And we are not sure that the baby will even live and how healthy it still is. It could already be suffering from many complications."

Jack nodded. "I understand your reasoning, Henry. It is sound logic and Doctor Webster's assessment of the situation is correct. Jenny is dying. The latest lab tests confirm the prognosis for both the mother and child. I am older than you and considerably older than Doctor Webster and Vera tells me each year to hang up my stethoscope but I love what I am doing. I can't begin to tell you after all these years how in awe I am over the human body and all its workings and how it strives to heal itself.

"God outdid Himself when He created man.

"Marvelous Hank, truly marvelous. I have lived long enough to see miracles before my eyes; impossible cases more serious than this, miraculously pulled through. And yes, I have seen unfortunate deaths and much sorrow as well. This is the life we live, Hank. At the end of the day we have to be obedient to God's laws and will and trust Him to turn it into good. If we place our faith in Him, He will turn it into good, perhaps not now, but at some time He will use our faith and suffering and sorrow for His purposes but we must give it to Him."

Henry nodded and listened to the wise doctor; it was so similar to what Jenny said the other day on the way in to the hospital.

Doctor Carter continued by posing a question, "What is God's will in this matter, Hank? Would He want us to abort the child or try to save both the mother and child?"

For the first time a surge of confidence swept through him. "The latter Jack, that's what God would want."

"Well then, what are our options?"

Henry thought for just a moment, those options had been floating in and out of his mind all day. "Well, we could do a C-section but the tests show the blood count is too low and she might bleed to death. The other is to induce labor. The problem with that is if it's a long labor with her high blood pressure, the stress might kill her." Henry was beginning to feel like one of the medical team weighing the options; as if he knew as much as the doctor next to him.

"But then again, Hank, the labor might be short and it's a small baby, the cervix wouldn't need to dilate that much. And what did I just say how God creates the body that always works towards healing itself and to follow His laws."

Henry nodded and for the first time in days felt his indecision and hopelessness began to lift...a surge of certainty flooded his being.

He had made up his mind!

He wanted to get up and hug the old doctor. "Yes, Jack, that's what we will do. I know Jenny would be in full agreement. I know if she had woken up to find out I decided to abort the baby, Jenny would forgive me but would never forget that the child was killed within her womb. She would be as good as dead for the rest of her life."

Henry was amazed not only with the doctor's assessment of the human body but how God works through people to minister to one another through His divine providence. Had he gone home, he would have missed the doctor. Why would he be making rounds at four thirty on Easter Sunday and not be home with his wife? Surely, at his age, he wouldn't have that many patients to see?

Yes, God answers prayers!

Henry gave his father–in-law a warm hug and told him to extend it to Vera. He couldn't thank Doctor Carter enough for coming in.

"So, tell me Jack, how many patients were you seeing today?"

Jack looked at Henry and replied, "Only one."

"That is my good fortune that you also stopped by to check on Jenny. "Who was your patient on this floor?" Henry wanted to know.

Jack smiled and softly said, "It was you."

HENRY RIPPLINGER IS the best-selling author of *Pewter Angels, Another Angel of Love, Angel of Thanksgiving, The Angelic Occurrence and Angel Promises Fulfilled,* the first five books in the seven book series "The Angelic Letters." The overwhelming response by readers to Henry's novels gives testimony to Henry's gifts as an author to write books that touch human hearts and offer direction to their lives.

Henry's empathetic abilities, combined with his lifelong experience and eclectic career as an educator, guidance counselor, professional artist and businessman, prepared him to craft this inspirational, spirit-filled love story and indirectly realize his aspirations of writing a self-development book.

Henry is also one of Canada's foremost prairie artists. His work is on display at private and corporate collections across Canada, most notably in Saskatchewan, his home province, and can be seen in the critically acclaimed book, *If You're Not from the Prairie.*

As both author and artist, Henry communicates from the heart, painting pictures with words that are so vivid and real that readers can feel and visualize every aspect of their own lives intertwined with the lives of his beloved characters.

Henry resides with his wife in the panoramic valley setting of Lumsden, Saskatchewan, Canada.

Please e-mail Henry at: henry@henryripplinger.com or visit the web-site: www.henryripplinger.com for more information on Henry's work and art. He would love to hear from you!

PEWTER ANGELS
BOOK ONE OF THE ANGELIC LETTERS SERIES

"He hath given his angels charge over thee; to keep thee in all thy ways…In their hands they shall bear thee up: lest thou dash thy foot against a stone."

PSALM 91:11-12

The summer of 1956 starts out like any other summer for 15 year old Henry Pederson: hot, long and boring. That all changes when Jenny Sarsky, along with her guardian angel and her family move into the house three doors down. From the moment their eyes meet, an earthly attraction unites their hearts while the spiritual energy travelling the length of the gaze they share joins their souls—spinning a web of love that transcends time and Heaven itself.

Mr. Engelmann, an endearing and wise mentor living out the word of God, comes into Henry's life, providing him with powerful insights and valuable life lessons that carry strength, wisdom and hope.

Pewter Angels the first book of *The Angelic Letters Series*, starts Henry and Jenny and their families on an inspiring yet tumultuous journey through life's struggles and victories, and the miracle of deep, enduring love.

Pewter Angels will grab your heart, squeeze it and hold it to the very last page.

ANOTHER ANGEL OF LOVE
BOOK TWO OF THE ANGELIC LETTERS SERIES

"God causes all things to work together for good to those who love God, to those who are called according to His purpose"

ROMANS 8:28

It was as if Jenny had vanished from the face of the earth. Two years after she and her family moved out of Henry's life, Henry still longs for her, their whirlwind romance gone from his life but not his heart. He was certain she would respond to his last letter, a pewter angel tucked inside —but there have been no letters, no phone calls. Nothing. A country apart, Henry and Jenny are unaware Jenny's parents have burned all the letters but the last… it is protected, it seems, by an angelic power.

Henry continues to rely on the love, support and powerful insights of his mentor Mr. Engelmann, and his secret plan to seek Jenny out sustains the hope that one day his love will return—until he meets Julean Carter.

But, is their new-found love deep enough and strong enough to overcome the heavenly touch that entwined Henry and Jenny's spirits when they first gazed into each others eyes?

Another Angel of Love…glows with moments of tenderness…deeply inspirational….will captivate the heart of every reader!

ANGEL OF THANKSGIVING
BOOK THREE OF THE ANGELIC LETTERS SERIES

This may be the single most moving book you will read this year—or in your life time.

Henry and Julean couldn't be happier. With a new baby, a new home and Henry's new job, everything is turning out perfectly for the young couple. Or is it? Henry can't seem to shake the memory of Jenny from his mind or the love he still feels for her. Little does he know, his wife is all-too-aware of Henry's hidden thoughts and feelings. Meanwhile, Father Engelmann, back from seminary school and creating a sensation as the new parish priest, is caught in the middle when both Henry and Julean confess to him about Jenny.

Will Jenny finally give in to James' persistent proposals, knowing that once married her chance to reunite with Henry would be gone forever? Spanning two decades, *Angel of Thanksgiving* takes the reader on an incredible journey of faith, hope and love. As we see Henry and Jenny's lives unfolding separately and so far apart, *will destiny bring them together again?*

Timeless Biblical themes as surrendering to God's will, forgiveness, and unconditional love are beautifully portrayed through unforgettable, real-life characters in this compelling, hard to put down novel.

Make a huge space in your heart before you begin to read Angel of Thanksgiving as it will quickly fill with love's beauty and wonder.

THE ANGELIC OCCURRENCE
BOOK FOUR OF THE ANGELIC LETTERS SERIES

Hailed by readers as one of the most inspiring works of fiction they have ever read, *The Angelic Letters* series is a story that is both riveting and life-changing...

After decades apart, Henry and Jenny's lives are poised to intersect yet again, when Henry's oldest son brings his new girlfriend home to meet the family. Bearing an unusual resemblance to Henry's first love, her name, Camilla, is not just unusual, it's also the same name Jenny had vowed to name her own daughter one day. Did Jenny get pregnant that fateful night in the park? Everything about Camilla seemed to confirm Henry's belief that she is Jenny's daughter.

As Henry struggles with this and other memories of his lost love, he also strives to pick up the pieces of his life after his wife Julean's untimely death. Can the lovely Ivania fill the void left by both Julean and Jenny? And what about Jenny herself? If only Henry knew that Jenny had been trapped for years in a loveless and lonely marriage, and that, more importantly, she has never forgotten her first love.

The Angelic Occurrence, book 4 in the series, is a thrilling and heart-stopping adventure of love. The twists and turns of fate will keep you gripping the book tighter and tighter as you witness the ever widening circle of influence Henry and Jenny's guardian angels bestow upon them in an effort to reignite a love that never died.

The Angelic Occurrence will touch your soul...
the essence of your being where faith is born.

ANGEL PROMISES FULFILLED
BOOK FIVE OF THE ANGELIC LETTERS SERIES

Reader after reader says the same: "The most awesome, inspirational, captivating series I have ever read. I cannot put the books down even when reading for the second time. The characters, the words, the spiritual content, consume my thoughts completely.

Henry couldn't get over the fact that he had purchased Jenny's home! Although separated for thirty-two years, their love was sustained by an angelic power that had never waned. It was all there in her diary that he had just discovered the day before. If only he had known sooner that his teenage sweetheart was critically ill just miles away ... the time they could have spent together!

Incredibly, Camilla, too, had just discovered the truth that Jenny is her birth mother. Even Father Engelmann had been astonished to learn that the Jenny he had been seeing in the care home for the past few months was the same young girl that had frequented his store so long ago—and Henry's first love. In his final act of love and in hope that the two lovers can finally realize their deep love for one another, Father Engelmann offers his life for Jenny's.

Will the Lord accept Father's plea to take his life for Jenny's? Can Camilla and Henry reach Jenny in time? And what of Jenny's wish to her guardian angel to see her beloved Henry and Camilla before she dies?

Angel Promises Fulfilled, Book Five in "*The Angelic Letters Series*," powerfully examines many life challenges, such as forgiveness, unconditional love and why God allows suffering and pain in the world. The insights revealed through the author's beloved characters will have an astounding, transforming affect on your life.

If You're Not from the Prairie, written by David Bouchard and illustrated by Henry Ripplinger, is a poetic and visual journey depicting the prairies and the people who have made this diverse land their own...a treasure for the mind and soul.

To contact the author and for further information about these books as well as other artwork, limited edition prints and other products, please visit:

www.henryripplinger.com

THE ANGELIC LETTERS SERIES

NOW IN:

AUDIO-BOOKS

Book One - Pewter Angels
Book Two - Another Angel of Love
Book Three - Angel of Thanksgiving
Book Four - The Angelic Occurrence
Book Five - Angel Promises Fulfilled
Book Six - The House Where Angels Dwell...coming soon

Available for purchase at audible.com

EBOOKS

All six books in the series are in ebook format and available for purchase from Amazon, Kobo and iTunes.

JOIN FACEBOOK

Join Henry's Facebook for words of wisdom from Father Engelmann, book signing tours and schedules, blog posts, future books and more.

VISIT THE WEB SITE: WWW.HENRYRIPPLINGER.COM

Ripplinger Fine Art Gallery

2175 Smith St.
Regina, Saskatchewan S4P 2P3
Tel: 306 791 7888

Ripplinger Fine Art Gallery is an award winning heritage style complex which includes:

HENRY'S CAFE', A CLOTHING BOUTIQUE AND SEVERAL GIFT SHOPPES

Ripplinger Fine Art Gallery, Henry's Cafe' and Boutiques is one of Saskatchewan's main tourist attraction visited by people from all over Canada, USA and abroad!

The ambiance, warm friendly atmosphere and heritage style create a memorable experience you will never forget!

Come, visit us soon!

Ripplinger Fine Art Gallery

Presents

FRAMEABLE ART CARDS BY
HENRY K. RIPPLINGER

Card size: 6 X 9 inches
Retail Price: $ 8.95

For a complete selection of all art cards in full color
visit the web site.

All art cards are also available as a Limited Edition Print.

For more details and shipping information visit
the web site:
www.henryripplinger.com

Ripplinger Fine Art Gallery

Presents

FRAMEABLE ART CARDS BY
HENRY K. RIPPLINGER

Title: Prairie Harvest
Image size: 5 X 7 inches

Overall framed size: 11 ½ X 13 ¾ inches
Retail price: $50.00 plus shipping and handling.

For full color image visit the web site:
www.henryripplinger.com

Ripplinger Fine Art Gallery

Presents

FRAMEABLE ART CARDS BY HENRY K. RIPPLINGER

Title: Prairie Harvest AND If You're Not From The Prairie
Overall framed size: 13 ½ X 25 inches

Retail price: $145.00 plus shipping and handling.

Note: the cards can be framed vertically and in sets of three art cards per frame.

For full color images of all art cards and framing visit the web site: www.henryripplinger.com

Limited Edition Prints as well as original paintings by Henry K. Ripplinger are available at **Ripplinger Fine Art Gallery** in Regina Saskatchewan.

Ripplinger Fine Art Gallery

Presents

FRAMEABLE ART CARDS BY HENRY K. RIPPLINGER

Title: Autumn Road
Image size: 5 X 7½ inches

Overall framed size: 11 ½ X 14 inches
Retail price: $50.00 plus shipping and handling.

For full color image visit the web site:
www.henryripplinger.com

Ripplinger Fine Art Gallery

Presents

FRAMEABLE ART CARDS BY
HENRY K. RIPPLINGER

*Title: **Hockey on the Creek***
Image size: 5 X 7 inches

Overall framed size: 11 ½ X 13 ¾ inches
Retail price: $50.00 plus shipping and handling.

For full color image visit the web site:
www.henryripplinger.com